ASSASSIN

BOOK ELEVEN OF THE
REVELATIONS CYCLE

Kacey Ezell & Marisa Wolf

Seventh Seal Press
Virginia Beach, VA

Chris Kennedy/Seventh Seal Press
2052 Bierce Dr.
Virginia Beach, VA 23454
http://chriskennedypublishing.com/

Publisher's Note: This is a work of fiction. Names, characters, places, and incidents are a product of the author's imagination. Locales and public names are sometimes used for atmospheric purposes. Any resemblance to actual people, living or dead, or to businesses, companies, events, institutions, or locales is completely coincidental.

Ordering Information:
Quantity sales. Special discounts are available on quantity purchases by corporations, associations, and others. For details, contact the "Special Sales Department" at the address above.

Assassin/Kacey Ezell & Marisa Wolf. -- 1st ed.
ISBN 978-1948485098

I could never have completed this book without the help and support of a whole host of people. Most obviously, of course, is my talented and amazing coauthor. Thank you, Risa, for playing this game with me. It's been a blast. Let's do it again sometime. Also, special thanks go to Mark Wandrey for creating this amazing setting and universe. Thanks to you and Chris Kennedy for letting us play in your creation. We hope our catsassins are worthy. Lastly, but never leastly, thank you to EZ, Roo, and Bear, without whom I would be nothing.

—*Kacey Ezell, December 2017*

If you get a chance to write a novel with Kacey, I strongly recommend it. Thank you, lady, for all the badassery and, incidentally, the amazing friendship. I could not have done this without you. Chris and Mark, this universe is fantabulous— thanks for letting me muck around in it. To my parents for not laughing at me when I majored in English (oh, wait, you did. Thanks for that, too!), to Jeremy for letting me endlessly talk about catsassins, even in the middle of the night, and to Mary for making me step up my writing game. Love to you all. Finally, to my Uncle Bob, who read my first (terrible) novel when I was twelve. I wish you had gotten to hold this one in your hands. We miss you.

—*Marisa Wolf, December 2017*

To my girls, because Mommy loves you. And to Pearl and Moxxi, my own sociopathic cuddlemonsters. Mommy loves you, too.

–KE

To Jeremy, for his patience when I disappear into my head, and to the dogs, for lack of same.

–MW

Author Note:

The Depik are a mammalian analogue, giving live birth to placental kittens after a gestation slightly longer than a season. Depik mothers, called damas, nurse their kittens for roughly a season after birth, though the young kittens can survive on raw meat almost immediately. Young Depik are capable of reproducing at three years of age and are considered full adults after four. The typical Depik lifespan is approximately 18–20 years, though some venerable Depik have continued to lead active lives well into their twenties. As some of the terms may be unfamiliar, a glossary and a distance/time converter is in the back matter of this book.

Hunting

He moved like water.

In the green dimness of perpetual twilight, the young male placed his fingerpads carefully on the thick, springy floor of the triple-canopy jungle. He glided forward as sleek muscles bunched and flowed into one another under his rusty orange fur. Long, moist plant tendrils reached down from above, brushing their wetness against his coat in the humid equatorial day.

Up ahead, his prey froze. The adult Cheelin had been grooming itself by the spring that bubbled up from the forest floor ahead. More than twice the Hunter's size, the hexapedal animal was considered one of the most challenging of Khatash's native prey species. Each of its six prehensile limbs ended in a venomous, stinging point that would deliver enough quintessential neurotoxin to kill an adult Hunter. This particular beast was male, as evidenced by his bulbous abdomen and triangular head. The females were sleeker and tended to hide better. Most male Cheelin didn't care to hide. They were too used to being the biggest and baddest.

Until a Hunter found them.

This particular Hunter, who had gone by the name of Choking Deluge since shortly after his birth, continued to slide through the undergrowth toward the Cheelin. Others, perhaps, might have chosen to pause, lest the Cheelin detect some movement in the jungle. But Deluge kept going, for he realized that *he* was not the threat the Cheelin sensed.

The Cheelin reared back onto four legs and craned its head to look up into the canopy above. It let out a sort of coughing roar, and the coat of fine, wiry hairs that covered all but the underside of its tentacles puffed up in an attempt to make itself look bigger and scarier.

The jungle echoed with an answering screech of warning, and death arrowed down out of the canopy above, right into both of the Cheelin's outstretched arms.

While dangerous, Cheelin were prey animals. They consumed only fruit and vegetative matter, and except for the adult males, tended to live in tightly knit family groups. Taking on a solitary male was challenge enough that very few predators on Khatash would try. In fact, Deluge knew of only two: Hunters like himself and the occasional Basreen.

The Basreen attacked from above, using the thin membranous "wings" that snapped out from its tubular body to slow its descent. Her descent, Deluge realized as he caught sight of her tail whipping through the air. Only females had ringed tails, with stingers of their own that carried a powerful paralytic.

She flew down and whipped her body around the Cheelin's form, attempting to wrap around his armored neck joint. Deluge knew if she could manage to fully encircle the neck and anchor down, she would flex her powerful musculature and begin to cinch in bit by bit, until the Cheelin's natural armor plate crumpled under the force, and he strangled himself. It was a slow process, but one good sting from her tail would dump enough toxin into his bloodstream to render the Cheelin immobile for a good long while.

If the Basreen could get her body fully around his neck. Which she didn't.

The wily Cheelin reached up and caught the diving Basreen in midair. He shoved one of his tentacles deep into her mouth, which snapped instantly shut. Her powerful jaws and armored palate severed the stinging tip, and the Cheelin roared in pain as dark red blood spurted from the wound. Nevertheless, his other tentacle successfully caught the Basreen by her ringed tail, and he whipped her out and away from himself, causing more of his blood to fly in an arc through the wet heat of the jungle scene.

It smelled delicious. Deluge took another step forward and crouched in the darkened hollow underneath a rotting Rizel stalk. He would have gone closer, but the injured Cheelin blundered by as it flung the Basreen around some more, and Deluge didn't feel like getting stepped on. Cheelin were heavy, and the suckers on the underside of their tentacles stung.

As Deluge watched, unnoticed, the Cheelin whipped the Basreen back across his body, which turned out to be a mistake. The Basreen managed to reach out and wrap itself around the joint where one of the Cheelin's aft legs joined his abdomen. When the Cheelin hauled the Basreen back the other direction, she flexed her muscles and held fast, and his grip slid off the end of her tail.

The Basreen had long since folded in her membranes, leaving her looking like nothing so much as an elongated tube of muscle, which, truth be told, wasn't far off. She used her strength to gather her body up and began climbing the Cheelin's leg. He let out a deep, hoarse-sounding howl of distress that shook water droplets from the leaves above. He tried to use his forelegs to pull at the Basreen, to sting her, to try and tear her loose. But Deluge knew that Basreen skin was thick and nearly impervious to puncture wounds. If there was such a thing as perfectly flexible armor, the Basreen was wearing it.

When the Cheelin turned his back on Deluge's hiding place in his frantic dance to escape, Deluge sprang. He leapt from the darkness under the wide, flat Rizel leaves and landed squarely on the Cheelin's abdomen. The Cheelin, mid-howl, faltered as the new threat presented itself. Before the hexapod could reach up to grab at him with one of its unoccupied limbs, Deluge slashed his claws across the creature's vulnerable eyes. The Cheelin screamed, and three of his arms flailed up, stingers glistening with drops of deadly poison at the tips. Deluge ducked one, grabbed onto another, and twisted himself up into a handspring that landed him on top of the creature's head.

The third tentacle followed, and Deluge swatted it away with brute force as he dove down to the forest floor, still holding on to the Cheelin's limb. The creature yanked and twisted, and nearly succeeded in getting away from Deluge, but the Hunter had wrapped the tentacle around his wrist and secured it by stabbing the stinger deep into the Cheelin's own flesh. The toxin wouldn't hurt him, of course, but it did prevent him from getting away.

Next order of business, Deluge thought, the Basreen. Less than half a heartbeat had elapsed since his initial leap from the undergrowth, and the arboreal predator was still working her way up onto the body of the Cheelin. Deluge reached out with his free hand and gripped her tail. She screeched in protest as he yanked hard enough to separate half her length from the Cheelin's leg. Had she been prepared for him, he never would have succeeded, but apparently Deluge had caught the Basreen by surprise, because he was able to get enough slack in her body for his idea to work.

The blinded Cheelin, warned by the Basreen's shriek, turned and surged in Deluge's direction. The Hunter ducked and then came up hard under the creature's abdomen, stabbing upward with the Basreen's stinger in the vulnerable spot between the foremost set of legs.

The Cheelin froze, shuddered, then began to crumple. Deluge flung the Basreen away from himself and dove out of the way of the Cheelin's toppling weight. The animal, wounded and paralyzed, crashed to the jungle floor. Deluge rolled up to his back feet and waited for a moment, but the Cheelin didn't move. It was fully incapacitated.

He dropped back down to all four paws and stalked closer, scenting the air. The Basreen was nearby, and he didn't know if she would contest his kill or not.

"Huntttr," she screeched in the way of her kind. Deluge froze and watched as she reared her elongated body up above the bulk of the Cheelin's still-breathing corpse.

"Basreen," Deluge said in return. Though a lower life form, the Basreen was a fellow-predator and deserved respect.

"Your kill," the Basreen said, which surprised Deluge. As a species, they were not known for their generosity.

"You helped," Deluge replied. "Shall we split the Cheelin?"

"Splittt," the Basreen agreed. "Young to feed."

"Ah, of course then. I will take the stingers and poison sacs. The meat is yours."

"Good Huntttttr," she said, and let out a kind of chittering sound that Deluge interpreted as pleasure. He blinked slowly at her and then drew his long knife for the first time in the process.

"Shall I kill the beast?"

"No kill. Meatttt bad."

"Ah. It will spoil the meat if he dies? Fair enough. I will just cut the stingers, then."

"Good. Young come now."

Basreen were not a populous species. While not as rare as the Hunters themselves, Deluge had only seen a Basreen in the wild once before, so he felt a particular thrill as the mother Basreen sent out a two-note screech and no less than twenty small, tubular winged animals dove down from the canopy above. The young Basreen settled over the bulk of the Cheelin, their multihued hides creating a dizzying display of pulsing color as they fed.

"You have many young, Basreen."

"Yes," she said, and Deluge wondered if such a simple creature was capable of something like pride. "Good young."

"Yes, it is good," he agreed, and got to work slicing up the tips of the Cheelin's tentacles. It wasn't hard work, but it was a delicate thing to extract the stinger apparatus without puncturing the poison gland inside. By the time he was finished, the Cheelin had been reduced to a bloody skeleton covered in offal, and the Basreen and her young had disappeared.

"Good hunting, Basreen," Deluge said as he slipped the last of the stingers into the pocket of the vest he'd worn for that purpose. The day had gone, and the darkness beneath the trees grew deeper as less sunlight filtered down from below.

"Good huntttting, Huntttttr," came the distant farewell screech from the trees far above.

* * *

Deluge hadn't needed the Cheelin's meat to survive, but as he journeyed through the darkened jungle back toward the City, his stomach began to growl its empty displeasure at him. It became so distracting that he broke off his journey long enough to kill a small creeper to fill his belly. Though it was hardly sport to kill the slow moving, bulbous plant-eater, eating it did the trick, and the young Hunter made it to the edges of the City by dawn.

"The City" was Khatash Starport. When he was a young kit, Deluge had accompanied his Dama to the City once. He'd been wide-eyed with wonder at the sight of so many beings in one place. The tall metal and glass buildings had seemed so alien compared to the long, low slung tunnels of their Den. And though he'd grown up speaking the language of his Human molly, Deluge had never heard anything like the lyrical patois of the starport. It had teemed with life and activity. He'd thought it must be the most populous place in the universe.

He'd been very young.

Still, though, the City was usually good for a few laughs, and Deluge felt his spirits lift as he approached the edge of the trees and the paved streets of the starport. As the City was one of the few places on the planet not buried under triple-canopy jungle, Deluge took a moment to pull his dark-tinted dawn-goggles on to shade his sensitive eyes before he sauntered out into the equatorial sunlight.

Instantly, the sound seemed to change. Oh, he'd been hearing the noise of the City for a while, but it had been background to the native sounds of Khatash's flora and fauna. Now, though, the hum of hovering vehicles and the dull roar of myriad languages all tangled together to take center stage in the Hunter's sensitive ears. Overhead, a formation of Basreeni fighters streaked by with a distant shriek. The deadly little fighters were capable of incredible maneuvering in both space and atmosphere, and would shoot down any craft that strayed from the cone-shaped extraplanetary zone above the starport. Deluge thought of the fighter's namesake he'd met in the jungle and smiled.

Though loud, the sounds were nothing to the assault on his olfactory senses. The musky wetness of the rainforest no longer dominated the air. Instead, he caught the scent of over a dozen life forms, native and alien both. Khatash Starport was the only place on the planet where an off-worlder could safely go without a clan sigil, and so it was quite the hub of interplanetary commerce. Having been out into the galaxy on contracts, Deluge had to admire the nerve of the merchants brave enough to come to Khatash. The deadly reputation of his people had spread far and wide, with good reason. Plus, Hunters valued their privacy, and the Council of Elders had decreed that alien could be summarily executed if it was determined they possessed knowledge they should not have.

Personally, Deluge found that particular law a bit capricious, but then, that was probably his unorthodox upbringing speaking. His Human molly was passionate about the thirst for knowledge, and she'd managed to instill at least some of that passion in each of the four of them. Susa had always told her kits that knowledge was power, but like all kinds of power, it had a danger and a price tag. He didn't know all the details behind why her wise Human eyes had always seemed so sad and ancient when she said this, but he knew there was a deep story.

In any case, Deluge figured it was his own thirst for knowledge that made him love the City. Even now, returning pleasantly tired from a good hunt and wanting nothing so much as to fall into his own bed at the Den, he felt the life and vibrancy of the City lightening his mood. Especially when his nose caught the faintest whiff of spiced Khava meat amid all the other scents swirling around him. Khava were one of the largest fish that swam in Khatash's great oceans, and when prepared correctly, their meat was a delicacy not to be missed. Deluge liked to think of himself as having a rather sophisticated palate, and after the bland nutrition of the jungle creeper, the taste of spiced Khava seemed just the thing. He turned his paws toward the source of that deliciously tempting aroma: the open-air market.

Located roughly five sprints (or, as Deluge preferred to think of it, a half-kilometer) north of the City's geographic center, the market functioned as one of the City's two hubs. The other hub, of course, was the starport terminal itself, where the roar of orbital shuttlecraft punctuated the din of commerce at regular intervals.

When the ancient elders had created the starport, they'd done so on the site of the research facility that had initially catapulted the Hunters towards the stars. The research facility had included a university with a central courtyard-type area used as an amphitheater. After the first space-going Hunters returned with tales of thousands of alien races and a complex, rough-and-tumble galactic economy, the Council of Elders had convened for a whole season. That time of deliberation had become legendary. Mollies still sang songs to their infant charges about the battles, both verbal and otherwise, that occurred between the various clan elders before the season ended. When it did end, however, the council presented their clans with a new paradigm. A paradigm that would define the Hunters as a race forever, and give them a new name: the Depik.

Of course, "Depik" was simply an alien word for "Hunter" in the native tongue of one of those thousand species, but still, it mattered. Because before they were the Depik, the Hunters were merely the apex predators on their lovely home world of Khatash. After becoming the Depik, they were the apex predators of the Galaxy itself.

At least, Deluge reflected with a grin, we certainly like to think so. Our arrogance would probably be more justified if we weren't constantly teetering on the edge of extinction.

"Something funny, Hunter?" a merchant being asked from a booth nearby. The being spoke from within the shadowed interior of a booth set back alongside the street. Wide swaths of brightly-colored fabric draped across the sides and top of the booth. The voice itself carried an electronic tininess that indicated the use of a translator.

"Almost always," Deluge said, turning to face the booth and raising up onto his back legs. He could hear the voice of his own translator weaving through his natural tongue. "I, Choking Deluge, greet you, unknown being. Welcome to our negotiation."

"I am Rurranach," the being said and stepped forward enough that the punishing light illuminated the lines of its form. An elongated head, maybe a bodylength long, sat atop a bulky trunk swathed in more of the rich fabric. He was obviously male from the impressively large size of his cranial crest. Female Sidar simply didn't grow that big. Dark, wiry fur covered the face of the alien, and traced along his muscled neck to disappear under the clothing. Two huge, intelligent eyes dominated the facial structure. "Fine fabrics and other luxuries suitable for a mighty Hunter such as yourself, if you'd like to take a look."

"A Sidar," Deluge said, letting his delight and curiosity infuse his tone. "I've never conversed with one of your race before."

"Ah," the Sidar said, dropping his jaw open in what Deluge presumed was a smile. "Well, I am honored to be the first, mighty

Hunter. It is only recently that we have begun trading here on mysterious Khatash."

"Welcome, then. And you can call me Deluge. Have you enjoyed it here?"

"What little I've seen of it, yes," the Sidar said. "I respect your customs, but I admit to a rather unprofessional amount of curiosity about your emerald of a planet. Does the jungle really cover every bit of land?"

"Most of it," Deluge said. "There are some barren places in the mountains, but everything else is pretty well covered."

"What of your polar ice caps? Surely the jungle does not grow there?"

"I would be surprised if it did, since both poles are oceanic," Deluge said, tilting his head and flicking his ears to indicate that his tease was meant to be gentle.

"How fascinating," Rurranach said.

"If you say so. Tell me about your wares. Are you doing well with your fabrics?"

Rurranach blinked his big eyes, then dropped his jaw again.

"I was warned that the Depik Hunters were blunt. An 'unrepentant mirror' someone called your kind. Many species would find such a question as that to be rudely inquisitive."

"I did not intend it to be so," Deluge said. "But you can be offended if you choose. I will not mind."

Rurranach's jaw dropped lower and a curious chittering sound issued forth. Laughter, Deluge realized, and slow blinked his own pleasure in response.

"Choking Deluge, Mighty Hunter, I believe I like you," the Sidar said. "I have not had the opportunity to talk with many of your race. Are all Hunters as entertaining as you?"

"Almost none, in fact," Deluge said. "I'm considered quite the wit."

"I can see why," the Sidar said, letting out more of the chittering laughter. "To answer your question, yes, I have found that my cloth—particularly the luxury fabrics—are in fairly high demand. Though I seem to be selling mostly to off-worlders like myself, rather than the native Hunters. I know that you Depik sometimes wear clothing over your fur…"

"Sometimes," Deluge said, and let his face twist in a little moue of distaste. "When we have to. It isn't very comfortable, as I'm sure you know. You're furred yourself, aren't you? How can you stand being swathed in fabric like that?"

"Well, I—" Rurranach laughed again. "That was clever, turning my question back on me like that."

"Thank you," Deluge said modestly. "But I genuinely do want to know."

"Well, I shall tell you," Rurranach said. "But only if you answer a question of mine."

"Done," Deluge said. "But if you ask the wrong question, you know that I will have to offer you a choice."

"A choice?"

"Between me answering or not."

"Why would I choose not to have you answer a question I had asked?" the Sidar asked, tilting his large head to the side. Deluge smiled in the Human fashion, letting his sharp predator's teeth be seen.

"Because on Khatash, knowing the wrong answers is a death sentence for off-worlders."

"Ah," Rurranach said, and he fell silent for a long moment while his eyes studied the Depik's face.

Deluge didn't mind the scrutiny and stood motionless under it. He maintained a pleasant expression on his face as he watched the Sidar trader study him. Behind him, the noise of the City continued as beings and vehicles moved in eddying currents through the market plaza.

"Why have I seen so few Depik?" Rurranach said, his voice low. "Is that the wrong question?"

"Probably not," Deluge said evenly, and his predator's eyes caught the subtle movements of Rurranach's massive shoulders relaxing. He slow blinked and went on to answer. "You've not seen many of us because there aren't many of us. Our population is much lower than most of the races in the galaxy. Some of the beings you sold to were probably sigiled to a clan though."

"Sigiled?"

"Sworn. Like a…retainer." 'Retainer' sounded better to alien ears than 'pet,' or 'slave,' Deluge had learned.

"Oh, so those who contract to perform a service for a clan?"

"No, that is different. Anyone, even another Hunter, can contract with a clan. Sigiled beings are…more. Special. Always alien, but in a very real way, members of the clan. Within their clans, some are as respected as any deo or damita."

"Deo? Damita? These are new words to me. I thought there was only the Dama, and the rest of the clan."

Deluge opened his mouth in a grin at the Sidar's fascination. He was like an attentive kit, hanging on every word.

"The Dama is the most important, of course," Deluge said. "She is our mother and queen, and the chief elder of any clan. But any larger clan will also have deos, male Hunters who have earned the title of elder, and damitas, lesser damas who have borne litters but do not lead the clan."

"Fascinating," Rurranach said, tilting his great head sideways. "Thank you for your answer, it was more than satisfactory. As to your question…"

The Sidar shrugged, and his cloth drape fell away from the top half of his body. Deluge felt his eyes widen in delight as the webbed wings that had been hidden under the cloak half-spread from Rurranach's shoulders, until the claws at the wingtip touched the booth on either side.

"Most know that we're a volant species," Rurranach said. "But in business, there are times when it is best to be discreet."

"In life, I'd imagine," Deluge said. "Your wings are magnificent. Thank you for showing me."

"You are welcome," the trader said. He dipped his left wing and with the prehensile claws that capped each finger bone, picked up the discarded cloak and swirled it around himself again. "I have enjoyed getting to know you, Choking Deluge."

"And I, you, Rurranach."

"Perhaps I can give you my contact data? In case you're ever in the market for luxury fabrics? Or if you wish to exchange any other interesting bits of information? If you have a slate, I can input it directly…"

"Just tell me," Deluge said, slow blinking again. "I will remember."

"Oh! Right. The Depik eidetic memory. Very well," Rurranach said and rattled off his booth schedule and off-market contact procedures. Deluge took the information in and stored it away. One never knew when the most esoteric bit of information could be useful. Another thing he'd learned from his Human molly.

"One more thing I'll tell you," Deluge said before he stepped away from the booth. "Do not try out those wings on Khatash. We have Hunters who fly, and we see in the dark at least as well as you with your sonar."

"I don't know how that's possible," Rurranach said.

"And that is why you still live. Enjoy your day, Friend Rurranach!"

With that and a final friendly nod, Deluge stepped away from the fabric booth and continued his saunter toward the scent of spiced Khava.

* * *

The klaxon blasted through the air, knifing through any other sound like a blade through soft flesh. Death From Above (simply Death to her friends and family) dropped the slate she'd been reading and leapt to her feet. Along with all the other aerial Hunters in her squadron, the lean, striped Depik female tore down the short corridor and into the launch hangar at her top speed.

Which, since she *was* a Hunter, was very fast indeed.

Her bird was parked in its designated bay, canopy already open. The crew chief, a young Hunter in flight training, was already there, ready to strap her in and confirm readiness to launch. As she had done nine times ninety and nine times before, Death vaulted into her seat and began running the scramble start procedures. As soon as she was in place on her belly, her helmet automatically came down over her head. The leads inside contacted her pinplants, and her heads-up display (or HUD) appeared in her vision.

"Start Engines," she thought. First one, then the other of the Basreeni fighter's atmospheric engines roared to life as the retractable roof of the scramble hangar finished its opening sequence.

"Good Hunting!" the crew chief called out as she toggled the canopy closed and leapt away. The canopy latched into place with an audible *click*, and Death brought up the command and control comm channel with a thought.

"Death ready," she said, her tone empty of emotion.

"Zaru ready." "Asash ready." "Royou ready…" The other members of the squadron checked in one after the other.

"Unidentified, unauthorized space and atmospheric craft sighted on three-one-zero heading for four ranges," the voice of the command and control Hunter came back into their minds. A map appeared on the HUD, with the target in flashing red as it swept on its flight path. "Your orders are to launch and destroy."

"Acknowledged," Death thought back. "Squadron, elements of three, stack altitudes per the standard. Launch!"

On her thought, the vertical catapult under the fighter bay fired, throwing the Basreeni up and forward through the open roof of the hangar. The engine whine increased as the maneuverable little fighter rode that initial momentum and began to fly under its own power. The Basreeni could take off on its own, but the short take off and land launch capability cut significant lag time out of a scramble start.

Plus, it was fun. Death found herself grinning as her squadron separated itself out into nine three-ship elements, separated by three thousand feet of altitude each. Her own element flew at the middle at one-eight-thousand feet...which just happened to be the target's current altitude.

"Funny, that," Asash, her squadron second in command, said across the private command net. "Looks like you picked the lucky altitude."

"It's not luck, it's skill," Death shot back. "And doing my homework. These bogeys usually camp out just below twenty k."

"And you want one." Asash's tone was teasing, and held no note of rebuke. Therefore, Death refused to feel guilty about setting herself up for the kill.

"Of course I do. I'm the squadron commander, and all of my people but the very newest have multiple bogey kills. I've only two, and—" she stopped herself before she said too much and focused instead on the flashing target icon in her HUD. It was moving toward them.

"Combat spacing," she snapped out to her element with a thought. The Basreeni on either flank moved outward slightly, gaining more room to maneuver and cover her, and each other. Death checked the position and angle of the sun, and felt a surge of savage joy when she realized it was behind her. This could not have worked out better.

"Cloak," she ordered, and she felt the ripple of reality as the fighter's neural interface system magnified her use of quintessence to bend the baryonic light of the sun. Her visual scanners confirmed that she and her two winghunters had effectively vanished from sight. Unless the pilot of the unidentified craft was a Hunter, he'd never see them coming.

And no self-respecting Hunter would fly like that. Hunters entering atmosphere from orbit announced their intentions, or they got shot down. Everyone else got shot down regardless. That was the law on Khatash, and it was well publicized. As a race, Hunters liked their privacy.

The blinking icon began to grow larger and larger in the HUD. Death confirmed her laser and magnetic accelerator cannon (MAC) were online and ready to go. She also had six rockets slung under her belly, just waiting for her order to fire. It was time to dance.

"Warning, multiple targets." The electronic voice of the Basreeni's audio warning system manifested in her head as the icon doubled, and then doubled again. Before long, there were eight flashing symbols arrayed in front of her element, and closing fast. Then the symbol changed from "unidentified" to one she recognized.

"Closing in. Watch the flanks. Likely only one is manned, the others are photo-recon drones. Don't waste your time with the drones. Find the leader."

Her winghunters acknowledged her orders with growls of assent. Death hovered her finger-pads over the trigger of her MAC as the formation pushed in closer and closer. Before too long, she could pick up the targets visually. Eight of them, flying in two diamond patterns, offset by about a sprint.

The law on Khatash was very clear. Except for correctly-marked Hunter aircraft, all other flight outside the extraterritorial cone above the starport was forbidden. And photo reconnaissance was a clear violation of the privacy statutes the Council of Elders had put into place millennia ago. The surface of Khatash remained a mystery to all but the Hunters themselves. Low orbit spacecraft even saturated the planet's stratosphere with enough electromagnetic jamming that satellite photos and communications with the surface were impossible. But occasionally, a small ship would slip through the orbital blockade and make it into atmosphere. They would then release data-collecting drones and attempt to take as much information as possible before blasting back out, presumably to be picked up just outside of Khatash's orbit. Death didn't really know.

None of them had ever made it. The credit for surface photos must be pretty good, though, because the poachers still kept trying.

"Fire," Death whispered, dropping her fingerpads as the point ship in the formation grew larger in her view screen. She felt the kick shudder through the Basreeni's airframe as the MAC began spitting hate.

The point ship faltered, smoke appearing in its slipstream. It lost altitude, but the others kept flying. A drone then, and not important. Once she took out the controller, the drones would either crash or self-destruct.

A warning shrieked in her ear. She rolled the ship on its side, feeling the buffeting of the air as a missile streaked by her belly. Another blast from the MAC took out the trailing ship, and then she continued the roll and pulled her nose down into a dive before the left and right wings of the formation could fire upon her. Her wing-hunters were hard at work, covering her as she dove, picking up airspeed before pulling up into a climb that formed the bottom of a loop. All that kinetic energy flung her up into the air as she poured on the power and rocketed into the vertical. The trail ship of the target formation banked hard to the right, preparing to dive, but it was too late. The arc of the target's flight brought it right across Death's nose, and she fired her missiles into the target's belly.

Explosions flashed across the sky, causing the light-reactive glass of the Basreeni's cockpit to gain down to near-opaque darkness. Death's HUD confirmed that the remaining drones went dark, meaning that the trail ship had been the controller. When the outside visuals returned, Death pulled back the power and kicked in a bit of yaw, which pivoted the fighter around a wingtip, and let her see the trails of smoke as the drones spiraled out of control toward the surface.

"Good shooting!" Zaru, her left winghunter, crowed through the interplane frequency. "I'm showing all drones dark!"

"Terminate, Terminate, Terminate," Death ordered in response, her voice the same, emotionless tone it had had been during the engagement. She toggled the autopilot on and monitored the formation as it reconstituted itself.

"Asash, take your element and sweep for unusual activity, confirm all drones are down and then return to base. All others, good work. RTB now."

With a thought, she turned the Basreeni formation back toward home, and finally slow blinked a smile.

* * *

Her target died peacefully.

And then everything fell apart.

Technically, it blasted apart, a series of explosions starting between the walls of the target's quarters and the hull of the ship, but it all meant the same to Silent Flame.

She was a successful Hunter, with an unparalleled stealth and an impressive number of successfully completed assassinations, but now a paranoid trader was going to be the death of her.

Silent Flame had stalked her target for months. Learned his habits, planned the rapid series of actions needed to disable and then re-enable his security systems to make his death look natural. The client required that no suspicion fall on them, and that no hint of an orchestrated death held up the distribution of his assets after death.

Invisible and undetectable in her quintessence field, Flame had even accompanied her target on a short trip from his large cargo vessel to Piquaw as he closed some sizable deal.

Her planning resulted in the sort of the death the client would likely pay extra for. The target regularly gave himself nanite shots, warding off surprise poisons or spontaneous diseases before they had a chance to root. An expensive hobby, but one that had served him well over his career. Flame doctored his shots, patient bit by patient bit, secure in her ability to remain hidden, until he ultimately poisoned himself so gradually it didn't register in advance. The auto-reports his pinplant sent on his medical condition would confirm it, and only hindsight would show his mistake.

His paranoid attempts to pre-empt death had killed him. A neat closed-circle that appealed to her, and in the moments after it was done, she took a moment to congratulate her cleverness.

Which gave her the perfect opportunity to hear the first *boom*, echoing between the hull and his quarters.

A deadman's switch, one she'd missed. She had been so *thorough*.

Entropy and waste, she thought as she ran. He'd been paranoid enough that blowing up part of his main ship had seemed a good idea, if he weren't alive to deal with it. The ship was large enough that she could hope the entire thing wouldn't crack open to the void, but one mistake was more than enough for one contract, and she wasn't going to wait to find out.

Flame had no transport of her own here. She'd slipped onto the ship when they'd docked with another trader and had planned to slide out the same way.

"Are we under attack?" A frantic voice from further down the corridor told her the halls were about to get crowded with confused passengers and crew looking for answers. Panic occasionally kept beings from remembering things like comms and their slates. Some species liked crowding together in a crisis, as weird as it seemed.

Flame just wanted *out*. One of the first things she'd done upon arriving on board was to scout the dropship locations in case of emergency. Another explosion, and she snarled to herself.

That she hadn't anticipated this one was annoying, but she would—

Everything brightened. Cold, then hot. Blindingly bright, and the bend of light that hid her in her quintessence field could not shield her from the blast.

* * *

Why was her face jammed into a wall? Where…

Right. Explosions. Ship. Escape route. She got up to continue her run and realized she hadn't moved. Tried again.

Something had torn, or broken. Something was leaking. Something was imbedded in her side and she would not look to see what it was. Breathe. Again. Once more. Then, slowly, push away from the wall. Only one arm worked, only one side of her body responded to her commands, but that would have to be enough.

Move.

The cargo ship, too large to ever land itself, had several smaller craft tucked all around its bulk, to ease planetary travel and multiply docking options at various stations across the galaxy. Her target had liked to be prepared. They'd had that in common.

Her thoughts scattered, and she tried to pull them back together. Flame had a plan. She would execute the plan. Just get to a dropship. She could send a command that would release several of the ships, making tracking her impossible, given no one would look for her. Some other beings would panic and board their own craft, so it would be a mess of flight signatures away from this behemoth.

Flame had stalked other Hunters, for fun. Followed them to their dens to see them at ease, learn who they were. If her own kind couldn't detect her, she could certainly weave through this bucking hallway, get to a ship, and get out.

Emergency supplies would keep her alive—blasted entropy. She couldn't leave blood behind. Unlikely someone would go around testing all the DNA they could find, but she wouldn't be responsible if they did.

This hallway was on fire, she noted calmly. Anything she'd already shed would burn away. Forcing each motion, she reached into a pouch on her belt, drew out a self-adhering bandage, and pressed it to her side so it would form around the wound. Smart enough to form around the shrapnel, too.

She didn't waste time looking at the injury. There would be plenty of opportunity to keep herself alive on the trip home. She'd patch up enough to make it, heal a bit on the way, and get fixed in the den, with a medic she trusted and beings she loved around her. Susa would…

Flame had been drifting again, and she hissed between her teeth. Move. Commandeer ship. Home.

Target was dead, client would be happy, and she'd learn from this.

Next time would be cleaner.

* * *

C unning Blade slept. At home, surrounded by his closest family, he allowed himself deep, boneless relaxation. He sprawled across a high perch, not a strand of fur twitching in the dim light from above.

Nothing else, not even the satisfaction after a well-planned and executed hunt, gave him the same refreshing rest, and yet he moved from sleep to alert awareness at the barest hiss of the door sliding open.

"Susa?" he asked, though he knew the answer. No other resident of the clan den would have made a noise, or allowed the scent of the air to change so quickly. Had it been Flame, he wouldn't have known until she cuffed him or yanked his tail. Once he'd believed his youngest littermate would outgrow such habits, but he'd once been a mewling kit believing milk to be the most important thing in the world, and he'd long since left both beliefs behind.

Their clan's Human molly tsked, but she didn't sound truly disappointed. Though she'd grown remarkably quiet for a Human, she would never reach even Deluge's level of stealth.

"You wanted to be sure to have time to review the contracts before meeting Dama ahead of the council," she reminded, looking both fond and concerned. Clearly, she'd expected him to wake on his own, earlier than this.

Blade stretched, yawned, and snapped his jaws shut with a satisfyingly audible click.

"Thank you, Susa. I should come home more."

"Why is that?" she asked, humoring him.

"I'm more rested from this nap than I've been for the last four months."

"You were on a contract," she said, wryly, then pointed at the food she'd brought. "And I do keep you well fed."

He slow-blinked at her, grateful for the loving way she treated him and his littermates, even now that they were long grown. His affection for their molly remained unspoken, but his slow-blink conveyed it enough that he was comfortable changing the subject.

"Flame and Deluge will be available for new contracts soon, and I'd like to stagger where we're going." It wasn't, technically, his job to do such things, but he'd never stop being the oldest, and he had a better eye for such things than most of his littermates. Not better than their Dama, but she was so busy that he was more than happy to help, and—usually—his siblings respected his opinions in these matters. Besides, Flame's last contract had taken the better part of a year, and though she'd earned a bonus for ensuring the target's death appeared natural, she'd also come back with a new scar and several broken ribs. Her next contract needed to be something that would allow her to use her unmatched stealth skills more efficiently...and would hopefully keep her a little safer.

"I know," Susa said, moving fully into fondness as the concern ebbed. She watched as he leapt down to take the snack she'd brought. "And they will appreciate your thoughts, as ever." As often, at any rate. "Will you be home for the evening meal?"

"I should be," he replied agreeably, turning from her to pick up his harness and work bag. Since he'd been barely weaned, Susa had been one of the few living beings he trusted deeply enough to turn his back on without any lingering wariness. "There shouldn't be many new contracts to sort, and I only have a few errands to run before going to the council with Dama." One of the metalsmiths had sent a message about a new batch of weapons, he needed to see a technician to be sure she'd truly fixed the catch in one of his guns' trigger, and it never hurt to browse the merchandise. It would keep him plenty busy ahead of the council.

"Very well." She paused, and he knew she wanted to hug him close, so he finished settling his straps and crossed close to her before leaving, rubbing his head against her hand as he passed by. Susa laughed at the extra fillip he gave his tail, and continued, "I'm sure Deluge will bring home enough from his hunt."

Blade chuckled in reply. The next youngest of their litter had been deep in the jungles, and would likely return with impressive spoils to show for his efforts. No matter how foolish the other male chose to be, his skills were not in question.

"Blade?" Susa asked just before he left the room.

He paused—for Susa, he would always pause.

"What do you think the council will bring?" She wasn't specific, but none of them were exactly sure what the council aimed for. Elders seemed to love their secrets.

"Interesting times for our clan," he replied, glancing back at her with a small smile. "As ever."

* * * * *

Interesting Times

A council of the galaxy's deadliest assassins appeared much like a gathering of elders anywhere else. Damas and their trusted few gathered, gossiped, and watched. Some spoke in small groups, some held haughtily apart, some observed subtly, and some overtly gawked.

Blade had never been a gawker, but here among some of the most successful Hunters of Khatash his ears swiveled to catch every sound, his nose twitched slightly to catch the nuance of scent and emotion in the air around them, and the tip of his tail curled back as his interest caught. Each motion itself infinitesimal, perhaps, but in a room of trained killers, he couldn't hope any of it went unmarked.

He was young still, compared to most in the large, rounded room, and he was among the least important, so perhaps his reaction would be taken as signs of deference and of knowing his place. Still, he waited until he had composed himself to glance at his dama, who moved through the collection of her elders and peers without hesitation.

And why not? Night Wind was still a new clan, rapidly growing and noticed at a planetary level. In a species that struggled with fertility, Reow had borne four living kits, all of whom had survived to adulthood, all of whom had become off-world Hunters of note in their turn. The odds of each part of that success were vanishingly small, and if that had been all that set the clan apart, still they be would be renowned.

Reow herself was an assassin in high demand; she had been the first to sigil a Human, making a pet and sponsored companion from the mercenary species, and she had taken increasingly higher value contracts over the years. Cunning Blade, as her oldest kit, had learned more by the time he'd been released from the den than many young Hunters learned their first year in the jungles.

Given all that, it was no surprise they'd been summoned to the council of elders to discuss a contract of importance to their entire species. The Governor for the Hunters had recently and unexpectedly died, and power and opportunities would always shuffle with such a significant loss. To Blade, it made utter sense that his dama would be counted as vital in a time of such movement.

"What do you see, my kit?" Reow murmured as they arrived at their assigned seating ledge. Though not as low as some of the larger, more powerful clans, Night Wind's vantage point was flatteringly close to the central speaking area. She leapt up to the spot with one surge of her powerful hindquarters and waited for her son to join her and answer the question.

Blade followed without hesitation, turning his attention from the elders of their species to his dama. He considered his answer, still processing all that was and wasn't on display in the interplays of clan and Hunter around them.

"Who believes they belong here and who does not," he said, twitching one ear back to indicate he did not mean himself.

"And have you drawn any conclusions from this observation?" she murmured as she settled into a resting position, tucking her front legs under her chest and cocking her head to the side in interest.

"That the council likes the uncertainty and perhaps wants to see what we all think of our standing. Why else would they not tell us what we're here to learn and leave us gathering time for such divisions to come clear?" Blade sat back on his hind legs, his usual thinking position, and curled his tail close around himself.

"The council is an interesting entity, my kit," Reow said as she began lightly grooming her face. "Never forget what it is: a loose confederation of elders, and that only. Within the clans, a dama may do as she pleases—or what her elders let her get away with, at least. For most here, obedience to the council's dictates are a matter of inconvenience at best, and pride-wounding at worst. They will obey, or at least give the *appearance* of obeying, because our place in the wider galaxy depends upon the council's appearance of control. If the Galactic Union thought for a second that the Council of Elders was less than omnipotent upon our world, we would be so much dust, as quickly as you can say Mercenary Guild.

"They fear us, my kit. The other races. This is as it should be, for we are fearsome by design. But it is also a liability. One which we mitigate through politics and playing the games of the Union. For we are ever teetering on the brink of extinction. And likely, we ever will be."

Blade was not one to dismiss something simply because it made him uncomfortable, and so the small noise he made in answer was less of protest and more a thoughtful sort of disgust, that they must placate lesser species and still their future balanced on the knife edge of fertility and risk.

"And the council knows well, this game they play?" Rarely had he met an elder or dama who did not take any and all control allowed, and he wondered how much the council believed in their control, rather than the appearance of same.

"Of course," Reow said. "It is why we participate in the Union at all. And why the council is a council of elders, not just a council of damas. For a clan's elder deos and damitas will have much influence over their clan's actions...and having them know the will of the council is important for that reason."

At that moment, a darkly-furred dama leapt up to the raised pedestal in the center of the room and sat, waiting for the conversations to die down, and the eyes to turn her way. Reow slow blinked a smile at her son and ceased speaking, turning her attention toward the waiting speaker.

Blade settled next to his dama, though his peripheral vision took in the reactions of the Hunters around them even as he turned attentively toward the older dama in front of them.

"There is a contract before us," she said, not wasting time with greetings or formalities—all knew they were here for a reason, "which affects all the clans, and to which we have a recommendation. With Governor Sissisk's sudden death, Peacemaker Hrusha will take the Governor contract."

Several clan leaders shifted at that, and Blade turned his head slightly to better observe their reactions. The Dama of Whispering Fear raised all the fur on her back before forcing herself back to stillness, and two of the elders of High Canopy let their jaws drop in disgust.

"The Peacemaker contract is therefore available." The stir of interest that provoked was inaudible, but obvious. Elders repositioned themselves, or pricked forward their ears, or in one case reared back. Blade did not hide his interest in observing their reactions, which meant even he showed a measure of surprise when the dama continued.

"Peacemaker Hrusha and the council recommend Reow, Dama of Night Wind, accept the Peacemaker contract."

Dama didn't immediately react, which was an indicator of her surprise, but only to one who knew her extremely well. After a moment, she slow blinked and pushed up to a seated position.

"I thank the Peacemaker and the council for this recommendation," she said.

"And the council is putting this to the gathered clans for discussion, rightfully." The Dama of Whispering Fear stood, her tail straightened tensely behind her. It was not a question, and she did not dip her head to either Reow or the council dama to acknowledge her interruption for what it was.

"A nomination is not an assignment," a deo from High Canopy said, lowering his head to Dirrys and the speaker in front of them all. "And Night Wind is still a small clan. What benefits us, in this recommendation?"

"Shall I speak in my own advocacy, then?" Reow asked, turning to look at the speaker. At her blink of assent, Reow flicked her ears and pushed up to her feet.

"A small clan might actually be an asset to a Peacemaker, if the clan is well-established. Small we may be, but Night Wind commands the fifth largest fortune of any clan on the planet, and each of my offspring has survived to adulthood and full Hunter status. One serves even now as a Basreeni pilot and commander of her Aerial Hunter unit. I, myself, am not beyond my fertile years, and either of my kitas may conceive at any time.

"We have new blood, but it is strong. Strong enough to make a sigiled pet out of the newest mercenary species in the galaxy, a feat as yet unmatched by the worthy clans in this room," Reow said in an even, respectful tone. She kept her tail and ears from twitching, and only someone as close as Blade would have seen the fine tremor of excitement that stirred the fur on the back of her neck.

"Then perhaps your clan will be ready in ten years, should the contract come open again," Whispering Fear's Dama murmured, her eyes half-closed in a not-quite insult. "All very impressive, of course, but the complexity of such a contract can only be understood by a dama with a depth of experience that a larger, ancient clan brings."

"Dirrys." The Dama of Blood Plague made the other Hunter's name sound like a spit of disgust. "Your clan has lost an off-world Hunter and the largest crop of *Malluma Songo* in your history, so surely you are not nominating yourself."

"Whispering Fear is the oldest clan in this room, and all growth comes with risk. The Peacemaker contract would be best supported by my clan's resources."

"Perhaps that is so," Reow said smoothly. "But Whispering Fear's recent losses have hit your bottom line hard, and most of your assets are tied up in your clan's extensive and valuable territory. Do you mean to say you will liquidate? And would that be wise for one of your years, Dirrys? Should not your resources be better spent on keeping your fertile kitas alive long enough to deliver live young?"

A barely audible hiss of shock at these blunt words. It was well known that Whispering Fear had suffered a rash of bad luck with its fertile females. For years, none but Dirrys, the Dama, had survived bringing a full litter to term. And before that, their infant mortality rate had been higher than most. Some said it meant that the ancient clan's blood was weakening.

Reow was clearly implying that to be the case.

"We would hardly need to liquidate to take on such a contract." Dirrys's derisive laugh carried the faintest edge of a hiss. "And that all you can respond with is the basest of...what is that? Insult? Limp threat? It indicates you have no business representing us outside of Khatash. Keep growing your clan, Dama," this with the subtlest twist on the word, a hint of mocking, "and perhaps you'll be ready to go off-world uncloaked someday."

Faintly, so soft that the sound couldn't have carried past his dama, Blade snarled.

Reow twitched her tail, a silent command to her offspring to remain calm. Dirrys's position could only be strengthened by their rising to her bait.

"Dirrys, do not start hurtling insults, lest we be here all day," the Speaker said, her voice carrying a note of irritation. "Peacemaker Hrusha has recommended Reow of Night Wind by name, citing her abilities, her relative youth and yet wide range of experiences, and her cosmopolitan views which will enable her to better integrate with the alien species in our galaxy. What say you to that?"

"I say Peacemaker Hrusha became Governor without the clans weighing in, and you brought this contract to us to consider." Dirrys sat more comfortably, her tail settling around her body, expression alert and inquiring. "So, let us consider."

"There's no reason to choose against the recommendation," a damita from Sweet Poison said, her gravid belly giving her the weight she needed to speak in this room despite her youth, her head lowered in deference. "The Peacemaker would understand best who her replacement needs to be."

Blade flicked an ear back in satisfaction, recognizing the clan as one that had lost out to Night Wind on several contracts. Likely they thought they could be better positioned if Night Wind became more occupied with the Peacemaker contract. His attention remained peripherally fixed on Dirrys of Whispering Fear, unconvinced by the too-obvious easing of her posture.

"I appreciate smaller, successful clans rising to notice," a deo put forth. "We should recognize the vitality and success that continue to grow our species."

Several clan heads shifted at that, some in agreement and some discomfited by the reminder their next generation wavered, as ever, on the edge of a claw.

"I agree," the first deo who had spoken picked up smoothly, "and so nominate Sirrus, Dama of Evening Tide. She has built our clan for nearly twenty years, bearing three litters and raising three adult Hunters, two of whom have had their own first litters. Offworld contracts and Khatash trade are equal anchors, and we have not," with a brief sideways glance to Dirrys, "made enemies at home or in the galaxy."

"All Peacemakers make enemies," Reow said, flicking her ears in respect toward Evening Tide. "I argue that we would want someone with experience dealing with such things in the position. Especially if that experience includes deescalating conflicts, or at least ending them quickly, with a minimum of collateral damage." Again, she very carefully did not look at Dirrys, but the barb was clear and well thrown.

Dirrys tensed, and Blade saw every one of her claws—she leaned on the edge of launching herself across the room before visibly restraining herself. No one else in the room reacted to the near breach of one of their deepest tenets, and Blade would have missed her loss of control if he hadn't kept his focus on her. Shock held him still, the idea that a dama would attack another dama, for nothing more than words…

The Speaker let the silence carry for a moment before sitting back comfortably, unaware of what Blade had seen. She looked from dama to dama, and flicked her ear to acknowledge no one else had anything to say.

"In light of these discussions, I hear nothing that outweighs Peacemaker Hrusha's recommendation. The suggestion carries." No one flinched, though several pairs of eyes and ears swiveled toward his dama. "Reow, do you accept the contract?"

"Provisionally, Speaker," Reow said. "I require a ninenight to travel home and consult with my clan before committing fully. But provisionally, yes. I would be happy to accept."

The Speaker's sound of acknowledgement was answered by a chorus of small noises from the gathered Hunters, and then with a brisk nod the Speaker turned her gaze from Reow into the general distance in front of her, signaling the matter was closed.

"There are smaller trade agreements to be discussed, for those clans affected. Our general session has ended, if you choose to return to your dens."

Not quite a dismissal, Blade understood more of the nuance now, where the council did not exactly dictate, but made clear all the same. The experience had given him plenty to consider, and he was glad there was a quiet night at home ahead, where he could give the proper time and attention to reflection.

* * *

When she landed, he was there.

Death taxied in from the runway, satisfaction running through her like a current. She turned off toward the alert hangar and cut the Basreeni's engines back to idle. With a thought, she coasted to a stop above her launcher, and began the shutdown sequence.

As soon as her canopy hissed open, she saw him approach.

Nine shadows, but her lover moved like poetry! He stalked like the Hunter he was, muscles liquid under his grey fur. Death felt a lick of desire curl through her as she pulled herself out of the Basreeni's cockpit and leapt lightly down to the hangar floor. He wasn't in her squadron, of course, but rather a pilot in their sister-squadron next door. And as her lover, he was always welcome here.

"Welcome home, Hunter," Mhrand said, slow blinking his striking amber eyes. "Eight kills! Impressive."

"Only one was controlled," she said. "The others were just drones. They hardly count."

"Drones are harder to kill than the manned fighter. More maneuverable."

"Which is why I went for the controller," she finished, dropping her jaw in a grin. "Take it out, and the drones kill themselves."

"That's my deadly love," Mhrand said, and answered her grin with his own. He leaned in to rub his cheekbone against hers in a quick kiss before turning to face the growing crowd of pilots and support Hunters gathering on the floor of the alert hangar.

"Eight kills," he went on, pitching his voice to carry over the noise of the crowd. "Seven of them drones…and on this, her last flight with the squadron before returning home to her Clan."

A sudden realization dawned on Death. She felt her eyes go wide and turned to look accusingly at her beloved. He merely grinned at her and stepped back.

An instant before the bucket of water upended over her, drenching her in an icy downpour.

Death let out a shrieking yowl and leapt toward Mhrand, who caught her, laughing.

"I'm sorry! I'm sorry! Peace, beloved, I yield!" he cried out amid the audible laughter of the squadron. Death swatted him handily on the head, then the body, then the head again before relenting and swiping her rough tongue over the side of his face.

"That was a dirty trick," she purred in his ear.

"I know. The tradition for final flights is that we tackle you and carry you to be doused...but be reasonable, love. None of us can take you. Subterfuge was the only way. The bucket has been rigged for the last ninenight, just waiting for you to get a launch. We disguised it as part of the fire-suppression system."

"Well. I see some of my training has taken root," she said, stepping back from Mhrand to address the members of her squadron. "I am satisfied. A clean kill to all of you."

The assembled Hunters let out a cacophony of celebratory yowls that made the rafters echo. Someone, somewhere, started playing music, and before Death could say otherwise, a fully-fledged party broke out right there in the middle of the hangar. She thought about trying to rein in the revelry...but it was her last alert shift, her last flight, and she'd just scored an impressive kill. They could afford to let loose a little bit.

"My squadron has picked up the alert," Mhrand murmured in her ear as he wrapped her up in an embrace. "I worked it all out with Asash. You did it, my love. You're all done."

Like many who chose to hunt in the sky, Death's contract had been for a period of four years, not including the required training time to learn to fly the Basreeni. Through her skill and determination, she'd been chosen by the elder dama in charge of the sky hunt to command a squadron for the last two of those years. It had been the hardest contract she'd ever completed. And the one she'd loved the most. She loved each of these Hunters as if they were her own littermates, and she knew they felt the same about her.

And Mhrand…the desire that always accompanied the thought of her lover curled deliciously through her body. They'd met in training, become lovers their first year on the contract, and had been inseparable since. She'd never met another being who moved her, who cared for her as well as he did, with his muscular strength and nurturing tenderness. Death had taken lovers before Mhrand…but none had captivated her as he did. And no other had caught her attention since.

"I wish to be alone with you," she whispered in his ear. "Now."

"Yes? All right," he said, giving her a wicked grin. "Let us sneak away, they can party without us."

* * *

"I want you to come home with me."

Death's words rolled out in the darkness of the space they'd found together, an unused alert sleeping alcove. Their bodies lay entangled, replete with love and satiated desire.

"When, beloved?" Mhrand asked.

"I will leave immediately. Your contract is nearly at an end as well. I wish you to come to my Den and meet my clan."

Mhrand's tail had been lazily twining with her own, but he went very still with that last statement.

"Death, what—"

"I love you, Mhrand," she said, cutting him off. "I do not wish to think of living without you by my side."

"Beloved," he said, his voice a low purr. "I will be yours for as long as you will have me, you know that."

"Yes…but I want more."

She shifted enough to come to a seated position. The darkness of the alcove was no barrier to sight. When they joined, so too did their quintessence fields. She could *feel* him, solid and strong, nearly as deadly as herself. A fitting mate. A fitting addition to the clan.

"My dama will approve of you," Death said. "Your kill record speaks for itself. You have chosen to hunt exclusively in the air, which is different, but not dishonorable. You come from an established clan of successful Hunters…and you have shown yourself capable of siring a litter of kittens."

"I have…what?"

Death slow blinked a smile, and with a wave of her right front paw, brought the lights in the room up enough for him to see her face baryonically.

"I feel them move within me already. At least three, but I suspect one or two more."

Mhrand's eyes went wide, and he scrambled up to a seated position opposite Death.

"Beloved...a litter? Kits?"

"Indeed. Does this please you? For if it does not, I will, of course, release you from our association." She managed to keep her voice steady as she spoke, though the thought of losing him sent a spike of icy dread through her.

Mhrand just stared at her, then dropped his jaw in the largest grin she'd yet seen from him.

"Don't you dare think about it, my beloved, beautiful, crazy love! Kittens! You are certain?"

Death slow blinked again, and she found herself grinning openly as well.

"I am. I expect they will arrive later this year. Perhaps a season from now."

"Have the healers been consulted?"

"Not yet," she said calmly. She must step carefully here, for males got touchy at times when their females were carrying young. "I would see my clan's healer for something with so much import as this. This litter will be the first of its generation in my clan."

Mhrand drew in a deep breath and reached out to stroke her ears with his fingerpads.

"Beloved, was that wise? You flew...today even. In combat! What if something—"

Death reached out and laid her own fingerpads on his lips, quieting him.

"Nothing happened," she said. "I am as well as I ever have been, and now my contract is finished. I will return to my clan and see our healer, and I will tell my dama and littermates the happy news. But…There is more that I would like to tell them."

"What?" Mhrand asked, eyes going wide again. A private corner of Death's mind wondered dryly if he would survive too many more revelations. He looked completely poleaxed.

"I would like to tell them we have formed a life-bond. That you will join our clan, and help me raise our kits. That you will stay beside me and be my partner when I, eventually, become the head of the family."

"Head—"

"I am the first to bear," Death said softly. "I will be Dama after my own is gone."

Mhrand's tail twitched, and his ears flicked back and forth as he processed this. Death watched him, her face and ears carefully expressionless, though she thought her heart might pound its way out of her chest.

"You, who will be the Dama, and could have any male you choose to sire future young…you want to form a life-bond with me?" His voice was low, his words precise.

"Yes."

"Beloved…" Mhrand trailed off, and simply reached out to caress her face. "I cannot…I have done nothing to deserve such fortune as smiles on me. I will happily go home with you. I would love you for nine times ninety and nine lives. I would love you forever."

Death slow blinked a smile, and reached to rub her face against his.

"Then forever it shall be."

* * *

Deluge closed his eyes and let the taste of spiced Khava explode over the inside of his mouth. It burned its way over his tongue and down into his belly, filling him with heat from the inside.

"You like it?" the Besquith trader growled. Deluge opened his eyes and looked up at the hairy alien. Besquith were not known for their charm, and this one seemed a representative member of his race in that department. It had somewhat beady eyes that glared at Deluge as he sat on the trading counter. Doubtless, the trader would have preferred for Deluge to remain on the floor in his bipedal stance. However, that didn't make sense in the Hunter's mind, given the immense difference between their two heights. Far better that he should spring to the counter and sit like a civilized being.

It wasn't his problem if his movements were too quick for the Besquith to track. Nor was it his problem if that fact made the other being nervous. Though Deluge had to admit it was amusing.

"I do like it," the Hunter said. "Your batch has a very good flavor."

"I have more," the Besquith said. "Five credits gets you the whole fish."

Deluge slow blinked at the outrageous price, and let his mouth fall open in his Human smile.

"And what would I do with a whole fish?" he asked. "Especially at that larcenous rate?"

"Larcenous?" the Besquith growled, its voice dropping lower. "Are you calling me a cheat?"

"Larceny means theft. Technically I'm calling you a thief," Deluge said. "But I suppose your language may not have such subtleties."

He didn't, truly, mean it as an insult. The Besquith didn't seem to care. It let out a low snarl and bared its teeth, then lunged at Deluge, snapping his teeth a hair's breadth from where the Hunter sat.

Or more accurately, where the Hunter had been sitting.

Because, of course, Deluge was in motion as soon as the Besquith started his lunge. He drove his powerful hind legs against the firm surface of the trading counter and leapt up into the air. A quick twist of his body allowed his front claws access to the large, pointed ears that sat atop the Besquith's head. He dug his claws into those sensitive ears and used them as a pivot point to anchor his leap. His lower body flipped up and around to the point where his back claws could grab on. One caught the alien's throat, just above the jugular, and the other hovered scant millimeters from the being's vulnerable eye.

"Hunter, your pardon."

The voice that spoke was Besquith, and female, unless Deluge missed his guess. It was also smooth and laced with respect, unlike the nervous, aggressive tone of the one he now had by the ears. That Besquith was busy whimpering in pain and fear as Deluge wrenched its head around so that he might look at the newcomer.

The newcomer stood in the curtained doorway at the back of the booth. She wore the rich silks of a wealthy Besquith trader, and the grey about her muzzle spoke of some experience. She inclined her head as Deluge met her eyes.

"I greet you," Deluge said. He didn't want to be rude, but he rather thought that in this particular situation, he might be excused the use of an abbreviated hello. "Welcome to our negotiation."

"I am Jhurrahkk" she said. "I am the alpha for our people here on Khatash. You hold the life of my pup in your claws."

"I am Deluge," he answered. "Your pup was rude and attacked me. His life is forfeit on my planet."

"This is where I propose we begin our negotiation."

"His life is forfeit," Deluge said. "I cannot change that. The clans are very clear."

"They are clear, Hunter. And we were very well briefed upon entry to your system. But there is a stipulation. His life is forfeit *on this planet.*"

"Which is where he stands."

"I am a mother, mighty Hunter. I would negotiate a period of time during which I might get my child off your planet and save his fool life."

Deluge slow blinked.

"I see why you are alpha, Jhurrahkk. Clever of you to mention your relationship to this unfortunate one."

"I have done my homework, mighty Hunter. I know how your race honors motherhood," Jhurrahkk said, inclining her head.

"Without our mothers, where would we be?" Deluge said, quoting an oft-recited maxim. "Very well, we will negotiate. What is your offer?"

"All of the goods in this booth, and all of my possessions here on Khatash, in exchange for one day to get him off planet and out of the system."

"That is rather a high offer to begin with," Deluge said. "You surprise me. Usually negotiations are much more…meandering."

"I am a mother whose child is threatened, mighty Hunter. I do not feel like wasting a lot of time meandering," Jhurrahkk said on a hint of a growl. She stood motionless in her trader's silks, but Deluge suspected she would be a vicious fighter.

"So you are," Deluge said, he flexed his front claws, causing the panting Besquith pup to let out another sharp whine. "I am tempted to decline and see just what kind of dance you would lead me, alpha."

Jhurrahkk tensed, her hackles rising along the back of her neck.

Deluge moved. Before either Besquith could react, he launched himself backward, diving for the floor. His front paws touched down on the gritty floor between the pup's heels first. His back paws followed, tucking up toward his belly where he kept a knife hidden in his hunting vest. The toes of his right paw curved around the hilt, and he slashed out with a kick that neatly severed the tendon running up the back of the Besquith pup's leg.

Deluge contracted himself back into a sitting position, conveniently hiding the knife beneath his body, and began to groom the fur on his left front leg. The Besquith pup collapsed, screaming. Jhurrahkk flinched at the sound.

"I accept your offer," Deluge said, his pleasant tone unchanged. "Provided you leave immediately with your pup for the starport. You do not have a day. You have until the next shuttle departure for anywhere."

The alpha mother let out a low, guttural growl and gave him a single nod. Then she bent down and picked up her injured pup.

"We have an agreement," she said.

"A pleasure doing business with you," Deluge said, as he watched the two of them leave the booth that was now entirely his.

* * *

"Mighty Hunter...you did what?"

Deluge dropped his mouth open in a laugh at the Zuul factor's expression. The large canid alien wore the sigil of Deluge's clan dangling from one of his ears, and had done so for as long as Deluge had known him—which was most of Deluge's life. Ruzeen had joined the clan as a pup long before Deluge's birth. There was a story there, but Deluge didn't know it. All that mattered was that Ruzeen was a devoted retainer. His race had a reputation for being both cunning and avaricious, and Ruzeen lived up to both qualities. In his case, however, all his cleverness and greed functioned on behalf of the clan. Which was why he was the clan's financial factor in the City.

"I bought a Besquith Khava trader's booth and inventory, Ruzeen," Deluge repeated, deliberately letting his voice sound as nonchalant as possible. To heighten the effect, he began once again to groom his front paws while the noon sunlight streamed through the windows of the clan's City offices.

"Yes, mighty Hunter, but...why? We have no interests in the Khava trade, and it is not really a growth industry at this time." Ruzeen's pointed nose wrinkled slightly in puzzlement. Like the Besquith alpha, his muzzle fur had faded from rich brown to grey with age. His large liquid eyes, however, were as keen and intelligent as ever as he sat next to a low table that held both a large slate, and Deluge himself.

"It just sort of happened. It was either that or kill a stupid kid who made a stupid mistake. You'll see to the disposition of the goods?"

"Of course, mighty Hunter."

"Ruzeen, you've known me since I was a kit," Deluge said.

"I have. You were an adorable ball of orange fury," the factor said.

"See? Why do you insist on being so formal with me now?"

"Because that is the way things are done, mighty Hunter. And also because I know it bothers you."

Deluge blinked, his ear twitching in surprise. Ruzeen eyed him sidelong and dropped his own jaw in a smile.

"Ruzeen!"

"You deserve it, young master. Especially when you come in here telling such stories! First you go out hunting Cheelin, then you return with nothing but the stingers and poison sacs—"

"And a booth full of Besquith Khava!"

"Oh, more than that, mighty Hunter. I know Jhurrahkk. She has entire warehouses full of goods. You did say you purchased *all* of her inventory, did you not?"

"Well...yes."

Ruzeen dropped his jaw again and this time let out a short, barking laughter.

"You have no idea! The Besquith here on Khatash were into much more than just spiced fish, mighty Hunter! You're now the proud owner of enough starship and atmospheric craft avionics parts to resupply every one of the Elders' Basreeni."

Deluge froze, paw halfway up to his face, mouth open, tongue out. The Basreeni fighter was designed by the Jeha, and while it wasn't overly maintenance intensive, the Council of Elders had wisely purchased a bench stock of parts from the insectoid alien engineers. Apparently, that deal had been brokered by the Besquith, and Deluge had just purchased himself into the very lucrative position of middleman.

"Well," Deluge said. "That is very interesting. I…ah…"

"Never fear, young master," Ruzeen said, his smile turning indulgent. "You may leave it with me. I know exactly how to play this to best benefit our clan."

"Of course you do," Deluge said, recovering his aplomb in an instant. He resumed grooming his face, and then stood up and indulged in a lengthy stretch on the Zuul's work table. "This is why I come to you with these matters."

"And because you don't know anyone else you can trust in the City."

"And because of that, too."

"So, you've hunted the deadly Cheelin and fleeced the even deadlier Besquith. What will you do now, young master?"

"I shall return home, I think. It has been a while, and Dama should likely hear of the Besquith affair from me. In case there are…repercussions."

"That would be wise," Ruzeen said, dipping his head as his smile dropped away. "You acted with propriety, but the Besquith can be unpredictable. You see clearly in this matter. Our dama will likely be returning to the den within the ninenight."

"Oh? Where has she gone? A contract?"

"No, young master, you did not hear? I suppose the word went out after you left last. A Council has been called. The Union needs a new Peacemaker."

"What of the current Peacemaker?"

"She will be promoted to Governor, representing the will of the Council to the Union. The former Governor has laid down this life," Ruzeen said.

"May she find her next one swiftly," Deluge responded. The platitude came automatically to his lips, but his mind raced through the possible implications of these events. "So, our dama will help choose the next Peacemaker."

"At the very least," Ruzeen said. Deluge looked sharply up at the wily old Zuul, but Ruzeen was known for his discretion. He merely closed his mouth and gave the Hunter a sly look and a nod.

Deluge let out a little sigh and then stood up to his back feet.

"Well, then I must certainly return home as soon as possible," he said. "Have you anything for me to carry? Messages or anything else?"

"An offer of contract came in from one of our dealers," Ruzeen said. "It requests your sister Silent Flame, though she may not be back from her previous commitment. Our dealer was very clear on the point that she might not be available. The client will accept a member of the clan in her stead. It might be a good offer for you, young master, now that I think of it."

"What is the contract?"

"A Lumar mercenary company is not fond of their commanding officer. Apparently, he puts them into terrible positions and then blames the rest of them. Discipline is overly harsh, according to them, and they aren't getting their appropriate share of the contract payouts."

"They must be getting some, if they can afford us."

"I believe they've saved up for some time for this purpose. One wonders why they didn't just take care of the commander during a mission…but then, the Lumar aren't known for being the smartest race in the galaxy."

"The name of the company?"

"'Proud Fist.'"

"How very…Lumar."

"Snobbery is unbecoming, young master. Please give our dama my love when you see her."

"I will, Ruzeen. Thank you."

Deluge dropped back down to four feet and walked over to where the Zuul sat watching him. With a low purr, the Hunter reared up and rubbed his face along the Zuul's cheekbone, mingling their scents together, marking Ruzeen as clan, as family. The canid factor let out a small rumble of pleasure and reached up to stroke Deluge's fur from ears to tail in return.

Without another word (because what more needed to be said?) Deluge leapt down from the factor's desk and walked out into the searingly bright sunlight.

*****

Recall

I t didn't take long to get home to the den.

Deluge hopped a suborbital, which rocketed him to the Clan's territory in less than half a Mrur. When it touched down on the familiar plateau, he felt a thrill of joy ripple through him. The door of the shuttle opened with a hiss, and the mountain air flowed in. While he wasn't the only passenger, he was the only kit of the Clan on board. And since his Clan paid for this particular shuttle service to their lands, the pilot ordered that the others remain strapped in their seats until he'd disembarked. He appreciated the courtesy, and gave the pilot a brief nod as he passed the cockpit on the way out.

The pilot lifted his paw, claws retracted, in response. Deluge didn't recognize the Hunter, but it wasn't unusual for his Clan to contract with the aerial Hunters who flew the Basreeni fighters to do this work for a season or two. Perhaps in a night or so, Deluge would venture out here and learn the pilot's name and Clan. It was always good to be sociable and make new acquaintances. One never knew when they'd be useful.

But not now. Now, he was home, and the moment the pads of his paws touched the soft, springy mountain soil, Deluge knew he'd been away too long. He broke into a run, his muscles burning pleasantly after too long immobile on the shuttle. He dove into the shadows of the jungle that ringed the shuttle landing pad and blinked twice in rapid succession. His sunlight goggles retracted smoothly into the harness he wore around his ears as the green darkness enveloped him.

The path from the shuttle pad to the Den wound for about three sprints through the undergrowth until it approached an ancient rockfall on the side of the ridge. Deluge headed straight for this, reveling in the feel of his body stretching and moving, his blood and quintessence flowing through him as he charged up the mountain slope toward the gap in the boulders that served as a front door.

By all the stars in the sky, how he hated sitting still!

Flushed and happy from the exercise, Deluge slipped through the boulder gap and slowed to a walk in the tunnel beyond. The floor dipped downward here, in a long, curving ramp that further cut the daylight from outside. Even Hunter eyes strained to see in this darkness, but Deluge knew every step like he knew the pattern of his own fur. At the bottom of the slope, a sharp right followed by a sharp left, and then a door that slid up into the ceiling as he approached.

Cool, comfortable light flooded the tunnel, causing his dilated pupils to contract quickly, and a voice spoke his name with the barest of lisps.

"Choking Deluge. I greet you, kit of my heart. Welcome home."

"Susa," he said and launched himself toward her tall, slender form. She reached out to him, laughing as he leapt into the slimly-muscled Human arms that had held him since he was a tiny kitten. Just as she had done back then, Susa pulled him close to her chest and bent her head so he could more easily rub his cheekbone against hers. Her scent filled his nostrils and, more than anything else, made him feel as if he were finally, truly home.

"I missed you, Del," the Human woman said, burying her nose in his fur. Deluge felt the warm rumble of pleasure start to fill his throat and move through his body.

"I missed you too, Susa," he said. "So much that I forget the niceties. I greet you, molly who raised me."

She let out a Human laugh, throwing her head back after the fashion of her species. Like most Humans, Susa's only real fur grew from the top of her head. Long and iron-grey, it moved as she did and carried her comforting, slightly spicy scent. Currently, she wore it woven together into something that resembled a rope and dangled down over her shoulder. Adult though he was, Deluge couldn't resist swatting at the tail of it while she carried him further into the Den.

"You know, just because I'm carrying you like a kitten doesn't mean you need to act like one, Del," Susa said. "I should put you down and make you walk. Any respectable molly would."

"You're better than a respectable molly. You're Human. Which means that besides being unique, you're also big enough to carry me as an adult. And don't pretend you don't enjoy cuddling us just as much as we enjoy you doing it."

Her laugh rippled out again, and she scratched deliciously behind his ears.

"Your sister-kita Death is here with her lover," Susa went on. "And Flame is expected any day now. Your brother-kit went with Dama to the council, as her aide."

"Mmmmrr," Deluge purred, "That sounds like Blade. He was always good at that kind of stuff."

"He does have an interest in politics and things beyond his own belly, that is true," the molly said, her gentle tone teasing.

"I will have you know, Susa, that I bested a Besquith trader in the City."

"Oh? Bested in what way?"

"I bargained her into a corner until she was forced to sell me all of her possessions and inventory on Khatash."

"I see," Susa said. "Very impressive. And what did this Besquith receive for her price?"

"The life of her child, forfeit by his own actions."

"Del," the teasing left Susa's tone, only to be replaced by mild censure. "If his life was forfeit, it was forfeit. You know the laws."

"It was forfeit for threatening *me*. He had no forbidden knowledge. All I did was give them time to get off planet. It was well done."

"If you do say so yourself."

"I did say so. You just heard me."

Susa laughed again and shook her head, causing that tantalizing rope of fur to bounce on her chest. Deluge thought about swatting at it again, but she had stopped walking, and the door in front of them was in the process of retracting into the ceiling, revealing the open space of the family gathering room ahead.

The room was large and round but managed to be comfortable and cozy just the same. The light was tinted slightly green, so as to mimic the natural light of Khatash outside. It filtered down on various steps and pedestals and ledges, all covered in plush fabric. They were arranged in clusters and provided plenty of spaces to sit or lounge for conversations.

Susa gave him one last Human-style kiss between his ears before depositing him on one of the pedestals.

"I will tell your sister-kita you are here," she said as she walked toward the back door. "And alert the kitchen. You must be starving."

"I ate this morning, in the City."

"What does that signify, Del? You are always starving," she said with a wink over her shoulder as she headed for the back door of the room. "Welcome home."

Deluge flopped onto his back on the pedestal and stretched out his arms and legs.

"It's good to be home," he replied.

* * *

The trip home took barely any time at all.

That might have been a factor of Mhrand's presence, though, and the joy that Death couldn't help but feel in his nearness. It was rather sweetly funny to watch him try to be solicitous as they boarded the suborbital. He refused to let her even wear the simplest of harnesses, citing that she shouldn't be carrying extra weight, and the binding couldn't be good for the litter.

"Mhrand," Death finally said in exasperation as they walked up the ship's ramp and to their shared couch. "You must stop this. I am well! Better than well. You are being ridiculous."

"Beloved," her fog-colored lover said, his voice thready with stress. "I know you are. And more than capable. It's just...the risk..."

"Gravid females have been flying aboard suborbitals throughout the long history of suborbital flight, dear one," she said drily. She stepped carefully into the couch and laid down. Unlike the cockpit of her Basreeni fighter, the passenger couch of this luxury liner was fleecy and soft. She curled into a comfortable sleeping position, legs tucked underneath, tail wound around herself, and looked up at her lover with wide, comfortable eyes. "No harm has ever come to a single litter because of it."

"I...all right," Mhrand said, his tail twitching nervously. But he climbed into the couch beside her and settled his muscled body around hers. Death breathed deeply of his scent and allowed her eyes to close. The one effect of pregnancy she'd felt so far was the fatigue. She was so tired. All the time.

The faint vibration humming through the shuttle's frame intensified as they prepared for launch. Safe in the warmth of the couch, coiled in the scent of her lover, Death let herself drift into sleep.

And woke, later, as the suborbital touched down in the mountains that were home.

"Beloved," Mhrand purred into her ear. "Come. We have arrived."

After four years, it felt surreal to step off the ship onto the soil of her clan's mountain. She'd been home during her contract, of course, but this was different. Her contract was complete; she was free of obligation. And the secret joy she carried in her body made what was always home even more *hers*.

The green light that filtered through the jungle painted patterns over her fur and his as she led him to the door of the clan's sanctuary and home.

"Be welcomed, love of my nights," she said as he stepped over the threshold. Mhrand paused then, and looked back at her with a slow blink.

"Thank you," he said. "I don't have your poetry."

She laughed then, and rose up on two legs so that they could enter with fingers entwined.

"No one is here to meet you?" Mhrand asked, disapproval shading his tone as they walked down the empty corridor inside the door.

"I sent no word ahead," Death replied.

"No? Why not? Surely you are due some ceremony?"

"Probably," Death said. "But I thought to make it easier on you. We will settle into our quarters and relax before forcing you to meet everyone."

Mhrand's paw tightened around hers.

"You show me too much care and not enough for yourself," he said. "You will be Dama…"

"Shhh. That has not been pronounced yet, and I would announce our news to my family in my own way."

"Of course! I am sorry, dear one, I just…"

"I know. You are careful of my dignity. Perhaps too much so."

"I love you," he said simply. "I only want to ensure you have the honors that are yours."

She stopped walking and turned to face him.

"Mhrand," she said, "I am well. It is well. We are home. You can relax. I did not ask you to come with me so you could be a guardian of my consequence. I asked you to come with me because I love you. Because I want you to meet my family, my Clan. Because I want you to join with me in a life-bond and help me raise our offspring here. Please, beloved. Relax."

Mhrand looked at her for a long moment, his beautiful eyes searching her face. Then he slow blinked an assent and leaned in to press his cheekbone to hers.

"You steal my breath," he whispered.

"And you, mine," she whispered back. "Even if you insist that you have no poetry."

This wry observation caused him to let out a short laugh, and he backed away from her a bit.

"All right," he said. "I will try."

"Good," she replied. "We are here."

A door in the corridor slid up into the ceiling, revealing a comfortable chamber with curving walls and a wide couch high on the far wall. Death recaptured her lover's paw in her own and led him through into the room that had been hers from the time she was a tiny kita.

Once inside, she used her pinplants to merge into the Den's network and inform the Clan's resident healer that she was home, and would call upon him in a ninth of a Mrur. Then she sent another message before retreating to the high couch for a rest with her lover while her luggage was brought in from the transport.

A ninth of a Mrur, and then they would see.

* * *

"So your molly is also a healer?" Mhrand asked later, as they exited Death's room and resumed trekking down the corridor toward the healer's suite.

"Not exactly," Death said, fighting a smile. "But she has studied for many years and could easily become one. She works well with Jhora, our resident healer, and it will be good for her to be present for the examination."

"Because of her expertise?"

"As I said."

"And it has nothing to do with the fact she's your molly? That her fingerpads were the ones that soothed you as a small kita when you were frightened?" Mhrand asked, a gentle tease in his voice.

"I am not frightened," Death replied. "I told you, all is well."

"My deadly love, there is no shame in being nervous. This is a momentous undertaking, and one which does not always turn out well. If the scent of your molly's fur brings you comfort, I am not one to judge you for it," Mhrand said, stroking her back with his tail as they walked.

Death couldn't help but let out a little laugh. She didn't tell him what was so funny, though. He would figure it out soon enough.

The Den had a private infirmary set deep in the mountain, past the main living quarters. Though small, the cluster of rooms was well appointed, with the latest in medical technology. Reow had always insisted upon it, citing the sometimes-dangerous nature of their work as Hunters. Jhora, the Healer, had been under contract to the Clan for as long as Death could remember. She was practically part of the family.

"I greet you, mighty Hunters of the Sky," Jhora said as the door to the infirmary complex slid into the ceiling.

"And we greet you, learned Hunter of Illness," Death said with a smile. She walked through the doorway a step ahead of Mhrand and rubbed her head against the small, cream-colored healer's cheek in an affectionate hello. "It is good to be home."

"It is good to see you home," Jhora said. "Please, come back into one of the alcoves. You are not hurt? I was told you wished to see me, but not why."

"Yes, well…we have something of a private matter to discuss."

"Should your lover remain here, then?" the healer asked.

"This concerns him as well."

"Ah. By all means, then, please step right in here," Jhora said, coming to her back feet and gesturing for the two of them to precede her into one of the examination rooms.

Death stepped into the room and hopped up onto the examination table before she realized there was someone else present. An unforgivable lapse of attention in any other circumstance, but her happiness at seeing that individual overshadowed any self-recrimination.

"Susa!" she cried, leaping from the table into the outstretched arms of the Human woman who had raised her.

"I greet you, mighty sky Hunter," Susa said, nuzzling Death's upturned face. "Welcome home, sweet kita."

"I greet you, my molly. It is so good to *see* you."

Death leaned into Susa's touch as she scratched the sensitive spot behind the ears and ran her hands down Death's back. Then Susa turned and deposited Death back on the examination table, before inclining her head toward Mhrand.

"I greet you as well, Hunter of the sky and lover of one I love," the Human said to Mhrand.

"I greet you as well…Human?" Mhrand said, his eyes wide and round. "You are the molly who raised my love?"

"I am," Susa said with a smile. "And you are correct, I am Human, sigiled to this clan. I have heard much of your fearsome reputation, Mighty Hunter. I am pleased to finally meet you in person."

"Dama brought Susa home when we were tiny kits," Death said. "Susa cared for us and raised us, just as a Hunter molly would have done. I am who I am today because of her."

"Well," Mhrand said and let out a little laugh. "I suppose I cannot argue with that. It is my pleasure to meet you, Human molly. Thank you for raising the Hunter that captivates me."

"Shall we begin our examination?" Jhora asked then. In all the excitement, the small, light-colored healer had blended into the background as she went about her preparatory tasks. Now she stepped forward on two legs, carrying a tray of interesting-looking diagnostic tools.

"Yes, please," Death said.

"And how far along do you estimate you are in gestation?" Susa asked gently. Death's eyes went wide as the molly surprised her for a second time.

"You knew?"

"I guessed. You sent a message that you needed to be examined, but you were not injured nor ill. That can mean very few things, kita of my heart."

Death shot a rueful glance at Mhrand and gave a grin and a shrug.

"Perhaps half a season. We are not exactly certain," she said.

"Are you...proud?"

"Oh, sweet little one," Susa said. "I am *always* proud of you. This is simply cause for even more joy. Let us take a look and see what we've got."

With confident, measured movements, the Human moved to assist the healer as she gave Death a thorough physical. They used both nanotech-based diagnostic protocols and more traditional methods. The nanomed procedures called for Death to drink some very foul-tasting liquid and then lie motionless while Jhora and Susa stared intently at an oversized slate. The more traditional ones were far more fun.

"There," Jhora breathed, as she moved the audio amplifier over Death's abdomen. "Do you hear that? That's one heartbeat...and here's another...three..."

Mhrand gripped tightly to Death's extended forepaw, his fingers tightening with every word as his eyes got bigger and bigger. The swishing rhythm of the fetal kittens' heartbeats echoed in the small chamber, and Death couldn't stop herself from smiling, nor her eyes from filling with joy.

"...and four," Jhora finished, with a satisfied smile. "I count four heartbeats. All good and strong, though with that many, one will likely be small and runty at birth. Perhaps that one may die, but the others should survive birth just fine. And the nano readout agrees. Four kittens. Congratulations, Damita."

"Thank you," Death breathed, feeling the word for mother sink in. "This is...that was unbelievable!"

She wanted to sit and listen to the sound of her offspring's heartbeats in that small room for much longer, but that would be a waste of everyone's time, and Mhrand was itching to leave. He didn't generally like infirmaries. The wide smile on his face spoke of his own deep happiness, though, and Death felt yet another wave of love for him wash over her.

"We did this," she whispered to him as Jhora and Susa cleaned up their instruments and put them away. "You and me, love. We made these kittens between us."

"Well, you did," he said, grinning. "I just helped a little."

That made her laugh, and she squeezed his paw.

Susa looked up and smiled at the two of them.

"I just got a message," she said, tapping the pinplant behind her ear. "Your brother-kit, Deluge, has landed and is on his way in. I must go meet him, since he saw fit to call ahead and give me some warning. I shall see you both later, in the parlor?"

"Yes, of course," Death said, reaching her free paw out to the Human woman. Susa took it, stroked it, and then leaned in to rub cheekbones.

"I am so deeply happy for you, kita of my heart," she whispered. "You will be a wonderful Dama."

"Thank you," Death said and slow blinked a smile.

"I will bring Del to the parlor," Susa said. "And I won't say a word. I suppose you'll want to surprise everyone."

"Of course," Death said. "I'm rather looking forward to it."

* * *

"I might have guessed I'd find you sprawled everywhere."

Deluge heard the soft, sarcastic drawl of his eldest sister-kita and opened his eyes. He hadn't meant to doze off, but the combination of travel and feeling finally safe at home had lulled him into a nap. Death's voice, though, was enough to have him wide awake and alert. He rolled over and pulled his body into a low crouch.

"Giving me warning before attacking? That's not like you," he said, dropping his jaw in a grin as he took in his sister-kita's form.

Death From Above's grey-and-brown striped fur made her look like a younger version of their dama. She returned her brother-kit's grin with one of her own and leapt lightly to a nearby shelf high on the wall. Whenever possible, Death enjoyed being above everyone else. She'd even gone so far as to become a qualified Basreeni and starship pilot. Deluge had always thought her particularly well-named.

She sauntered along the shelf, followed by the grey bulk of her chosen lover. Mhrand, of the Creeping Fog clan from down in the lowlands somewhere. For the past two seasons, wherever Death had gone, Mhrand stalked right behind her. Like Death, Mhrand was an aerial Hunter, one of the pilots who flew the Basreeni fighters to ensure the integrity of Khatashi atmospheric and orbital space. He was big, and loud, and jovial.

Deluge liked him a great deal.

He got to his feet and waited until Death had walked almost precisely half the length of the shelf toward him. Then she stopped and sat, and began grooming her face nonchalantly. Deluge grinned again and shook his head.

"You still haven't grown out of your kittenish games, sister?" he asked as he made a leap up to the far side of the shelf. Her ears twitched in a silent laugh, but she otherwise ignored him, appearing intent on washing her face. Deluge looked to Mhrand, who lifted a paw and smiled, as if to ask what he could do about his love's stubborn nature. Deluge dropped his jaw in a chuckle, because all three of them knew the answer to that.

Not a single thing.

So, as always, Death got her way, and he came to her.

"I greet you, little brother," she said in that demure voice that clearly said she was scheming something or other. She lifted her face, angling her cheekbone in offer. With pleasure rumbling forth from his chest, Deluge bent to nuzzle her face and mingle scents—

Only to find himself flipped to his back and falling toward the floor as she swept his legs and rolled them both off the shelf. Deluge heard Mhrand let out a yowl of surprise and fear as they fell.

Of course, it wasn't that far, and it was easy enough to flip around and land on his feet, but as soon as he did so, Death was there, tangling up his arms, pulling him down to the ground despite his greater mass. He managed to get one of his arms up in between the two of them, and flexed his claws enough that it broke the skin on her chest. She let out a hissing sigh and shoved away from him. He rolled and came up in a crouch.

"Nice," she said. "I wasn't expecting the claws. Good work. You've gotten better."

"As have you. I greet you, sister, and I'm glad to see that all the soft living of a pilot hasn't eroded your wrestling skills," Deluge answered, grinning.

"Hey, easy with that," Mhrand said as he hopped from shelf to pedestal to lower ledge to the floor. "It isn't all 'soft living.'"

"I greet you, aerial Hunter," Deluge said, turning to include the gray Hunter in the conversation. "And I hope you know I'm merely teasing my sister-kita."

"I greet you, Hunter of the surface and stars. And I know. You Night Wind clan play rough, whether the sparring is verbal or physical. I have learned this." As he spoke, Mhrand came up next to Death and pressed the side of his body affectionately close to hers.

"Speaking of which," Mhrand said, dropping his tone and looking over at Death, trying to catch her eyes. "Was that wise, dear one?"

"It is fine," she said. "The clan healers all say that I am in excellent health, and it is early enough that I should have no ill effects from my usual sorts of exercise."

"Yes, but did the healers know what all you considered your 'usual sort' of exercise?"

"What?" Deluge asked, confused. "What are you talking about? Death, are you ill? Why are you seeing the healers?"

His sister-kita met his eyes and gave a small smile.

"I'm sure you can figure it out if you try, Deluge. I'm not ill, but I won't tell you before I tell the rest of the clan. Susa said they should be here any minute."

Deluge felt his brow wrinkle, and he sat down hard to think about it. Death looked over at Mhrand with a smile and a softening of the line of her body. She suddenly looked so intensely happy that she seemed almost to glow…

Deluge felt his eyes open wide with shock as suddenly, he understood.

"Death!" he gasped. "Are you serious?"

She turned her beatific smile on him and nodded.

"Don't say anything. I must tell Dama first. You know this."

"I…yes, of course! Oh, but…congratulations, I'm so happy for you!"

Mhrand started laughing out loud, his own purr heavy in the sound.

"You were right, dear one," he said. "You nailed Deluge's reaction exactly."

"Reaction to what?"

The far door had opened, and in walked the most important figure in Deluge's life. Susa was his molly, the female who raised and nurtured him, but even she could not supplant the role of the Hunter who entered the room on her back two legs. Even here, safe at home, she moved like the wind for which she was named. Every line of her body whispered of a quiet lethality.

"Dama," Deluge said and dipped his head in respect to his mother.

* * *

"I greet you, my offspring," Reow, Dama of the Night Wind Clan said to her children. "And you as well, sky Hunter beloved of my kita."

She dropped to her four feet just inside the threshold of the room and leapt to the central pedestal. Behind her, Cunning Blade, Deluge's only male sibling sauntered, murmuring his greetings to Deluge, Mhrand, and Death as he did so.

"Susa informs me that Flame has just arrived on a suborbital," Reow said as she began to nonchalantly groom her face. "Blade and I must have just missed her. As soon as she arrives, we can begin."

"Begin what, Dama?" Deluge asked. "Is there…I just came home. I didn't know that you had called a gathering."

"I haven't," Reow said. "But you are all here, and I have news. As do some of you, I suspect." She turned her penetratingly blue eyes on Death, and slow blinked a smile before continuing to wash her face.

Blade leapt to his own perch next to Deluge, and took a moment to rub his cheekbone against his brother-kit's in affection. The two of them had always been allies and close friends, especially when their sister-kitas would gang up on them.

"How was the council?" Deluge asked in an undertone. He had no doubt that Reow could hear him if she chose to do so, but she seemed completely content to groom her lovely fur and wait.

"Interesting," Blade replied. "Dama will tell you all about what took place."

"I'm sure," the big Hunter pressed. "But I want to hear your interpretation as well."

"My interpretation? I'm not...That remains to be seen," Blade said, and turned to look at his brother-kit with an appraising eye. Deluge slow blinked a smile at him and then raised his paw to his face in a deliberate echo of their dama's unhurried mannerisms.

Underestimated me again, did you? Deluge thought while satisfaction curled through his mind. Someday, my dear brother-kit. Some day you will learn that just because I am big and jovial, that does not make me stupid.

In the meantime, Death and Mhrand made their way over to rub against Blade and exchange scents and affection. Deluge listened with half an ear to their pleasantries, but kept an eye on the doorway. Before more than a few breaths had passed, the panel slid up into the ceiling again and Susa reappeared, holding Del's smallest sister-kita in her arms.

"Susa," Reow said, putting her paw down. "Really, she is a Hunter grown! You should not carry them like kittens any longer."

"Dama, she—" Susa started to say, but Silent Flame cut her off by leaping out of the molly's Human arms and onto Reow's center pedestal.

"Dama," Flame said, "I greet you."

Deluge sat up straight at the sound of her voice. Flame was usually very soft spoken, but her words flowed with ease when among family. Now, though, her tone was tight and briar-bramble rough. He cocked an ear forward to listen more closely. What was wrong?

"I greet you, my kita. Your contract is fulfilled, I see. You are injured?"

"It is of no consequence," Flame said. "An inconvenience, only. Else I would have gone to the infirmary to see Jhora first. But Susa said you were gathered here, so I asked her to bring me."

"We can wait, little one," Reow said. She reached out a paw and stroked her youngest kita's ear. "If you are injured—"

"No," Flame said, her rough voice firm. "It is as I said, an inconvenience. I will seek the Healer after."

"As you choose, mighty Hunter," Reow said, slow blinking her approval. "Then, I suppose that we are all assembled, and we should begin."

"Shall I give you privacy, Dama Night Wind?" Mhrand asked. Reow looked at him for a long moment and then twitched her ears in the negative.

"You are beloved of my kita and welcome to this council. I believe that some of our discussion today will concern you, unless I miss my guess," she said.

Reow stood up on her hind legs then and reached inside one of the pockets on the utility harness that she wore. Deluge could see her withdraw some kind of token—something shiny—but he couldn't make out the details before she palmed it and closed her fingerpads around it.

"I have been offered a contract," she said. Deluge's tail twitched in surprise before he could stop it. Beside him, Death shifted as well. Blade, however, was conspicuously still. Reow looked at each of them and then held up the token, angling it so that the light fell full on the face of it.

It was round and blue, with a tree embossed on it. Deluge felt a thrill of shock and recognition zing through him. A Peacemaker's badge?

"Word has come from the galactic Capital. Less than a standard month into her term on The Commission, Governor Sissisk has died. Peacemaker Hrusha recovered her body, and has been selected to represent our race as Governor. Thus, she will retire her badge, and the Council has nominated me as Peacemaker Hrusha's replacement."

Deluge drew in a breath as the questions threatened to bubble out of him all at once. Around him, his siblings gave voice to their own excited concerns and curiosities. Reow held up her other hand, and the babble ceased. She slow blinked at the instant response and then folded both paws around the Peacemaker badge, which she returned to her pocket.

"The contract pays extremely well, and will double our liquid assets within the first galactic year," Reow said. "I am of a mind to take it, but you are grown members of this clan, and therefore, I would hear your counsel."

She turned first to Death, her oldest kita and slow blinked a smile.

"Perhaps now would be a good time for your news, dear one," Reow said softly. "As it very well may factor into your siblings' thoughts."

If Death felt any disappointment at her apparent failure to surprise Reow, she did not show it. Instead, she nodded gravely and stood up on her four feet. Deluge felt a surge of pride in his magnificent sister-kita as she began to speak.

"Mhrand has sired a litter of four upon me," she said, her voice ringing proudly through the space of the parlor. "Jhora says that I and the kittens appear well engaged in a healthy, normal pregnancy, and I expect them to arrive after perhaps a season."

Noise and congratulations tumbled out of Blade and Flame then, and Deluge happily added his own felicitations to the tumult. Reow, however, said nothing, merely slow blinking and holding eye contact with her oldest daughter-kita.

"I greet you, Damita," Reow said then, her words soft, but cutting through the noise like a knife through flesh. "And name you my Heir."

Deluge was close enough to Death that he could see her swallow hard as she fought to contain her emotions. She remained very still, eyes locked with her mother's, until finally her composure broke open, and she grinned wide in the Human style. Mhrand let out a short howl of triumph and threw himself into an embrace with the Hunter that he loved.

"The rest, tell them the rest," Death's lover urged her, and Deluge could see that the sky Hunter's own grin split his face.

"We have decided," Death said, a little breathless. "That is, I have asked Mhrand...and he has agreed...to form a life bond. To join our clan. To become one of us!"

This part Deluge didn't know, and so he was one of those who burst into noise this time. He also came to his feet and leapt at his sister-kita's lover in joy. The two of them went down in a tangle as Mhrand, laughing, tried to fight off his soon-to be brother-kit.

"Very well," Reow said, and as before, her words stilled the wrestling chaos. Deluge pulled himself out from under Mhrand's grey shoulders while Reow watched them all with indulgent eyes. Mhrand turned and inclined his head to the Hunter who had borne his love.

"Dama," he said softly. "I am grateful for your acceptance."

"When the litter has arrived," she clarified. "Then I will become your Dama. I ask you both to wait until then, just in case."

In case of what, she didn't clarify. Deluge could see in the twitch of Mhrand's tail that he didn't like the idea, but Death inclined her head obediently, and therefore he had no choice but to do the same.

Better that he learns to accede to Death's will now, a tiny, sardonic corner of Deluge's mind whispered. He will need that skill, if he is to be her life-mate.

* * *

After the announcement of Death's pregnancy and heirship, Reow decreed that they would adjourn for a feast. This caused Mhrand no end of confusion.

"Why are we going to eat now?" he murmured softly in Death's ear. "Nothing has been decided!"

"Other than my heirship," Death corrected.

"Well, that was always going to happen. You're the first to breed, beloved, who else was she going to choose? No, I'm talking about her contract as Peacemaker. Didn't she say she wanted your input? Especially yours, I should think, as Heir!"

"She did. And she will get it. She is just giving us time to consider what we will advise. Beloved, we should go," she said, standing up on her back legs and looking around the parlor. "Everyone else has left. We will be late."

Mhrand stood all the way up, too, and stepped up so their chests were touching. He rubbed his face against hers, and stroked his fingerpads down the length of her back as far as he could reach. She felt her breath leave in a sigh and relaxed into his touch.

"Beloved, I hope you know," he said softly. "There is nothing in the universe as important to me as you and our offspring. You are the center of my galaxy."

"And you are mine," Death responded on a purr. "Come what may, we will have each other and our kittens."

"Come what may."

Death pressed her cheekbone against his again and then stepped reluctantly away from his embrace. He flicked his ears flirtatiously at her, which made her slow blink a smile as she dropped to all fours and padded out of the parlor.

While they had been the last to leave, they were not, it seemed, the last to arrive in the dining room. Flame and Deluge were both missing, but the others were gathered in a rough circle, eating bowls of spiced, shredded Khava meat. Reow looked up as Death and Mhrand walked in.

"Sit anywhere," Reow said. "Deluge took Flame to the infirmary, so we're not being particularly formal."

"So I see," Mhrand said softly. His tail twitched over and brushed Death's, and she followed his gaze to see Susa seated cross-legged next to Blade.

"She is our molly, and she is part of the family," Death said. "You knew this."

"Yes, but...to eat with a Human? I've never seen it done before."

"Where have you seen a sigiled Human before, love? Do not be tiresome," she said with a sigh. Mhrand's ears flicked, and he turned to her with a slow blink.

"You are right. I am sorry, beloved. Let us sit with your family and eat."

"Your family too, soon."

"Soon," he agreed, but it was too late. All of the golden, buoyant happiness of their embrace moments ago had drained away, and now Death merely felt tired.

Still, one had to eat. Especially when one was carrying four lives within oneself. She lowered herself to the padded surface of the room, and a service bot appeared from a doorway in the far wall. The bot carried two bowls of the delicious Khava over and set them down in front of Death and Mhrand, then chimed and began to roll back the way it had come. The scent of the meal wafted up to Death, and she suddenly felt ravenous. Her instincts pushed at her to devour the entire bowl as fast as possible.

She reached out daintily and took a small sliver, then placed it in her mouth and savored the taste. Self-discipline was paramount. Always.

They ate in relative silence for a few moments, until Mhrand looked around and spoke up.

"Dama of my beloved, may I ask something of you?"

"Of course, you may ask, beloved of my heir," Reow said in measured tones after swallowing her bite. "What would you have?"

"I would know the story of your clan, mighty Hunter. I would raise my own offspring with the stories of their clan-founder's might ringing in their ears."

"Then perhaps you would speak too loudly," Reow said. Mhrand blinked, unused to her brand of dry humor. He glanced over at Death.

"She is joking with you," Death said quietly. "She likes to play with words."

"Indeed, I do, Mhrand. My apologies. Your question was well phrased, and I mean no offense. You should know our story, after all, so I am pleased to grant your request."

She sat up and gently pushed her bowl away with a delicate forepaw. Another service bot materialized out of nowhere and whisked it away as she began to wash her face.

"I do not know the name of my original clan, nor that of she who bore me," she said. Death, who had heard this story many times, felt Mhrand stiffen in surprise beside her. Reow paused in her washing and looked over at him.

"Does that surprise you, young sky-Hunter? I suppose it must. I have come to learn that kittens, such as I was, are greatly prized in our society. I have no idea why I was the exception, but apparently, I was. My first memories are of hunger and loneliness. I came to awareness all alone, and when my infant eyes opened, I saw only the dirt and roots of the melik trees around me. My claws were soft still, and yet I knew that I *must* eat. I had just begun my life. I was not yet ready to surrender it."

Death felt something twist inside her at the familiar story. She'd always felt a great deal of pity for the kitten her Reow had been, but this time, something was different. Perhaps it was the four strong, fierce heartbeats she'd heard earlier that day, but a slow rage began to build within her mind. Who could take something so precious as a newborn kita, and leave her to die all alone in the jungle of their home world? She had lived, of course, but that didn't change the monstrous nature of what had been done to her. Death thought that, perhaps for the first time, she could finally begin to understand the depths of that monstrosity.

"My first attempts to assuage that hunger were nothing to sing about," Reow said wryly. "But eventually, I found a newly-dead carcass and was able to eat. Then I slept, and was nearly killed by a Basreen. I think she thought I was already dead, because when she realized what I was, she began to teach me."

"Teach you?" Mhrand asked, incredulous. "A *Basreen?*"

"Yes," Reow said. "She was a very good teacher. From her I learned the two fundamental laws of the hunt: watch, then find a way."

Death slow blinked at the memory of her dama repeating those words over and over again as she and her siblings grew in size and prowess. Reow had always emphasized that hunting was a mental activity before it was anything else. She had required the four of them spend entire nights observing vids of different species around the galaxy, learning their language, their customs. She would quiz them on what they had learned and would require them to use that information to make conclusions about those species, based on logic, and what they'd observed. The four of them had planned out thousands of hypothetical contracts on myriad different targets…but in the end, it always came down to those two principles. Watch. Find a way.

Soon, Death thought, joy pulsing through her. Soon I will teach our young ones those lessons, beloved. And you will be beside me.

"I stayed with my teacher for three years," Reow was saying. "By that time, she was very old. She put me in the way of other Hunters, and left me so that she could die in peace. I have always honored her memory."

"Of course," Mhrand said. His ear twitched, and Death slow blinked at him again. He didn't understand yet. Of course he didn't, it was such a strange story! But he would, in time.

"The Hunter that found me was a healer, and he and his lifemate allowed me to stay with them until I reached my majority. Then I went out and accepted my first contract. It was a well-paying one, and from there I started to amass the fortune that I would need to build this den and begin my Clan. When the time was right, I found a willing male, and conceived my children. Shortly after their birth, I found Susa and brought her home…and now soon, you say that you will join us."

"It is my greatest desire," Mhrand said, and Death pressed her shoulder against his as the love inside threatened to overwhelm her.

* * * * *

Discussions

Much to Deluge's delight, a feast followed.
Reow announced it was time to eat, and they
left the discussion and followed her through the
twisty corridors of the Den. It might have seemed abrupt to some,
but Deluge knew her ways enough to realize this was just Reow's
process. She had dropped the bomb of her nomination during the
initial gathering, now she would give each of them time to reflect and
would probably solicit their individual opinions later in private.

He fell into step beside his youngest sibling as they walked. Well,
he walked. Flame limped, heavily favoring her left side, broken ribs
marked by a deep scar.

"Rough contract?" he asked softly. He let his shoulder bump
gently against hers. He didn't think he'd hurt her, but apparently, he
was wrong. Flame let out a hiss of air between her teeth.

"I am pleased to see you," she said. "But please don't do that
again."

"My apologies. I can see that it was. You are headed to the infirmary?" He kept his tone pleasant, but underlaid with steely intent.
Flame had always been the smallest of them, and though she was
fully grown, that hadn't changed. He, on the other hand, was quite a
bit larger than the average Hunter. Polite questions aside, she *would*
go to the infirmary next, one way or the other.

She looked over at him, a question in her eyes. He twitched his ears in the affirmative. If it came to it, he would simply pick her up and carry her.

Flame let out a sigh and took the next turn to the left. Deluge kept pace beside her as they started to wind their way back to the infirmary section.

"Care to talk about it?" he asked.

"Not much to tell," she said, her tone stiff. "I underestimated some of the mark's security measures and paid the price. But his death appeared utterly natural, the client is pleased, and I am still alive."

"Flame—"

"Do. Not." Her voice cracked out like a whip. "I am not a kitten. Small I may be, but since Dama's semi-retirement, I've earned more credits for this clan than any of us. It was just a mistake. One I won't make again."

"All right," he said. "It's just that we love you, littlest sister."

"I know. I love you all too."

They walked the rest of the way in silence broken only by the occasional muffled grunts that Flame made. Despite his worry for her, Deluge was impressed. She hadn't given any indication that she was in such pain during the gathering. Only now, when he was her only witness, would she allow her weakness to be known.

He was about half a heartbeat from picking her up and dealing with the consequences of her wounded pride when they reached the door to the infirmary complex. Healer Jhora looked up from a slate as she walked in.

"I greet you, Hunter of hurts," Flame said, a little breathless. "And I'm happy to say that I've brought you some of your prey."

"I greet you, lethal one," Jhora said. "I would thank you, but I do not enjoy seeing my patients injured. Can you jump to the table?"

Perhaps she could have, but Deluge didn't give her the chance. Heedless of her pride, he rose to his back feet and scooped his sister-kita up in his arms. He felt her body tense, and so he deposited her on Jhora's examination and treatment table as quickly as he could and then backed away before her claws and fangs could make her displeasure known.

"I'm helping!" he said, giving both females his widest, most charming grin when they separately pinned him with their icy stares.

"Thank you for your help, Del," Jhora said, her voice soaked in sarcasm. "Perhaps you can help yourself out of my infirmary?"

"No. Wait, please," Flame said, struggling to push herself to a seated position. Jhora murmured something that Deluge didn't hear and reached out to stroke the back of Flame's neck. The injured Hunter ignored the healer and stared at her brother-kit. "I will get you for that, Del. But stay. I have something to discuss with you."

"Of course, littlest," he said, and rose to his back feet to touch his chest in a gesture of love. "Whatever you need. You know that."

"Fine," Jhora said. "But don't be in my way."

"I wouldn't dare, Healer."

The older Hunter-of-hurts let out a kind of harrumph and turned away from the table to gather the tools of her trade. Flame reached out a paw and beckoned him closer. When he hesitated, she sighed and renewed her motions with more vigor.

"I'm serious, Del," she said. "This is not a ploy to get back at you. You know I'm subtler than that."

"You are," he conceded and shrugged. With Flame, it was not a question of *whether* she would get her revenge, it was just a question of *when* and *how*. He accepted his eventual fate and walked close enough to touch her paw with his own.

"I need some help," she said, her voice close to a whisper. Something twisted painfully inside Deluge. She must really be hurt. Flame never asked for help.

"Anything," he said, his tone deadly serious.

"I accepted another contract to be accomplished after this one, but Blade is right. I will need time to recuperate." she twitched her ears in a shrug. "Extending it for too long will draw out the client's suffering."

"Who's the client?" Deluge asked.

"The second-in-command of a Lumar mercenary company."

"Lumar?"

"Veetanho."

"Ah. And the mark?"

"Her sister. The commander."

Deluge narrowed his eyes and attempted to think this through.

"Why would a Veetanho mercenary with a company of Lumar at her bidding take out a contract on her sister? Even if the mark is her superior officer, it seems easier to just do it herself. It's not as if she wouldn't have the combat skills."

"I gather that the commander is impressive in single combat, and that she's a sadistic wastrel of lives as a merc commander. She seems to enjoy watching the Lumar under her command get chewed to pieces by overwhelming firepower, and takes contracts that support that."

"Well, the Lumar aren't known for their mental prowess—"

"Exactly! But the Veetanho are. And yet this company continues to bleed and bleed with no surcease. It's just…wasteful."

Ah. There it was. Flame was passionate in her convictions, and though she was an excellent and lethal Hunter, like many Hunters she found wholesale slaughter only acceptable if done in pursuit of some objective. Any objective would do. But to just waste lives felt...dirty to her. Deluge knew that, because he felt the same.

"All right, littlest," he said, slow blinking. "I'll do it, on one condition?"

"What's that?"

"Well, two conditions. One, that you obey Jhora's instructions *to the letter*, and you let yourself fully heal. I don't like listening to you stifle whimpers while you're simply trying to walk."

"Done," Flame said. "And the second?"

"That you hold your revenge until after I return." He stretched his mouth wide in a Human-style grin and had the pleasure of seeing her slow blink a laugh in response.

"Very well," she said. "But the second the contract is marked fulfilled on the 'net, your amnesty ends."

"I would expect nothing less," he said. Then he bent to rub his cheekbone against hers as Jhora returned to the table, her forearms full of instruments and slates. "Now rest and heal. We've made a deal."

"So we have," she said. Her eyes started to close as Jhora injected something into her system. "I thank you, Del."

"Anytime, littlest, anytime."

* * *

Deluge didn't go down to the feast after all. Flame's description of the contract made it clear further delay would only exacerbate the hideous waste of the Lumar mercenaries' lives. It was important enough that she asked him for help. Therefore, it was important enough for him to move on it immediately.

Instead of the dining room, he followed the twisting hallways back to his quarters. The door slid open at his approach, revealing his luggage stacked neatly in the center of the room. One of the family's contractors had brought it in while he'd been busy with the gathering and Flame, as he'd expected. The Night Wind clan's contractors were very good at that sort of thing. Details were managed, and one never need concern oneself with how.

It was one of the things he always appreciated about being home.

Of course, one of the things he appreciated about not being home was the opportunity for fun and adventure, and this contract should provide plenty of both. Which reminded him, he needed some details.

"Please send Susa to my room at her earliest convenience," he said aloud. The lights flashed, indicating the voice-recognition software had accepted his instructions and would send the message.

"And ask her to bring some of the food from the feast," he added when his stomach let out a gurgle. Another flash of the lights. Good enough.

Now to unpack. Or was it re-pack?

As far as luggage went, he didn't really have much. A spare harness or two, a compact emergency nanomedicine kit, some physical credits...but mostly it was weapons of all kinds and shapes. Chemically fired projectile guns, energy pistols and rifles. Explosives, small and large. Vials and vials of poisons and antidotes. Fourteen different gauges of garrote wire, enough to cut off the breathing apparatus of about 90% of the species in the galaxy. Intense portable light sources that would burn the synapses of some of the dark-adapted species. Even a few live, incredibly venomous species of various small lifeforms he kept in carefully-protected carriers.

And blades. Everything from a needle-like poniard to a knife as long as his foreleg. One never knew when one was going to need a good edge. Claws would often do in a pinch, but blades were...

...well, they were fun.

"Quite a collection."

He'd been expecting Susa, so Deluge hadn't flinched when the door to his quarters slid open. But it was Reow's voice that preceded her lithe form into his small quarters. Deluge put down the throwing knife he'd been cleaning and padded over to greet her properly.

"I thought you would still be at the feast, Dama," he said.

"I thought you would have attended. But you were looking after Flame?"

"I was. I apologize if you missed my presence."

"We missed you, but there is no need for apology. I taught you four to care for one another. I am glad to see my lessons were well received." Reow arched her back and stretched, then padded over to hop up to his sleeping ledge. "Blade told me about Flame's contract. You are taking it in her stead?"

"I am. It is important to her, and it seems like a fun, lucrative venture."

"Good. Susa also told me about your encounter with the Besquith traders in the capitol," Reow said as she curled herself into a ball and watched him from above.

Deluge picked up the knife again, interpreting her actions as permission to get on with his packing.

"Did I do wrongly, Dama?" he asked.

"Did you?"

"Not in my judgment. Perhaps I stretched the limits of the law a bit, but she was a mother trying to protect her wayward child. I knew she would get him off world as soon as possible."

Reow looked at him for a long moment, her motionless ears and tail giving no clue as to her inner thoughts on the matter. Deluge forced himself to finish wrapping the throwing knife and put it into his case. His unconcern over the situation began to fray under Reow's relentless regard. He wondered if she would say more, but she eventually twitched her ears and blinked slowly, causing him to feel a surge of relief.

"Very well. It was lucrative, at least. Well done in that. And now you will take your sister-kita's contract. Be wary, my kit. Remember your lessons."

"Always, Dama," he promised.

She slow blinked again, and Deluge's earlier relief warmed into the glow of certainty. His dama loved him, and she was pleased with him. All was right with the world.

"Now, tell me, my rash one. What do you think of the contract I have been offered?"

"To be Peacemaker? Well, it is certainly prestigious, Dama, you can't argue that."

"No."

"And it would be lucrative." She had liked that about the Besquith affair. Reow had never been shy about her desire to amass great wealth. It was what allowed her to build her Clan. Hunting for riches was both necessary and honorable. She had taught them that.

"It would."

"Then I think you should do it, Dama. Because it sounds like fun."

Reow blinked again, ears twitching, and then let out a Human-style laugh.

"That is your driving concern, isn't it, my brash one? Will something be fun?"

"Well, it is certainly not outside of your capabilities," Deluge said. Though he kept his tone light, he wondered if he should feel insulted. "And it is honorable work for a Hunter such as yourself. It will bring much prestige to our small clan...I do not see why fun shouldn't be a consideration alongside those things."

Reow rose to her feet and leapt down from the sleeping ledge in one fluid motion. She took a single step toward her son and rubbed her cheekbone lovingly against his.

"And that is what I love most about you, my Deluge. I thank you for your counsel, and I wish you good hunting."

"Good hunting to you, too, Dama." Deluge said, pressing into her. "I will come find you on your Peacemaker business after my contract is completed."

"I hope that you will," she said. Then she gave him a playful swat and sauntered out of the room as silently as she'd entered.

* * *

Deluge had just finished packing when a chime announced he had another visitor.

"Enter," he said, and slow blinked a smile as the door slid up into the ceiling. "Susa. I though you would come sooner."

"Dama wished to speak with you first," the Human woman said, stepping inside his room. Though she had none of Reow's liquescence, there was still a kind of heavy grace in the way Susa moved. Deluge had not had much opportunity to observe other Humans. He wondered how his molly's movements compared to that of a Human merc, for example.

"I am almost ready to go," he said, sitting down on the floor next to his packed luggage. "Flame said you had most of the information on the contract."

"I do, and I've uploaded it to your ship," Susa said. "You will get the full intelligence briefing as soon as you link in, but the short version is this: a Lumar mercenary company is being mistreated by its Veetanho commander, and the second-in-command is loath to take her on directly."

"Seems cowardly," Deluge said.

"Or smart, if she knows she can't win," Susa said.

"Or that," Deluge said, slow blinking as he conceded the point. "Flame told me this. What else is there?"

"You'll be traveling to 'Tlor, the Lumar home world," she said, articulating the glottal stop at the beginning of the world. Sounds like that were difficult for Hunters to pronounce, and Deluge found himself distracted by the name for a moment or two.

"...are you listening, Del?"

"What? Yes! ...What were you saying?"

Susa snorted and shook her head.

"I was saying the trip to the Praf region will give you time to study the details of the contract. It may prove useful in this case."

"Why? Was something out of order about the contract?"

"Flame didn't think so," Susa said, "But when I watched the vid of it, there was something that seemed off to me. Nothing I can put my finger on. And certainly nothing you can't handle," she added with her wide, Human smile.

Deluge twitched his ears in response.

"But you tell me this as a warning."

"I do. Because I love you, and if you are warned, you will be on your guard for surprises."

"And so I will," he said. And then, because he loved her too, Deluge got up and leapt into Susa's lap. Once again, she cuddled him close and stroked his fur as she'd done when he was a kitten.

Deluge had never been one for depriving himself of comfort. He was tough enough to cope with spartan conditions. He'd done it and proved that fact to himself. But that didn't mean he enjoyed it. To him, self-denial for no good reason seemed as useful as cutting his flesh so he could practice bleeding...that is to say, not at all.

So he snuggled himself close to Susa's soft warmth and let the scent of her skin wrap around him. He had no reason to think the contract would keep him away for long, but that was no reason not to revel in the feeling of home while he could.

She squeezed him tight and then gave him her habitual little toss. As he had always done, he turned it into a leap and landed lightly on four feet before turning back to her.

"You should get going," she said, "Dama has said for you to take *Iora*."

Deluge's body stiffened in surprise. *Iora* was the name of the fastest ship owned by the clan. Reow had named her after her old molly, saying that Iora was the epitome of grace, and so was the little ship. He had his own ship, of course, but it wasn't anywhere near as sleek or powerful as *Iora*. Susa smiled at his reaction.

"Dama thinks that she will not have much of a chance to use her in the coming season," the Human clarified. "She will take *Sarru* to her investiture as Peacemaker, as it is likely she will need the space and grav-ring of the larger ship."

"That makes sense," Deluge said, his eagerness growing. Susa laughed again.

"Of course it makes sense to you," she said. "You would agree with anything just to be able to take *Iora* out. Be careful with her, Del. She's a lot of starship rolled up in a very pretty package."

"I'm always careful, Susa," he said. And when she snorted to show her opinion of that statement, he dropped his jaw to grin at her in the Human style. "I am!"

"Yes. Well. See that you are. We love you, Del. Come home safely."

"I love you too," he said. She gave him another smile and then turned and left. He looked after her for a moment, wondering what about this contract had made the usually imperturbable Susa nervous.

* * *

D eluge didn't wait for dusk. He left as the sun rode high above the canopy, which meant the green half-light under the leaves was slightly brighter and greener as he exited the den. He took the same path he'd used upon arrival, but instead of veering toward the suborbital station, he continued straight through the thickening jungle until he reached a long, narrow clearing on top of the ridge.

The minute he stepped into the sunlight, his goggles extended and covered his eyes with dark lenses. He blinked to readjust his vision and stretched out with his quintessential senses. A faint ripple under his skin told him the aerial disguise mesh was in place, bending the light so that the clearing would disappear from baryonic detection. Visual or electronic scans from either orbit or atmosphere would show unbroken canopy, ensuring only Hunters could find the clearing with the clan's smaller ships. The largest one, the luxury star yacht, resided in orbit.

Deluge liked the smaller craft better anyway. The sleek lines of the ships looked sexy and fun. Plus, the act of piloting them tended to be more immediate, more visceral. He could *feel* the movement of a little corvette as he flew it. The star yacht didn't give that kind of feedback, luxe though it was.

And he was going to fly *Iora*. Anticipation tangled with joy and fluttered through his system as he caught sight of her tailfin flash. The ridge supervisor perked his ears up and walked over as Deluge approached the launch cradle where *Iora* stood ready.

"I greet you, Choking Deluge," the aging Hunter said. He slow blinked and stood up on his muscular back legs, his front paw out in a friendly gesture of welcome.

"I greet you, Murrron, old friend," Deluge said, and reached out to tap his paw against the other's in hello. "It is good to see you again."

"And you, Del. It has been a long time."

"Well, you were home visiting your clan," Del said. "And I was out doing some local hunting. No need for anything exorbital."

"Nice. A little pleasure hunting to keep sharp," Murrron said with a nod of his rusty orange head. "I did as much in my day, before I settled down to work this contract for your dama."

"I still think it's funny that this is your retirement job, Murrron," Del said. He looked at the other Hunter out of the corner of his eye. "It's full time work, and then some, with as much as we travel. And you're the maintenance lead for the whole clan!"

"Night Wind is strong, but small, yet. And while I completed a few contracts in my day, machines always fascinated me. So, when I decided to retire, and your Reow needed someone to help her with her ships, this seemed a natural fit."

"Plus, you like Dama," Del said slyly. Murrron let out an amused rumble but did not say anything else. A wise Hunter knew when to hold his tongue. Deluge laughed at the look on Murrron's face and remembered when the older Hunter had taught him that maxim.

"I imagine your contract is time sensitive? Given your uncivilized departure hour?"

"It is," Deluge said, laughing again. "Your pointed hint is well taken, Murrron. I should be going."

"*Iora* is ready for you," the older Hunter said as he began walking toward the launch cradle. Deluge fell into step beside him. "We've just upgraded the docking points, so the coupling process should be faster and smoother. Your defensive armament is loaded and shielded so as to be nearly undetectable. Your cover identity and transponder codes have all been loaded."

"Who am I?"

"Luxury goods merchant. Besquith registry. Primarily spiced fish and other foodstuffs."

"Ha! So, you heard about my encounter in the city?"

"I did, young Hunter. Take care you do not overstep. The clans are clear on the laws for off-world traders."

"They are. But he was just a young pup. It seemed harsh to kill him when his life had just begun."

"So instead you maimed him and cast him and his mother into poverty, then sent them off world with nothing to their names."

"I doubt that, Murrron. She would have to have other assets even to get here. We're not exactly a crossroads of the galaxy here on Khatash. And I only took what she offered, which was everything that she owned on planet. I doubt that was everything she called her own."

"But you do not know that it was not."

"No, I do not know."

"A wise Hunter makes sure."

"Yes, Murrron," Deluge said, suppressing a sigh. Murrron slow blinked at him, then stood up and toggled open *Iora's* cockpit hatch.

Deluge gave the older Hunter a playful swipe and then leapt up through the hatch onto the pilot's couch. He settled himself, belly down, paws on the control pads. As Murrron closed the outer hatch, the pinlink cradle came down and settled comfortably over Deluge's head. He inhaled as his pinplants made the connection, and suddenly he *was* the ship.

"Your orbital escape window starts now," Murrron's face appeared in his vision.

"Keying launch sequence," Deluge responded, and the instant he thought it, *Iora's* powerful engines hummed to life.

"Good hunting," Murrron replied. "Launch in 3, 2…"

The last number was lost in the cacophony of thunder and the sound of Deluge's own blood in his ears as the launch cradle catapulted him into the sky. *Iora's* engines answered with their own throaty roar an instant later as they caught the momentum of the launch and kicked into full power. He imagined himself as a bright streak against the blinding brilliance of Khatash's rarely-seen sunlit atmosphere. Even behind goggles and his own closed eyelids, Deluge could feel the piercing light battering at him, trying to penetrate the sleek metal skin of his ship.

Hunters, he reflected as the ship fought through the buffeting effects of the atmosphere, preferred the dark for a reason. The light was too damaging for the secrets they carried.

Soon, though, his patience paid off. *Iora's* flight smoothed out as she exited the last surly bonds of Khatash's atmosphere. With a thought, Deluge brought up her current intercept course toward the free trade orbital zone. He ran through the calculations in his mind and confirmed that they all looked and felt correct. With a little luck, he'd find a dockable freighter ready to leave the system within the ninenight or sooner. Hopefully sooner.

He'd dock and be dragged to the Praf region, and then he'd fulfill his littlest sister's contract for her. Because he loved her, and because when it came down to it, he was a Hunter, and that was what he did best.

* * *

Death luxuriated in bed the next evening. She had never been so sleepy in her life. The Healer had told her to expect this, but it still felt disconcerting to sleep away an entire day and still not be ready to rise at darkfall. Mhrand had risen, rubbed his face along hers, and left to find her brother kits, or to train. She didn't really know. All she knew was that the soft fur of the bed still carried his warmth and scent, and she wanted to roll both of those all along her body.

Therefore, she was still lying in bed when Reow came calling.

"Still abed?" Reow asked as she padded quietly into the room. "Are you feeling ill?"

"No, Dama," Death said. "Merely tired. Healer Jhora said this wasn't unusual."

"It isn't," Reow said, leaping up to the elevated platform that held the bed. She stepped delicately over to Death and laid down next to her, curling her body around Death's back. For just a moment, Death closed her eyes and remembered being a small kita, held safely in the warmth of her dama's fur.

"Were you tired all the time?" Death asked.

"At the beginning, yes," Reow said. "Pregnancy is hard work. Your body is building the bodies of your kittens as we speak. Such things require much energy. That is why you must have a care for your proper nutrition during this time."

"I know," Death said. "Jhora told me, and I noticed Susa watched every bite I ate at dinner."

"She loves you and is proud of you. We all are. Are you frightened?"

Death shifted slightly as she considered the question. Truth be told, there wasn't much in the known universe that frightened her.

Like any predator, she thought in terms of risk and reward. Risk was to be considered, mitigated if possible, and then ultimately accepted. But feared?

"I don't think so," she said.

"That is both good and bad," Reow said and ran her rough tongue along the back curve of Death's skull, grooming her like she was still little. "Many are lost in the birthing fight. But you are young and strong, and I think you will survive."

"I will do my best to do so," Death said, allowing a bit of dryness to leak into her tone. Reow flipped her tail against the bed with a *thump* of laughter.

"I am sure that you shall. My kita, I must ask you something, and it may displease you."

Death fought not to stiffen in her dama's embrace.

"If you must, then you must," she said softly.

"Are you absolutely *certain* this lifebond is what you want? That binding yourself to Mhrand is the wisest choice for yourself?"

Death did stiffen then, and her words felt etched in ice when she spoke.

"Do you object to him? Is there a reason you believe him unfit for our clan, Dama?"

"No," Reow said, her tone patient. "I have no specific objections, nor reasons to believe he would not be a valuable addition. I just want to make sure *you* are certain."

"I am," Death said, ice turning to steel. "You may be sure."

"Then I am assured," Reow said, running her tongue over Death's head again and again in the grooming ritual that millennia of damas had used to soothe troubled kittens. After a few minutes, Death relaxed into the caress once again.

"I am very proud of you, my kita," Reow said.

"Because of the litter?" Death murmured.

"For many reasons. The fact that you have successfully conceived is but one joy added upon millions. You have brightened my life, little Death. Before you and your siblings were born, I was alone. You are my clan, and everything I have done in my life has been for you four."

"We know, Dama; we love you too," Death said. A rumbling started deep within and poured out of her on a low purr.

"I did not know which of my kitas would succeed me as elder of the clan. You and your sister kita would have had very different command styles, I think. I am interested to see in what direction you will take the Night Wind Clan."

"Dama! What are you saying? You will be here to lead us."

"Perhaps I will, but if I take this Peacemaker contract, sweetling, you must know that I will be gone more often than not. Much of the clan leadership will naturally fall to you at that point."

Death closed her mouth with a snap. Reow let out a soft rumbling chuckle.

"Do not think to tell me you don't feel ready. I have been training you and Flame for this since you were born."

Death blinked, and realization broke open in her mind. She thought back to the exercises of her youth. Reow's training had always emphasized problem solving and stealth, but now that she reflected on it, she could see how she and Flame were encouraged to take the lead during any cooperative ventures. Clearly, Reow had engineered some of their training scenarios to demonstrate how concepts like delegation and empowerment made for a stronger overall team. She'd actually utilized a lot of what she'd learned during her recent term as commander of the Basreeni squadron.

But leading a squadron for a term of two years was quite a bit different from being head of the family.

"I don't know that any training could actually make me ready, Dama," Death said. "Is anyone ever ready?"

Reow rumbled again.

"I don't know, kita. I've not asked the other elders. I imagine it's much like taking your first contract. It doesn't matter if you're ready or not. The situation is what it is, and you must either succeed or die. Simplicity itself. Remember the first lessons."

"Watch, then find a way."

"Watch," Reow said, rising up to rub her cheekbone against Death's. "Then find a way. Our clan must do two things to survive, Death. We must prosper, and we must grow. Watch which way the wind blows, and find a way to do those two things. That is how you must lead."

"Yes, Dama."

"And now, I have a question for you, my heir," Reow said, lying back down. "What are your thoughts on the Peacemaker contract?"

"I think you should take it," Death said, without hesitation.

"Just like that?"

"You said it yourself, Dama. We must do two things. The Peacemaker contract is a very lucrative one, which will only help our prosperity. And it is prestigious, which won't hurt, either. It takes you from us for a longer timeframe than I'd like, but...perhaps that's not entirely unwelcome, given recent events. I imagine you'll want to use this time as a training exercise for me. To help us grow."

"Not just you, kita. All of you. If Flame conceives, she may elect to form a cadet branch, and will need practice leading as well. And do not neglect the potential of your brother kits. Strong male elders are something every clan desires, with good reason. The day may very well come, my lovely, when you are in dire need of council unclouded by the emotions of motherhood. Only your brothers will be able to provide that for you. They will be the very backbone of the clan we are building. Especially if Flame branches off."

Death felt her uncertainty of moments before return. Those were angles she had not even considered, but as Dama, she would have to do so. And though the Night Wind clan was small, things would only get more complicated as it grew. She would be responsible for the lives of each member of her family...and not only them, but to a lesser extent, the Hunters and other beings off world who contracted with the clan as support personnel. All of them depended on the Dama to make decisions and determine policy.

"Do not fret, sweetling," Reow purred, and began grooming Death once again. "You will not be alone. I will help you as I can, and your siblings will always support you."

"Yes," Death said. "And Mhrand."

"And Mhrand," Reow added. And if she was a little slow to do so, well, Death figured it was just because her thoughts were elsewhere. She had no doubts about her lover. He would support her till the last breath in his body. Reow would see. Mhrand would win her over.

Eventually.

* * *

The next ninenight passed in a surreal sort of blur for Death. Surreal, because she felt trapped in a constant pendulum swing from joy to misery. Joy in her pregnancy, in her love, in being at home. Misery in the sickness that the pregnancy caused, and in the unrelenting fog of fatigue that constantly pulled at her. She took to sleeping for nearly eighteen hours every night, rising only long enough to eat, and then promptly throw up what she'd eaten.

Four nights in, Jhora put her on intravenous supplements.

"This isn't uncommon in pregnancies," the healer said briskly as Death wiped her mouth with a shaky paw. Mhrand had brought her to the infirmary after she'd been unable to keep anything down, and Jhora had shooed him out just before Death started heaving again. Jhora waited another heartbeat, and then whisked away the basin in which she'd caught the last remains of Death's evening meal. "Uncomfortable for you, certainly. And dangerous if left unchecked. But we'll ensure you've good nutrition and hydration, and you and your kittens will be just fine. I'm going to give you a little anti-nausea medication along with the supplements, and we'll see how you do."

"I just wish I didn't feel so weak and tired all the time," Death said, hating the whining note in her voice.

"It will pass. Give me your forearm."

Death obeyed, ignoring the quick sting of the needle as Jhora started an intravenous line.

"Nanites can't do anything?"

"What would you have them do?" Jhora asked. "They are programmed to repair damaged tissues, whether from injury or illness. You have neither. This is a normal part of your life cycle, Hunter. At most, the nanites could abort the pregnancy, but I do not imagine you want to go that route."

"What...Why would anyone...?"

"There are reasons, Death. Medical and otherwise. It's not up to me to judge whether or not those reasons are valid."

"But kittens are so rare!"

"Yes. Which is why it is often a last resort. I should not have mentioned it to you. I didn't mean to make you upset."

Death felt her eyes widen with horror, her tail twitching in distress. To her shame, she didn't seem to be able to bring her body under control. Lately, anything she felt became immediately and obviously manifest in her body language. It was maddening.

Jhora reached out and stroked her head, her touch soothing.

"I am sorry, Death. I did not think. Put it out of your mind. You and your litter are safe here at home. Between the prowess of your clan and my skill, nothing will harm you or your kittens. I promise."

Death closed her eyes and tucked her head down. She focused on taking deep, calming breaths. Slowly, the horror began to recede as she forced her thoughts to move in another, more useful direction.

"How long is your contract with us, Jhora?" she asked after a few moments.

"Hmmm?" the healer asked as she watched a readout scroll across her slate. "My contract? Nine years. I just re-upped last year."

"Good," Death said as her eyes started to drift closed once again. "My kits will have the best medical care available. You must never leave us."

"It would take something quite extraordinary for that to happen, Hunter. Quite extraordinary indeed."

* * *

A few nights later, Reow announced she would formally accept the contract to serve as the Hunters' next Peacemaker. In typical Reow fashion, she didn't waste any time, planning her departure for the station above Capitol for the following night. She would take *Sarru*, the clan's largest ship, and would likely not return for several galactic standard years, except for visits.

"So," Reow said at dinner, speaking both to her offspring and the gathered retainers. "I will leave you in the capable care of my heir. While I am otherwise occupied with Peacemaker business, you may refer to my daughter, Death From Above, as your dama. She speaks for me in all things, and her decisions will be as mine."

Shock rocketed through Death. She felt her eyes widen, and her tail and ears start to tremble. So soon?

"You will find that she is more than up to the task. Her experience as a Basreeni commander and the number of contracts she's fulfilled speak for themselves. And, as I'm sure you all know, she has proven herself fertile. We expect the first litter of a new generation of Night Wind kittens in a couple of months." As Reow spoke, those present turned to look at Death in twos and threes. She felt the weight of their eyes, their smiles. They trusted her, Reow trusted her…but she still had so much to learn.

"So tonight," Reow said, raising her voice slightly to cut through the murmur of approving conversation. "Let us celebrate a chance to be with one another before we depart on our separate ways…all but my wayward son Deluge, who is already gone on contract." A ripple of amusement followed this dry observation, as Reow had no doubt intended. Death watched her mother play the small crowd like a master and wondered if she'd ever be that skilled.

"But he, like each of us, works toward a singular goal: the ascendancy of the Night Wind Clan," Reow continued and turned to fix her penetrating blue eyes on Death. Death suddenly knew without a doubt that *something* was expected of her in this moment...but she had no idea what. She felt out of her depth and lost, but the words of her mother's most important lessons echoed in her mind.

Watch. Find a way.

So she stood up on her back feet, stretching her spine as tall as she could. A memory of old tales told by her Human molly teased at her, and on impulse, she lifted her drinking bowl in her forepaws.

"My friends and family," she said, pitching her voice to carry through the room. "I invite you to take part in an ancient ritual from a faraway land. Drink with me now, to the ascendancy of the Night Wind Clan."

"To the Clan!" Blade answered, his eyes intent on hers. He would recognize the origin of the ritual, at least. As would Flame, probably.

"To the Night Wind Clan," Flame answered, quieter as always. The two of them lifted their own bowls, and one by one, the retainers and contractors of the clan did the same. Lastly, Reow lifted her own bowl and nodded her approval to Death as they all drank in unison.

After that, the feast began in earnest. Though they'd had a feast scarcely a ninenight ago, the clan's staff had still managed to create another wonderful panoply of dishes and delights. This feast was larger, too, since all of the retainers and contractors had been invited to hear Reow's announcement.

Mhrand, seated beside her, made it his personal mission to see that Death was given the best parts of every dish presented. She appreciated it, and him, but his solicitousness did nothing to stave off

the grinding fatigue…or the growing nausea that started about halfway through.

"My love," he asked at one point, turning to look at her with his
ears cocked forward in concern. "Are you well?"

"It is the pregnancy sickness again," she said in a low tone for his
ears only. "But I fear I should not leave. This is an important night
for the clan, and my departure may be seen as weakness or insult.
Neither is a good option."

"No, but…"

"Please, love. I will handle it. Just…let me be."

She took care not to let her tone snap as she said it, but he recoiled in hurt anyway. Death fought the urge to sigh and simply
turned back to the assembled clan. She focused, as Jhora had told
her, on keeping her breathing steady and even, and tried to distract
herself with conversation. Meanwhile, Mhrand sat in a discontented
lump at her side.

Well. One problem at a time. She'd finish this meal, then smooth
things out with him. Emotions were running high all around with
Reow's announcement. He would forgive her shortness. Because he
loved her.

She looked up to see Reow regarding her closely. She slow
blinked at her mother, trying to reassure her that all was well. Reow
didn't return the expression. Instead, she merely watched her eldest
daughter and heir, and the Hunter she'd chosen to love. Death
opened her mouth to say something, but the nausea rose within her
at that exact moment, and she was forced to close her eyes and
breathe. Breathe it down and away, lest she disgrace herself in front
of the clan she was supposed to be leading.

Again, she drew the air in and forced her mind and body back toward calm. Calm enough to open her eyes, at least. Calm enough to laugh and talk lightly with her siblings and the contractors lounging nearby, while the serving bots brought in dish after dish of spiced delicacies and food that would normally be quite appetizing, but tonight...

No. Breathe. Slowly. She forced herself through the calming exercise again, and yet again. Until finally the dinner was over, and she could drag her fatigue-frayed self to bed. She'd thought to speak to Mhrand, but he laid himself down without a word and slept, and she was just too tired to push.

So, Death laid herself beside him and fell into sleep, knowing that when the sun set the following evening, her dama would be gone, and she would be left to stand on her own.

* * * * *

Cataclysm

All went relatively smoothly for Death for the first ninenight.

Reow departed the first evening. In contrast with the large feast the night before, she'd wanted only her offspring and Susa to see her off on the ridge. Mhrand had come, too, of course, walking shoulder to shoulder with Death after they made up from their spat the night before. He pressed against her as they wished Reow well, and then again as they stood back from the ridge and watched her ship burn its way into the night sky. Death drew strength from his presence and from the knowledge that even if they argued, he'd stand beside her, come what may.

"Well," Death said as the last burst of light from the *Sarru's* engines faded. "That is that. We shall hear from her in a little less than two ninenights, I suppose, when she arrives at Capitol. In the meantime, let us go back inside and figure out what we're going to do with ourselves."

Blade nodded sharply and twisted around. He moved stiffly, Death noticed. Unlike him.

"We should ensure Mhrand brings all the best kills to you while you gestate," Flame said, glancing back at Blade. Her ears twitched as if she were considering something, and she sounded as if she were trying to lighten the mood.

"I'll get my own, thanks," Death said. "I'm pregnant, not an invalid." Though as she said it, Death's innards began to roil in their standard evening revolt. She forced herself to breathe through her nose and began walking back toward the entrance to the Den.

"What is your plan, Flame?" Mhrand asked in the awkward silence left by his beloved's abruptness. He cocked his ears in invitation and started to follow Death's path. "How long will it take to recover from your injuries?"

"Not long," the youngest sister answered. "Though Blade would prefer I wait longer before taking my next contract. Even now I'm only slow, not—to use Death's words—an invalid." It was not entirely true, but close enough. Flame always considered consequences, and she knew that even at a slightly reduced rate, she could excel as needed.

"Will you seek another contract, then, littlest?" Death asked. She'd stopped just under the edge of the jungle canopy to wait and watched the three of them as they moved toward her. "Or will you abide yet awhile?"

She would have liked to have said that her question was disinterested, but that would be a lie. Sudden hope punched Death in the gut. If Flame and Blade would stay with her for a time, perhaps they would keep her from making some grievous error that would cause the downfall of the clan. Or something like that.

Pausing as they drew even with her elder littermate, Flame leaned her weight more to her unwounded side and used that to brush fondly against Death.

"I will rest a short while and weigh which contracts might best serve our clan." A flicker of amusement there; of course Flame would carefully consider all options—that had ever been her way.

"And you, Blade?" Death asked. "What will you do? I...well. I don't want to influence either of you, but...what plans do you have?" She had noticed, of course, that something seemed off with their brother. Perhaps he didn't wish to speak about it in front of everyone, but if something were wrong, Death felt she needed to know. She was, after all, supposed to be acting as the dama. It was her business to know what bothered her family.

"Stay, for some time at least." He looked ahead, always scouting the path regardless of how needless it might be. "There will be contracts to sort, and—if that's helpful to you, of course." Blade had certainly known he wouldn't be named heir to their clan. Still, now that it was real, it sat...oddly.

"It is, of course," she said. "In truth, I'd hoped you would. I could use your counsel. I confess that I'm not feeling at all ready for this. Dama said you would be an asset. Flame, too. I'm glad to know I can count on you both...not that I'd expect differently." It was so strange. Why was it strange? What was happening here?

"I always knew it would be you, Death, and of course you'll be ready." Flame said, her tone slightly too neutral to be only observing the obvious. She gave Blade a sideways look.

Blade's tail twitched twice before he stilled it.

"Dama makes her choices as carefully as any of us," he said after a moment, fully meeting Death's eyes for perhaps the first time since the official announcement. "You have our support." Much of the tension left his bearing—not all, but enough to be noticeable.

"All of our support," Mhrand said, leaning against her. In that moment, Death felt torn. On the one flank, she loved and appreciate Mhrand's unwavering devotion. But on the other, there had been an important moment of connection there between Death and her siblings. Though he was welcome, Mhrand wasn't quite one of them yet, and it caused a discordant note in the whole process.

"I thank you all," Death said, trying to ease past the awkwardness. "For now, let's head back and get something to eat. I've been reviewing the clan's business records, since there's not much else going on. Fortune grant there won't be, at least until we hear that Dama's been safely invested as Peacemaker."

"Surely you don't think anything would interfere with that, do you?" Mhrand asked.

"Probably not," Death said, and for no reason she could name, her eyes were drawn to Blade.

"The council—" Blade began, the stripes around his eyes seeming to ripple as he considered his words, "they…" Another pause, and then he shook his head once, sharply. Clearly, he wanted to think further over what he'd seen before talking about it. Or perhaps it was Mhrand's presence that stopped him. Either way, he continued on a different track, "They were as interesting as ever. I imagine Dama is prepared." He met Death's eyes again, a silent signal that they should talk later.

* * *

Flame paced through the den stretching the bunched muscles down her recovering side. She decided she would take a contract soon—she was mostly recovered and knew their dama would soon be ensconced in her new responsibilities.

Something kept her bound here, though—her sister, or perhaps the changes in her littermates' dynamics. She had pushed herself to consider if her injury caused her hesitation in taking another contract, but that didn't seem right. A buzzing sense of restlessness had started to outline her thoughts, and yet she still had not claimed a contract.

Blade and Death had gone out to inform key contractors and contacts of their dama, both sharing updates and continuing to build connections vital to the success of their clan, and though there were surely others still at home somewhere in the den, she didn't come across them in her wanderings. It gave her time with her thoughts, to consider her next step and try to understand what was holding her back, but for once, introspection and reflection weren't helping.

Flame made a small noise in the back of her throat and turned her steps toward the main entrance to continue her walk outside. She'd just cleared the cave-like archway that protected the doors when a buzzing from her comm pulled her up short. The notification sound indicated a call that had been generally placed to the den, then routed to her. Though their clan had grown over the years, Flame and her littermates held priority over other Hunters, both for their prowess and their ties to the dama. As the one of her siblings closest to the ping, Flame received the routed call to their clan, though no one she could think of would have run a general call rather than messaged one of them directly.

She accepted the connection and made a sound to indicate her presence, listening to the swell of activity on the other end.

"Night Wind," an official voice stated briskly, "this is the suborbital station."

Intrigued enough to push away her restlessness, she continued her walk outside of the den, though at a slower pace than she'd begun. "This is Silent Flame," she said, knowing her name would be on record for her clan, and the Hunter calling wouldn't know who the general call had gone to.

"Silent Flame, your clan has a visitor." A slight decrease in the crispness of his tone, knowing he wasn't speaking directly with the dama.

"A visitor." They weren't expecting anyone. Off-worlders, rare as they were, stayed in the city around the starport. Hunters messaged directly if they had some reason to go to another clan's den. Flame could think of no reason someone working at the transport station would call her rather than forcibly rebuff some other being attempting to leave the city.

"From the Peacemaker's office. Says she's to report to Night Wind den, and nowhere else."

Flame's slight interest deepened fully into curiosity. Her dama couldn't have sent someone so soon after arriving. In all likelihood, Reow had yet to be invested in her new position, meaning the current Peacemaker, soon to be their Governor, would have sent her. No one but a Hunter could leave the city of Khatash, except for a Peacemaker, or someone on Peacemaker orders. Why would Peacemaker Hrusha send someone to their den, rather than simply waiting on Reow's arrival? It didn't make sense, and Flame wouldn't let a mystery wait for her littermates to return.

"Put her on a transport. I'll meet her at our station." She'd already been moving in that general direction, and by the time a non-Hunter had been cleared through to a ship and arrived at the station, Flame would be there to meet her.

She could decide what to do with the stranger then.

* * *

The station was small, with a warren of rooms and mostly automated systems. Given the specialized traffic of their area, there was little needed here. A room for pilots to rest, if necessary, storage for fueling, a communication hub in case of emergency, some perches in case one had to wait. Few ever came out this way, other than Hunters coming home and heading out, or contacts delivering something face to face. Flame didn't bother going outside, choosing to stay close to the exterior wall and watch the shuttle land.

She dropped to all four legs to provide stabilization for her weakened side, and she considered pulling her quintessence field close to study their unexpected guest uninterrupted. After a breath she dismissed the thought—it would be rude to hide from someone on Peacemaker orders, and unnecessary to boot. Her natural stealth was flawless enough for her to pass under nearly any species' notice without needing to become actually invisible.

The shuttle opened to release only one figure, and Flame sat back on her rear legs.

A Human.

Not many Humans made their way to Khatash, and only one that she knew of had ever moved outside of the city. Perhaps no other Human but Susa had ever been welcomed to a Hunter's den, and now Night Wind would have both Humans to step foot in the jungle.

Flame slipped around the corner soundlessly, melting into the shaded cover and studying the approaching visitor.

Nothing like Susa, for all they were both Human females. Susa radiated warmth and love, intelligence and sweetness, a combination uniquely hers. This Human was taller, more tightly wound, her furless skin darker than Susa's. Her hair was coiled close to her head like an angry tail, her clothes the sort of form-fitting no-nonsense uniform that marked Human fighters or those who wished to be seen as such.

The Human moved easily, aware of her surroundings and wary enough to show she had sense. Flame slid back out of the cover, walking on her rear legs, and moved into the Human's eyeline. The woman noticed her almost immediately and didn't startle. A credit to her species.

"What brings you here today?" Flame asked once the Human had reached an audible range.

"I'm on Peacemaker orders," the woman replied, not knowing her arrival had been called ahead. She halted and took a position somewhere between fighter attention and casual lounging. "Is this the Night Wind clan home?"

"Which Peacemaker?" she asked, the humor faint in her tone. The question she ignored for the moment. "You are?"

"Tamir Alcuin, contracted to Depik Peacemaker Hrusha. And you?" There was some wariness in the woman's voice, though Flame would not have registered it without a long history with a Human.

She softened her body language, communicating she was not feeling predatory. "Silent Flame. Our dama recently arrived at Capitol to meet Peacemaker Hrusha." Again, she wondered why Hrusha had sent an aide rather than simply waited for Reow's arrival, given the timing.

A small huff of impatience answered that, though Tamir didn't let anything register on her face. "I missed her then. Silent Flame, may I seek rest in your den?"

She'd certainly learned something about Khatash, though she used the galactic species term 'Depik,' rather than the more natural term 'Hunters.' Flame regarded her another long moment, taking in the Human's tension and alertness, and wondering at it.

"We will share shelter," she replied, not quite fully welcoming the Human in with all privileges, but allowing for safety and at least a short stay of companionship. "It is a walk to our den, if you are willing?"

The woman Tamir glanced back at the station building, something wry passing across her face, but she only nodded.

They had walked in silence for several minutes before Flame voiced the question she'd had since the suborbital official had called. "I am surprised the Peacemaker thought to find our dama still here."

A hesitation, which told Flame that perhaps Tamir was wondering the same thing, and then Tamir shook her head slightly, and they continued walking, the clearing around that station replaced by the endlessly stretching trunks of the jungle's anchor trees and the spirals of vegetation.

"Is your den in the canopy?" Tamir asked, with a cautious glance above them. Between them and the lowest level of the canopy were countless predators and prey, enough for a diverting afternoon for Flame and half a dozen painful deaths for Tamir.

Flame contented herself with a noncommittal noise, deciding they could both be unhelpful, and continued to lead her guest deeper into the greenish-gold light of the jungle.

The walk remained uneventful, the path trod often enough that Khatash's non-sentient species knew to be wary of the Hunters. Flame took them on a spiraling path away from the main entrance as they approached the cliff face, for no other reason than she wanted to, given Tamir would have no way of knowing where or what anything was beyond tree, stone, path, greenery.

She led them toward an overgrown alcove, barely visible behind draping vines and paused before pushing aside the vegetation to enter the den. Perhaps she should have sent a message to Death first before bringing someone new into their home, but no. Peacemaker orders, and better she get a sense of what it was all about before interrupting her elder siblings' day. It would be good for all of them if Death and Blade could fully erase the tension that still existed after Death's elevation.

Tamir followed her without hesitation, though some might have thought twice before following a Depik into a dim, enclosed space. Flame took them deeper into the cave. Given Susa's long residence in the den, the entrance was more than tall enough for a Human, though Tamir did not seem nearly so impressed or grateful of that fact as she should have. Flame wondered idly how observant the Human was, given she didn't seem interested in why a species that barely reached her waist would have an access point that stretched over Human height.

The stone around them changed subtly, from natural and rugged to slightly too smoothed to be natural, and then ended in a curved cubby studded with rocky outcropping, the surfaces too perfect to pass for untouched nature any longer. Flame leapt to a perch that put her at eye level with her new guest, steadying herself so as to show no hint of her lingering injury. While the Human claimed Peacemaker orders, it was better to trust and verify rather than continue blindly, and Flame wasn't sure why the Depik Peacemaker would have a Human in her employ.

Tamir looked around as the air changed subtly around them, taking in the smoothed stone walls, rounded edges, and numerous niches and ledges that served as resting or launching points for the den's residents. She visibly braced herself and then forced out a breath.

"My orders are to speak only to your dama," she said, meeting Flame's vividly blue eyes directly. "And what I have to say is not for the open air."

"Any part of our den is as secure as any other." Not entirely true, but all this Human needed to know. "And, as I said, our dama is not here. She is with your Peacemaker, and she should have been there for a week. Perhaps you should just turn around and return to them?" It was not quite a jibe, as she kept her tone level rather than mocking, but the overly interested tilt of her head gave her words a bit of a barb.

From Tamir's suddenly visible frustration, it landed with more than a hint of bite, though the woman channeled her annoyance into needlessly straightening her sleeves. Wondering if that would reveal hidden weapons, Flame shifted her own position subtly, and then the tension broke in an unexpected way.

Tamir threw her head back and laughed. Flame didn't relax entirely, but eased at the sound.

"What's funny?"

"Not funny, Silent Flame. I don't know what to do, but I certainly wouldn't choose suicide. I'm not here to attack you in your own stronghold with something I've strapped to my arm."

"Ah." She shed a bit more tension, allowed her tail to relax and twitch idly over the side of her small ledge. "I have yet to kill a Human, so I'm glad to not change that in my own den this morning. All the same, I don't know what to tell you. Dama will not be back soon, though our Heir will be."

Tamir shook her head and looked around the room again. Flame let the moment stretch and then finally yawned.

"I have no other options for you, Tamir Alcuin of the Peacemaker's office. Peacemaker Hrusha had to know our dama was on her way, so I can't think of why she would send a Human message, rather than wait to see her in person. We have no dama to take your message, except my sister, Death From Above. You can stay and talk to her or go and try to catch up to my dama, but otherwise—"

"The dama is your mother?" Tamir's attention sharpened as the realization formed from the tweaks in Flame's language. Perhaps she was truly observant after all.

"She is."

"I would like to wait for your Heir, thank you."

Flame sighed internally and jumped from her ledge to one much higher on the wall. She reached into a hidden cubby and entered a code on a pad Tamir couldn't see, then nodded to her left where a wall had begun to slide into the floor.

"This way then, if you will."

"Silent Flame—"

"Just Flame is fine." She moved easily across to the new opening, only pausing when she realized Tamir had started, and then stopped, moving.

"Why?"

"Why what?"

"Why 'just Flame'? Peacemaker Hrusha dislikes when any of us call her anything but Creeping Agony; she says it's worth the effort to get her name right." In fact, Tamir's accent was not purely terrible—nowhere close to accurate, but not a disaster. Flame was impressed.

"I have been Flame since I was very young," she replied, feeling no need to bring Susa into the discussion at the moment. "Come along." She continued moving again, taking them down a long hall into another rounded room, this one bigger and set with various styles of furniture, some appropriately sized for a Human.

"Make yourself comfortable. Do you require a beverage or food?"

Tamir was staring at the cushions, and then glanced back at the hall they'd walked down. Before she could ask the question, Flame crossed the room and gestured at a cold closet with an interrogatory noise.

With a quick shake of her head, Tamir focused back on the Hunter. "Yes, a drink would be nice. Do you have coffee?"

"Of course. I don't know how long Death will be." She wanted to ask for the message again but busied herself getting drinks and channeling Susa as best she could.

"The Peacemaker had concerns," Tamir said upon accepting the hot mug of coffee.

"About?" Flame was surprised the woman had said anything on the topic, after she'd shown Tamir how content she was in silence.

"About the transition. Not your dama, of course, or else she wouldn't have sent me to talk to her. I just…she said I wasn't to talk with anyone but the dama."

"If you want me to give you an answer, I'd say we are each of us trusted by our dama. If you were to tell her, you could tell Death, or me." She kept the words neutral, carefully so, burying the tendril of exasperation rising in answer to the Human's apparent indecision. "I am otherwise out of options for you."

Tamir looked troubled, though she tried to hide it and said nothing else.

* * *

It was a few days more before Death was able to have that conversation with Blade. More than she would have liked. Despite Reow having left everything in working order, Death found her time taken up with administrative tasks. The clan held roughly a thousand service contracts, and she had to review them all so she knew what they contained. Susa was of great help during this time, as was Blade himself, but it wasn't until the night Reow arrived on Capitol that they had a chance to talk about Blade's concerns with the council.

After a morning of endless conversations with various clients and contractors, Blade paced restlessly beside her as they walked.

"You're taking the long way home," he said at one point, when she angled away from the most direct route back to the Den.

"You look like you could use the exercise," Death said in her dry way. "And it will give us a chance to talk, since you can hardly avoid me now."

"Was I that obvious?" Blade asked.

"Not at all," Death said. "We've both been busy. But it has been several days, and something has been on your mind. I will wait as long as you need, though. You know that."

"Yes, well," Blade said, his tail twitching in frustration. "No time like the present. That all went well."

"I think so," Death said letting out a sigh. It wasn't flying Basreeni or stalking targets, but the morning's work had been exhausting just the same. "I was pleased to be able to reach out to some of our contacts and tell them of Dama's new contract."

"Interesting to do so face to face, in some cases. Some are not as satisfied with our dama's new contract as I would expect," Blade said, his twitchy ears indicating that his thoughts were elsewhere.

"We're a young clan, Blade," Death said. "You know that better than I. Especially compared to some. Our quick rise to such heights is going to twist some tails. I'm sure you saw it in the council meeting."

"Mmm. Indeed. What do you know of Whispering Fear and High Canopy?"

"Powerful clans, both. Good Hunters. Whispering Fear supplied several of my pilots in the Basreeni, and one of my higher leaders was a deo of High Canopy. Why?"

"Some clans were neutral in council, given Dama taking the Peacemaker contract neither hurt nor helped them immediately. Those two were strongly against." He paused again, the hesitation unlike him. Death looked over to see the fur on his forearms rippling with tension.

"Well, I suppose they had their reasons. Did they put forward their own candidate?" Death felt the soft skin between her eyes wrinkle as she tried to wrap her mind around what Blade was telling her. He had always been the subtlest thinker of the four of them, and she couldn't quite grasp the nuance he was trying to convey.

"Evening Tide pushed for their own Dama, but Whispering Fear..." he trailed off again, flexed his claws, and frowned. "Their Dama hated that ours was suggested and wanted it. Nothing she said directly, but there was a moment I thought she would attack in front of the whole council."

"Oh. That's…significant. Dama never told me of any enmity between our clan and theirs." Clan rivalries were common, certainly. But the life of another Hunter was so precious that to personally attack one seemed obscenely outrageous. "What did she do?"

"She was so surprised when the contract was offered to Dama that her eyes fully slitted and claws flexed—I happened to be looking her way by luck. That made me pay more attention to her reactions than I would have otherwise, and everything she said was just slightly off." Blade shook his head, his eyes distant. "When Dama accepted, she tensed all in a ripple—I saw her, barely a breath, but she lost control." His voice carried a note of wonder at the sheer audacity and blasphemy of it all.

"What stopped her?" Death asked, caught up in the story despite herself. "If she was ready to attack, why didn't she?"

"How could she have, in front of every major clan?" Hunters fought, of course, it was only the taking of a life that was forbidden. But two damas, that skilled, wrestling among the most experienced—and therefore likely deadliest—of their kind? "I think she decided something else, in that place. And I wouldn't trust whatever she decided."

"So, we must be on our guard," Death said, twitching her ears. "With a clan as large as Whispering Fear, any kind of attack will likely come from an unexpected quarter, too. Perhaps it is good that I am having to go through all of our financials and accounts. Do you think High Canopy may also be maneuvering against us?"

"They will likely block us from the front—try and steal contracts, skew a trade, if anything. Whispering Fear, given its size and influence, and their dama...they're the ones I'm worried about."

"And so this is what's been troubling you?" Death asked softly.

"I have worried."

Blade turned to look at his sister and stepped closer so that their shoulders rubbed against one another as they walked.

"It is," he said. "And I'm sorry. I should have spoken to you earlier. I didn't want to make you worry, what with the kittens and all."

"But I worried anyway," Death pointed out. "You know better than that, Blade. We're a team, always."

"Yes," he said, slow blinking. "We are."

They turned to follow the small creek that wound up the hillside toward the back entrance to the Den and continued the rest of the way in silence. Death suspected Blade continued to chew on his thoughts and suspicions about the other clans, but that had always been his way. Of them all, Blade was the strategist. As for herself, she was content to wait and see, trusting that her clan's defenses were all they should be.

No sooner had they stepped in through the back entrance when Susa emerged from a crossing hallway nearby.

"Blade, Death," the woman said, slow blinking while smiling in her Human way. Her hands trembled, though Death smelled no fear in her scent. Excitement? What could get their unflappable molly so worked up as that? "I am glad you have returned. Flame is asking for you, Death, and you may wish your brother's counsel for this one. She brings a visitor. A Human bounty hunter here on Peacemaker orders."

"Another Human!" No wonder Susa was excited! "Are you...?"

"I am fine," Susa said, smiling again. "She appears to be very nice. It's just...strange, after so long."

Blade moved first to press against her, rub his cheek against the hands she stretched down to him. Death followed, keeping her eyes on Susa's face. From all appearances, the molly really was fine. Death would have expected her to exhibit signs of sadness, or even a little uncertainty or fear. But then, Susa rarely did the expected.

"I really am fine, Damita," the woman said, reaching her right hand out for Death as her left continued to caress Blade. "My home is here, with you all. Now, shall we go see what the Peacemaker Guild wants with our clan? I've put her in the small parlor. Flame is there with her, as is your Mhrand."

Susa never did anything by accident, and so Death interpreted the molly's use of her new title as a reminder. In Dama's absence, she must speak for the clan. Well enough. She'd certainly been practicing that lately.

It wasn't far to the little parlor, and the three of them entered together. Death took care to watch Susa's face as the visitor stood and held out her hand in greeting to them all. Susa glanced down at her and slow blinked. A reassurance. She really was fine.

"I greet you, Damita Death From Above of the Night Wind Clan," the bounty hunter said, drawing Death's attention back to her. "My name is Tamir Alcuin, licensed bounty hunter, and I'm here under orders from the Peacemaker Guild."

"I, Death From Above, Heir of the Night Wind Clan, greet you, bounty hunter Tamir Alcuin of the Peacemaker Guild. Welcome to our negotiation," Death replied in English as she padded into the room and leapt up onto the central pedestal. Usually, Dama occupied that spot. Today, it would have to be hers. "You know our customs well."

"And you speak excellent English, Damita," Alcuin said, settling onto a cushion when Susa gestured she should do so. Mhrand leapt up to curl beside Death, and Blade and Flame took their own seats. "I was surprised to see another Human here. I was told that off-worlders are seldom allowed in your dens."

"Susa is a part of our clan," Death said in a tone that invited no further discussion on the matter. "What can we do for you and the Peacemaker Guild, bounty hunter?"

"I was sent with a message for your dama from Peacemaker Hrusha, and I was told to give it to no one but her."

"Ah. The Peacemaker will be able to give her the message directly, then," Death said, slow blinking. "Dama should have arrived on Capitol seven days ago."

"Ye-es," Alcuin said, her voice troubled. A wrinkle appeared between her brows, and she had opened her mouth to say something else when a complex series of chimes echoed through the air in the small parlor. Death felt her fur stand on end, for that particular sequence was reserved for emergency messages from a member of the clan back to the den.

An image appeared in the air between Death and the doorway; it was the canid face of Ruzeen, their Zuul factor in the City.

"Damita, Hunters, greetings. I don't have much time," the Zuul said, his tone curiously hushed. His eyes stretched wide, and his breath came in quick little pants as he spoke. "The word has only just gone out, and there is to be no warning...the elders have declared Night Wind Clan anathema. They say that Dama killed the old Peacemaker. I'm sending the video packet they used to justify it all.

I…I am so sorry to tell you this, but our dama—" he broke off with a whine and lowered his head. For just a moment, Death caught sight of the ear that usually carried the clan's sigil. It was a bloody ruin, as if someone had violently torn the sigil out of his flesh.

"Our dama is dead," he said. "They attacked my office and took my sigil. They didn't hurt me otherwise, so Susa should be fine, but the rest of you…"

He trailed off again, whipping his head from side to side, causing blood from his ear to splatter red on the bottom of the image.

"The rest of you, you Hunters. You must flee. They're coming for you!"

Ruzeen's face disappeared, replaced by an image of an open area that Death recognized as the major orbital shuttle station above Capitol. The bounty hunter sucked in a sharp breath as they watched Dama and another Hunter wearing a harness with a Peacemaker badge walk out of the shuttle dock. They headed down a short corridor to enter an airlock that led to Dama's large ship, the *Sarru. Sarru* pulsed her way back from the station's docking arms, clearly visible through the external view cameras. A moment later, an explosion blossomed across the black, blotting out the stars and the view of Capitol below.

* * *

The attacks started immediately.

In retrospect, Death always thought that should have told her something, but in the moment, she was too busy trying to survive to piece things together. Plus, when it came right down to it, they were caught completely flat-footed.

They'd been taught to anticipate every threat imaginable…but no one had ever imagined a scenario like this.

Shocked silence followed the video, broken only by the soft whirring as the serving bots hovered their quiet, efficient way into the room. Death had requested food and drink for this meeting, as a courtesy to the bounty hunter and her Peacemaker masters. Death's body felt wooden, but she forced herself to reach out and take a drinking bowl from the nearest bot's tray.

A thin trail of smoke started issuing from the vents underneath.

"What…"

"Death!" Susa yelled. "Get down! They've been hacked!"

Death hunched her shoulders and curled herself around her belly just as Mhrand launched himself at her. She felt the impact of his body covering hers, dragging her to the floor an instant before the bot exploded with a deafening *boom*. A high-pitched ringing began to sing in her ears, and she fought to recapture the breath that had been knocked from her lungs.

"Beloved. Beloved! Are you all right?"

Mhrand's voice sounded very far away and tinged with an edge of panic. She felt a lessening of his weight, and the air whooshed into her starving lungs in a rush. She forced her eyes to focus and nodded.

"Yes," she said, barely hearing herself. "Yes, I'm fine. But you?"

"Shrapnel, it's nothing," he said. And then another bot exploded, sending them flying backwards. Death managed to tuck her body into a roll this time and landed on her feet on a nearby ledge, but she felt slow and wrong-footed. What was going on?

"Death?" That was Blade's voice. The small parlor had filled with smoke, and it was hard to see.

"Here, Blade!" she called. "With Mhrand! I'm all right, but he's hit!"

Suddenly, three more bots appeared through the swirling smoke, converging on her position. She let out a snarl and leapt up, reaching with her claws to flip herself onto one of the highest ledges of the room—the one that ran around the entire circumference of the place, with openings onto the little used upper hallway system. Death flattened herself on her belly and reached down to her lover.

"Beloved, up here," she said. Her hearing was coming back rapidly now, thank all that was good. "Before they blow!"

Mhrand looked up and leapt, stretching his forepaws out to clasp with hers. Rather than try to change the vector of his leap, she simply went with his momentum, using her body as a pivot to toss him high enough into the air that his tail grazed the arched ceiling, and he had plenty of room to flip and land on all four feet beside her. He winced as he touched down, and Death caught sight of the dark stain of blood on his back fur.

Before she could do anything about it, though, a whirring sound warned them that the serving bots were hovering up toward them. Death grabbed hold of Mhrand's arm and pulled him after her into the dark, disused tunnel of the upper hallway. The bots might follow them, she knew, but the tunnels were small enough that only one could approach at a time…and no mere serving bot could outrun a Hunter.

"Stealth," she whispered, pulling her quintessence field around herself as she did. Her skin came alive with awareness, and a heartbeat later, she felt the pull under her fur as Mhrand did the same. She sprinted down the tunnel, tail whipping behind her as she ran into the darkness.

The corridor curved ahead, which was excellent, because it meant that when the first bot exploded, it did so before the curve, and partially blocked the tunnel for the two bots that followed. Several more twists and turns, and she could no longer hear the high-pitched whirring whine of the bots' hover engines. The tunnel sloped downward for a bit, and then opened up onto a gallery that had her nearly sitting down as she skidded to a stop.

"What—" Mhrand asked as he nearly barreled into her and dropped his quintessence field. She did the same.

"I'd forgotten this was here," she said. "Sloppy of me, I know, but we so rarely use these upper passageways. See those doors there? They lead to our sleeping quarters. That gives me an idea. We need to get you to the infirmary, but I know I'd feel a lot better with some weapons. What about you?"

Mhrand answered with a predatory snarl, and Death felt her chest tighten with love for the tough, indomitable Hunter. With weapons and his love beside her, what need had she to fear?

She pressed her cheek against his for a split second before bounding toward one of the doors.

"This one," she said, slapping her fingerpads against the lock plate. The door creaked a bit from disuse, but slid upward easily enough, letting the dim light from their room shine into the inky darkness of the corridor.

Death didn't have to urge Mhrand to move quickly. He bolted through the door as soon as she had it open, and she slipped through right on his tail. Once inside, she turned to slap the lock plate on the inside again, and made the door slide down and locked securely into place. None too soon, as she heard a pair of muffled *boom*s through the solidity of the door.

"Down here," she said, leaping down to the floor and heading to the cupboard that held her harness and weapons. She shrugged into her harness straps, looking over her shoulder at Mhrand while she fastened the belt portion.

Her lover was picking his way down ledge by ledge, moving slower than before. Anger surged through her at the sight of his pain, but she swallowed it, locked it away as something to deal with later. Survival came first.

Death turned back to her cupboard and began sheathing blades and clipping various weapon holsters onto her harness. As a Hunter, direct combat wasn't her primary skillset. Most often, her contracts had involved getting in unseen, ending a life, and then getting out undetected. But she could run and gun if she had to, so she grabbed several personal energy weapons that would be good for taking out the stupid service bots, at least.

"Are you ready?" she asked, turning back around as she sheathed the last thin, needle-like blade she liked to carry. She was about to speak again, when the sight of Mhrand stopped her. He stood in front of the open cupboard where he'd stored his gear, a slate in hand, a sick look on his face. His ears flattened back against his skull as he looked up at her.

"Beloved?" she asked,

"I can't go with you," he said, his voice harsh.

"What? Is something wrong? Your family—?"

"No. Yours. Your Zuul was right. Night Wind Clan has been declared anathema," he said, turning the slate so she could see it. "Your dama's crimes couldn't have happened without help, so you're all being held responsible for the death of Peacemaker Hrusha."

"What are you talking about?" Death asked, her voice going shrill. "Dama didn't kill her! She wouldn't do that! And you know that there's no conspiracy! When would I have conspired with anyone? I'm always with you!"

"In light of this, my true dama has called me home."

Icy cold dread stabbed through Death. She felt her ears flatten, her tail fluff up.

"You would leave me?"

"This says I should *kill* you," he said, his words bitter and biting. "The law is clear. You're responsible for the death of a Hunter without her consent."

"I didn't kill the Peacemaker, and neither did Dama!" She spat the words as the cold dread spread throughout her body. What was she saying? What was *he* saying? "And you are welcome to try."

Mhrand flipped his tail in negation.

"You know I can't. I—I love you still, Death. And you carry our offspring—"

"My offspring," she said, her voice flat as her ears. "If you will not stand beside me now, Mhrand, you will *never* stand beside me! So, if you will abide by the letter of the interdict, then make your move, false beloved. I will not sell our lives cheaply."

"I won't attack you."

"Then you had better leave, before I attack you." She delivered the words on a snarl, and leapt over his head toward the highest shelf and the upper hallway, just as the ground-level door slid open and another serving bot appeared. The bot exploded, and Death heard Mhrand's yowl of pain, but she didn't look back. She pulled her quintessence field around her and sprinted down the hallway.

In her searing rage, Death didn't know where she was going. Nor did she care. Her only concern was getting out, away from Mhrand before her sudden desire to feel his flesh tearing beneath her claws took hold.

She rounded a corner and nearly ran bodily into Susa and Blade. The bounty hunter, Alcuin, followed close behind, gun trained to cover their path. Quick as a thought, Death dropped her quintessence field and leapt into her molly's arms.

"Good," Susa said, her voice clipped and calm. "I was looking for you. The bots all left when you did. I think you're a target. We must get you out. Where's Mhrand?"

"Gone," Death said, her voice cracking as anguish flooded through her. She fought it, tried to burn it away with rage. Sadness was incapacitating. For now, anger was better.

She'd be sad later.

"Oh?"

"Ruzeen was right. We're under interdict. All being held responsible for the Peacemaker's death, according to the message from his dama. He wouldn't attack me, so I left."

"Oh sweetling…"

"No. Not now. Let's just get to the ships and get out."

"We can't stay together. It will be better if we split up," Susa said. "Flame, you stay with Alcuin, go to her ship. Interdict or not, no one would dare fire on a Peacemaker vessel. Blade will get out on his own. I'll stay with Death."

And though it would have been faster for Death to run on her own, she felt Susa's arms tighten around her as she held her close to her chest and ran for the exit toward ship ridge.

* * *

The sun was coming up, filtering through the green of the jungle canopy, turning the darkness to merely dim. Death could feel Susa's heart pounding as the Human ran, carrying her down the path through the trees. It wasn't far to the ridge and the sleek starships that waited there, but the path was twisty and Human eyes weren't as sharp as a Hunter's. Death knew she should jump down and lead the way, but she couldn't bring herself to move from Susa's embrace.

She felt a pain in her chest, a tightness. Mhrand's words had caused a cold core of dread to form inside her, and it radiated icy pain that made it hard to breathe. Her mind kept replaying the scene in her sleeping chamber. She could see Mhrand's face, bewildered and angry. She could see his ears flatten in despair. She could hear the questioning in his voice. And most of all, most dreadfully of all, she could feel his hesitation hanging in the air between them.

He hesitated. In the moment she needed him most, he hesitated to remain by her side.

Unforgivable, and yet…

And yet, hadn't *she* been the one to push him away? Wasn't it *her* words that reverberated in her memory?

If you will not stand beside me now, you will never stand beside me…you had better leave, before I attack you.

Death tried to breathe past the glacier of pain in her chest, but all she could manage was a mewling sob.

"I know, sweetling."

Susa, still hustling through the trees, put her face down and brushed her lips against the top of Death's head, just between her ears. Try though she might, the Hunter couldn't seem to make any other sound than the soft crying.

"Just hang in there, kita. We're nearly there. Let us get to the ship and safely away, and then you can fall apart as much as you need. But stay with me now. I fear—"

A bolt of energy fire blasted through the trees, momentarily blinding Death as it fluoresced.

"Fuck," Susa muttered as she leapt to the side, off the path. "You'd better pull quintessence, sweetling. I'm no match for a Hunter, but if they don't know you're here, you might be able to make it on your own."

"Not without you," Death said, unable to keep the wet anguish out of her voice.

"I'm not the target, little Dama. You are."

And just like that, with two words, Susa changed everything. Little Dama. For that was what she was now. Queen of the clan, mother to her unborn kits. While Death herself might have been tempted to succumb to the agony of heartbreak, a dama could not afford such luxuries. Her children must survive. And so, she must survive.

Fair enough.

"Give me ten heartbeats, then run all out for my ship. It's right in the middle of the pack. Go direct, but use what cover is available," Death said, her voice firming up with every word. She reached up to rub her cheek hard against Susa's jaw. "Stay alive, my Human. I need you."

"I will do my best," Susa said.

Death supposed that would have to be good enough. Another energy bolt split the air to Susa's right, causing her to flinch. The scent of ozone and scorched wood wound through the night.

"Ten heartbeats," Death said as she pulled quintessence and leapt. "Go."

The moment her paws touched down on the spongy under-growth of the jungle floor, Death leapt upward again, touching her pads lightly on the upright trunk of a tree and springing back the other way to catch a low hanging branch. She swung around this, using her momentum to whip her body up and onto the rough sur-face of the tree's bark. From there, it was another short leap to an-other, higher branch nearer to the edge of the clearing, where she could see who was shooting at them.

A lone Hunter stood in the meadow, an energy rifle to his shoul-der, and his rusty orange ears flat against his skull.

Murrron.

"I see you, Human," he said. "You can come out. It's not you I'm after."

"May I suggest that you cease shooting at me, then?"

"Wasn't shooting at you. Was shooting near you. If I was shoot-ing at you, you'd be dead."

"Thank you for missing."

"You're welcome. Can't forever, though," he said, and Death heard real regret in his voice. "Can miss you, but not the kita. Wish I could."

"Who would know?"

"Someone. No one. *I* would know. I've lived a good long life, and in all that time, I've never willingly disobeyed my dama's com-mand. I'm not about to start."

Something in his words caught at Death's mind. His phrasing was odd. Never *willingly* disobeyed...Was he giving her a subtle out? If he could be compelled to disobey...

She spared a thought, wishing Blade were here. He was far better at such nuances. Not that it mattered, for Murrron stood between her and escape, so she was going to have to go through him regardless. But maybe he was giving her a chance to succeed.

Death threaded through the tree branches, taking care to move as silently as possible. She reached the edge of the clearing just as Susa's ten heartbeats were up, for the Human exploded into action below her. Murrron fired three bolts right at her, and likely would have hit, if not for one thing.

She was named Death From Above for good reason.

Death struck from her position, diving down, claws extended. He looked up at her an instant before her forepaws smashed into his face, causing his aim to go wild. She whipped her back legs under herself and down as they caught on his rifle. She stripped the weapon from his grasp as they both tumbled to the ground with the force of her leap.

But Murrron was a Hunter in his own right. And if he was a little slower than he'd been as a youngster, he more than made up for it in age and treachery.

"I loved your dama," he hissed as they rolled on the ground. He brought one of his claws up in a strike toward her throat, but she managed to turn aside and take it as a glancing blow on her shoulder. "I never told her, but I did. I'll always regret that."

"She cared for you a great deal," Death grunted in return as her back legs scrabbled for purchase near his belly. He kicked them aside and managed to gash her inner thigh hard enough to break skin.

"She did. And that was always enough. I'm as proud of you four as if you were my own," Murrron said, and bit her painfully on the ear. Death let out a hiss, and drove her claws into the flesh of his chest. Murrron yelped, releasing her ear, and let her go from the grapple.

Death rolled backwards, over her head, and came up in a crouch, her tail rigid. Murrron did something similar, but slowly. Nearby, the sound of starship engines rumbled to life.

"Susa started the ship," Death said.

"I had it ready to go."

"Did you now? I get the feeling you don't really know what you want out of this encounter."

"You may be right," Murrron said, and slow blinked. "But then, that's never mattered much. Not for me."

"What does matter?" Death asked, fighting down the icy pain as it tried to resurface.

"Doing a good job," Murrron said, "Being with those who matter."

"You could come with us," Death said. "Join our clan. I can—"

"No," Murrron said, shaking his head. "Had she wanted me like that, she would have asked. And it's fine that she didn't. But I can't join with you without it, don't you see?"

"I do," Death said, swallowing hard against the fullness in her throat. And then she struck, faster than she knew she could move. She pivoted on her front legs and kicked out with her back ones, connecting just below Murrron's jaw on the side of his neck. His head snapped to the side, and he slumped to the ground. Unconscious or not, she didn't know. Nor did she have time to figure it out.

Drowning in regret, she leapt over his crumpled form and resumed her sprint for her ship. The hatch stood open, and she vaulted inside, landing on Susa's lap. Death felt one soft, long fingered hand come to rest on her back while the other slammed down on the canopy control. She was vaguely aware of the light dimming as the hatch closed and sealed. Then there was a kick of acceleration, and she could finally let herself spiral down into blessed oblivion.

* * *

Blade's ears buzzed, the explosions' repercussions lingering as he forced himself not to look back. He had no way of knowing which way Death, Flame, or Susa had gone, and knew better than to follow even if he could make out scent or sound in the pungent mix of fire, blood, and smoke overlaying the thick jungle brew that closed around him as he pushed forward.

Pain began to make itself known along his back and limbs, a combination he could not separate into burns or cuts or bruises. With an experimental shake of his head that only made the buzzing worse, he focused on each loping step, forcing a count to keep his pace steady. If he kept himself aimed at a target, it felt less like fleeing from his home. A purpose ahead, not a defeat behind.

The attack had been sudden, and thorough. Although targeted most viciously at Death, someone wanted them all dead. The Human Alcuin had helped turn the momentum, and he was sure his littermates and Susa would survive. He was sure he would, too, though that last explosion had...

Someone had known about the explosion that took Reow and the Peacemaker before it happened, because a random attack made for too much of a coincidence, and they had planned in depth. To have reprogrammed their probes, to have Hunters in waiting—that took time, and effort.

Skill, the combination of talents each of the siblings had honed, the Peacemaker's bounty hunter, and a fair measure of luck had only barely saved them—the attack had been designed with overkill in mind. In the face of all that planning, whoever had waged the attack would not hesitate to follow through. Their lives had become forfeit, and he couldn't simply run through the jungle to the city and appear as though nothing had happened. As though he weren't under interdict. The fact that the attempt had been so meticulously designed and yet failed signaled that someone, somewhere on Khatash, could not afford for him to live.

His thoughts circled these facts as he continued counting, working his way deeper into the jungle and away from the wreckage of his clan.

Reow had no reason to kill the Peacemaker, but someone had determined she had.

Someone hated Reow and all she had built, enough to kill her and the Peacemaker, name her clan anathema, and sentence them all to death.

Someone had managed to put together the pieces and conduct a stunning attack in their most guarded dwelling, and they had nearly succeeded.

Someone had resources and experience.

It had to be Dirrys. It had to be Whispering Fear.

The realization beat against him, increasing his pace, so obvious it quickened his breath. Of course it was her, the angry dama who had nearly attacked his dama in council. He didn't know how, or the entirety of why, but it was enough. He knew it had to be true. He would go to Whispering Fear, and challenge her in front of her clan, pull out her teeth and use them to carve out her eyes. He would tie her with her own tail, pull strips of skin from it and feed them to her. He would mark her fur—

Mid thought, mid count, panting, he toppled into the undergrowth, unconscious before the ground slammed against him.

* * *

A high, skittering cry shocked Blade awake, and he leapt to his feet with his front claws extended even as his eyes opened. The motion immediately sent pain racing from the base of his skull to his back legs, and he hissed.

The hiss saved his life, giving the poisonous slipskin reason to be elsewhere immediately. Covered in blood, smoke, and dirt, Blade's scent had been faint enough to give the long, scaled creature confidence in its unchallenged stalking of the flier who had shrieked. The hiss of a deadlier predator kept it from spitting its venom at the flier, and Blade saw only the blur of its scales as it fled.

For a moment Blade wavered on his feet, then crouched, panting. The pain refused to ebb, but adrenaline helped dampen it, giving him room to take stock of his injuries. A rib, cracked or broken, and pressure down his side indicated it might cramp his breath, but likely hadn't punctured anything. A mass of blood dried into his fur down his back where he could just reach. Some projectile or shrapnel had lodged itself there, but he wouldn't reach to dig it out while unprotected in the open jungle. The slipskin might have fled at finding an unexpected predator nearby, but there were plenty of other creatures who would flock to the smell of fresh blood, and several of those could strike him down, given his weakened state.

Smaller lacerations marked him all over—there had been several explosions—but not enough to keep him from moving. He turned his head, ears swiveling, marking the direction he'd come from and orienting himself in the sprawl of trees and vegetation.

As a kit he had roamed much of the jungle near their den, finding clever hiding holes and mostly hidden small caves for his treasures, and he'd kept some of them as he grew—less for shiny playthings and more for quiet space to research and consider a contract, away from his siblings. Being Blade, he'd also stocked a few with supplies and gear, because tools were often as helpful as knowledge in executing a hunt.

Without climbing into the lower canopy, he couldn't be certain, but he was fairly sure he'd pushed himself north and slightly east, closer to the small river that wound around the empty hills between their den and the city. The undergrowth was exceptionally layered and tangled that way, with enough animal trails and moving vines that his path would have been hard to trace. The same undergrowth likely meant Blade hadn't gotten nearly as far as he'd wanted to, so if he continued to move north and slightly east, he should reach the river and be able to find the way to one of his better supplied caves.

He briefly weighed the idea of climbing and using the lower canopy paths for a more direct journey, but that would push his already strained body and put him in contact with more nimble competitors besides. Any part of the Khatash jungle could be deadly, but the lower levels of the towering trees that interlocked across their planet hosted some of the fastest creatures, and he'd been lucky enough so far that he knew better than to push it.

Opening his mouth to better scent the air, Blade took a deep breath, ignored the jab of pain that resulted, and moved.

* * *

The edges of his vision broke up into gray sparks, but Blade's pace held steady as he slipped past the tangled vines and piled rocks that concealed the deceptively small cave entrance. Inside, he paused only to ensure nothing had moved in—Hunter scent would keep most, but not all, invaders from roosting—and stepped carefully across the rough ground of loose stones and fluttery, stinging fungus.

Toward the back of the cave, where the high arch of the ceiling began to narrow in closer to the ground, a cracked boulder leaned against the irregular wall. A much younger Blade had been exceedingly proud of his own cleverness in moving it, positioning it perfectly to hide the low opening to a corridor branching further into the cave system. He spared a fond thought for that smug little kit as he climbed the boulder and slid on his back into the small opening left between the cleft of the boulder and the opening of the rocky hall. It wasn't as perfect as the hidden entrance to their den, but as far as he knew, not even his dama had discovered this particular hiding place.

Two more turns through near-perfect darkness, and he unerringly reached for where he kept regularly-refreshed lamps, turned a switch, and slitted his pupils against the low light that flooded his hidden cave.

The scrape against stone had set the wound in his back to stinging, so he went directly to the cabinet he'd long ago fashioned out of fallen branches and sticky vines, digging out one of the nanite shots he'd so carefully stored. Hunters learned by failing just as much as succeeding in their early stalking of prey, and better to be prepared with a cache of nanos than bleed to death because some desperate creature got in a lucky blow.

He held the shot in one hand and leaned sideways against the wall, ignoring the flare of pain from his rib as he twisted back to get the claws of his free hand dug around the hard nugget of metal in his back. Breathe, tear, hiss, press the shot against his leg. He stood there, staring at nothing, pushing through as pain and healing chased each other through his body.

He told himself to go and get a container of water to drink, but instead dropped to the ground, curled into a defensive circle, and let consciousness go once more.

* * *

When Blade woke, he rolled to his feet, testing his range of motion. Stiffness, a hint of dull pain, but no catch to his breath. He opened the cabinet again for rations and drank half the stored water without regret. As he ate, he considered his whirling thoughts when he had left den and siblings behind. While he could tell now that some of his decisions had been motivated more by emotion than actual knowledge, he was sure of his realization—Dirrys had been behind this. It had to be either Whispering Fear or High Canopy that had moved against them, and High Canopy had fewer off-world contacts and less on-planet resources. Dirrys's momentary lapse of control at council reinforced his decision that Whispering Fear was the leading contender—and was the target to aim himself toward. Of course, he couldn't simply accuse their volatile dama, nor was there any public recourse given his clan's destruction.

No, he thought to himself, fur prickling up on his arms in pleasure, *nothing public*. He would hunt, as he always had. Invade their den, learn their secrets, and confirm who had brought this chaos to their door. And then, destroy them, root to crown.

His claws itched to bury themselves in blood and meat, but he sat, curling his tail close around himself, eating calmly. He considered what he had to do and cut away the damaged fur on his side and back, adapting it to the shapes other clans favored. He must disguise himself—Cunning Blade of Night Wind would never make it to Whispering Fear's den, nor far into the city. Disguises were below Hunters, but in the service of this particular prize, he would be a fool to put pride over necessity.

A story. He would be someone else, a Hunter who knew nothing of clan politics, of hatred for a dama of his own kind, of plotting the downfall of an ancient clan and burying its den in death.

This time when he slept, it was with the boneless satisfaction of one who knew his business.

* * *

Flame desperately wanted to look back the way Death and Susa had gone, but she knew if she saw even a hint of them she would abandon Tamir in an instant and leap after her sibling and molly. As she knew just as strongly what a terrible idea that was, she maintained her awkward pace, quintessence pulled close, undetectable in the bounty hunter's footsteps as they approached the station from which the Human had so recently arrived. The shuttle should still be there—at the very least, it was their best option, and Flame had no other ideas. After a lifetime of nesting plans under plans to adapt quickly when reality twisted around her, this lack of options felt like stepping off solid ground and plummeting through every layer of the jungle canopy.

Two Hunters appeared in front of the station. Neither had been there a moment ago, and Flame, lost in an obsessive attempt to decide what to do if the shuttle had been called back, reared back. Had they been lying in wait, under lightbending? The long, low building of the transfer station had been built seamlessly from metal to discourage any jungle creature from attempting to nest, which removed hiding places for even the cleverest Hunter. Hunters wouldn't be in their quintessence fields at an outlying station, on this night, for no reason.

Flame spared a thought for Death. Her sister should have been safe from attack. They should have let her alone as long as she carried young. Everyone had to have known—Reow had registered her as the clan's heir. That could only mean one thing, to take such an official step. So, she should have been safe, protected by the miracle of the lives she was growing.

But they'd attacked Death anyway. Targeted her, which could only mean the clan as a whole was to be wiped out. If they'd attack a pregnant damita, the clan Heir, Flame knew her own life carried no value at all. Why were strangers here? For nothing good, so Flame remained invisible, close to the Human's steps.

"Human," one of the Hunters said with a purr, while the other vanished again. Flame wondered if others crouched nearby, hidden in their bent light. Not many were as skilled at stealth as she, but there were some. It was possible she and the bounty hunter were vastly outnumbered here. Unlikely, but possible. She tensed low to the ground, poised to move, and hoped the Human would proceed carefully.

"Depik," Tamir replied levelly. "My business here is complete." Unspoken but clear, they had no business interfering in her execution of Peacemaker orders.

"Are you taking anyone with you?" the visible Hunter asked, studying his claws, tail flicking idly.

"My business here is complete," Tamir repeated, tone hardening.

"And does that business supersede mine, on my own planet? You are far from the city, Human. Helping a criminal under interdict would not help you."

Susa had told her, but here, from this uncaring stranger, the word interdict struck her so hard she nearly stumbled. At the same moment, Tamir startled slightly, glancing down, looking for something that wasn't there. Perhaps the invisible Hunter had crossed over to brush against her, intimidate her—Flame had played the same game before, but for the moment she didn't care. They'd declared her clan anathema. Her life was forfeit, not just here in this moment, but on all of Khatash. Anywhere a Hunter found her. Her life, her littermates,' that of anyone claimed by Night Wind. Two unfamiliar Hunters, lying in wait for them, made it real in a way the attack and Susa's words had not.

Belatedly, Flame realized these other Hunters were making clear they could become invisible—even if the manner of it wasn't obvious, they would never do such a thing unless they intended that the Peacemaker's bounty hunter never left Khatash. She wondered why she had taken so long to put it together, and cursed herself for an addled kita. She had to focus. She knew better than this.

With a small shake of impatience, Flame moved away from Tamir, keeping her quintessence field tight. She closed her eyes and pulled in a breath. Listened, breathed, and reached to grab the

Hunter she knew had to be there. Luck gave her a firm grasp, and she followed up with skill, wrapping around him fast and hard. Cutting off his air before he could make a sound. As soon as he went limp, she sprang away, leaving him to crumple to the ground, visible in unconsciousness, but apparently untouched. She was fairly certain he'd live. She was absolutely certain she didn't care.

While his partner stared at the newly revealed body, she bounded across the distance between them, wrapping closely against him before he could react.

"My life is already forfeit," she snarled low, directly in his ear. "What do you think will keep you safe from my claws?"

"Do you dispute the Peacemaker's authority here, Hunter, or may I go?" Tamir might not have understood what was happening, but she was adept enough to react, keeping her tone neutral even as her body tightened slightly.

The pause lengthened between them.

"I do not dispute," he choked out. "Go." As soon as the words were out, he collapsed, and between one breath and the next, Flame appeared, standing over him.

Tamir visibly jumped, but they didn't have time for an explanation. They had to get off-planet, if Flame were to have any chance to figure out why any of this had happened.

Flame stopped only long enough to survey the two fallen Hunters, then twitched her tail dismissively. After a moment, she pulled her quintessence field close around her again, disappearing, and ran through the station and into the shuttle ahead of Tamir.

"Anyone on Khatash will be able to scan and see you have a Hunter signature with you," she said as Tamir caught up and sat at the controls, "but it is custom to ignore a Hunter they can't identify, when she is invisible. Custom and your status on a Peacemaker warrant should carry us through."

"You know," Tamir managed in a conversational tone, "it's weird to hear a voice floating from a body I can't see."

"Pretend I'm the comms," Flame said, voice flat in dismissal. "You talk to disembodied voices all the time."

"Not ones that can kill me on a whim."

"You just saved my life." Disgust ran through her, and she didn't bother to keep it out of her tone. "Do you consider Depik stupid? Why would I squander that just to kill you before I'm off-planet?"

"Why get you off the planet if you'll kill me in space?"

"Humans." Flame spat, pacing on silent feet. She glanced at the screen before resolutely ignoring the sight of her home receding behind them. "Killing you serves no purpose for me. You didn't lead that attack on my clan."

"I did not. Whoever did seemed perfectly happy for me to die alongside you."

"Yes."

"Who do you think did it?"

Flame wanted the Human to shut up and let her think, wanted to drop her field and send out a message demanding to know what had happened, wanted to go back and ensure those Hunters at the station were dead, that Susa was okay, that her littermates had survived...More than what she wanted, she needed to get off Khatash and get the distance the find out what, and why, and who.

"Whatever truly happened between Dama and the Peacemaker, the attack happened too quickly after we saw the video. Someone knew before we did in order to have a plan in place."

"How else were the probes programmed?" Tamir stared at the controls in front of her, though the course to the suborbital station was locked in and there was nothing she needed to do. Flame supposed that was easier on a Human than glancing around for a Hunter she couldn't see.

"Someone knew something they couldn't have. Unless they did it. Planned to kill Dama and the Peacemaker, and knew they had to wipe us out so we wouldn't find them."

"But here we are."

"There's more here; more than it appears. Has to be."

"Peacemaker Hrusha sent me here for a reason." Tamir might have been convinced, or convincing herself; her tone was thoughtful. Flame wished the Human's voice weren't so neutral, giving her something to take offense to, something to provoke an attack. No, she knew that was stupid and short-sighted. If the Human were going to betray her, she would have done so already. Unwilling or no, they were all the other had for the moment.

"So, we find who did this and why."

"And then?"

This was a job more important than any contract, and who better to complete it? Dama had named her, and taught her, to be who she was—silent. Patient. Matchless in waiting, able to avoid notice and bring death with impossible accuracy. Whoever had done this to Reow, to their family...

"We end them, as they tried to end us. It's only a matter of time."

And they'd never see her coming.

* * *

The shuttle docked at the suborbital station without incident. No one, at least no one visible, awaited them at the airlock. Tamir stepped out from shuttle to station, walking with the confident, unhurried stride that seemed to be her custom.

Flame paused once they crossed over, deploying every sense to determine if they were being flanked, trusting in her own superior stealth to keep from being detected in turn.

It disturbed her that no one waited in the hall. If there would be an attack, then it would be further down, when they were on the move. Tamir didn't seem concerned, though from the way she was holding herself, it took effort for the woman to keep from glancing around to try and see Flame.

Flame sighed and followed this new Human, understanding that most Hunters wouldn't be able to read such nuance of Human body language. No other Hunters, beside her siblings, had been half-raised by the species, and few others cared to learn more than it took to kill them when contracted to do so.

Tamir navigated each turn with a minimum of hesitation, though she could not have spent much time in this station. That meant she could read Depik and used the signage and flashing figures on the wall screens to proceed without fuss. Or perhaps the Peacemaker ship had been allowed to talk closely enough with the Depik system to navigate its pilot through the halls, though that seemed a far less likely scenario.

Flame tucked it away to answer later and noted they made it through four turns and two lifts before getting even a sensation of another Hunter passing by. Trap? Attack? Clearing out of the way of the one visitor to their planet they couldn't toy with to their fullest whim?

A checkpoint ahead slowed their steps, the oversized door to the external docking passageways closed, a Hunter sitting on his back legs, aimlessly revealing and sheathing his claws. The airlock quality seal should have dwarfed him, given it was over twice the height of an average Human, to allow passage for the tallest of species that might have need of it. Tamir demonstrated she was not so ignorant of Hunters and their culture as to be fooled, and before he launched what was sure to be a lazy sort of challenge, she stopped and held herself at attention.

"Peacemaker business concluded on Khatash. Getting back to my ship," she said briskly, keeping her eyes aimed at roughly his midsection. Respectful but not deferential, a smart line to hold.

"Did Peacemaker business include wiping out an errant clan?" he asked, flicking a glance at her and then away, as though the matter had no importance to him. "No, that timing wouldn't work, would it. Aiding them, then?"

"I came to Khatash to do a job for Peacemaker Hrusha, and I did it. With Peacemaker Hrusha's death—"'"

"Murder," he interrupted, dangerously pleasant.

"I am bound to return to Capitol for a new assignment. I am still on Peacemaker duty, unless you intend to take your issue up with galactic law."

"If you worked for the Depik Peacemaker for any length of time, you might imagine how much I care about galactic law." Scorn etched through the word 'Depik,' but his lounging manner didn't shift.

"I know you can kill me before I blink," she replied, sounding just short of bored. "And I know just how much retribution you'd bring down on your entire small species, and yourself in particular, if you did. Doesn't seem worth the momentary satisfaction. Do you dispute my right to pass?"

Flame glanced up at Tamir with a measure of surprise. She walked the line well—neither defiant, which the Hunter could easily meet challenge for challenge, nor overly meek, which would be answered with violence.

The Hunter didn't answer, coming to a similar conclusion, and without perceptible motion from him the door spiraled open behind him. More than likely he had an invisible counterpart, but she remained secure in the fact neither of them would sense her.

After they cleared the doorway, Flame paced ahead. Thwarted aggression flooded her system and left her with too much energy for Tamir's casual pace. More than once she sensed the edges of another Hunter's quintessence field, and more than once she skirted a little too close to see if she could determine which Hunter passed. But these halls were crowded with several species' worth of arrivals and departures, and it was a foolish risk. She forced herself to ignore the temptation of other Hunters, to focus only on moving undetected. She had to pay attention. She could not start a fight. This close to leaving her world, she certainly couldn't be caught.

Not before she'd hunted this prey to ground.

* * *

A t every connection between the main airlock and the smaller one that connected to the bounty hunter's ship, Tamir's voice remained nearly bored, unaffected by whatever had happened on the ground. Perhaps few knew of the attack after all, given how uneventful the brief conversations were. Flame watched, invisible in her field, and saw the rage collect in the Human's shoulders.

Susa had rarely carried such emotion, but Humans seemed determined to carry tension in their upper body. Protecting their delicate necks, perhaps. Flame filed it away as something to ask Susa.

A pang almost made her miss her step—had Susa survived? Hunters wouldn't go out of their way to kill a Human, even if her clan had been interdicted. There was no profit in it, nor glory; only the Hunters of the clan would have been targets. Flame tried to convince herself, knowing that Death would have done everything in her considerable power to protect Susa.

But the guards at the station, and that one at the airlock, had been willing to attack Tamir while she served Peacemaker orders, so Flame could not have faith Susa would have been left unmolested.

Knowing that Blade, Death, and Susa could so easily have come to harm did her no good, and it only amped up her agitation. She pushed the line of thought down, taking deep breaths as she slipped through the halls. Focus. She would deal with all of that later. Right now, she had to stay in control, not let her emotions push her to foolish action. That effort took her all the way through the clearance and launch of the bounty hunter's ship. Flame curled tightly into an out of the way corner, to process and bury what needed to be cleared away to center her thoughts.

Perhaps it was minutes or hours into their voyage, but either way Tamir showed remarkable discipline in waiting before clearing her throat and spinning her flight couch to get a better view of the bridge.

"You still with me?"

Flame stood, shaking off the lingering emotions of the loss of her family to compose herself, then dropped her field. Tamir did not jump, but better angled herself in her chair to face her visible companion. For long moments the two stared at each other, their alliance too new and unexpected to give them much of a starting place.

"We've saved each other's lives," Flame said, waiting for Tamir's nod. "Do you care, what happened to Hrusha?"

"She was my boss, and a damn good one. Whoever took her out had no compunction about trying for me too, and I have a problem with that. And taking out a Peacemaker should have consequences."

"Where to now?" Flame asked, her bright blue eyes steady on Tamir's brown ones.

"I wasn't joking about headquarters. They'd expect me to return for reassignment. And…" the Human trailed off, looked away, but the anger was still clear in the way she held herself. "Peacemaker Hrusha knew something was off, that's why she sent me. My job isn't done, and your dama didn't kill her. She suspected something was wrong on Khatash, and it wasn't with your clan or she never would have sent me to you—and she had to have chosen me for a reason, not some other Depik. Doesn't make sense otherwise. So, we go back and see what happened."

"We saw what happened," Flame said, sounding out the words deliberately, testing her.

"Sure, we did." Tamir's voice was all scorn, and Flame relaxed. "We agree your dama didn't kill the Peacemaker, and there's no motive there that makes sense. So something else happened. Some*one* else happened, or how else was that attack on your clan already planned and so quickly executed?"

Flame made a noise of agreement, hearing the belief as the Human echoed Flame's words. She lowered her head, gesturing Tamir should continue.

"We go back and see if there were any witnesses. I'll get the formal report. Peacemaker Hrusha said..."

Without thinking, Flame crossed over to Tamir as the woman paused, put a front paw on Tamir's knee, whisper soft. They were both still wary, but it was enough of a gesture to get the woman talking again.

"She said the meat had gone rotten deep inside. It still looked like a fresh kill, but corruption had spoiled the whole thing, from the inside out. She wanted answers and indicated they would be important to me, too. I never saw her misjudge a situation."

Flame withdrew, gaze going distant as she considered. "A Hunter doesn't reach her age or position without skill to see what is underneath. We will find the rotten core and burn it out."

* * * * *

The Contract

'Tlor was a grey, dismal place. Like Khatash, very little of the actual terrain could be seen from orbit. Unlike Khatash, this was because the Lumar home world was covered, nearly pole to pole, in densely crowded cityscape.

Nor was it interesting cityscape, Deluge reflected. The rows and blocks of buildings were of mostly uniform height and shape, giving the view a depressing sameness as he watched out the window of the orbital shuttle. His own ship was parked in a geosynchronous orbit just outside the cone-shaped Galactic Free Trade zone that extended up over 'Tlor's largest starport. He'd caught the shuttle down to the surface, and had enjoyed the exercise of blending in with the crowd on board.

Which crowd was particularly diverse, almost surprisingly so. One could make a lot of credits on 'Tlor. Besides the always popular Lumar mercenaries, the planet boasted multiple rare and valuable resources in the form of both planetary and orbital metals, some inert gasses, and several popular hallucinogenic compounds that several species used for recreational and other purposes. By rights, the Lumar should have been counted among the richest of the Union species...but they were not. Common opinion held that they were just not up to the intellectual challenge of managing their inherent wealth, and so certain other species had stepped in to do it for them.

Not the least of which were the tactical geniuses, the Veetanho.

Deluge's target was one of these—a Veetanho mercenary commander by the name of Rhaabou. She was tall for her species, nearly twice his height, according to the information his ship had fed to him during the journey here. She cut a formidable figure in the stills and video he had, with her well-muscled body and commanding, arrogant stance. She certainly looked the part of a tactical expert and single combat master.

And she was even more impressive in person.

Later that night, Deluge found her carousing in a mixed-clientele establishment. He'd donned a long cloak, and kept his hood up and his head down as he found an unoccupied corner with a good view. Rhaabou and another Veetanho sat in the thick of the debauchery, wreathed in clouds of colored smoke as music thumped through the air. Beings ebbed and flowed around them, some bringing food and drink, others dancing or moving. Mindful of the first lesson, Deluge made himself comfortable and watched.

Rhaabou's companion turned out to be her sister, Apeya. Where Rhaabou was tall, Apeya was much shorter. Still, she carried herself like one who had won her share of fights, and though her build tended toward the wiry rather than muscular, she was obviously quite strong.

She also had, by far, the worse temper of the pair of them. She snarled menacingly at every passerby who ventured too close. Once, a dancer bumped her, and she leapt to her feet and attacked. Deluge watched as the ensuing fracas was quickly dismantled by the establishment security and Rhaabou herself, who interceded to get her sister to calm down and retake her seat. A moment later, a serving bot stamped with the establishment's logo appeared carrying a tray of something that was either food or drink, and appeared to be entirely intoxicating, if Apeya's reaction to it was to be believed.

And the more intoxicated she became, the more extreme her behavior became. She acted even more violently toward the other revelers, and even more lovingly toward her sister. All night, until Rhaabou carried her nearly-incapacitated sibling off to one of the ubiquitous ultra-short range urban shuttles that crowded the skies above 'Tlor's endless city.

Susa was right, Deluge reflected. This didn't add up at all. He needed more information.

So, the next evening, back on *Iora* after a rest, he tried a different tactic.

Mercenary company records were, to a certain extent, public information. At least, the contracts that came out of a merc pit were. It was nothing at all to look up the details of Proud Fist's contracts and see when they'd been entered into, the name of the client, and the status of the contract. The recent contracts all had a status of "fulfilled," with riders indicating that combat loss bonuses had been paid. Combat loss bonuses weren't unusual, but looking at them made Deluge wonder just how large those bonuses were. He turned his attention to tracking down the name of the banking house that handled the financials for Proud Fist...

And nearly fell out of the pilot's couch with laughter. Clearly, serendipity smiled on him for this strange contract. For the banking house was a Sidar company, and the chief officer had a very familiar name.

* * *

It took almost no time at all to make arrangements for a meeting. The meeting itself, however, was slightly delayed. This was only to be expected, since the last time Deluge checked, his new Sidar friend Rurranach had been on Khatash. The Sidar hadn't mentioned that he was an operating officer for Theela Financial, one of the mid-level banking houses in this arm of the galaxy. All of the research that Deluge found on the company indicated they were concentrated in the Praf region, but market reports on the GalNet hinted that Theela Financial might be making a move outward and trying to establish a presence in the Centaur region.

So, when Deluge reached out to Rurranach, he'd offered to discuss exclusive banking opportunities for the Night Wind clan. As he'd predicted, the Sidar jumped at the chance, and after a delay of almost exactly the transit time for a message to get to Khatash and back, Deluge and Rurranach met up once again in a busy market setting.

"I greet you, Mighty Hunter and my friend," Rurranach said as Deluge dropped his quintessence cloak and appeared on the cafe table the Sidar had selected. It was a credit to Rurranach's training and self-mastery that his only reaction was a slight stiffening of his wings under the cloak.

"I greet you, Keeper of Secrets and mover of funds," Deluge said lightly, dropping his jaw in a grin. "Thank you for coming so quickly."

"How could I not, when you dangle such tantalizing prey before me? Handling your clan's fortune would make us both rich beyond our imaginings, my friend. I was very happy to get your call."

"I am already rich beyond my imaginings," Deluge said with a slow blink. Something about the Sidar made him want to tease. "As a matter of fact, I came into a very lucrative business venture shortly after we last saw one another."

"I heard," the Sidar said, dryly. "Well done."

"You are the first to say so," Deluge said. "I thank you."

"It was well done, in my view. You saved the life of a Besquith pup and gained a not inconsequential amount of wealth in one masterful stroke, mighty Hunter. I think you would be quite formidable should you ever choose to take up hunting profits full time."

"I appreciate that, Rurranach. I do. But now that you mention it, I *am* under contract."

Again, the slight stiffening of the cloaked wings. Deluge slow blinked another grin.

"Do not worry," he said, "You are not my target."

"Good to know," Rurranach said, matching Deluge's dry tone.

"I imagine it is. However, I need some help."

"If I can give it, I shall."

"I need to see the financial records of the Lumar Proud Fist Company."

Rurranach leaned forward, tilting his magnificently-crested head to the side.

"That is...a difficult request, my friend."

"Which is why I offered to aid your house in your quest to establish more of a foothold in the Centaur region."

"I see. Forgive me, my friend, but...is such a thing within your power to give? When we met, you were very clear that you are subject to the whim of your dama, and you seem a bit young to be given the title of deo," he added with a twist of humor in his tone.

"It is," Deluge said, slow blinking, "Because currently, the Night Wind clan does not engage with a banking house. We handle our finances internally. So, if I contract with you for the use of my own funds, that will be an exclusive contract, will it not? At least for the time being."

"Clever Hunter," Rurranach said, letting out that chittering laughter Deluge found so charming. "I think you know it does not work that way."

"Perhaps not, I concede. But my own fortune is not insubstantial, and it *would* be an in to my clan. My brother-kit Blade could tell you better, but I believe none of the other major clans use a banking house either. You could very well be the first if you begin by contracting with me."

"And the terms? I turn over the financial records to you and in exchange you contract with me to manage your personal fortune?"

"Yes. For a trial period of one year. If you are as good as I think you are, that will be ample time for you to demonstrate how you can make me richer than my current mark beyond my imaginings," Deluge said, slow blinking once again.

Rurranach regarded him for a long moment, then bobbed his head up and down in a slow, ponderous movement.

"Done," he said. "I will have the records for you tomorrow, though I doubt I can let you keep them."

"That is fine," Deluge said. "I only need see them once."

Despite his caveats, though, Rurranach did, in fact, deliver copies of the records for Deluge to keep. The following day, he transferred the entire data stream of every financial transaction made by Proud Fist to the *Iora's* storage banks. Then he and Deluge caught a shuttle back to the orbital station, where the small ship had docked in obedience to Deluge's quintessential commands. Though it was close quarters, the two of them hunched together in the cockpit and combed through the debits and credits, identifying the ones which corresponded to the payouts made by the company's mercenary clients...and the combat loss bonuses which were so interesting.

"Yes," Rurranach breathed as he looked at the data spread before them on the ship's view screen. "See here? I never noticed it because I never looked at all of these payments together like this, but the date of the first combat loss bonuses corresponds with the date that Rhaabou was raised to command of the company. But what's interesting is that each one of these bonus credits is accompanied a day or so later by this payout here...looks like Rhaabou was skimming off the top."

"How can you tell?" Deluge asked.

"Because these payouts are simply transfers to different accounts, rather than payments drawn against the account and paid to an outside source. Like these payments here for refitting...must have been an ugly mercenary encounter. That's a really big payment. They must have refit with top of the line equipment. What was it...energy rifles?" Rurranach said with a *tsk* sound that conveyed great disapproval.

"But that doesn't make sense," Deluge said, "Because look, there are additional payments later that year for energy rifles, only this maker is far inferior to the first...why buy inferior rifles if you already had more of better quality from an earlier purchase?"

"That is an interesting question," Rurranach said. "I wonder..."

The Sidar tapped the command pad and brought up several more records onto the view screen. He stared at the numbers and code scrolling by, and let out a subliminal hum.

"Yes," he said again. "Every one of these payouts follows that pattern. And what's more, a quick GalNet search tells me that each of these companies are subsidiaries of this pinpeck farming conglomerate."

"So, all the payments were made to the same entity...someone is using the Proud Fist to launder credits and obscure their trail," Deluge said, catching on.

"Yes," Rurranach said, with more of the chittery laughter. "Yes, they are. You should be a Hunter of profits, Del. You'd be quite good at it."

"I'm quite good at what I'm doing now," Deluge said.

"I believe you. Which is why I think you'll find it fascinating to know who is on the board of this pinpeck conglomerate," Rurranach said. He tapped the control pad again and the columns of numbers and transactions disappeared, replaced by a single page document that looked like the charter of a company. It was in a language Deluge didn't recognize, and couldn't immediately read. Through his pinplant connection to the ship, he ordered *Iora's* translator to convert the text to English.

"Rhaabou?" Deluge asked, as *Iora's* translator processed his request.

"No," the Sidar said, "Interestingly enough, it's her sister, Apeya."

* * *

Further investigation of the company's financial transactions turned up a few other interesting discrepancies as well. For instance, based on the draws against the account, Rurranach pointed out that Apeya was the one traveling to the various merc pits during the time that the disastrous contracts were enacted.

"So it was Apeya who made the agreements? In her initial message to us, she indicated she knew ahead of time the contracts were a terrible idea. 'A dreadful waste,' she called them," Deluge said. He had the feeling the pieces to this strange puzzle were very close to falling into place, if only he could find one last bit. "Why would she do that?"

Rurranach angled his head so he could meet Deluge's eyes.

"Why did you take this contract, Del?" he asked, using the familiar form of address. They hadn't known each other long, but digging through this data and unraveling this mystery together had brought the two of them rather close.

"Because my sister-kita couldn't. She was hurt on a previous contract, but she'd already accepted this one. So, I will fulfill it in her name."

"Yes, but why? Why not just buy it out, or let it wait until she healed?"

"Buying out contracts is incredibly expensive," Deluge said, "Even for someone like me. But as for waiting...well. I didn't want to."

"Why?"

"Because of the waste." Deluge slow blinked as the connection started to become clear. "Because I am a Hunter, and killing should at least be done for a reason."

"The Veetanho are clever as a race. It is likely that Apeya knew the idea of a capricious waste of lives would engage you, or your sister, and persuade you to take the contract. It was a very clever manipulation."

"Yes," Deluge said. "It was. Except for one thing."

"What is that?"

"She forgot exactly who she was manipulating." He yawned then, deliberately flashing his pointed teeth in a move calculated to underscore the deadliness of his bite.

"I don't think she did," Rurranach said. "Remember, she's Veetanho. She knows a Depik clan will always fulfill a contract. And if her sister dies, she takes over the command, and she eliminates the one skimming off the kickback payments. I wouldn't be surprised if there were other members of the board of the pinpeck conglomerate who were putting pressure on her to do this."

"And meanwhile, the Lumar still die."

"Lumar die every day, my friend," Rurranach said. "Careful, or your image as the perfect killer will suffer."

Deluge slow blinked a smile at that, and gave the ship the command to leave its orbit and approach one of the orbital shuttle port stations for offloading.

"I recommend you stay here, aboard *Iora* or on the station. I will return in a short time," he told the Sidar as the little ship's powerful thrusters kicked in, pushing both of them into to their couches.

"And you?" Rurranach grunted against the acceleration.

"I am under contract," Deluge said. "I have a task to complete. I will notify Apeya as soon as the contract is fulfilled, and I will request payment to my account. It would help if you could expedite that."

"Since you are now my client, I can," the Sidar said.

"Perfect. Let me know when it's done. I stay linked with *Iora*, so if you are aboard, we can talk to one another using her comms."

"Of course."

They rode out the rest of the short burn in silence, while Deluge considered his approach. He didn't imagine that it would be terribly difficult. The contract was, at its heart, a straightforward one. No requirements for the appearance of an accident or anything exotic. Simply get in, make the kill, get out. And get paid.

Once on the surface, Deluge wrapped himself in quintessence and bent the light to shield him from sight. He returned again to the same establishment where he'd encountered the sisters before. Sure enough, they were there again, partaking in the revelry and noise that worked so well to cover any remaining hints of his presence.

Something that felt like liquid light trickled through him as he stalked between the gyrating bodies of dancers toward the Veetanho table. He breathed in the taste of alien bodies on the air, felt the vibration of the pulsing music brushing through his fur. It all combined into a heady focus, a knowledge of his own deadly capabilities…and the purest form of joy—he would soon use them.

In the end, it wasn't particularly dramatic. He flowed through the crowd to the table and removed a syringe of poison from the harness he wore. With quick, decisive movements, he plunged the very thin, very strong, very long needle into the joint behind Rhaabou's left knee and depressed the plunger. Instantly, a lethal dose of poison entered her bloodstream, where it would filter through her circulation and end up in her lung apparatus. Deluge removed the needle and stepped under the table to watch the aftermath and make sure the poison did its job.

As a Hunter he respected had recently reminded him, a wise Hunter makes sure.

Rhaabou twitched and then coughed. Then she coughed again. Deluge heard something shifting on the table above him, and then Apeya's high-pitched voice.

"Sister?" she asked. "Are you..." she broke off, then let out a scream as something heavy hit the table above his head. Deluge pulled his quintessence tighter around him and eased out from underneath the other side of the table. A glance back showed the former commander lying on the table, a spreading pool of very bright blood oozing out of her mouth. Apeya was on her feet, screaming as the crowd swirled around her in chaos. Deluge slipped between the feet of the panicked revelers and wove his way out the front door.

* * *

It took several hours for payment to be posted to his account, according to Rurranach's transmissions from *Iora*. Deluge wasn't particularly worried about it. He figured it would take Apeya some time to handle things, especially given the fact she hadn't (per her request) known when or where the attack would happen. Nor how. She had seemed quite distraught in the club. Either she was a tremendously gifted actress, or the sight of her sister's body was genuinely upsetting to her.

Deluge was willing to believe that both were possible. Either way, she would need time to make the payment. He spent that time stalking her from a distance, hiding mostly in shadow, but now and again using his quintessence to aid in his stealth capabilities. He watched her from a building ledge outside of the club. He rode on the floorboard of the ground transport that took her back to the Proud Fist headquarters. He followed her into her private quarters and made himself comfortable on her sleeping surface as she worked to put herself back together.

Eventually, finally, she picked up a slate and tapped in a few commands. Almost instantly, Rurranach's muted voice came through the tiny earbud inserted in Deluge's ear.

"Paid in full," the Sidar said. "With a note of thanks."

"You're welcome," Deluge said out loud, dropping his quintessence cloak with an internal sigh of relief. He'd held it for longer, in the past, but it was wearying after a while. Apeya let out a most undignified squeak and turned around, firing an energy pistol at the wall near his head. Deluge had angled himself so that the chance of her hitting anything was slim to none, but he leapt free of the bedsurface anyway.

"And here I was, just being polite," he said.

"Why are you here?" Apeya asked, her voice ragged with something that might have been pain or sadness...or even anger. Deluge didn't know, and it was fascinating to speculate upon.

"I wanted to talk to you," he said. "I wanted to make sure you knew the contract was fulfilled."

"I know it is," she spat. "I was there when you murdered my sister!"

"You murdered your sister," Deluge said calmly. "I was merely the weapon. Do you hate that pistol you hold in your hand?"

Apeya looked down at the energy pistol still pointed at him and lowered it to point at the ground.

"I *loved* Rhaabou," she said, still in that angsty hiss. Her ungoggled eyes were a striking red-rimmed green. "I hated her for making me kill her. But she left me with no choice. She was skimming off of our payments, and she had to be stopped."

"And now she is," Deluge said. "Will you continue to throw your hapless Lumar lives away on bad contracts so you can continue to disguise the money trail you are obscuring?"

"What—? No! The contracts will be…"

"Wrong answer," Deluge said, and moved before Apeya could fire the pistol she'd been raising to shoot him. He leapt to the side, got all four feet on the wall and pushed off a nanosecond before she sent a bolt sizzling into the concrete where he'd been. He twisted his body and managed to catch hold of her ears with his outstretched foreclaws, which yanked her head backwards, and she stumbled.

He got his feet up on either side of her neck and bent his head to whisper in her ear.

"And now you see why one does not play false with Hunters when it comes to our contracts," he said. She snarled and beat at him with her fists, but her angle was bad, and he shrugged off her ineffective blows. "We are killers for hire, but we are not your patsies. I would tell you to remember that, but you will not have the chance."

With that, he flexed the claws on his back feet, driving them through the layers of fur and skin and sinew to find the twin vessels that carried blood to and from her brain. He shredded these circulatory superhighways with a single slash.

Apeya let out a gurgling sound and fell to her knees as blood began to pulse out of her wounds onto the floor. Deluge let go of her ears and leapt free as she toppled forward, then bent down to look at her near side eye. He slow blinked a smile, so that it would be the last thing she would ever see as the light dimmed in her red-rimmed green eye.

That should have been it.

It would have been it, had not something completely unexpected happened. Something that was enough to make Deluge suspect that he was the butt of some sort of cosmic joke.

The door to Apeya's room opened, and a Lumar wearing the company's uniform walked in.

"Commander?" the merc said, then stopped and looked at the scene in front of him. Deluge should have pulled quintessence and vanished. It was unforgivable that he did not. But the truth was that his extensive use of stealth had tired him out, and in the end, he just froze. Just for a heartbeat, but it was enough. The Lumar had seen him.

So, he decided to own it.

He made a bowing kind of gesture from the waist, a gesture his Human molly had taught him long ago.

"Your commander is dead, compliments of the Night Wind Clan," he said. "Who are you?"

"Uban. You kill Commander?" The Lumar took a step inside the room and looked around, his four large, muscular arms hanging loose. Deluge surreptitiously let one of his favorite nerve-poison-treated knives fall into his hand from his harness.

"Yes. Does this anger you?"

"No. You new Commander?"

"I?" Deluge asked, his tail stiffening in surprise. "No. I can't be your commander. I'm no mercenary."

"You kill Commander. You next Commander. I help you. Lumar listen to me. I strong. Big. I make discipline." Uban puffed out his already impressively massive chest as he spoke, and Deluge thought he detected pride in the big creature's tone.

"Do you? Then you are obviously the best person to be the next commander, Uban. You should do it."

"No. Not smart. Need real Commander. Make contracts. Give orders. Keep Lumar safe. Not bad commander," he said, looking over at Apeya's cooling corpse. "Good commander."

"Ahh—"

"You could get him a real commander," Rurranach said in Deluge's ear. He'd nearly forgotten about the Sidar back on his ship in all the excitement, but now Deluge felt a flood of relief at the sound of his voice.

"What do you mean?" Deluge asked, and then put up one paw-hand to tell Uban he wasn't speaking to him.

"He's right. They'll just get slaughtered without real leadership. The Lumar are almost perfect mercenaries, except for that one fatal flaw. You need someone from another species, preferably a species that is ruthless and creative and capable of caring for the lumbering creatures. But the commander of a Lumar company stands to make a great deal of money if they're handled properly. You would not have a terrible time finding willing applicants."

"Applicants?"

"Of course, you're not just going to hand them over to anyone, are you? That would be just as wasteful as letting the Veetanho live."

"That's underhanded of you, Rurranach," Deluge said, a trickle of warning in his tone. "The last being to try and manipulate me lies cooling at my feet."

"It's true, though. You know it is, Del. You're sentencing them to a slower, painful, less meaningful death if you don't get them a good leader."

Deluge sighed heavily, because he did, indeed, know that it was true. He lowered his paw-hand and looked at Uban.

"I am not your commander," he said with great resignation. "But I will help you find the one who is."

* * * * *

Egress

The dye itched.

It shouldn't have. Blade wasn't allergic, there had been no reaction, and the darkly orange spots and stripes shone just as healthily as his original dark fur and subtle stripes had done.

Still, a nearly overwhelming urge rose to rub in every dirt pile and against each stubby melik trunk he passed. Disguises were below Hunters. A waste, an acknowledgment that strength and cunning were not enough to accomplish a task.

He restrained himself from rolling with an effort. The simple truth remained evident—his skills alone were not enough to accomplish this task. Someone on Khatash wanted him dead, and anathema to take another Hunter's life or not, it had to be one of his own. Or a group of them. He had no way of knowing if his siblings had survived the escape routes Susa had suggested in those last hurried moments. Had Death kept Susa alive? Had Flame gone with the Human Alcuin? If so, what would they do? Attempting to reach them, even to search to confirm they had made it, would only bring death upon them.

Nothing good would come of it.

Someone was trying to eradicate them, like they were some infestation of groundlings.

Death would keep the kits safe. There would be a future for their clan.

That most of all. Death and Susa would be safe. That had to be true. It was the most important and valuable mission—as long as Death could bear her litter safely, their clan had a chance at recovery. Flame would take care of Flame, hopefully the Peacemaker's bounty hunter would be of use. Deluge was out on contract, maybe they hadn't been able to find him.

Most pressing was what he had to do, to make their long-term survival possible. Stay on Khatash and ensure they had a home to return to, once the blood settled. Which he couldn't do as Blade.

And so Chirruch stalked the market, newly arrived from the deep jungle, the only Hunter of his generation from a small clan without off-world Hunters. Orange-striped and darkly spotted, alert and unfamiliar.

And stalking.

Whispering Fear kept their den near the starport city, which gave him plenty to go on. He could play the newly-arrived yokel, contained and staring without staring, which gave perfect cover for a hunt that had to go unnoticed among experts.

"Weapons, fine sir?" A cheery voice called, a long appendage snaking out from a covered stall to catch his eye. "Something to outfit you for off-world perhaps? Or the closer confines of the city?"

Blade paused, balancing the hesitation of a newly-arrived jungle Hunter with his own unwillingness to test his disguise so soon.

"I have all the knives I need," he said haughtily, boldly meeting the top row of the merchant's eyes.

"Ah, everything you need for a rousing run through the canopy, I've no doubt. Sharp edges, some energy weapons, a claw set I'm sure. But I have beauties to make you knock down a sepsi tree, eh? Come in, take a look at least."

Blade knew the merchant, as Fip had gotten Blade's attention with a similar spiel when Blade's first off-world contract had been looming, and the young Hunter was sure one more addition to his arsenal would make all the difference. It turned out the Sipset talked the usual patter and had the goods to make it worthwhile. Clever merchant or no, the multi-limbed trader could hardly have stayed in business on Khatash with subpar goods, but even among the city's carefully curated merchant class, Fip had great, and sometimes extraordinary, merchandise.

Any clan of note had Hunters who would buy from Fip, and if he made an ally of the trader—if *Chirruch* made an ally of the trader, he could cross paths with a member of Whispering Fear sooner, rather than haphazardly later.

"I'm not looking to trade with a..." Blade trailed off, sure no deep jungle Hunter would recognize an atypical Sipset at first glance. Fip had been into body modifications long before Blade had been born and would likely be proud some half-trained Hunter didn't recognize him. And when Fip felt proud, he was more likely to take a liking to a stranger, meaning Blade could cultivate a relationship all over again. It might take more time than Blade wanted, but every lead he could build was a step further than he had, and who knew which step would put him on the path to make his clan safe again?

"Oh, no, my fine Hunter. Many a Depik has found exactly what he needed, from this old Sipset. I've been on Khatash for over twenty years, leaving only for the most exciting of vacation opportunities. You know how it is, when the familiar becomes, well, too familiar. The itch to travel, the drive to the stars, and of course the return to the rich earth of Khatash. All jungles and deadly encounters, only the best, wouldn't you say? Take a look. I wouldn't steer you wrong. Generations of Hunters have chosen my wares."

Visibly reluctant, Blade stepped closer to the tent, seeming not to notice the pleased way Fip's tentacle-like limbs curled around the displays and pulsed comfortably. Sipset had no exceptional sense of smell, or fine registry of electromagnetic pulses. Not a single processing ability except visual that might betray a visiting yokel as the established off-world Hunter of Night Wind. It made him an excellent test case, and nothing of Fip's manner indicated he had recognized anything of Blade here.

It was a start.

* * *

B lade slept high in the canopy through the days, walking back into the city each late afternoon or dusk. Not a regular schedule, clearly exploring, wandering in the way of a Hunter new to the city with an undefined agenda. On the fourth day his persistence paid off.

As he strode in the direction of Fip's stall, he caught sight of a smoky gray Hunter stepping inside the stall. She had symbols shaved into her fur, but nothing that identified her clan. Her ease in the market indicated familiarity with the city. She had to be from one of a number of clans that sent Hunters through for goods.

"Ah there he is, Chirruch! Still considering your next purchase, are you? Perhaps a long blade, for those leaping reaches?"

The other Hunter turned her head, considered the new arrival, and tilted her head in silent welcome.

"I have not decided," he said, coloring his tone as one willing—but not eager—to be guided.

"You can trust Fip's judgement," she put in, her front paw gliding gently over a well-ordered display of claw sets without touching them. "It took me some time to adjust, when I first started coming to the market."

"Is it that obvious I don't know the city? I thought surely after four days I would blend with you starporters." Blade ducked his head with the appropriate amount of deference for an unfamiliar female and allowed some measure of humor into his voice and bearing.

"I greet you, Hunter." She slow blinked at him once after the greeting and made a huff of amusement. "Very close," she said, tail curling to show it was meant to be a gentle tease. "Just another day or two more, and I'm sure no one will know any differently."

"I greet you, Hunter," he replied. He let her see his pretending to be relieved, and she made the amused noise again. They browsed in silence a bit longer, Fip calling out to passerby, confident enough in earning a sale from each of the Hunters inside to call for more.

"Good thing I'll be here a while longer then," he said into their companionable silence, lifting a folding weapon and admiring the fine craftsmanship. "Be a shame to come all this way and not learn to blend."

"Jungle, then?" she asked, looking him over again. "Let me guess. Southwest, deep in, *Malluma Songo* crops."

"Jungle, far north, mining contracts," he said, slow blinking at her in turn.

"Aah, so close." She made a snapping noise, and they both smiled. "Well? Where do you place me?"

"Hm. City raised, off-world Hunter, dips into the jungle for fun."

She flipped her tail at him, clearly entertained. Fip pointed a series of eyes at them, then away, evidently as amused by the pair of them as they were with each other.

"One out of three, jungle boy. I hope you have better luck in your city endeavors ahead." She shifted the claw set she'd slipped over her left paw, studying it. "This one, Fip."

"Already charged your account, Ichys."

Another slow blink, and she waved the additional metal claws over her own at Blade.

"Fip has given me away. I was going to leave you wondering, make you find me in the market later."

"Chirruch, Deep Night." He dipped his head to her again. "Now we're even. Or close to."

"Whispering Fear," she said with an overdone sigh, giving him her clan name in answer to his hint.

An electric charge zipped from the tips of his ears to the end of his tail. If Fip or Ichys noticed the slight shiver of motion, they'd attribute it to his obvious interest in Ichys, not the sudden discovery of a target.

The hunt had clarified.

* * *

He and Ichys met for a meal here, browsing there, and after another two days, a hunt together in the jungle outside of the city.

It was an excuse to show off for each other, lounge on branches as wide as a room, use any excuse to chase each other through levels of the canopy. There would be a kill, of course, but this chase was more interesting to both of them, and they gave only a fraction of attention to stalking of prey.

"Dama had only me," he said, his tail curling loosely around hers as they ostensibly surveyed the tangle of vegetation below them. "There have been no kitas since she was young, and no other kits. One by one over the years, Hunters went into the jungle…"

She didn't need him to finish the sentence. Deadly as the Hunters were, they were not the only predators in the jungles, and even they could fall astray. Instead she leaned slightly closer to him, the edges of her fur brushing the very tips of his, the feel of electricity between them.

"Contracts then, and trade." Not quite a question, but a gentle prod.

"Or another clan." He said it low, reluctant. Clans ended and began all the time, Hunters needing to find advantageous positions and more fertile damas. It wasn't rare, or a tragedy, but who would choose it, all other things being equal?

"Your dama would accept that?"

He glared down at the twisting nest of vines, as though willing some venomous creature to appear and challenge them. The silence settled around them, both comfortable and charged. Finally, he let the fur down his back ripple and audibly blew out his breath.

"Yes. It was her suggestion. I could have roamed the jungle looking for other clans, but it seemed smarter to start at the city. I don't know what I have to offer a city clan, but…"

Her turn to be quiet. What Blade knew, but Chirruch couldn't possibly, was that Whispering Fear had lost a sizable *Malluma Songo* crop recently, and a rising young off-world Hunter not long before that. Ichys could no more offer him a place in their clan than either of them could fly above the uppermost canopy line. But she could build a path toward such a thing, for him.

"Where are you staying?" She didn't look remotely surprised when he gestured around them; it made utter sense a deep jungle Hunter would feel comfortable taking his rest in what came closest to his home. "Our den is large—our clan is one of the oldest, and we have outlying warrens that aren't the den proper, but in our domain. You can stay in one of those. Meet the other Hunters. Perhaps...it is not my place, but there is always room for someone strong and talented, who will work hard to further the clan. Perhaps Dama will see this in you and offer you a place."

He snorted but leaned his arm against hers. "If your clan is so large—how well do you know your dama?"

"She is *my* Dama," Ichys replied, the emphasis in her tone indicated that, like both Blade and 'Chirruch,' her dama had borne her. Given Dirrys had had two kitas survive to adulthood, there was every chance Ichys could prove fertile and be named Heir herself. Chirruch didn't have that context, of course, but Blade felt satisfaction settle in his mind. He had no doubt he could prove himself, especially with Ichys as an ally.

He would channel Flame, and hide so well they forgot he existed. He would listen. He would learn. And when he discovered proof that it was Dirrys, that Whispering Fear was to blame, and he worked out the why, he would tear them apart.

Their clan would be destroyed, and any Hunter worth saving would be spared. Their den would be struck to rubble, their contracts traded away.

With the blood lust rising in his mind, he didn't notice how much closer he'd leaned to Ichys, and how comfortably she leaned back.

* * *

Death woke, disoriented. She inhaled, tasting the recycled air. A ship?

Her ship. With Susa on board.

Memory crashed in, and she opened her eyes to see her molly's abdomen, encased in a shipsuit. Death stretched, noting the stiff, weak feeling in her limbs as she reached up toward the face of the Human who had raised her, loved her.

And now, saved her.

"How are you feeling?" Susa asked quietly. She bent her head and dropped a kiss between Death's ears, and used one hand to stroke beneath the hinge of Death's jaw. The other hand rested on the ship's control yoke.

"I see you reconfigured my ship," Death said as she looked around. It sounded snappier than she meant it, but she didn't want to think about how she felt just then. So instead she thought about trivialities. Susa just chuckled and continued to stroke her fur.

Reow had given her the ship upon completion of her first contract. It had space enough for four Hunters, or one Human and a Hunter. The cabin area was designed to be as comfortable in close quarters as possible. Currently, Susa had toggled on the Humanoid control system, and she sat strapped in a semi-recumbent position that looked completely unnatural and uncomfortable to Death. Rather than the pressure-sensitive paddles she would have used, Susa had activated the half-wheel of the control yoke that extended "down" from the forward bulkhead toward the seat. In front of them, the panoramic viewscreens showed an unrelieved white void surrounding them.

"We're in hyperspace," Death said. "Where are we going?"

"Karma."

"Bit out of the way, isn't that?"

"It is, and that's the point, my dear. Every Hunter in the galaxy will be looking for you. I'm hoping to hide you somewhere they'd never think to look."

"And where is that?"

"My home. Earth."

Death blinked and slid her body back down in the zero gravity to a sitting position in Susa's lap as she turned this concept over in her mind. Earth. It was certainly the back end of nowhere; that much was certain. Humans were such a new species. Most still considered them exotic savages, barely out of their own planetary orbit. Susa was known to some on Khatash, because she was the first Human pet to be sigiled by a clan. But no one ever asked where pets originated, and Reow had only ever said she picked her up on some space station.

"All right," Death said. "You have a plan?"

"Sort of," Susa said, leaning back in the couch so the security blanket that lay strapped over them both shifted along Death's fur, causing prickles of static electricity down her spine. It felt like a portent.

"And?"

"Houston," Susa said.

Death waited.

"Houston Starport is the biggest city on Earth. Or at least it used to be. It's a galactic free trade zone, so we shouldn't have any problems getting there, once we get to the Tolo Arm."

"And once we're there?"

Susa took a deep breath before speaking.

"I brought approximately twenty thousand credits in chips and red diamonds with us. Earth is very poor, you understand. This is a fortune to them. Many fortunes."

"Will many fortunes buy safety for my offspring?"

"I am hoping they will, if we can find the right seller."

"Such as?"

"What do you know of Earth's history, Death?"

"Only what you have taught me," Death said, swishing her tail impatiently.

"You know Earth was first contacted by the Buma, but were then found to be a mercenary race after they attacked the MinSha guards traveling with the Union delegation, yes?"

"I suppose," Death said. "I've not had reason to pay much attention to Earth, except as needed to care for you, Susa."

"Well, this is important. We *are* a mercenary race. And unlike a lot of other merc races, Human mercs run the gamut of specialties. There is one company in particular, one of the survivors of the Alpha Contracts—"

"Alpha Contracts?"

"Humanity's first mercenary contracts. Hundreds of companies went out. Only four returned."

"Oh! I have heard this story. They're called the Four Horsemen, right? Cartwright's Cavaliers, Asbaran Solutions, Winged Hussars, and—"

"The Golden Horde, yes. The company that saved the production of 'Galactic Guardians, Part Two.'"

"You propose to purchase the services of the Golden Horde to protect me?"

"If possible. From what I understand, they don't keep much of a presence in Houston, but I suspect they at least have a small office. They'd have to, as it's the major starport."

"How do you know these things?" Death asked, "You've never left Khatash, not since you came to live with us."

Susa laughed and stroked Death's fur under the blanket.

"I can read, Death. I know how to search the Galnet. As a race, I find you Hunters tend to be rather blind to anything that doesn't directly affect you or the execution of one of your contracts. But we Humans are endlessly curious. I've kept up with whatever stories I can find about Earth and my race. It seems...well. It will be an interesting ride for humanity, that's for certain.

"But in any case," she went on, "That's neither here nor there right now. What's important is that Earth is way, way off the beaten path, and I think we've got as good a chance of hiding out there as anywhere. Marginally better, perhaps, since I know the territory. Or used to, at any rate. And we'll be able to blend in."

"Of course," Death said slowly as she warmed to the idea. "You won't appear remarkable or special at all on your home planet, and I am modestly good at stealth."

"Thanks," Susa said dryly. Death flicked her ears and grinned up at her in the Human style. "But I actually don't think you'll need your quintessential stealth all that much, to tell you the truth."

"Oh?"

Susa nodded, and reached out with her left hand to tap a short command on the view screen interface. Immediately, the white nothingness vanished, replaced by a picture of a gargantuan Hunter.

Or not really a Hunter, Death realized as she wormed her way up higher onto Susa's chest so that she could see better. The resemblance was remarkable, though there were definite differences. The animal appeared to lack a hinged pelvis, so it wouldn't be able to walk bipedally. Its paws had shortened, stunted fingers, and its head was rounder and proportionally smaller compared to the rest of the body. It was clearly a predator of some sort, though, as even in the format of a still picture, the creature's intense focus shone through. It crouched, its orange- and black-striped coat blending into the tall grass that surrounded it. Its eyes were fixed steadily on something outside the frame of the scene, but Death had the distinct impression that whatever this strangely similar predator stalked didn't live long after the picture was taken.

"What is that?" she asked.

"That is *Panthera Tigris*," Susa said. "Commonly known as the tiger. It is the largest species of feline predator native to Earth."

"It looks a lot like a Sirra'Kan."

"We thought so, too, when we met them," Susa said. "*Panthera Tigris* is a member of family Felidae, which is one of the most prolific families on Earth."

The picture of the solitary predator blinked out, replaced by a collage of several animals. Large, small, shaggy, and sleek, they all carried an unmistakable family resemblance, and every one was unmistakably a predator. After a moment, Susa tapped the interface again and the pictures began to wink out of existence one by one, until only a solitary photograph remained.

"This," Susa said, tapping the interface to zoom in on the remaining specimen, "*Felis catus*, the most successful feline species on Earth. They live on all continents, including Antarctica, and even on ships at sea. They are the domestic cat."

"Ahhh," Death said, her ears perking up in interest. "These are your pets."

"Yes, some of them. But 'domestic' is something of a misnomer, because a statistically significant percentage of their worldwide population is feral or semi-feral. In other words, for the most part, cats can take us or leave us."

Death turned to look away from the screen and study Susa's face. Her calm expression seemed normal, but something in her voice had changed.

"We would never leave you, Susa," Death said, not really sure why she did. "You are a part of us."

"I know that, sweetling," Susa replied and caressed Death's ears. "And I would never leave you. Bonds of love cannot be broken."

Memory stabbed through Death like a blade. She gasped and felt her ears flatten in sudden misery.

"Can they not?" she whispered.

"No," Susa said, her voice taking on a stern note. She let go of the view screen interface to cup Death's face in her hands and stroke her ears. "They cannot. Not when the love is real, Death. Not when it is true and strong and returned."

"My love was real," Death's voice was small and mewling as she spoke. She hated it, but she couldn't seem to help it.

"I know, kita. And he was always undeserving of it. But you are strong, and not alone. And you will survive this and return stronger than ever. What doesn't kill you—"

"Just pisses me off," Death finished in a whisper. It had been a joke between them, a corruption of one of Susa's Human proverbs. It had always made Susa laugh in the past, but she wasn't laughing now. Instead, she just nodded.

"That's right. The domestic cat is not the largest or the most powerful of the felines on Earth, but they're the most successful because they're smart enough to ally with humanity. So are you, sweet Death. You pretend to be my cat, and we'll blend in long enough to get your litter born. Then, when they are grown enough, we will take all of that anger, that 'pissed off-ness,' and we will find those who have hurt our family…and the one who hurt you. And we will see to it that they will never, ever harm our family again."

"Yes," Death whispered. "Yes, we will."

* * *

Humans were disgusting.

At least, that was Death's first impression.

The shuttle touched down on a primitive landing surface that looked as if it were held together with inert wire and scrap metal, but it seemed to do the trick. In her role as Susa's animal companion, Death made the journey inside a closed box whose sides were made of a mesh fabric. It wasn't ideal, and seemed a lot like a cage, but Death knew how to swallow insult and embrace her cover identity. She wouldn't be much of a Hunter if she didn't.

So, she curled inside the carrier and watched through the mesh as Susa carried her past rows of blocky buildings stretching up to a steel-grey sky. The air felt close and wet, but lacked the healthy green scent of home. Throngs of Humans streamed this way and that. Death had seen them before, of course, but never so many in such a small area. It was a bit overwhelming, especially when she considered that each one of these beings was an individual thinker with their own will and thoughts. Typically, when she'd encountered a species willing to live packed in such close quarters, they tended to be non-predatory and herd like. Some even had a fully-fledged hive mind construct. But Humans were different. They had the numbers, but they also had their individuality. That made them interesting…and possibly dangerous.

Despite herself, despite everything, Death slow blinked a smile and began to relax. She could understand a dangerous creature. She was one.

Susa walked out to an area where grimy, primitive-looking machines rolled up on inflated tires and excreted clouds of noxious gasses out the back. The stench was overwhelming and made Death's eyes water. She shunted some of her attention away from her baryonic senses, just enough to blunt the reek of the vehicle's fumes, and dialed in to her quintessence field to compensate. She didn't bend the light, but it made it easier to function while being effectively nose-blinded.

"Where to?" the vehicle's driver asked as they approached one. He stuck his head out the window and grinned at Susa in an aggressive manner. Susa's smiles had always been sweet and love-filled, but Death quickly saw how the Human bearing of teeth could have other, more sinister overtones.

"Downtown."

"You got cash?"

"I've credits," Susa said pleasantly. The driver's eyebrows went up, and his leer deepened. Susa smiled. "I've also got an energy pistol and a very large knife. As well as off world weapons you wouldn't recognize. I advise you to deal straight with me, and I'll do the same with you, got it?"

The leer faded into a frown, then a snarl.

"You're a bitch."

"Perhaps, but I'm a busy one. Will you be taking me to my destination, or shall we escalate our confrontation further?"

"A full credit."

"Done," Susa said without hesitation, despite the outrageous price. "Go now, please."

She handed over the tiny chit, and as soon as the driver had it in his dirty fingers, the vehicle lurched into motion. Death's carrier slipped backward and bumped up against the upholstery, jarring her so that she nearly lost her footing.

"He is unpleasant," Death said, speaking in her native tongue. "I would like to kill him."

"That would draw too much attention," Susa murmured. Death saw the driver's eyes in the mirror ahead flick up at them.

"He is listening."

"Probably, but I think it's fine. Humans sometimes talk to their cats. He probably thinks that I'm one of those."

"Does he understand our language?"

"Highly doubtful," Susa said with a smile. "As far as I know, I'm the only one who ever studied it, and you remember how well I spoke when I first came to you."

"Like a lisping kitten with a damaged brain," Death said, blinking slowly at the fond memory. She sighed and laid herself down in the carrier. "Very well, then. I will suffer his rudeness. I would like to kill him, though, so do but say the word and it is done."

"I will keep that in mind, Little Dama."

Death shoved down the pain that title brought and slow blinked at Susa once more. She then turned her attention to looking out the grimy window at the cityscape. More buildings stacked one on top of the other loomed over the streets like the trees back home. Earth seemed to have cultivated her own artificial canopy built by the hands of her Human children.

The view shifted several times as the carrier slid and skidded with the driver's abrupt changes of direction as they careened through the streets. Though sound, like scent, was somewhat muted by Death's shunting of the baryonic inputs, she could hear a kind of mechanical wailing sound that seemed to coincide with the driver's maneuvering. Someone protesting, perhaps, as he aggressively threaded through the streets and stacked concrete?

Finally, they lurched to a stop. Death felt the carrier skid and nearly fall to the grimy floor of the vehicle. Susa shot out a hand and caught her at the last minute, for which Death let out a grateful mrrow.

"Thank you," Susa said as she opened the vehicle's door with a thick *ker-chunk* sound. The driver grunted something unintelligible to Death's ears, and Susa let out a sigh. Then she grabbed the carrier's top handle and stepped out into the stinking air once again.

"Are all Humans that unpleasant?" Death asked.

"No," Susa said. "We run the gamut. You're just more likely to find the unpleasant ones in densely packed territory like this."

"That's right. Individuals. Law of averages. Etc."

"Exactly. Let us hope that these next ones are rather more agreeable."

"Indeed. Who are they, exactly?"

"They," Susa said as she started walking toward an unassuming building, "are The Golden Horde."

* * *

Wrapped in her quintessence field, Flame took advantage of the chance to evaluate each of the Peacemaker contractors and fighters Tamir interacted with on their way from their dock to the level she usually worked from. Or perhaps had worked from—given that Hrusha had hired her, it was possible that Tamir wouldn't work on Capitol for much longer. Yet again, Flame wondered who would take the Peacemaker and Governor contracts with Reow and Hrusha so messily dead, and once more she filed the thought away as unhelpful. No matter who took those contracts, Flame wouldn't be able to trust them, and it seemed impossible that either newly-elevated Hunter would work with someone from an interdicted clan.

Since thinking of events on Khatash served no use, Flame kept her focus on the individuals of various species Tamir did—or pointedly didn't—speak to along the way. Fighting-shape, most of them, though there were some scurriers as well, moving to complete tasks rather than handle other bodies.

"Dek!" the Human called, with apparent affection. "I didn't know you were back on site."

Another Human, this one with a metal arm, picked up his pace to greet her. "Closed out my bounty in record time. Do you know that idiot had the nerve to post up two rocks away from the station he tried to blow up? Made it too easy, and now they'll send me on some backass quadrant dusting to find some mass-swindling yahoo, and I won't have a decent beer for three years."

"Yeah, except you'll bring enough beer to last you, but otherwise..." she laughed with him for a few seconds, then twisted the hand closer to Flame, loosening her wrist. Flame noted it as another tell of the woman's, an easing of tension before she said something she didn't especially want to. "You hear anything?"

"Uh, about Hrusha getting murdered? Or where you're getting assigned? You don't want the next killer kitty to keep you on your toes?"

Tamir's spitting noise answered too quickly to be a show for Flame's benefit. Flame studied the male anew, paying closer attention to his pulse and all the weak little joints and folds of skin that opened so easily under a Hunter's claws.

"Unless you have the balls to say it in front of a Depik, don't say it at all, dumbass. I mean, say it to one who's not in the best mood, and it'll also be the day you get to taste your own colon, but, your choice. You hear anything about me, is my question. I'm not getting involved in any Depik contract mess."

The edge of Flame's tail twitched in amusement. Such a simple tactic, saying the opposite of one's intentions. How refreshing, when simplicity worked.

"Nah. I only got back two nights ago, and all anyone's talking about is the explosion, when that level will be repaired, how far around they have to go to be sure Pelasivet of Gonorrhea or whatever gets his afternoon drug fix. You know the drill—speculation and gossip and angling to get better assignments."

"Shit. I better still get paid for this last trip I did for Hrusha. Who's taking point on the investigation? They'll probably know who I need to see about credits."

"Diaden, the Cemarap aide. You know the one, all wavy flappy edges and smart investing tips?"

Flame took her eyes off his jugular to watch the trickle of other bodies passing them, noting which ones took a bit too much notice of Tamir along the way. She hadn't killed a Cemara, so her study of them had been brief. Blade could likely have told her the highlights of their current governing state, but she remembered they were hugely complex organisms that looked like a Human-sized single-cell paramecium. Lots of moving little globules on the inside, and countless long, sensitive strands all around their outside, digit-like in their dexterity. She remembered thinking shaving one would disorient it enough that their famed calculative powers would flounder, making them easy to kill. Unlikely that she'd have to kill this one, but at least she remembered the important parts.

"Diaden. He really loves poker, right, always gambling and then lecturing people on their cards after he wins?"

Dek nodded, glancing away as a group of loud Oogar poured out of the nearest lift, purple fur momentarily taking up all of the air.

"Yeah, I got it. Thanks, Dek—meet you for a beer before you ship out?"

"Better—you still owe me three from Piquaw."

"You got that flipped, skinsack. But I'll buy you one if Diaden gets me paid, then you buy the next five."

"Inflation, huh? Picking up some bad habits out there on the run, Tam-a-lou."

"Six then, for the shitty nickname," she threw that over her shoulder, already moving for the still open lift. Flame cast another considering glance at him before following, wishing she could afford to drag her smallest claw against his leg as she passed, for that kitty comment. That Human needed to remember how very fragile his species were.

On the lift she brushed Tamir's arm to let the Human know she was still there, then sat between the back of Tamir's legs and the lift's wall, to keep from weaving around if too many other bodies got on board. Del would find that hilarious, but Flame had always valued stillness. Besides, it gave her a moment to center herself. Which was useful, given that she couldn't just attack the big glob they were about to see. Flame realized she'd been a hair too ready to split Dek down the middle when she didn't like what he said. Not something that would serve her well with the Cemarap.

* * *

"I don't know what else to tell you," Diaden's voice box snapped for the third time, his furry cilia waving infuriated patterns that the voice box interpreted into tone. "Peacemaker Hrusha's records were not clear, and there are still some we haven't unlocked. Nothing we have on record justifies payment."

"And I'm telling you that I was sent on a job, I did a job, and now I get paid. You've worked with the Peacemakers long enough, you know how this works."

"And whose account should I pay you from, bounty hunter? The Peacemaker account that's locked until a new Depik Peacemaker is installed? Hrusha's account that's been transferred back to her clan? Maybe Reow's, now that all her clan's assets have been seized and reallocated to some jungle cave, for all I know?"

"I don't give a shit, investigator. I don't know what else to tell you. I did my work. Pay me. Isn't that why you were put in charge?"

"I was put in charge because Governor Kelket is angry about the death of her friend, and wanted someone she could trust!" The throb of frustration in the Cemarap's tone perked Flame's ear. She leaned closer to his curved bubble of a chair, hoping for more unguarded disclosures.

"I was put in charge because all sense has left Khatash, and if the Depik are killing each other right out in the open now, we have no idea what else they might get up to, and we can't afford to offend a race that is much more mercenary than your own, so don't think you can intimidate me."

Tamir took a deep breath, making such a show of it that Diaden moved back, with the instinctive distrust of anything that had to work so hard to absorb air. She visibly relaxed, making that so obvious Flame realized the Human was over-exaggerating her body language in the hopes that even a large blob could read it.

"I am not trying to intimidate you, Diaden," Tamir said, leaning on the table between them and speaking in a soft, almost lilting tone. "I know you're very well connected, or you wouldn't be in charge of such an important investigation. I am tired, and cranky, and would like to be paid and reassigned so that I may continue to get paid, but I know none of that is your fault." She varied the pitch of her voice, calmer, more convincing.

"Given how much time you've spent on this investigation, is there anything you might be able to tell me about what Hrusha did or her meetings in the time between her sending me and when she...died? Perhaps I can find someone who can corroborate the job she sent me on, so my account can be settled, and I can see about taking on some other office's work? You are the expert here, and I need your help." She spread her hands, sitting back in her chair, inviting his expertise.

The flattery and vulnerability mollified the Cemarap, judging by the way his cilia slowed around the top half of his body.

"I can't share any files with you," he said, shifting to a more opaque color and obscuring the churning motion of his inner mechanisms. "But let me look through them and see if anything catches my eye."

Flame had taken her perch on the table for comfort and convenience, but at this she leapt lightly to the top frame of his chair. She opened the pouch belted to her hip to pull out her recorder, and leaned forward to better examine what Diaden was opening. As he toggled through files and notes, she scanned each. Nothing had been written in a legible language, but the recorder would get it back to the ship for translation. It would take more time, but she was satisfied to have at least something from this interminable meeting.

"Beyond Governor Kelket, she met with Peacemaker Essey from the Cochkala and Governor Griveserk of the Zuparti several times while you were gone, and you know they won't recall anything. You can talk to Griveserk's aide Karvoch, since he's still on station and has no role in the investigation. Maybe he has something. We both know neither a Peacemaker nor a Governor are going to remember some passing talk about a bounty hunter's schedule. Otherwise you're on hold like everything else for the Depik Peacemaker office, until everything's settled."

"Then let me help settle it, Diaden. I want to get paid, and you know I do good work. A *Depik* repeatedly hired me. Give me a list of things you need done or sorted, and then I'm closer to payment, yeah?"

The voicebox made clicking sounds as the Cemarap considered, the cilia down his left side all moving in unison like a Human tapping fifty fingers. Flame wanted to pull a handful of the thick strands, as though that would push the aide to a decision.

"That's not a bad idea. Here, I'll send the video over—did you know we have video? Depik are so legendary at killing you'd never think they'd forget about a camera, of all things—and the witnesses. I've only talked to half, so just get their general statements."

Busy work, and of course they'd seen the video, but Tamir had Flame and some confiding notes from Hrusha. With that, between the two of them they could piece some order to what Hrusha had been putting together, sending Tamir to Khatash with that cryptic warning.

Blade was the littermate who most enjoyed digging into information and forming the right pattern, and Flame didn't know where he was, but she could honor him in applying what she'd learned from him. She had not become a devastatingly effective assassin by accident, and she would apply herself here, alongside this Human bounty hunter. In the end, there would be someone to kill, and it would mean clearing their dama's name, reinstating their clan, and honoring her siblings and Reow in the resulting blood and death.

It was worth a little busywork.

* * *

The interviews had been so boringly unhelpful that Flame took a break and returned to the ship to watch the video again. They had both watched it on a loop through most of the night, and studied it with every program each knew, but no part of it turned up faked or doctored.

Reow and the Peacemaker walked, focused on something, toward the ship. They walked at a normal pace, looking natural, until they walked directly into an explosion. Neither of them could have gotten out of the way.

Flame had seen her dama hunt many times, and every shift of muscle, fur, claw, indicated focus. She did not know Hrusha, but her reactions looked genuine as well, before both Hunters disappeared in the explosion.

But why would Reow have been visible at all, going after such a dangerous—and forbidden—target? No, regardless of how skillfully edited or created, the video had to be faked, at some or every level. Her dama would never betray their kind, their clan, and her kits in such an unforgivable way.

Impatient at giving into another cycle of the same thoughts, Flame stood and shook herself thoroughly. She rubbed the backs of her front paws briskly against her cheeks and over her closed eyes, then forced her body to adopt an air of easy calm. No one would see her once she left the ship, but she would know.

The airlock remained open, so she moved unnoticed through it and back to the station proper, using the walk to expend all her excess energy. She'd spent long stretches of time covered by her quintessence field while completing contracts before, so she shouldn't be so restless only days in, given that she freely prowled the ship when it closed up for the sleep shift. Tamir refused to sign it back to the Peacemaker pool before she got paid and formally closed out the last job. It was the small leverage the Human wielded, and Flame supposed she should be grateful for it.

She remained ungrateful regarding the time spent interviewing the witnesses, few of whom had actually witnessed anything at all. Few of the species represented had any special senses, and none of the individuals had any training in discerning the subtle differences of explosions, so 'I heard the boom' had unfortunately been the theme of most of Tamir's interviews. Flame had suggested that if anyone had actually seen something of import, Diaden would have already talked to them, and Tamir reluctantly agreed.

Perhaps she would have the opportunity to slice globs out of the Cemarap aide after all, if this waste of time continued. If no one knew she stalked the Peacemaker halls, no one could blame her or the Depik race. Even were she to be caught, her life couldn't be more forfeit, and her clan had already been destroyed.

Again, she pushed calm through her thoughts and forced each joint to relax as she moved through corridors and around oblivious beings. It had become a mantra, reminding herself not to do anything stupid, do nothing that would keep her from discovering what had happened to Reow and the Peacemaker. Nothing that would stop her from clearing her clan's reputation and allowing all of her siblings to come home. The accomplishment would never repair what they had lost, but it was enough to keep her from indiscriminately carving into the useless beings that filled Tamir's days with their idiot talking.

She paced outside Tamir's borrowed interview room until the door slid open. Flame gave a cursory look at the older Human female who slouched out. She was clearly worn, tired, and no threat at all. Flame assumed she'd given a detailed account about seeing a flicker of motion, or reeling back from a percussive force, and dismissed her from any further thought. She let the woman pass, then slipped inside the small cube of space.

Desk, chairs, refreshment table, darkened screen, Tamir already slamming back down into her seat as the other Human left.

"Close record," Tamir said, and the computer beeped softly to confirm the record had stopped. Flame brushed a paw against Tamir's hand and leapt onto to the table, glancing half-heartedly at the notes still visible on the desk.

"Anything?" she asked, whisper too soft to travel far, restraining herself from flopping onto her side over the pad. Invisible she might be, but a measure of discipline remained required.

"I'm beginning to think these interviews are a waste of time," Tamir muttered, as though talking to herself. Her tone was rueful, conveying either sarcasm about the interminable task she'd asked for, or the oddness of pretending to talk to herself when really she was communicating with the invisible assassin who haunted her steps these days. Both, probably.

They'd agreed Flame should remain undetected. It served their investigation best to have a secret weapon, especially when they had no way of knowing what enemies were in plain sight around them. That didn't keep it from getting frustrating for both of them at times, but it was still the right call. Especially when they weren't even sure what, or who, they were trying to find.

A tentative knock clanged against the frame of the open door, and a small blue figure in a bright orange wrap leaned inside. Flame looked over, mildly interested—she hadn't smelled it coming. A Terling, maybe? They ranged a body length taller than the average Hunter and were able to alter their scent trails with impressive thoroughness. She thought they were more green than blue, but perhaps there were variations. She had never gotten to kill one. They had a reputation for being gentle, advice-suggesting trade partners. They also had a knack for giving their customers the better end of the deal, while still making a profit. If any of them had ever been put under contract, Flame hadn't heard of it.

Tamir sat more professionally upright in her chair and raised a hand in a gesture that conveyed both 'come in' in Human and 'let's begin negotiations' in Terling. Flame would have found this most impressive, except that she was busy trying to remember the best way of taking out the spindly trader. She had just remembered that blue Terlings tended to be non-fertile males when the other being made a series of fluting noises and scurried inside on its base of fifty little feet-pods.

"Sorry to interrupt." His small slit of a mouth managed Tamir's language surprisingly well, and Flame thought, all other things being equal, she could jam a front paw in there and claw out his throat from the inside, rather than wasting time on the thick hide of his neck.

"I have time before the next interview." Tamir tilted her head slightly, offering the empty chair across the desk to her unscheduled visitor. Flame sat up straight now too, interested, and stopped idly weighing options for bloodshed at the hope something useful might happen.

"Yes, yes. Uh. Yes. No need to record, I am just passing through, and remembering when you allowed me the first word of Tirric Station's need for grapples. Yes?"

"Yes," Tamir said, smiling without teeth. Flame supposed it was proper etiquette for Terlings, and resisted the urge to bare all of her own teeth to move this along. No one would know, and she was the most patient of her siblings. She had to remind herself of her own patience at least twice more while the blue creature levered itself into the chair and shifted until half of its foot-pods were folded comfortably under him and the other ones dangled off the front and sides of his seat.

"Yes. Yes! Passing through, and heard the saddest news about Peacemaker Hrusha. She liked pinpecks from the Cemarap home world, and I had a deal, and she was very happy to have pinpecks. Yes. It is sad news." After Tamir had made the proper noises to agree that the news was, in fact, sad, the Terling shifted and kicked a dozen or so foot-pods.

"Sad, yes. It is strange, that her friend the Governor Kelket did not bring her pinpecks, from her own world, yes? The Cemarap Governor knows so much about her friends and usually brings gifts, but this time did not. I ordered extra pinpecks to make up for it, thinking the Peacemaker Hrusha would like it even more, after seeing so much of a Cemarap, but not having any pinpecks."

Flame hoped Tamir understood this better than she did. Hrusha was friends with Kelket, Kelket usually brought Hrusha presents, but hadn't this time, and yet had spent more time with Hrusha lately. Without presents. Fascinating. She considering returning to ways to pick the Terling apart, but the blue male had more to say.

"Governor Kelket did bring presents for her friend Governor Sissisk, who also sadly died. Old for a Depik, yes? Thirty or nearly so, but healthy, yes, we all thought. Maybe just how Depik are, Hunters to the last moment. But that was before Governor Kelket started to get sick, too. Oh! I have to bring some oquet to a friend before it spoils, so delicate. Yes? So nice to see you, yes, see you again soon!" Abruptly he hopped back off his chair, foot-pods propelling him with alacrity, and he scurried out still fluting 'yes' before Tamir could answer.

The bounty hunter took a breath, typed a command to reschedule the rest of her interviews, and stood just as abruptly as the Terling.

"I need a bath," she said, and left.

Finally, Flame thought, knowing something was happening, and jumped down to follow Tamir back to the ship.

* * *

Tamir did not waste time with a second cleansing for the day, though she did change into a flowing sort of casual outfit while Flame did a scan to ensure there were no new listening devices installed while they were gone. It wasn't a perfect system, but it gave her something to do, and Diaden had tried to leave a subroutine in the comms system the first time he wobbled through. Better to be thorough than surprised.

"The Cemarap Governor was friends with the Hunter Governor and the Hunter Peacemaker," Flame said as Tamir returned draped in goldish-oranges long enough to hide her practical boots. "You knew that already."

"The gift thing is weird," Tamir said, pacing around the small galley in a way that made the space smaller. "Cemara pride themselves on gift-giving, even if you just saw them, and the higher ranked they are, the bigger deal giving something is—especially because they have the aides to get it done properly. The Depik Governor's death isn't…" She frowned and stopped talking, and Flame reminded herself once more how patient she was.

"I didn't think the Depik Governor's death was connected, because Hrusha acted normally after it happened." Tamir spoke slowly, eyes unfocused as she thought back through the series of events. "But it's weird for a Cemarap to be so close to both Peacemaker and Governor from Khatash, but to only gift one...I need to talk to Gerren."

"Does that mean anything to me?" Flame's tail lashed once, but she lounged comfortably on the galley table with every other indication of calm attention.

"Gerren knows the gossip. Runs one of the smaller bars, sees and hears enough to know when to shut his face and when to open it. We had a falling out, or I would have gone to him first."

"You have a source, who knows things, who you know knows things, and we've wasted ninenights on hand-fed idiots?" Flame's voice held steady, but her ears flattened, and her tail snapped back and forth across the table.

"He wouldn't know anything about an explosion thirty decks away, and we needed a picture of what happened there. And if he won't talk to me—"

"He'll talk." Flame's eyes rolled in the Human gesture of disgust as she moved for the door. "And if you don't want him to talk while holding his own kidney, I suggest you get him to do so before I have to drop my field."

* * *

The bar was built into the curve of the station, up in the further edges, away from the spin that gave them gravity. Its first proprietor had put up only two walls, leaving the final side open to the branching hallway that deposited traffic directly into the rounded triangle dominated by the dark mek-wood.

The bar was surrounded by tables, benches, and chairs of various heights and configurations that changed location more often than should have been practical. Open for every shift, the clientele ebbed and grew in a cycle only Gerren and his employees had figured out.

Given the scarcity of customers, the mid-part of the third cycle appeared to be an ebb, and no one moved behind the bar. A standard 'buzz for service' glowed above the multilayered blacks and greens that shaded the bar, and Flame resisted the temptation to jump ahead of Tamir and do just that.

Before either of them reached the bar, a spare, tall figure rose from the table closest to the wall, and Tamir stopped short, muttering 'Gerren' under her breath. Flame had already guessed the Humans' falling out had been of the torrid lover variety, and found herself mildly disappointed. Gerren had the webwork of lined and sagging skin that suggested at least triple the years Tamir had lived, and though he moved well enough, Flame doubted it was enough to provoke any kind of passion from the bounty hunter. Boring.

"Thought you'd taken to drinking at Midships." Gerren stood between Tamir and the bar, arms crossed across his chest.

"Not here for a drink," she replied, dropping her arms to keep from mirroring his posture.

"Apology then?"

"Wouldn't say no to one."

Gerren snorted so hard his arms uncrossed. He turned his back on her and moved toward the bar, cocking his head back to listen for her. Halfway to the bar he slowed.

"You coming?" he asked, turning his head and speaking over his shoulder.

She snorted as well, muttering something under her breath obviously not meant for Flame's ears. Maybe this encounter wouldn't be entirely boring after all. Flame dropped to all four legs to run ahead, stretching out to make the most of the short distance. She aimed for a tall stool near the bar rather than the bar itself, knowing mek-wood was often prized for the ability to insert electronics between its layers, and not wanting to set off any weight sensors. She'd chosen well, as Gerren walked around the bar and Tamir leaned against it, casting up next to Flame's stool.

"Well?" He poured something dark and sharp smelling halfway to the top of a fat, beveled glass. After a moment, he added a splash of something golden with bubbles, and Flame leaned closer to get a better sniff.

"How often do Governors visit Peacemakers?" she asked, picking up the glass in one hand and turning it in the glow of light from behind the bar. "Cross-species, I mean. Rough guess."

"Here and there." After a moment of consideration, he poured another glass with the same dark liquid, drank it swiftly, and refilled it, leaving the squat bottle on top of the bar. "Not the most common, but we've had a fair number of Governors pass through the Corner."

"The Depik Governor come through?"

"Depik don't spend a lot of time in bars, Tam. Not a whole lot of us provide ongoing entertainment to them, unless they're thinking about eating us."

Flame, not needing to keep her composure, dropped her jaw and scrunched her nose in distaste. Eating a Human would be a waste—they weren't nearly enough of a challenge to hunt to enjoy the resulting feast, and she'd probably just see Susa's face the whole time, which would extinguish any speck of joy in the kill.

"No one's trying to eat a toothpick, Gerren. They like meat and the chase, and you'd give little enough of either." She took a hefty sip from her glass and tapped the fingers of her free hand in a random pattern against the bar. "What about the Cemarap Governor?"

"Those ooze-rounds? Yeah, she likes to come here and soak up the gasses. Wish she'd put on some drapes like her aides." Neither the term nor his supposed disgust had any heat, and Flame considered him curiously. His attempts to insult seemed more some sort of ritual than any kind of judgement, which made some sense given they were aimed at two species so demonstrably his superior, one physically and one mentally.

"Yeah, they're just as grossed out by Humans' need to go expel waste every couple of hours, so you're probably even. Done playing the cranky old man, or do we need a few more rounds of this?"

He put his glass down and stared at her for a long moment, cementing for Flame that it was some sort of routine they did, him hating everyone and her refuting it with some insult toward humanity. Her cutting it short meant either she fought the same impatience Flame had been dealing with, or she remained uncertain enough of Flame's temper to keep from going down any lines the Hunter might take violent issue with. Hopefully both.

"Temper, Tam. I don't owe you anything."

"You owe me your grandson's life, and that twice over." She drank more, holding the glass in the air rather than putting it down, and dipped it toward him as she continued, "You also owe me for your boney ass being in one piece after those Oogar had a rough night, if I remember correctly."

"I paid you for that in whiskey." He snorted again, louder this time, and refilled her glass. "Yeah, when the Cemarap Governor's in her visiting cycle, she usually comes by. Usually just with Cemara, though she's met with a few other species now and then. Maybe the Depik Peacemaker once, now I think of it."

"What'd they talk about?"

"Eh. It was a while ago, Tam. I don't know. Seemed friendly enough."

"You don't know, or you need credits alongside your grandson's life?"

He tapped his nose and drank, and she blew out her breath with more force than necessary, putting her glass down to pull out her slate and type up a transfer.

"That won't clear unless it's worth it, Gerren."

"They had a casual wager on some merc companies. Kelket's picks were doing better, and Hrusha was giving her shit, saying there was no way a Lumar company could have outplayed a Tortantula. Kelket offered to let her throw in some Depik clan's contracts, Hrusha laughed in her face and picked up the Winged Hussars instead. Sounded like a regular thing they do."

"But?"

"Her tail was flicking pretty fast for a second there," he said, shrugging and taking another sip. He spread out the fingers of his free hand for emphasis. "Don't think Kelket coulda seen, the way their table was set up, and Hrusha stopped it quick, but that is innersting, no?" He drew the word out in a dramatic drawl. "Sign of some peeves, if I know my Depik stories."

"You don't have to make a show of it, to make it sound more valuable." Tamir sounded bored as ever, but Flame picked up the small signs of interest in her Human sidekick. "You know I'll pay you." Another tap, and she confirmed the payment, then picked her glass back up and polished off the liquid. "Anything else come to mind about Hrusha?"

"Besides your boss getting blown up, you mean? That surprised me, and I'll tell you that for free. I know a buncha species have that 'we never do whatever' rule, but I also know almost all of 'em have individuals that go and do whatever they want. Depik though, I believed they didn't go running around killing each other. Can't imagine there'd be any left, given how good they are at it. Or they'd never be able to take a paying contract, 'cause they'd be stuck avoiding or hunting each other all over the galaxy."

"It does seem unlikely," Tamir murmured, helping herself to a refill from the bottle when he didn't make any moves to pour for her again. He didn't pretend to protest, so her payment must have been fair.

"Heard a bit about her replacement, the one who took her out. The normal buzz you get with a new Peacemaker, only thing that stood out is this one was maybe fond of Humans, and folks were wondering what that meant, if she'd go around collecting some."

"Mostly we just call them aides," Tamir replied with humor in her voice, and he snorted something close to a laugh and shrugged.

"You been spending some time with Diaden, and if he isn't a little lapdog...Much good it'll do him, with Kelket about to retire herself. Been getting sick, you know, wavy around edges." Another shrug, and Gerren grabbed the bottle to stow behind the bar, with a slight detour to top off his own glass. "Had a group of Sidar that was pretty chatty about the possibilities with the new Peacemaker, and you can talk to Althagar, but they lost face after that Elgon IV incident, so I'd say it was just normal jockeying."

Tamir's turn to shrug, and she sipped her drink with both hands for something to do besides fidget. After a minute and a fair amount of drinking, she tapped her glass to Gerren's and left it on the bar.

"Tell your grandson I said hello," she said as she stood, Flame taking the moment to stretch while they said their good-byes. "And try not to piss off any more bounty hunters while I'm away."

"Only my favorites," he said, and Flame assumed that meant they'd apologized to each other in a decidedly Human manner.

Still unable to talk to each other, Human and Hunter walked down the furthest hallway to the most out of the way lift to minimize stops back to their level, both occupied with their own thoughts. There was little traffic at this time of day, so Flame relaxed her vigilance slightly, not having to watch for unexpected legs, tentacles, or carts who wouldn't see her to get out of the way.

Their silent bet paid off, the lift dropping every level without stopping, and as the doors opened, Flame considered if she and Tamir had taken the same information from the old man. She didn't notice how much lower the lighting level was in the hall outside the lift, her pupils widening automatically to give her a clear view.

"The fuck?" Tamir asked, and Flame focused, realizing it was too dark for unassisted Human eyes to make out more than shadows in gloom.

"Don't you have goggles?" Flame pitched her voice for hopefully only Tamir's ears and moved forward smoothly. Tamir's noise of disgust indicated the bounty hunter did have goggles that would give her night vision, but stowed and not on her. Humans. All these tools to help them adapt to an unfriendly universe, and they go wandering about in their thin skin with their barely functional senses, leaving all those toys at home.

"Hall's clear." It smelled off, bright and bitter with some sort of smoky chemical mix. "For now." The nonstop lift felt slightly more suspicious now, but all Flame could think, for the second time that day, was *Finally*.

It seemed stupid to herald an attack by turning the lights off and not immediately pouncing, but then whoever was coming thought Tamir was alone. Joy bubbled through Flame, washing away the restlessness she'd fought since they left Khatash.

They made it partway down the hall, just out of sight from the door that led to the main corridor. As they approached the curve, Flame ran ahead, and nearly laughed. Five Human figures, no protective shields, no special armor, barely more than the minimum tactical spacing. They didn't think Tamir was an easy target given their numbers, but they weren't worried enough to prepare well.

Fun.

"Five," she announced, startling all of them with the sound even as she passed undetected between them. In the middle of their grouping she leapt, digging her claws into and through the protective padding on number Three's thigh, cutting deep into the skin below. She used that to swing her momentum through his legs and up, landing on his back, which made for the easiest access to reach around to his throat, cutting the burgeoning scream into a satisfying gurgle. Even as he fell, the Human in the point position lifted a knife and went high for Tamir as she slid low around the corner.

Flame spared a passing thought to wonder why they weren't using force weapons, but that could wait until after the fight. She flung herself back from Three as he fell, landing on Four's chest and clawing him across the face for the sheer fun of it—the Human's panic when he couldn't see her, but could certainly feel her, almost made up for all the boring interviews she'd watched.

The Human was well trained enough to bring up his knife, not just grab at whatever was sticking to him, so Flame kicked off with her back legs and flipped over his head, cutting his helmet free and non-fatally slicing the sides of his neck in the process. He was still making shriek, panicky sounds, slashing around with the knife, so Flame dropped back to the ground to give him a second. Five rushed forward, going for Tamir or whatever had dropped his friends, and Flame made a low sound of approval. Die brave, little Human. As he passed she lunged and moved up his body in precise fashion, slicing both his achilles, digging into his inner thigh where the largest of arteries waited, skipping his spine only because it was too much work to cut his vest free, and taking out the jugular just for kicks, given he'd be dead within seconds of flopping to the floor.

She had a moment to see Tamir throw a knife at Two—it missed his face but hit him enough to throw off his run, which Flame found impressive for a Human in this lack of light—then turned back to Four, who was still slashing at nothing and had moved on to incoherent yelling. It was nice when they put on a show, but better to cut this short in case they had backup. She unsheathed a knife from her side, since that seemed to be the weapon of choice in this brawl, and stabbed him twice in the leg to get his hands aiming lower, then backed up to throw the knife directly into his throat.

Even as he sank to the ground with his hands wrapped around the hilt, the shouts tried to bubble up out of his throat along with the blood. Humans really were determined things, sometimes.

Rather than delay the inevitable, she reached forward to pluck the knife out of both his hands and throat, letting the blood pour free, and turned again to check on Tamir. One was down, still attempting to get up but incapacitated in some way, and Two slashed at her with far more discipline than poor Four had managed. As Two also had the benefit of night vision, while Tamir had to count on her other senses, Flame decided a bit of support was in order. Two's boots were higher and thicker than Five's, so slicing his achilles wouldn't be nearly as convenient, and she didn't want to jump too high and end up in Tamir's altitude of attack.

Disappointed, she sheathed her knife and unholstered the smallest of her guns. When Tamir threw herself back just ahead of a jab, Flame fired, the air sizzled, and Two fell hard to the ground, his momentum carrying him nearly into Tamir before he fell. Flame darted forward to grab his knife, used it to finish off One, and took the barest moment to enjoy the overwhelming victory. "All down," she said, not bothering to lower her voice, because who cared at this point.

"Why the hell didn't they shoot?" Tamir asked, working her way forward in the low light. "Grab one of their weapons, maybe we can—"

"Got it. Let's get to the ship—this wasn't great, so they probably weren't alone, and now they know you aren't either."

Tamir made a noise of agreement, and picked her way over the sprawled bodies. Five was still moving, but weakly, so Flame paused only long enough to flip off his goggles and dip the knife into and back out of his eye. Someone on the station would be experienced enough to identify the wounds, perhaps, but they didn't need a last-breath whispered account of what had happened. Flame had never been a fan of witnesses.

"You don't even have blood on you. Walk to the ship, nothing happened, I'll stay next to you." Flame narrowed her pupils before the door slid open into the brighter main corridor, almost disappointed that no more shadowy figures had collected during their fight in the hall.

They still had a few ports to go before their ship's dock when Flame got another chance.

"Tamir Alcuin, formerly on contract with Peacemaker Hrusha, by order of law you are bound to stop." The voice was officious, skewed machine-like by the security helmet obscuring the Lumar head underneath. Other passing beings moved quickly out of the way, leaving the path clear between Tamir and the taller figure ahead.

"Identify yourself," Tamir snapped, her pace confident, not swerving a single step.

"You are bound—"

"The hell I am. You have no badge and are not Peacemaker security, and I don't know you."

"You are—"

"Someone call security!" Tamir bellowed, and before Flame could get a third step, someone fired a bolt gun—it went wide of Tamir, could have been poorly aimed at the helmeted figure, or a warning shot meant to clear everyone else out, but either way, it was clear what they needed to do.

Another shot, some ululating cries from a Sidar in the crowd, and Flame bolted forward to foul the Lumar's legs, rather than aiming for a nonexistent vulnerable spot. Her momentum and angle provided just enough force, knocking the Lumar to the ground and giving Tamir room to run. The woman kicked his gun away as she passed.

The helmeted attacker bellowed, and Flame turned to see Peacemaker-marked figures closing in on it, their own guns trained on the prone figure. No one was paying attention to Tamir, which seemed like the best time to get out.

Tamir ran the rest of the way to the ship, shouting back the shortest of answers the few times someone ran by the other way. Whatever that had been, they needed to be clear of it, and their ship was the best option.

Flame, still in her quintessence field, kept pace and thought about the next move. They'd have to trade the ship out for another as soon as possible. For someone to attack here, at Peacemaker headquarters, meant the benefits of a Peacemaker ship wouldn't be worth the obviousness of it. They'd have to make haste to some backward station to leave the ship and get passage to a smuggler shipyard. If Tamir didn't have untraceable credits stored away somewhere, Flame was fairly sure some of her smaller accounts would have been missed in the clan freeze.

If not, things were going to get even more interesting.

* * * * *

Dilemma

Deluge had Rurranach join them at the Proud Fist headquarters in order to formulate a plan.

"Where do we start?" Deluge asked as he sat with the Sidar and Uban in the room that the Lumar merc had indicated was best for a conference. It wasn't a large space, but it was comfortable, with a large table and chairs that would suit a number of different species. Several viewscreens hung on the walls at various intervals, and the corner cabinets held a variety of consumables generally considered to be luxury offerings. The Veetanho commanders of Proud Fist had obviously not been overly concerned with living a spartan lifestyle.

"Well, what is it we need?" Rurranach asked. He looked up at the big Lumar who stood beside his chair. They'd offered Uban a seat, but he'd declined. Apparently, the chairs were for commanders only. Deluge, of course, sat directly on the table. "Uban, you said your company is back up to full strength, yes?"

"New troops. Green. Strong but need training. Need experience. Need commander."

"Yes," the Sidar said, "we are working on that. So ideally, we're looking for an experienced mercenary commander. Or sub commander looking for a promotion. Someone with an idea of how to train, equip, and lead a full company."

"And good. Need good commander. Not butcher," Uban put in.

"Yes. That too."

"Well, that shouldn't be too hard to find," Deluge said, his tone dry and deadpan. "I'm sure there are hundreds of paragons like that just floating around the galaxy, waiting for a company to fall into their laps."

"Your sarcasm is noted, my friend," Rurranach said, "but I think you'd be surprised. I have a feeling that if we were to journey to one of the larger merc pits, we'd find someone who fit the bill quite well. I suspect you'd even feel rather good about some of your choices."

"Oh? And why is that?" Deluge asked.

"Because many of the beings I have in mind happen to be Human."

Deluge's ears twitched as he digested this information. Uban's face pulled into something that might have been a frown, and he crossed both sets of arms over his chest.

"Humans weak?" he asked. "Need strong commander. Smart commander."

"Not at all," Deluge said. "Perhaps one on one, they might be. They've begun to make quite a name for themselves, however, using increasingly sophisticated battle armor to make up for their natural deficiencies. And more importantly, they're cunning and creative. I was raised by a Human, Uban, and she taught me well how to stay alive. Rurranach is right. A Human commander might be just what you need. If we can find the right Human."

Somewhat to his surprise, Deluge realized he felt a fair amount of responsibility for the Proud Fist company. Not because he'd killed their commander...that was a contract, and he'd been paid well to do the job. But more because he'd made the call to kill their deputy and left them without a leader. If his reasons for killing Apeya had been valid, then those reasons were enough for him to see that these Lumar mercs were given into hands that would do right by them.

And so, he cared. Inconvenient, perhaps, but there it was. He cared, so he would see to it that they got a decent commander, and then he would be on his way.

"Good. Right Human, then," Uban said. "Not weak Human. Good Human."

"Yes," Rurranach said. "We must definitely have a good Human. And as I said, I think we will find what we're looking for in one of the larger Merc pits. The closest one is Telpa. We can be there in a single transition. Though we won't all be able to fit on your ship, Del."

"Uban stay," the Lumar said quickly. "Get ready for Good Human Commander."

"That works," Deluge said. "I suppose this means we have a plan. Do you have any reason we shouldn't leave right away?"

"No," Rurranach said.

"All right, let's do that. We can sleep in hyperspace."

* * *

Deluge had visited merc pits before, but he never ceased to be impressed by the air of such places. The excitement and aggression-soaked atmosphere raised his fur and caused his aggressive nature to come to the fore.

"I doubt we'll have much luck in the main bidding pits," Rurranach said shortly after they arrived on Telpa. "We're not looking for someone in a position to be seeking contracts. The person we're looking for is hoping to be found by a company in need of experienced fighters. For that, we go to the bar."

"I bow to your wisdom in this," Deluge said as he fell into step beside the Sidar. They both wore the kind of nondescript cloak favored by those looking to avoid notice. Since a fair number of other beings were similarly clothed, the cloaks worked pretty well.

As they walked past the entrance to one of the pits, noise and light, and some of that particularly unique atmosphere spilled out. So, too, did a pair of Goka, who had apparently been getting a bit rowdy for the establishment's staff. Deluge dodged the carapaced aliens and kept his hood pulled down low. He may have hated wearing clothing, but it *did* come in handy from time to time.

"This place looks good," Rurranach said a moment later as they approached a quieter, seedier looking place next door to the pit. The light inside was dim enough that Deluge retracted his glasses, and the air reeked of various different forms of intoxicating substances. Tables of diverse heights stood scattered around the room, and a decrepit-looking serving bot covered in old stains wove through them carrying a tray. At a midlevel table in the back, a single figure sat hunched over a small glass. A tall bottle half-full of clear liquid sat in front of him, and as they watched, he poured some of this into the glass and drank it all at once. Deluge had to fight not to wrinkle his nose as they approached. That stuff smelled like what Murrron used to clean engine parts.

"He must be tough, if he's drinking that. Perhaps he'll decide to attack rather than talk." Deluge said softly, for Rurranach's ears alone.

"I'm certain you can take him, Hunter. And I always carry a Medkit," Rurranach quietly replied. But the figure must have heard, for he lifted his head and stared at the two of them with a slightly unfriendly look.

He was Human. Taller than Susa, and powerfully built. His eyes were dark and large, and his square jaw and somewhat prominent chin were covered under a layer of dark stubble, though not enough to be considered actual fur. Like Susa, his legitimate fur was confined to the top of his head, though his was shorter, and sort of stuck out in several directions at once.

He gave off an air of muted menace, and he lifted his eyebrows as they walked up to his table.

"Wasn't looking for company," he said.

"Were you not?" Rurranach asked, tilting his head and giving his version of a smile. "I rather thought you might be interested in what we have to say."

"You rather thought wrong."

"Who pissed in your cereal this morning?" Deluge said, using an idiom that he'd learned from Susa. Back when he and his siblings were going through their difficult adolescent year, she used that phrase in exasperation more often than not.

The Human blinked, then let out a short laugh.

"Where'd you learn that expression?" he asked. "We're a long way from Earth."

"I am acquainted with one of your race," Deluge said, and took the opportunity to leap up to the surface of the table. Once there, he opened up the clasp on the annoying cloak and let it drop. The Human's eyes widened slightly at the sight of him.

"That makes one of us," the Human said. "I recognized the Sidar. What are you?"

"I am a Hunter," Deluge said. "Your kind call us the Depik. My name is Choking Deluge, and I greet you, Human. Welcome to our negotiation."

"Negotiation?" the Human said, letting out a flat kind of laugh. "Is that what we're doing?"

"Are we not? I have something you want, and you have something I want. We are in a position to benefit each other."

"What could you possibly have that I want, cat?"

"A mercenary company."

"You want to hire me for your mercenary company? Neither the Sidar or the-whatever-the-fuck-you called yourself are recognized mercenary species."

"No. But the Lumar are. Unfortunately, they're not equipped to lead themselves, so they require a leader from a different race. My familiarity with Humans led me to conclude that a Human commander would fit that bill nicely."

"You have a Lumar mercenary company?"

"Yes."

"And you want me to command it?"

"Perhaps, yes."

"What's in it for you?"

"I don't have to command them. As you noted, I'm no mercenary myself. My skills lie...elsewhere," Deluge said, slow blinking and opening his mouth with a smile. Behind him, Rurranach chittered softly. The Human reached for his bottle.

"I gotta say, this is not how I expected to spend this evening. My name is Gage, by the way. Alton Gage."

"A pleasure to meet you, Alton Gage."

"That's another Human phrase."

"You are clever," Deluge said, slow blinking. "And observant. Are you interested in my offer?"

"Hell, why not?" Gage said.

"Excellent. Then perhaps you will not mind telling me about your background as a mercenary?"

Had Deluge not been watching closely, he might have missed the way Gage's shoulders and jaw tightened, just a bit, at his question. But as it was a reasonable question, politely phrased; the Human could hardly refuse to answer. He took a deep breath and looked up, eyes narrowing as he started to speak.

"I started when I was just a kid. Barely twenty or so. I honestly forget. Anyway, I went out on the Alpha Contracts with a bunch of guys. Shit got bad...I survived. Luck, I guess. And the caprice of a Veetanho I've never seen again."

"What do you mean?"

"I mean they were all dead around me, all of my guys. Goddamn Goka massacred us, and I was nearly dead, too. But when the enemy comes through, they're led by this Veetanho, and she slaps a Medkit on me, and I survived. She said I reminded her of her young, all hairless and vulnerable." He broke off and poured another small glass of the clear liquid and drank it all down at once. Deluge held still, despite the pungent scent of the drink. With a story like that, perhaps Gage needed to drink his engine cleaner, or whatever it was. Deluge would not stand in his way.

"Anyway, I healed up, went back to Earth. Didn't like it, didn't fit in. Not after what we'd seen. So, I went back out, picked up work here and there for whatever company came through. Eventually, I got my hands on a CASPer and started learning how to use them. Got a few jobs training new recruits how to use 'em, too. Did some user testing on the Mark 3 that's in use now…it's a good rig. Just finished another gig as a trainer, and decided I needed a drink."

"Have you ever commanded?"

"Me? Not in combat. Nothing larger than a platoon, anyway. But I've run training courses that had several platoons of recruits and all their instructors. So that's something."

"One last question, if you don't mind," Rurranach said, leaning forward to enter their impromptu interview. "Mr. Gage, I apologize for the bluntness of my question, but it is important to our situation…if you could go back and speak to your first commander, during the Alpha Contracts, what would you say to him?"

Gage was silent for a long time, his haunted brown eyes boring into those of the Sidar. Deluge could see the hinge of his jaw working as he ground his teeth together, and a fine tremor came over his hands. Finally, after several tense moments, he let out a long exhale, and reached for his bottle again.

"I'd tell him to back the fuck out of that contract," he said, looking down as he poured yet another drink. "And I'd shoot him if he didn't."

"And that is why you are perfect," Deluge said.

* * *

In a private bet with himself, Deluge gave even odds that Gage would actually use the transport ticket they'd provided for him to show up on 'Tlor. But sure enough, when he and Rurranach showed up at the arrival gate for the shuttle, the Human merc stood up from where he'd been leaning against a wall and walked toward them. Though he still towered over Deluge, he looked small compared to the various Lumar milling around the place. Perhaps that accounted for the scowl that creased his face as he approached.

Perhaps that was just his customary expression.

"I greet you, Alton Gage," Deluge said, holding out a paw.

"I greet you back, Deluge," the man said. He walked up and bent to place his own hand, briefly, under Deluge's fingerpads. "Hello, Rurranach."

"Hello, Gage," Rurranach said. "Would you like to follow me? Our transport is out this way."

"Sure," Gage said. He hefted the bag he carried up onto his shoulder and fell into step behind Rurranach as the Sidar turned and weaved through the shuttle port pedestrian traffic. "This place is crowded. Do you...ah, are you all right down there?"

"I can care for myself," Deluge said, a glimmer of humor in his tone. "But it might be easier for us to talk if I ride on your shoulder."

"Oh. Um. Sure, if you want," Gage said.

"I don't need to, if it makes you uncomfortable."

"No, it's fine. I just wasn't expecting it. Come on up."

Deluge slow blinked, and then dropped down to all four feet before making a simple leap. He gripped Gage's shoulder with his front paws, careful not to extend his claws. Then he hauled his back feet up and adjusted his balance to account for Gage's gait. It wasn't, perhaps, the most inconspicuous way of traveling, but he'd been on 'Tlor for quite some time at this point, and there had been no problems, so he was willing to relax a little bit.

"I'm very excited to see you," Deluge said once he was settled in place. "I was half afraid you wouldn't come."

"I almost didn't," Gage admitted. "Part of my brain kept trying to convince me that you were a vodka-induced hallucination."

"Well, I'm glad you're here. I think you will find the Proud Fist to your liking, and I remain convinced you are exactly what they need."

"Why do you care so much?" Gage asked. "If you don't mind me asking, that is. Why do you care about what happens to these Lumar? I read everything I could get my hands on about your race—which wasn't much, by the way—and they all agree that you Depik are pretty much sociopaths by the standards of any other species."

"That's not entirely true. We are highly social as a race."

"I meant in the sense of being amoral."

"Well, that's not entirely true either. Some things are right, and others are wrong. Our definitions may vary, though, compared to those of other beings."

"You don't mind killing in cold blood."

"No. We don't."

"And you don't mind killing for profit."

"No. But then, you're a mercenary. You don't mind it either."

"It's a bit different."

"Is it?" Deluge slow blinked and let his jaw fall open. "You use your skills to enact violence; so do I."

"Yeah, but I'm enacting violence against other mercs…combatants who know what they signed up for."

"Do not kid yourself, Gage. If someone is willing to pay my fee to take your life, you know what you've signed up for, too. My services cost too much to be squandered on innocents."

"That seems…inexact. How do you know in advance?"

"I don't, but the market would suggest it. As would the evidence. Take this company, for example. The commander was an embezzler and a thief, as well as a sadist who allowed her sister and deputy to enter into suicide contracts that killed hundreds of her troopers for no reason other than to better enable their money laundering and embezzling schemes. Add to that, she cheated her own sister on top of everything. She was not an innocent being, not in any sense of the word."

"And you killed her because of that?"

"No, I killed her because her sister paid me to do so. I killed her sister because of that. And almost immediately regretted it, because now I have a Lumar merc company on my hands."

"Ahh…so who paid you to kill the sister."

Deluge said nothing for a moment. He felt his tail twitch down Gage's back in irritation at himself.

"No one," he admitted finally. "I did it because I did not like the way she wasted the Lumars' lives."

"So, taking suicide contracts is wrong in your eyes?" Gage asked. When Deluge twitched again, he spoke quickly before the Hunter could reply. "Don't get me wrong, I'm not trying to judge. I just want to understand."

"Waste is wrong," Deluge said with a sigh. "Though I think perhaps not all of my kind would act as drastically as I've done. I blame my Human upbringing."

"Wait…what?"

Deluge twitched his ears and felt his good nature return. This clever Human merc hadn't expected *that*.

"Yes. Remember, I told you I'm acquainted with one of your kind. The woman who raised me like a second mother is Human. So,

I wouldn't be surprised to find that some of my racial sociopathy, as you call it, has been diluted by Human mores."

"Oh," Gage said. "Okay. Fair enough. Is that why you wanted a Human? Because you like the way we think?"

"I suppose so," Deluge said. "I didn't overthink it."

That got a laugh out of the man, and a few heads turned to look as they passed out of the shuttle terminal and into the bright daylight of 'Tlor. Deluge's goggles snapped out and into place. Rurranach led them to the thoroughfare that was typically choked with vehicles on- and off-loading passengers and luggage. Deluge leapt from Gage's shoulder into the cabin of the well-appointed vehicle, and the other two followed.

"Headquarters, please," Rurranach said, and the automated system beeped in acknowledgment as the door closed, and the thrusters pushed them into the crowded sky.

* * *

Uban had outdone himself.

When they returned to headquarters, the Lumar Merc had rounded up all of his fellows and organized them into blocky formations. Each of them carried an energy rifle and wore his full battle kit as far as Deluge could tell. They stood arrayed in the open basement room of the headquarters building, looking like proud, formidable, uniform warriors.

Even the Hunter had to admit, they were impressive. Maybe it wasn't his way of enacting violence, but it was impressive just the same.

"Greet you, Hunter. Sidar. This new commander?"

"I greet you, Uban," Deluge said as the three of them walked in-to the basement. Uban stood in the center front of the formation, and he walked toward them with a puffed chest and formal, stilted movements. "Your troopers look formidable. Well done."

"Thank you, Hunter," Uban said and looked pointedly at Alton Gage, who stared back with something that might have been a tiny smile curving his lips.

"Ah…this is Alton Gage. A Human mercenary commander. We brought him to see how well you liked each other," Deluge said, feeling somewhat at a loss for words.

"Is smart?"

"I'm smart," Gage said for himself.

"How smart?"

"Smart enough to help develop the tactical manual for the Mark 3 Human CASPer suit."

A murmur of sound rippled through the ranks of the Lumar, as if nearly all of them had inhaled sharply at Gage's words.

"Are you familiar with the Mark 3 CASPer?" Gage asked softly, his smile deepening.

"Fought CASPers in Kendry mining belt operation. Hard to fight. Most died," Uban said, and though his words were clipped and professional, Deluge realized that there was real pain in the big Lumar's eyes.

"Yes. I'm sorry for your losses, then, Uban," Gage said.

"Bad contract," Uban said quietly. Very quietly.

"Yes. I don't like bad contracts," Gage said.

"No." Uban said in agreement. He paused for a long moment, looked Gage up and down, then looked at Deluge.

"Good commander, Hunter. Uban thanks."

"You're welcome, Uban," Deluge said, his ears twitching in laughter.

"Commander," Uban said, turning back to Gage. "Come inspect."

"Ah...well..." Gage said, glancing back at Rurranach and Deluge. "That's not...I haven't..."

"You might as well, Gage," Deluge said, lifting one paw and beginning to groom his face. "You're eventually going to do what Uban wants anyway. He's uncommonly good at getting his way."

"Yes," Uban said. "Come, commander."

"Fuck," Gage whispered, and he dropped his head down, shaking it from side to side briefly before straightening up and throwing his shoulders back. Deluge continued to groom his face, and he heard Rurranach stifling his chittering laughter behind them.

"All right, then, First Sergeant Uban," Gage said, his tone firmer, his voice carrying through the ranks of massed Lumar. "Let us proceed with the inspection."

Deluge settled in to wait, fascinated despite himself. The interplay between Uban and Gage had been amusing, to say the least, but the near-instantaneous transformation in Gage was something he'd never seen before. The changes in the Human merc's demeanor were enough that he would probably have noticed even had he not been familiar with Humans and their non-verbal communications. With every step, every look at a Lumar weapon, Gage seemed to solidify and harden. Like a being given purpose, or another chance at life.

Fascinating.

He was still raptly watching the inspection process when the southern wall of the basement exploded inward, spraying concrete

and metal shrapnel in a deadly cloud right into the ranks of the assembled Lumar.

Deluge picked himself up off the floor, only then realizing that
he'd been thrown across the room from the force of the explosion.
A high-pitched ringing in his ears deafened all other sounds, and he
couldn't see anything but dust, couldn't smell anything but flame and
fear. He stretched out with his quintessence, using it to locate the
bodies around him. Most were still living, warping the quintessential
web the way vital beings did. Some were not, that warping starting to
fade as they ceased to live and became more like the objects surrounding them. Deluge bent the light around himself and began
searching for Rurranach, or Gage, or even Uban. What had happened?

The ringing in his ears was just starting to fade when he heard a
series of short, staccato pops. Somewhere, he caught the faint edge
of Gage's voice, shouting commands. A rumble came from the
southern wall, and Deluge turned just in time to see a flood of Goka
scuttling on the ceiling through the breach left by the explosion. Before he realized what he was doing, he had two knives in his hands
and was snarling up into the mass of attacking insectoids.

It was an almost fatal mistake.

Something heavy hit him in the back, and pain like fire erupted in
a searing line behind his ear. He fell forward, collapsing his body
around himself in a defensive roll. Something caught at his hind feet
and followed him through the roll, preventing him from regaining
his footing. He found himself flat on his back, barely able to bring up
his knives to defend his face, before his assailant was atop him.

She dropped her quintessential cloak and snarled in his face.

"You're mine, murderer," the female Hunter said, her teeth snapping in exhilaration.

"*Me?*" Deluge gasped as she bore down on his throat. "You're the one attacking a fellow Hunter!"

"You're under interdict," she said, spitting the words out. "Your whole upstart clan is, for the murder of Peacemaker Hrusha!"

Deluge twitched at this news, which nearly killed him. His attacker brought her back paws up and attempted to stab at his vitals with the wicked hooked knife she carried with her back foot. He brought his own back paw up and blocked it, barely. He felt the sting of a cut, and the warm wetness of his own blood as she nearly severed one of the fingers there. A cool, spreading numbness brought immediate physical relief, but whispered to him that he had very little time. She must have poisoned her blade.

Well, fair enough. If that was how this was going to go, he would go with it. And luckily for him, he was bigger and stronger than she was.

He wrapped the now-numb fingers of his back paw around her ankle and held her off with brute strength. He balled the fingers of his other back paw into a fist and kicked her as hard as he could in the pelvic region. She let out a gasp of air and would have recoiled, but he wasn't about to let that happen. He dropped the knives he held in his front paws, and, while one paw grabbed her crossed wrists, the other gripped her throat hard, squeezing with everything that he had. At the same time, he reared up and sank his teeth into the forearm that held his knife-paw immobile. She let out a scream, and raked her front claws at his vulnerable eyes. He closed his eyelids and took the slash, feeling agony tear into his face as more warm wetness began to drip down into his fur.

She struck at him again, and this time, he took her movement and forced the two of them into a roll across the debris-covered floor. She continued to scrabble at him with her poisoned knife, but his strength held out for the moment. He squeezed harder on her throat, feeling the bones and tendons under his paw grind together, and she began to drag at the air with ragged gasps.

"If not me, then someone will kill you," she whispered, her eyes triumphant. "My poison taints your blood even now."

"Yeah, well, I've got a lot of blood," he replied. Perhaps it wasn't the pithiest thing he could have said, but to be honest, her pretentious prattle was getting on his nerves. He squeezed harder, watching her eyes start to bulge in their sockets as he held the rest of her body immobile.

"Scramble," he said, as her tongue began to loll out of her mouth. "It will be faster and better if you do it. In fact…"

He leaned close and tongued loose the little pouch he always carried sealed to the roof of his mouth. While her struggles grew progressively weaker, Deluge skinned the pouch open with his teeth and dropped the single pill it contained into her open, gasping mouth. He then let go of her throat and clamped his hand over her mouth and nose, preventing her from taking the deep gulp of air she had started to take. Instead, she swallowed the scramble pill, and her eyes went wide for a second before rolling back in her head.

The dissolution protocol started immediately and smelled terrible. But at least she was properly scrambled.

The rest of the world came back to Deluge all in a sudden rush. Chaos reigned around him. Goka dropped from the ceiling, knives first, and slashed at enraged Lumar who battled back with all the fury their heavy fists could bring. Even though he knew it would highlight him to any other Hunters lying in wait, he pulled quintessence and bent the light around himself once more. He had to find Rurranach. The Sidar had a Medkit under his cloak. He had to stop that poison.

Quintessence couldn't identify one individual being over another. At most, it could give Deluge an idea of the size of a living being. Fortunately for him, Rurranach wasn't as big as the Lumar. So, when Deluge felt a moderately large, but still smaller than a Lumar, living being under a swarm of stabbing Goka, he knew it had to be either Rurranach or Gage. And as he could still hear Gage shouting commands, he was fairly certain it was the Sidar.

Goka liked to attack from above, it seemed. Well, he could certainly play that game.

He took a second to retrieve his knives, and then used the piled rubble to leap up to a vantage point that overlooked the Sidar-sized scrum. Then, remembering his dama's lessons about how the Basreeni hunt, Deluge dove into the fray, knives extended, and began moving with as much speed as he could muster. He hacked a wing here, sprayed a blast of brightly colored ichor there. He struck out with his clawed back paws as often as he did his knives, and he twisted and dove as he struck, staying in constant motion, leaping from one insectoid body to the next. He stabbed down between a carapace and a thorax, and kicked himself up and backward, twisting in the air to avoid the counterstrike as he landed on something that was softer. Quick as a thought, he pulled his quintessence cloak around himself, causing the Goka to pause for a half second in confusion.

Which was more than long enough.

Deluge kicked aside the flap of Rurranach's cloak under his feet and reached for the Medkit strapped to the Sidar's waist. His back-foot fingers toggled open the clasp and removed two nanite injectors. He stabbed one into his numb leg, depressing the plunger and letting out a hiss of pain as the agonizing lifesavers shot into his bloodstream. He crouched down and stabbed the second deep into the Sidar's shoulder.

"Wake up," he whispered. "Come on, Rurranach. Wake up and spread your wings! Get them off of us and I'll get us to safety."

Deluge never knew if the Sidar heard him or not, because a voice started yelling for everyone to hold. The Goka around him backed up a step, knives still at the ready. Slowly, the enraged Lumar were persuaded to leave off their pummeling of the attacking force, and the noise of combat slowly subsided.

A large Goka stepped forward, rustling its wings.

"Where is the Depik?"

Deluge pulled a small cylinder from his harness. It didn't look like much, but it was a sleek kind of projectile weapon that carried a particularly nasty nerve agent-filled dart along a laser-designated path. All he'd have to do is point it and lase his target, and that target would die within seconds. He fervently hoped that if this went bad, a few seconds would be enough time to save his life.

"I'm here," he said, releasing his quintessence and letting the light reestablish his presence.

"Not you," the Goka said, clicking its antennae impatiently. "The female. Our client."

"Oh," Deluge said, surreptitiously readying himself to use the weapon. "She's dead. See that pool of goo over there?"

"Burning black entropy!" the Goka cursed. "Are you serious? She hadn't paid us yet!"

Deluge's ears twitched in surprise. That was not the reaction he'd expected.

"Should have...insisted...payment up front," Gage said, stepping forward out of the tight knot of Lumar clustered around him. He was breathing heavily, and carried a wicked slash down the side of his face, but he appeared to be otherwise well enough.

"I tried," the Goka said. "She threatened to kill me if I 'impugned her honor' by suggesting she'd fail. Stupid cat."

"She was overconfident," Deluge said.

"How...much?"

A fierce triumph leapt in Deluge's chest. The ragged voice that spoke came from the crumpled form beneath him. Rurranach lived!

"What?"

"How much did she promise you?"

"Five thousand."

"Double...it," Rurranach suggested to Deluge. "You can...afford it."

"Excellent idea," Deluge said. "I'll pay you double if you'll go away and keep silent on this affair for as long as possible."

"I can do that," the Goka said. "I can easily do that. You can transfer credits?"

"My Sidar friend here can," Deluge said. "In the meantime, we've both got wounded to see to. Gage, would you be opposed to opening up your infirmary to our new friends here? Uban knows what to do, I'm sure."

"Uban know," the big Lumar said. "Good fight. Need medics."

"Fine," Gage said. His voice was clipped, but Deluge couldn't figure out if that was because he didn't like Goka, or because he was unhappy about extending medical treatment to their erstwhile attackers. In the end, it didn't really matter, he supposed. Gage's issues were his own business.

"Excellent," Deluge said. "Let's get started then. I've much to think on."

* * * * *

No Plan Survives First Contact

Then well-built den tunneled deeply into a rock fall that appeared ancient. Though the more he looked at it, the more convinced "Chirruch" was that it had been at least partially deliberate. Or added to, perhaps, as the clan grew and needed more space. The buildings on the outskirts were a mixture—some in stone, some in the ground, and some, Chirruch had been grateful to note, pressed in the trunk of a towering melik tree.

Blade had developed Chirruch's background partly to make it difficult to investigate, and also partly because he had enough experience in the deep jungle to fake it properly. Reow had insisted her kits spend a full season in the jungle, away from the safety and comfort of the den. She charged them to learn from the Basreeni, observing the primitive predator species, and living in the trees as they did. In that time, Blade had learned more about the peculiarities of tree-dwelling than many Hunters knew. Lucky, or his disguise would have been burned almost immediately. Not for the first time, his dama's unusual upbringing paid unexpected dividends.

And so Chirruch settled in the tree with every evidence of contentment. This emboldened Ichys, and she offered to introduce him to their dama in at the next evening meal, which was happening tonight.

He had to slip away to ensure no hint of black showed in his orange fur. Of course, there was no flaw—the dye would far outlast this mission, or he had failed spectacularly—and he justified his absence by purchasing a torque of shimmering blue-green metal, deftly fastened into the shape of the sleeper vine found in the far north stretches of the jungle. It would make for an excellent guest gift, hearkening to his supposed home and showing the deep jungle guest had picked up some understanding of city customs in the handful of days since his arrival.

* * *

Ichys fetched him, an honor he recognized. He had entered the den briefly to be introduced, so no one tried to attack him for trespassing in the tree; therefore, he could have gone to the evening meal unescorted, though he likely would have wandered until finding someone to guide him. But she chose to make the effort to bring him, and he warmed at her presence.

She grabbed the torque out of his hands and examined it, turning it this way and that, holding it up to the light, pulling it close and holding it at arm's length. Her ears flicked briefly toward him and away, making the tease of it clear.

"Does it meet with your approval?" he asked, wanting to laugh far more than her actions deserved.

"It'll do, Chirruch. As, I suppose, will you." She turned, tossing the torque back to him in the same motion. She kept the corner of her gaze on him, watching him snatch it neatly out of the air.

"Testing my reflexes?" Blade pitched his voice low, making a challenge of it.

"Always." Flicking her tail at him, Ichys left his little alcove and he, momentarily helpless, followed without even thinking about it.

"Are we going the long way?" Blade asked, after the walk had stretched longer than he expected, and his head cleared to notice more than the wave of Ichys's long gray tail. They were too close to the city for true jungle to surround them, but vegetation pushed closely to the paved path on all sides. Greenery tangled above so tightly it formed something of a tunnel around them, making direction harder to gauge.

"Are you in a hurry?" She glanced back over her shoulder, daring him to challenge her, and he slow blinked a content smile.

"Hungry, maybe." He meant it to be flirtatious, and she took it as such, flipping her tail and flicking her ears at him.

"Eager little jungle Hunter. Dinner will be late; it usually is when we gather together." Her ears flattened slightly, as though she were considering whether to say more. She apparently decided against it, and they were quiet until the path branched ahead of them. One turn curved off into a tangle of undergrowth, and one in the vague direction of the den. Down that path the upper vines reached lower to the ground, wrapped densely enough that they could only clear it on all fours, not by walking upright. Blade knew that was the one they would take, vague direction or no.

"Showing me a hidden entrance already?"

"Pull it in, kit," she replied, her tone keeping it a tease rather than a rejection of his deliberate double entendre. Ichys dropped to all four legs, tail waving gently as she sauntered down the tunneled path.

He followed, scenting the air and finding no recent Hunter traffic. If this route into the den were well known, it didn't seem well traveled. Chirruch could enjoy this time alone with Ichys, but Blade needed to separate himself and file away this approach to the den. If it weren't well traveled, and his scent would now be expected here, he could use this several times to scout the den, and find other ways in and out. Observing Whispering Fear and its Dama might have just gotten easier.

Their walk remained uneventful, the tube of vines blending almost seamlessly into carved rock, carved rock into natural rock, natural into smoothed. Blade examined the stone, appreciating the subtle carvings and embedded patterns of gems and contrasting minerals that had been carved and set at irregular intervals. This had been a better-used entrance once, or perhaps the special project of an artistically minded Hunter. When he caught himself thinking about doing something similar for Night Wind's den, he pushed away Blade's reactions and tried to think of only Chirruch's.

"Ready?" A rhetorical question, because as she asked it, Ichys straightened to two legs, casually leaned on the wall, and the dead end ahead of them opened into a warmly-lit corridor. She didn't wait for him to answer, slipping inside and vanishing the moment she crossed the doorway.

Blade laughed, because he should, and because he wanted to. He should have worried how often those two impulses combined with Ichys, but he didn't.

Not yet.

He didn't pull his quintessence field up, daring her to attack as he moved casually into the den. The hall had been built high and wide enough to accommodate larger sigiled species and kept clear of furniture or clutter. Small niches and smoothed projections studded the wall, allowing Hunters an alternate path to the honed polish of the floor.

Blade stayed on the ground, guessing if he leaped for a ledge he'd be knocked down mid-air by an invisible female somewhere near him, hidden in her bent light. He turned left, was rewarded with a hiss, turned right, and felt the purr more than heard it.

Without looking he reached to the side the purr had sounded from, poking the invisible Ichys in the shoulder. She dropped her field with a laugh, bumped him fondly, and gestured to their left.

"Now the games truly begin, jungle kit."

* * *

The gathering room was a long, low chamber; its dim lighting and scale were pitched perfectly for Hunters. Few sigiled companions came here, he guessed, or if they did, they were not meant to be comfortable.

Cushions and some low benches scattered near the table, several of which were occupied by the six Hunters in various stages of repose. Five males and a female, each of whom wasted no subtlety in examining the new arrivals. The female, younger than the rest, jumped from her perch on a far bench and raced over, bumping her cheek against Ichys's.

"Sister," Ichys said, tone warm with pleasure. "Sivand of Whispering Fear, I introduce you to Chirruch of Deep Night."

"Hunter, I greet you," Blade said, dipping his head to the grey-and-black-striped Hunter before him. She looked him up and down, blatantly evaluating, and slow blinked a smile that was all mischief.

"I greet you, Hunter," she replied, flicking her ears forward and back. "Handsome," she added to Ichys. "How does that orange work in the jungle? Do the Basreeni find you in the dark?"

"I wouldn't know," Ichys answered, with a stiffness that was entirely pretend. She swatted at her sister, who swatted back, both of them easy with the other. Blade observed the relaxed tails and loose body language, and missed his littermates with a pang so sudden it flattened his ears. Catching the slip, he hastened a question.

"Sisters? Were you so lucky to be littermates?" Few Hunters reached adulthood with a littermate. It had been an advantage for him, to grow alongside so many of his kind, test and push his skills nearly from birth. Not for Chirruch though, who would regard such a rarity with the appropriate awe.

"No," Ichys said, tweaking Sivand's ear. "We are some years apart. Siv still yearns to be out in the world more than the den."

"Not quite so young," Sivand retorted, flicking her tail. "Wouldn't you agree, Chirruch?" She added a throaty purring noise, causing Ichys to swat her again, then rolled away, laughing.

"You both do your dama proud," Blade offered, choosing his safest option. Ichys poked him with a claw, not hard enough to break skin, so he had walked the line well enough.

"No sign of Dama," Sivand said, returning to her bench.

"I've time to introduce you then." Satisfied, Ichys gestured to each Hunter as she spoke. "Firnt, who knows every merchant in the city. He introduced me to Fip when I'd barely left the den."

"Fip has excellent merchandise," Firnt said, after their greeting.

"I met him my first day in the city," Blade replied, flicking his ears toward Firnt in a display of respect. If Firnt knew all the merchants, he likely knew how the clan spent much of its credit. A Hunter to cultivate. "I knew his goods were quality and am glad to know how lucky I was to meet him."

"Chirruch was lost in wonder with Fip's stall the day I met him. Fip seems quite fond of our jungle Hunter." Ichys tugged Blade's closer ear, then tweaked his tail when he reached for her hand.

Firnt flicked his ears to Blade in return, amused by the small show of deference and perhaps by the interplay between Ichys and Blade.

"Uchir, who has hunted for Whispering Fear since our dama was a kit just leaving the den," Ichys said, Blade's tail still grasped in her hand. She paused long enough for each male she introduced to exchange the traditional greeting with Blade, and continued, "Girrip, more often off-world than home in the den. Jres, who also grew up in the deepest of the southern jungles, and still finds our city ways baffling. Echrys, who leaves us tomorrow for a contract, and sleeps more than he wakes when he is at home."

The affection and warmth in the room was real. Chirruch sank into it with a wistful sort of envy, which only made Blade's resentment grow. He missed his clan. He missed Susa, always bringing snacks. Reow, pushing them and loving them, her expectations and approval all in a mix. He missed his littermates, the unguarded joy they indulged in the safety of the den. He missed *home,* and there was a not insignificant chance some or all of these Hunters had played a part in taking that from him.

Blade watched with Chirruch's yearning to be a part of a growing, successful clan, covering his own weighing of the interactions. Why this combination of Hunters, for this dinner, for Ichys to introduce him more informally to the clan? Were they the trusted council around the dama? Was this the group Dirrys had consulted, before choosing to burn his den to the ground? *Watch. Find a way.* His dama's words echoed in his head.

He listened more than he spoke, telling only one story—a self-deprecating one, mostly true, of how he ended up stuck, hanging upside down in a Basreeni den, and all the hijinks that resulted in getting in, and out, of said situation.

The Hunters laughed, a little at him, a little with him, and Ichys beamed at him in approval. When she turned her head to speak with Uchir, Sivand slid from her seat and lounged over to Blade, shoving him over on the bench to sit next to him.

"She has decided to mate with you," the younger female said, ears swiveled toward Ichys and eyes on Blade, a sparkle of trouble all throughout her posture. "Surely you know. This was your last test, with some of her favorite Hunters of the clan. I think they like you."

"They?" Blade asked, his eyes wandering over to Ichys without his making a choice to look at her. He wondered if this meant Dirrys wasn't coming, and there wasn't a dinner at all. He wondered if this was a good idea. He wondered why he didn't care whether or not it was.

"Oh, I think you're fine. I'll decide if I like you if Ichys decides she likes mating with you. If she's happy, I'll have no cause to take your tail for a trophy." She flashed her claws, giving her light tease the very edge of a threat. Death would have approved.

"Am I here for the dama's approval as well?" he asked, acknowledging her comment by dipping his head and not arguing it.

"Oh, no. Dama will wait until we are all assembled and restless to make her appearance with the food. It makes us appreciate her more." Bitterness touched her tone, there and gone, glancing enough that he could have imagined it. "Ichys has learned how to take advantage of the pauses." She shrugged expressively, and bounded away to tackle Echrys.

Blade filed the information for later reflection, pulled his thoughts away from the idea of mating with Ichys, and determined

Firnt and Uchir were his targets for the evening. Before he could move, a scent distracted him.

All the Hunters lifted their noses slightly, smelling the meat coming their way. Underneath it, a sharper scent. Hunter. Female. One he recognized, faintly.

The dama had arrived.

Each Hunter pointed their face attentively toward the entrance, and Dirrys paused between hall and room, looking them over. A mechanized wagon behind her was loaded with food.

"Dama, we greet you," Ichys said, inclining her head. A murmurer of the same words rose from each of the Hunters, and Dirrys blinked an acknowledgement, flicking her eyes over both her kitas, and then the other Hunters. Her ears pricked in interest, seeing Blade, but he kept his eyes low. Easier to hide his hate by pretending deference, easier to tamp his rage when he only saw her in the periphery of his vision.

"My kitas. My clan." It was a version of completing the greeting, Blade supposed, though not a gracious one. Indicating all in the room belonged to her, which would roughen the fur of even the most loyal clan Hunter. "And a new arrival."

"Dama," Uchir spoke, as the eldest in the room, "Chirruch, of Deep Night."

"Yes, Ichys's guest. I suppose you must be quite…impressive, Hunter."

"Dama," Blade murmured, keeping his eyes low.

"You all have waited most patiently for me while I completed my business, very well, very well. Let us eat." She stepped into the room, tail and head high, confident in her ownership of all within. The wagon apparatus rolled in behind her, and Sivand moved to meet it.

Though her ears flicked in barely muted resentment, she unloaded the food to the table while Dirrys made herself comfortable.

Conversation resumed, and Blade noticed how much less warmth there was. A measure of ease still, as none seemed frightened of their dama. Conversation centered about contracts, and a new trade agreement, nothing scandalous or interesting or fraught with danger. But the companionship that had made him long for home had ebbed, and for the first time Blade considered that he may not have to kill everyone in the room.

The relief should have worried him.

* * *

Nights turned into ninenights. He interacted little with the dama, but cultivated the relationships he'd begun all around her.

With Firnt, he wandered merchant stalls, asking questions about off-world contracts with all the hidden eagerness of one who had not yet taken one—and learning more about the state of the clan's off-world income. Who took the most contracts, who was in disgrace with the dama, whose jobs took so long it seemed they were avoiding the den.

With merchants, he learned more about the finances—by being a charming, slightly naive customer, he learned which of Whispering Fear's Hunters owed money, or overpaid.

With Uchir, he drank Cooz and laughed at the older Hunter's sharp observations, learning about clan dynamics, and where alliances had solidified or might have more room to push.

With Ichys, he sometimes forgot his aim. They talked about everything, hunted with savage joy, and after several days of late meals, acknowledged they had been courting without purpose, and made it quite spectacularly purposeful.

The closest he got to losing everything was late one evening, walking with Ichys after a midday meal, when he saw Mhrand, casual and leaning.

Anger rippled through him at the sight of the aerial Hunter. Last Blade had seen him, Mhrand had been following Death as she fought to help him escape the explosions in their den. The fact that he was here, now, meant that he must have killed or abandoned Death and his own growing kits in the midst of that overpowering attack. Had Death survived? Had she died when Mhrand abandoned her? Had he run when staying would have meant everything?

"Hackles down, little male," Ichys purred in his ear. "I'm only taking one wandering Hunter back to my den these nights."

Blade smoothed his fur with effort, forcing his muscles to ease, and turned his face away from Mhrand's idle conversation with Firnt over Cooz. A newly arrived younger male could be excused from tensing at the sight of a similarly sized and aged rival appearing without warning in territory not yet claimed, but Chirruch had no reason to know Mhrand enough to challenge him, nor any standing to do so. Whispering Fear had not reached its age by encouraging internal rivalries, and Chirruch would prove nothing but his own weakness by being threatened by someone as newly arrived as he. He could be forgiven this one slip, given how recently and casually he'd been taken to mate by Ichys, but Blade had to ignore the pulsing need to rip Mhrand's eyes from his skull and braid his tail into his spilled intestines.

"His fur is patchy and dry," Blade sniffed dismissively, rewarded by her low laugh. "Is it only nights, or...?"

Laughing again, she turned them away and back to her den before Mhrand even looked their way.

* * *

"He mated with a damita from Night Wind," Firnt explained, matching his pace to Blade's as they circled the market, considering what they wanted to eat. "Realized the clan was rotten and left, heard a few days later how deep the rot had gone. Spent some time in the jungle getting his balance back, figuring out how to choose a clan so as not to make the same mistakes. Nasty business."

"If they were that rotted, more likely they kicked him out—why risk letting him stay, if he's so honorable," Blade offered, apparently distracted, putting more effort into scenting for the best midday meal option than paying attention to his fellow Hunter's take on the newest arrival to Whispering Fear's outskirts.

"That's a point. Always more than someone says about what they've been up to, eh?"

"When it comes to you off-world Hunters," Blade added, making sure to keep himself out of that category, even in only Firnt's head, and pulled his lips back in mock scorn. "Always so sneaky and playing five games at once. Give me a plain old jungle hunt, just stalk and harry, no plan needed."

"Who needs a plan when hunting with Ichys goes so well," Firnt replied, teasing in turn, dropping his jaw in a grin when Blade chuffed in acknowledgement of the hit. "It is a point Mhrand didn't go back to his own clan after all that, now that you mention it."

"His own clan doesn't have such fine females, I wager." Blade gestured at a food cart up ahead, not wanting to seed his dislike of Mhrand too obviously. Let the points itch at Firnt until the blunt male wondered aloud to Mhrand. Firnt would be likely to mention he'd been talking with Blade, and if Blade knew Mhrand, that gray male would charge right up to a newly arrived jungle Hunter with few allies. Mhrand had no subtlety, and Blade had never been so happy for that truth.

* * *

"How many clans should a Hunter consider, before the Hunter becomes the problem?" Blade asked lightly, throwing down the dice as Uchir drank.

"Bored of Whispering Fear already?" Uchir asked, spitting in disgust at the roll and throwing down a chit. "Or is it Ichys hinting you should move along? I thought you'd last longer."

"Hilarious." He rolled again, then made a noise of disgust annoyance and refilled both their mugs. "All right, sure, say it's me," his tone made it obvious it wasn't, as did the heated glance he unthinkingly sent Ichys's way. "I came in from Deep Night, poked around Whispering Fear, got some interest from a female, then leave with my tail low when she shoos me off. Can I go to Split Trunk, or will they wonder about me? In the jungles we like decisiveness, but maybe in the city you get more options."

Unfortunate, that the sound ebbed and his words landed clearly enough that Mhrand heard, across the room where he sat discussing contracts with two other Whispering Fear Hunters. Uchir's rasping laugh landed in that semi-silence, and the other male scooped up the dice in turn.

"Ichys looks ready to eat you fresh from the hunt, kit, so I don't think you have to worry about being shooed off just yet. Let's finish our round before she pounces."

* * *

Even Blade could have planned it only slightly better, when Mhrand finally came for him. Tender tree-grugs had recently finished their breeding season, leaving the new batch of wrigglers unattended by their erstwhile brooders, and Blade made it a point to brag about his plan to fetch a newly fledged morsel to present to Ichys, as though not knowing how trite such a move was in city circles. He headed for the upper canopies, and left just enough of a trail to prove he had nothing to hide.

He'd caught and bagged two grugs, and draped himself over a thick collection of tangled branches to consider if he wanted a third. There was a fine line to showing off, and he didn't want to stay out so long it seemed that he was avoiding anything.

The mass of branches and vines vibrated slightly beneath him, and for a second he let himself be surprised that he hadn't sensed anyone following him sooner. But then, no matter how unworthy Mhrand had ultimately proven himself to be, Death would never have selected him if he'd been completely useless from the beginning.

"I don't think Ichys likes grugs enough for us to both bring her some," Blade called into the jungle, as though he didn't know exactly which direction Mhrand was stalking him from.

The vibrations faded, then resumed slightly fainter than before. Blade's pulse picked up in excitement, and he rolled onto his side, visibly uncaring. It gave him the leverage to push off at an unexpected angle, when Mhrand launched himself from the layer of vines above, bursting from the tightly wrapped collection of leaves to strike the empty patch Blade had left behind.

Blade nearly laughed at how simple it was—not for the first time, he considered how lucky he had been to have so many surviving littermates. The training they'd given each other from their earliest days continued to benefit him—after a lifetime of trying to dodge the aptly named Death From Above, Blade would never fall victim to a barely-skilled lunge like Mhrand's.

He doubled back with breathless ease while Mhrand was still realizing his attack had missed, and Blade swiped a handful of claws down Mhrand's side with utter satisfaction.

"Oh!" he declared, eyes wide and pupils huge, "Mhrand! I thought you were a slipskin, trying to make lunch of me. No one answered," he leapt over Mhrand as the other male turned lightning quick to answer the attack, and left matching stripes of blood down Mhrand's other side, "so I assumed I was wrong. Thought maybe I was smelling a bilge-pest." It was a childish insult, given the rage seeing this traitor provoked in him, but even now, Blade could not be Blade. Chirruch had no reason to hate Mhrand, but every reason to antagonize a rival Hunter who had attacked him first.

To compound the insult, Blade channeled Del at his most infuri-ating. He lounged on his hind legs, lifting a front paw to groom him-self as though Mhrand posed absolutely no threat whatsoever.

Mhrand spat on the ground between them, tail bristling, some-thing like a yowl gurgling in his chest. Blade cocked his head curious-ly, pretending to try to understand words that weren't being spoken.

"How silly of me. You don't smell like a bilge-pest! I mean, of course you sound like a two-legged caseera looking for its other legs, but we're both surprised, aren't we? Did you want to try and catch a wriggler?"

Mhrand launched himself again, as of course he would, and Blade threw himself low, close to the bark of the tree, and twisted as he passed under Mhrand to add a third set of claw marks down the ex-posed belly. Fast, brutal, and disappointingly empty of the satisfying spill of intestines. He couldn't kill Mhrand, as much as every bit of him yearned for it. He couldn't whisper any intense warning, nor do anything that might show Chirruch as having depths the young jun-gle Hunter shouldn't so much as know existed.

Dirrys was his true prey, and nothing else was worth shaking Chirruch's path. Killing Mhrand would satisfy something in him, but would neither avenge nor clear Night Wind, and so he would resist the overpowering urge. Humiliation though, that would be well with-in a talented young Hunter's claws.

"You're bleeding like prey," he observed, resuming the insultingly at-ease posture of a moment ago. "I don't think you'll be able to sneak up on a wriggler in that state, but if you want to play bait for a slipskin, I'm sure I can kill it before it eats you. I'm not nearly as tired from today as you look."

Mhrand panted, pulling himself back up to his back feet with a growl. He met Blade's eyes, his own slitted with pain and rage, and gathered himself to spring again.

"Really? I had no idea you city clan-hoppers were so stubborn. Maybe you could make it up in the deep jungle after all. I mean, not like this," Blade gestured to the freely bleeding wounds streaking Mhrand's gray fur, "but in general." He was overdoing it on the insults, but he could see Mhrand wavering and was running out of opportunities to siphon off the bloodlust.

The air pressure shifted, and a shadow dropped between them, resolving itself into Uchir. The older male had a mixture of amusement and boredom in his bearing, ears pricked forward in a neutral alertness.

"Enough of that then, younglings. Whispering Fear needs Hunters, not rutting animals. Get yourself cleaned up," he added to Mhrand, who sagged at the sudden cutting of tension.

Inwardly, Blade fumed that Mhrand had been idiot enough to let someone follow him, but then supposed his own trail had been enough. He'd had to leave it for Mhrand, but of course any other clan member could have let curiosity take them this way as easily. Outwardly, he maintained the insultingly unconcerned lounge and groomed himself.

"Enough showing off, you," Uchir added to Blade, but there was a rough fondness in his tone that meant Chirruch had passed a test. "We're going to put all that energy of yours to work for the clan. I think Ichys might take you off world."

Moving into their off-world contracts meant a significant step closer to the inner workings of Whispering Fear. In some way then, Blade owed a debt to Mhrand, for taking him forward. It was a debt

Blade would only ever repay by drawing more blood, and perhaps an organ, but a debt all the same.

* * *

There were over a dozen Hunters in the room, gathered in a cavern that had been carved long ago to ensure nearly fifty Hunters could be in one place without crowding against each other. A sensible precaution—Hunters wouldn't kill each other, but that had never meant they wouldn't fight, and many Hunters were better off only occasionally seeing others of their kind. Putting too many prickly, highly-trained killers in a too-enclosed space was a fine way to court disaster, and whoever had built this audience chamber in the middle of Whispering Fear's den had planned for it.

With a smaller group though, sound carried oddly, and the room seemed too big. There were no obvious perches or ledges for resting above the floor, though the walls seemed rough enough to allow for a determined climb if one wanted to go around their peers. An elevated section across the room from the entrance held a cushioned bench, clearly meant for the dama, as there were no other seats or places to rest.

This room was meant for the clan to gather, hear what the dama had to say, and leave. Faint wear marks in the ground indicated this might not always have been the way, but Dirrys had been dama for twice as long as Blade had lived, and only two members of her clan were old enough to know what it had looked like before, so this was how Whispering Fear ran.

Blade allowed himself a brief moment to remember Night Wind's gathering room, the chairs, cushions, and shelves scattered around. How Deluge had loved to slip into whatever seat Susa was about to choose, and surprise her. How Flame had gotten good enough to sometimes surprise Deluge at his own game, sneaking onto the chair first in her quintessence field, and pouncing on him.

There were no pranks here, and while some of the Hunters grouped together with evidence of warmth and existing bonds, this room meant business first and last.

He made another effort to see it objectively. He didn't trust Dirrys, and so he wanted to see this clan negatively. It was more than a family group, larger and older than his own clan, and of course it would operate differently. Until recently, it had been one of the wealthiest clans, and therefore "differently" did not mean the same as "worse." The Hunters all carried the healthy wariness that came of being summoned by their dama, but otherwise carried their conversations with ease. No one appeared in fear of some unexpected, unprovoked punishment.

Chirruch, from an even smaller clan, would have no idea how to judge it, and so he observed without worry that it would make him stand out. Watch. Find a way.

* * *

"This is barely half of our Hunters, maybe a third of the clan," Ichys murmured at his shoulder before her scent had a chance to register.

"I had no idea," he lied, then glanced at her when she laughed.

"Of course, you did. You researched Whispering Fear the day you met me at Fip's."

"I…" Blade blinked quickly, one ear swiveling back as he tried to remember where he'd slipped, what she knew. Were they gathered because they knew who he was?

"When we went hunting," there was amusement in her voice, and she slow blinked to signal he could calm himself, "you knew a bit more about my clan than the day we met. Hunters like to know what they're getting into—I would never be angry at you for that."

Foolish. Nearly gave himself away on the mistaken notion he had already somehow revealed himself. That would be a truly embarrassing way to go, after all this work and time. He lowered his eyes, both ears pricked forward in rueful acknowledgment.

"I didn't want you to think me a lost yokel. I am, of course, but I hoped you'd see more."

She laughed again and leaned to rub her cheek against his. Several of the other Hunters noticed, one turning to watch more obviously that the others. A rival lover, perhaps, or an aspiring one. Ichys didn't pay attention.

"Have you adopted a wanderer?" a new voice asked, from a space Blade knew was empty a moment ago.

"Arow." There was fondness in her tone, and Ichys moved slightly away from Blade to greet the arrival. "This is Chirruch, new to the city and visitor to our clan, from Deep Night."

Blade took the time of her introduction to fully observe the Hunter who'd managed to appear without warning, to even his senses. Arow had deep brown fur with a rich shine, unshaven and barely scarred despite his age. The male was older than any Hunter he'd met before, including the elders at the council. Though he did not need to, he dipped his head to this deo, and the older male rumbled deep in his chest.

"He'll do. I didn't know they taught such manners that far in the jungle."

Despite the warmth in the older male's tone, Blade stiffened, as Chirruch must. Young, untested in the city, with much to prove to win a place in Whispering Fear, it was exactly the reaction he would be expected to have.

"Just because life is harder for us there, doesn't mean we don't learn equally as deeply as you city-dwellers."

"Well spoken. I like the little claw point of insult in return, most skillfully done. Not too witty or angry, just enough to show me you have teeth." It should have been ridiculous, this older Hunter narrating the balance Blade had struck, but instead it felt like...praise. Indeed, Ichys made a pleased noise deep in her throat, and Blade straightened further, though he couldn't have said if that was his reaction, or what he thought Chirruch would do.

"You didn't think I'd bring just anyone here, did you?" Ichys rubbed against Blade again, then moved away to greet others before Arow could answer.

"Ichys has only sponsored two Hunters before, both females," the deo said, ignoring Ichys's rhetorical question with his dark yellow eyes locked steadily on Blade's. At Blade's obvious surprise, he nodded. Rarely would a female in line for Heir, but not yet confirmed, actively welcome a potential competitor into her clan. Rarer still, to purposefully sponsor her inclusion. It wasn't entirely unheard of, given that the best Damas put the needs of the clan far above their own, but unusual enough to remark upon.

Before either of them could say more, a stirring in the crowd indicated Whispering Fear's Dama. He couldn't imagine this dama modeling Ichys's actions and wondered where the younger female had learned such goodness.

Arow melted away as invisibly as he'd come, and Blade was sure it had nothing to do with quintessence. The old Hunter could have given Flame a competition, and it gave him a momentary pang to consider how much Flame would enjoy someone to push her skills so thoroughly.

Dirrys took her time moving to her elevated bench, accepting greetings and deferential gestures. Blade categorized it as preening, and he could have been much less gracious. He tracked her as she moved through the crowd, or allowed the Hunters to move around her, as Chirruch would be expected to do. He put years of experience erasing his feelings to use, showing only the vital interest of one whose position depends on the dama, rather than one who would like to like to slice her from top to tail and roll in the blood.

"We have a number of new contracts to choose from," she said after taking her due, settling comfortably on the bench and surveying those she had invited. "Opportunities for both our experienced Hunters, and for some potential clan members to prove their value to Whispering Fear. Of course, we can take no joy when other clans falter," her voice was appropriately neutral, though the lazy motion of her tail hinted at unseemly satisfaction, "but all we can do is step into the unfortunate void they leave behind."

Better business for the successful, the implied message echoed, and Blade felt the confirmation of her part in Night Wind's destruction as a blow. Despite the control holding his emotions in check, he curled his fingerpads close against his palm to ensure no hint of claw showed. Attacking her here, now, had only the slightest margin of possible success, and none of clearing his clan. He would be better than her, in all things.

"Our best honor for other Hunters is to succeed wildly and ongoing, to ensure the survival and flourishing of our kind. And so, we grow our clan, by influence and with strong Hunters. And, we may hope, with kits of our own." She did not glance at either of her offspring, but stretched comfortably instead. Blade wondered if she'd actually insulted them, her own kitas, in front of the gathered Hunters, though he knew better than to glance around to study them in answer to his question.

"I have the contracts ready, for you to review and request. Some, of course, I will assign as I see fit, but as ever I will not waste your time including those in the shared files."

That damas could choose who took certain contracts was no secret, but to openly acknowledge her use of power served only to remind the Hunters in the room that she could do so and to engender their interest in what they wouldn't see. Blade did look around then, not needing to see Dirrys's indolent posture to note her smugness. A new arrival had every reason to see how established clan members reacted to the dama's statement, though Blade had other motives.

A small handful of Hunters shifted, showing what could be subtle hints of unease or simply a poorly-settled lunch. Either way, it marked additional beings for him to casually talk with, in order to continue to grow his understanding of the reputation of this particular dama.

His gaze snagged on Ichys, standing at an alert attention rather than resting on her hind legs as was her right. He watched her too long—Dirrys had started talking again, and he'd missed the first words, and then he saw Arow, across the room. The older male watched him watch Ichys, and Blade had to smooth down the fur on his back with a conscious effort.

Neither Ichys nor the old deo would break his focus, he told himself, and tore his attention back toward Dirrys, who paced now, ending a declarative statement about trade. That other species, while perhaps not as deadly as the galactically-feared Depik assassins, could serve as great profit partners to Whispering Fear, if only they had the right Governor.

Blade had left the council with the understanding that Dirrys wanted the Peacemaker contract his dama had taken, but he reconsidered, watching this show. The Governor contract may not have been as immediately lucrative, yet there were sizable perks. For a clan that had grown ancient and fat on both trade and off-world hunts, Whispering Fear could act decisively with the sort of advance picture of trade negotiations and upcoming contracts a Governor had access to.

He had no proof for his actual mission, so the sudden interest in finding out more about what had happened to the former Governor had to be pushed aside. It was tempting though, because of course a dama who had chosen to wipe out an entire clan on the basis of some inconclusive video and no motive would certainly be capable of killing one of their own for gain.

Blade hadn't thought he could think any lower of Dirrys, but in this, at least, he had been mistaken.

The gathering broke apart as soon as Dirrys jumped down from her bench, indicating the formalities, such as they were, had closed. Hunters made noises and gestures indicating they would review the public files in privacy, or that they should like to approach the dama later on one or the other, and began to leave. Ichys slow blinked a smile at him, then turned to leave with her half-sister, Sivand, and Blade took the opportunity to follow two strangers out of the room, both of whom glanced at him and dropped into their quintessence fields.

That gave him all the permission he needed to pull his own field around him, wait until he was fairly sure the hall had cleared, and make his way back to the audience chamber he'd just left. If he kept his distance from the dama, she shouldn't be able to sense him. And while he didn't entirely believe she'd be so foolish as to throw out something incriminating in a place where so many assassins could still invisibly linger, stranger things had happened. Regardless, it gave him the opportunity to see her in action without needing to monitor his own reactions, which allowed him to pay much closer attention.

"None of the contracts are worthy of you, Grissik," Dirrys said, her ears pointed forward and her gaze earnest on the rangy Hunter. "You should reconsider the opportunity to monitor the *Malluma Songo* crop in the southwest. You know we cannot have another failure, and there are few I trust as much as you to ensure profits accumulate in that corner again."

Blade knew it was meant to be inspiring, but he felt his fur lift in disgust. There was a threat there—perhaps Grissik had failed off-world, or had played some part in the spectacular crop failure referenced at the last council. Something in how Dirrys leaned in, or how her tail held perfectly still and straight behind her. Grissik may or may not have read it, but ducked his head and retreated quickly enough that Blade assumed he had.

"Shall I send you off-world again, Arow?" Dirrys asked sweetly as the last of the other Hunters made their way out. Her tail lifted in an idle curve, and she didn't turn to face him.

Arow settled comfortably on all four legs, supremely unconcerned with the tone and bearing of his dama. She finally turned around as his silence outpaced her patience, and he pricked his ears politely toward her and tilted his head.

"No," she purred, sitting back on her hind legs, unconcerned by every measure, "how could I risk you? You've become so grandly aged, and all the young Hunters must have someone to look to. You always were such a good teacher."

The briefest flicker of his flattened ears showed she had scored a hit, though not one Blade could entirely decipher. Arow must be easily thirty, an unusual age for any Hunter, and doubly so for a male, so her reference to his age couldn't have wounded him. Teaching, then, some loss of a student, or she had found a way to keep him from leaving Khatash, and he missed the space between stars.

"Have you chosen one of those new arrivals to train, then? Ichys seems fond of the orange one, though I like how the big gray one from Creeping Fog moves."

"Have you chosen one of the new ones, then, Dama?" Arow asked, solicitous. "The clan always benefits from the new blood of outside Hunters, but of course there is much to be said for having our own kits around."

Her tail dropped from its smug curve, flattening to the floor behind her, and Blade caught just a waft of searing rage from her, quickly stifled. Instead, she lifted a front leg and smoothed the fur over her cheeks, uncaring.

"Such standards you have, Arow, asking others to do something you were never quite capable of yourself. Whispering Fear is lucky I care as deeply as I do, both bearing and raising two surviving kitas and bringing us the most lucrative of contracts."

Despite the calm of her tone, Blade saw the fur ripple down the middle of her back, and how precisely she held her face toward Arow. She was not furious enough to attack the male, but she balanced on a claw tip. Arow's tail twitched once, either acknowledging that fact or daring her to lunge, followed by a half-blink nearly as insulting as grooming himself in front of her.

"Contracts that nearly offset our losses," Arow agreed, dipping his head in something like deference to her. Blade appreciated that Arow hadn't mentioned the loss of the Peacemaker contract, given how likely that would have led to bloodshed, and Blade wasn't sure which way such a battle would have ended.

"Our finances are stronger than they've been in a long while," the dama snapped back, goaded into blurting something, and Blade leaned forward so quickly Arow flicked the barest of glances his way. There was no way the deo could have seen him, but Blade clamped down on his emotions doubly hard all the same. It was equally impossible that Whispering Fear's investments could have offset the loss of the *Malluma Songo* crop and several dropped contracts, never mind the hints he'd heard from Firnt and others about failing deals. Able to recover in time, surely, but stronger than before? Impossible.

Unless the dama was not only holding contracts for certain clan members, but also taking secret contracts herself.

Secret contracts such as attempting to wipe out Night Wind, for instance.

Arow inclined his head again and stood, and Blade cursed his eagerness—despite his quintessence field, Arow must have sensed
something of his movement.

"So you say, Dama, and of course you know best. I'll not keep
you any longer."

Blade held still at every level until both had left, then silently
cursed the whole invisible walk back to his den.

* * *

Flame sprawled dangerously on the floor of her small
cabin. It wasn't proper ship behavior, since any sudden
stop or course correction to avoid an attack would send
her flying into a bulkhead, but they'd been flying through empty
space for what felt like seasons, and it wouldn't end for another double ninenight. Beyond that one joyfully bloody hallway on Capitol,
she'd done nothing but stalk or wait or force herself to patience since
they'd left Khatash.

Fled it. The thought itched in her mind, leaving without knowing
what had come of her siblings, of her Susa. No way to search for
them now, when the best-case scenario—that she'd find them—
meant the potential of calling down the wrong kind of attention on
them…

Yet again she pushed the thought away, shoved herself up to her
feet, and stalked out of her cabin. Tamir was either in the galley or
strapped into the command couch; she bet on the latter and got it in
one.

"Anyone out there?"

"Nothing in sensor range." Tamir rolled her couch around to face Flame, exhaustion clear on her face. Flame wasn't the only one sick of travel. "We've already hopped two gates, without a tail. I don't think they'll find us here, and Briglen isn't top of the list they'd guess for me to run to."

"Because you have higher priority shadowy ship drops?" Flame hopped into the second couch, but didn't reach for the belts. Her ears flicked back, indicating it was a rhetorical question.

"Briglen is just the waypoint. We'll leave the ship there, get to my contact, and he'll get us over to the shipyard. They've moved it a couple of times already, and I don't think a name has stuck yet. I've tried not to pay too much attention, just in case they ever go cross-ways with the Peacemakers."

Flame made a noise, knowing Tamir had explained it already; she still did not especially care much about the details. While they usually consumed her, given how important details were to successfully completing a contract, now each new piece of information that didn't lead to an answer about her dama, what had happened on Capitol, or how her littermates fared, only made her want to scratch through armor while someone inside the armor tried to kill her.

"We can ask my contact what he's heard in the chatter about Governors and Peacemakers, but otherwise all we have is the video, the Cemarap Governor being dodgy on gifts, and Hrusha's ambiguous message to your dama. And that something is definitely going on, if someone is trying to kill us. Did you turn up anything on that knife?"

"I've never wished I hadn't killed someone before." Flame shook her head, ears flattening in distaste. "Not that I regret the killing itself; I'm glad we killed them, but I should have left at least one alive

for a little while so we could question him." It had seemed clever at
the time. Take one of their weapons and trace it back. There must
have been some reason the group had been equipped with only basic
knives, rather than any of a multitude of more effective weapons.

"Nothing on the knife then," Tamir said, "Or the blood?" At
Flame's second headshake, she sighed. "Of course not. Don't kick
yourself too hard. I should have stopped and called in the Peacemaker staff, even if we ran to the ship first and just holed up there."

"Yes, they would have instantly been able to tell us where the attackers came from, given us a motive, and couldn't *possibly* have been
involved."

Tamir blew out her breath hard enough to make a loud noise
with her lip-flapping, and Flame almost smiled. The Human dropped
her head back on the couch and sighed again, most dramatically.

"To pull off an attack on Capitol, someone had to be very
plugged in, or at least know the right people," she said, giving voice
to what they both knew.

"How did they predict our route back to Gerren?" Flame asked,
extending a claw for each point, "How did they hack into the
Peacemaker systems to turn off the lights without anyone noticing?
How did they drop a random Lumar in the middle of a public walk-
way and hope that would work? How did they manage to keep it off
GalNet?"

"All of that makes it risky to reach out to anyone on Capitol. And
you missed a few: who the hell are they? What the hell do they want?
Why are they stupid enough to confirm for us that something was
going on, when we didn't have any real proof of anything?"

"That one's easy—they thought you were alone." Flame considered her extended claws and then waggled them at Tamir. "Not a mistake they'll make again."

"Hrusha said it was rotting from the inside." The Depik Peacemaker hadn't been talking about Capitol, but she'd played it all close to her vest for some reason, so maybe it had included some part of Capitol as well.

"Better we get some distance and figure it out." Sheathing her claws, Flame settled more comfortably into her couch.

They certainly had distance, but had they run themselves directly into a dead end?

"Where do we go once we have the new ship?" Tamir asked as though following her thoughts.

"To talk to the Cemara Governor, if that's all we have. I've looked up everything I could find about her if you want to compare notes."

Tamir laughed, shaking her head, though she ignored Flame's inquiring look as she pulled up her own files. She shared them to the Hunter's slate, put the notes she'd taken on a screen they could both look at, then laughed again.

"Just go talk to the Governor, easy as that. A bounty hunter who sometimes takes contracts for the Peacemakers, and a Depik who doesn't currently exist."

"A Hunter who's gotten in front of harder to reach people than a public Governor," Flame corrected, amused in turn. "At worst I have to leave you behind and get there myself, but as long as you stay out of dark hallways, I think you'll be fine."

"Thank you for saving my life," she said dutifully, though there was an edge of a laugh in her voice. "I suppose that makes us even."

"Even?" Flame sat up, interested.

"Even. I saved you at the den, shooting out that bot. You saved me at the shuttle station. I got you off Khatash. You saved me in that hall."

"Pardon, Human bounty hunter. There was also the Hunter at the door on the suborbital, who would have liked to play with your stringy bits."

"Pardon, fierce Depik Hunter. That Lumar who tried to shoot at us might have gotten you if I hadn't kicked his gun away."

"Oh, was that what happened?" Flame asked innocently. "I thought you tripped."

"I'll give you a half step up from me, then. It seems before this is done we'll have a chance to even our score."

"I've heard worse suggestions." And for the first time, Flame slow blinked a comfortable smile at the Human. It didn't erase the restless urge for answers, but it helped.

* * *

Leaving the Peacemaker ship behind, to be towed or stowed somewhere at a surprisingly fair price, left little impression on either Human or Hunter. The two took their small bags of supplies and boarded the smaller shuttle without a look behind or much care for their surroundings. Briglen was a nothing of a station, seemingly put together with scraps and held together by spit, though it functioned at a higher level than its looks credited.

Flame filed it away as a point of interest, her thoughts focused ahead, weighing branching possibilities of what they should do if Tamir's contact did not have any new information. Del would have found a way to charge ahead, Blade would already have had three solid plans, and Death would know the right thing to do; Flame wished any of them were with her. Watch. Find a way. They had all learned that central lesson from their dama. She had to believe they would all apply it well.

A waste of a thought that changed nothing, she told herself, checking the straps on her bench seat out of habit and glancing across the aisle at Tamir. The woman leaned back against the slight cushion of the wall, eyes closed, ignoring the searching looks of the two other passengers who were trying to figure out if she was traveling with a Depik assassin.

They did not meet Flame's eyes, which was just as well. She'd chosen to drop the quintessence field for this part of the journey, given the practical considerations of the logistics of their travel. The secret was out, at any rate—Flame was a spectacularly-talented assassin, but sudden hand-to-hand fighting had never been her specialty. The release of pent-up aggression and complete surprise had served her well, and it had also blown her cover. She should have paused to take stock of the situation and used weapons that could have pointed to Tamir or any other species, not her own claws. If their attackers had been better prepared, better trained, better armored than half-ready Humans, she and Tamir might have been in trouble.

And why Humans? It continued to snag her thoughts; that question, as neither she nor Tamir determined a motive. What did an attack squad of Humans, potentially with a Lumar backing them up, have to do with a Depik Peacemaker's death? Even if they had offended the Cemarap aide in some manner, why would he send Humans?

Her ears flicked rapidly, dismissing the spiraling round of thoughts. Everything they knew or didn't know just led back in an endless circle, and she wasn't entirely sure how they would press forward. Contracts were often puzzles—learn about the target, make a plan that matched what the client both needed and wanted, and drive toward the clear objective that made the puzzle possible. Flame enjoyed building the puzzle nearly as much as successfully closing a contract. This though…. the objective was clear: prove Reow didn't kill the Peacemaker by figuring out what had really happened. How to go about that, without client or any idea of what actually happened, rapidly formed into a flier's funnel nest of frustration.

At least she was visible, if nameless, out here on the edges of galactic travel. It meant other beings moved out of her way, and it eased some of her restlessness. There was security in her stealth, but what good was security with Reow dead and her clan scattered?

She rooted so deeply in this sucking cycle of thoughts the docking of the shuttle surprised her, and the fact that she'd been unaware enough to be surprised soured her mood further. Flame wandered away from Tamir until the other two passengers had cleared out. If there was a dedicated search for a Human woman traveling with a Depik, that small distraction would hardly throw off detection, but it was enough, especially given the clientele here, to keep it from being an easy lead to find or follow.

She made her way back when a squat, deeply-gray being of an unknown species came into the open docking area and turned its body directly toward Tamir. It didn't look directly at Flame, which she appreciated, and made a waving motion with the three limbs lining its left side to the Human.

"Leeb," Tamir greeted, holding her left arm to the side and doing some sort of kick with her left leg. Flame took a moment to appreciate how comical it looked.

"Tam. Show you your ship." A minimum of small talk. Flame liked that too, which helped push her mood back to center.

They moved through a warren of airlock tubes, and Flame kept her attention on their surroundings, to be sure she could find the way back to the shuttle if needed. Then, realizing the shuttle was likely temporary, she noted that whoever ran this 'shipyard' could just as easily blow an airlock connection if it came down to it. She turned her focus back to their silent guide. It resembled a lumpy boulder more than anything, with a jumpsuit that matched its hide exactly. Three limbs on each side, two longer than the third, thick trunk-legs only barely defined from the overall body.

She opened her mouth to ask what it was when their guide halted, gesturing at the junction directly ahead—sealed airlock door to the left, and a narrower corridor curving off ahead.

"Here," Leeb said. "Ship is here." All the limbs pointed to the airlock. "Food is down there." All limbs shifted to point to the corridor. "You want to go or talk?"

Tamir gestured to the corridor, and they walked in silence for another stretch. The food hall was the first non-airlock tube structure, a large shipping container-looking box with a handful of stalls and a lot of well-spaced seating options.

"Looking for a job?" it asked after they'd each collected food and settled at a table well away from anyone else.

"In one," Tamir replied. "Got something interesting?"

"Here and there. Your job good?"

"Enough." She allowed them all to eat in silence for a minute before leaning forward, suggesting it was time to get to business. "How much attention do you pay to the Governors?"

It made a gesture that Flame was fairly sure meant 'more or less,' and sat quietly, waiting for the point.

"Lot of movement that way, sounds like. Dead, retired, forced to retire."

A complicated shrug at that, indicating Governor turnover was usual. With so many of them, at any given time, some were bound to die or leave or be replaced for reasons both prosaic and scandalous.

"Some of it's been affecting the Peacemakers, too."

Now Leeb looked interested, widening both sets of eyes.

"Both the Depik Governor and Peacemaker died recently. Heard anything there?" Tamir moved away from subtlety, meaning either this being was trustworthy, or she felt the pressing of time against them. No one would be able to track them easily, and this 'shipyard' wasn't high on the galactic radar. Still, they hadn't expected an attack on Capitol either. Flame didn't know which of those motivated Tamir, but either way she respected it. Tamir had been good enough at what she did for long enough that Hrusha had regularly retained her. That and Flame's own observations indicated sound judgement on Tamir's part. And Flame felt that creeping tension down her spine that kept her wariest, so better to get to the point. Unlikely they'd be attacked was not the same as impossible.

"Beings like to talk about Depik," it said, glancing at Flame as if to gauge her reaction. She stared back, unsurprised by such an obvious statement. "But can't say there's been much seems real. Secretive."

"Imagine that, assassins being secretive," Tamir answered, deadpan.

Leeb fluttered some appendages, a gesture that neatly crossed species, and Tamir typed on her wristpad to transfer credits.

"Governor didn't just die. Word is someone tried to shop a contract around on a few Governors, trying to use another merc species. Depik don't take those contracts anyway. Maybe a Depik was one of the targets. Heard the Governor wasn't in bad health. Old, sure, but too healthy for sudden sick to make entire sense. So, like the Peacemaker, yeah? Taken out."

Flame wanted to care about that, given any dead Hunter was a blow to their fertility challenged species, but she didn't. A dead Governor wasn't what they were after, what had happened with the Peacemaker—the realization that it could be connected crashed on her half a heartbeat later. Her ears swiveled, as though searching for a clue to why that realization had not occurred to her sooner.

Someone set up her dama, killing her and the Peacemaker she'd been sent to replace. The Peacemaker about to take on the Governor contract, which had opened…unexpectedly? She hadn't much thought about it at the time, given how far the Governor's concerns were from her own. She paid equally little attention to the council on Khatash—Reow handled all that with Blade, while she'd been more than happy to focus on her off-world contracts and hunting the jungles to improve her skills.

"Got anyone who would speak to that?"

"Just general word." Another complicated shrug. "Depik are interesting, but who wants to get in their business? Best case you learn something, sure, worst case you get their attention."

Flame couldn't argue that, though satisfaction and frustration conflicted on the matter.

"Know who the other Governor targets were?"

"Nah. Zuparti Governor died around the same time, but he'd been sick, and the MinSha and Terling ones rolled off, unsure of status. Maybe something on the Sidar Governor, though that was last session. Heard that's why the Cemara Governor resigned early. Old and lost a lot of friends."

"Cemarap can be sentimental like that," Tamir agreed, finishing off her noodles. "What's the take on the Peacemakers?"

"Business as usual," it said, with another shrug that asked for money. When Tamir just stared, Leeb fluttered some limbs a bit more. "A little more activity, some side deals getting squashed, some action on the Buma and GenSha sides. Any need there?"

Tamir shrugged in turn, visibly losing interest, and Flame judged their conversation about to end. She finished the last of her neatly-cubed meat and yawned, giving Leeb a healthy opportunity to see each of her perfect teeth.

"Those extra credits are a thanks for your discretion," Tamir said as she stood, pulling its attention back from Flame's closing mouth. "Nobody followed us here, and we don't want to be followed from here."

It nodded eagerly, and Flame thought it genuine. A combination of her own presence, Tamir's money, and whatever past experience had made it a contact of Tamir's in the first place, added up to something like loyalty. She didn't put much faith in it keeping its mouth shut, but they should get enough of a head start. This moving ship-yard hardly wanted more attention, and pulling the tail of someone with Peacemaker connections seemed as smart as climbing a poison-sticker vine to avoid the river.

The walk back to their new ship was brief and uneventful, giving no outlet for the tension branching through Flame's body. Tamir glanced at her a few times, but she shook her head tightly, and they went through the pre-flight checklist in relative silence.

What passed for flight control gave them three hours before they could undock, so they took time for a proper tour. The small ship they'd acquired had five separate sections in the middle of its long ovoid. Galley, bridge, two crew quarters, and head. Cargo holds had been built into the edge points, making the ship more efficient by balancing the spin, and holding extra space outside the environmental protection needed for living crew. The records had been transferred to them—which appeared mostly true—showed the ship had been designed for a small family of Cochkala, and the edges of the walls snagged the eye with faint wrongness. Cochkala were solid traders, and understood the importance of doors not sliding shut on tails, but they moved differently from most species, and it showed in their design choices. Flame registered and ignored the oddness, appreciating that Tamir seemed to do the same. Working for the Peacemakers, and as a bounty hunter in general, Tamir had certainly had plenty of opportunities to adapt to or suffer through the occasional weirdness that came from other species' functional and stylistic decisions. Not entirely comfortable, but they would have time ahead to adjust.

They settled their belongings in their small quarters and met in the middle to check provisions in the galley. Though the quiet had held for most of their review, it did not last long into their galley inspection.

"Milk-eyed fool," Flame muttered, tail lashing as she paced, opening storage drawers and checking them against the manifest the ship recorded. The bitterness in her voice indicated her disgust was self-aimed, though the flexing claws still drew Tamir's full attention.

"I thought you revered your elders," she said, deciding to try for a distraction.

It worked, in part. Flame stopped short and stared at her in confusion. Her brightly blue eyes bore into Tamir's brown ones as though to unlock the meaning of the Human's non-sequitur.

"Milky eyes," Tamir repeated, more slowly. "An old Depik, right? Why is that an insult? Because they can't hunt as well?"

Flame chuffed a noise that wasn't quite amusement, but didn't mean imminent violence either.

"Milk eyes." Now it was Flame's turn to sound overly patient, and her tail jerked irregularly. "Babies, not elders. Until they're weaned, kits aren't much more than stomachs and a few sharp edges, and their vision is poor and cloudy through most of it. Milk-eyed means you aren't suited to be on your own outside the den, as something will almost certainly eat your round little self before you see it coming." The pacing picked up again, slower, but still anger fueled. "I can't believe I didn't consider it—the possibility of a connection between the Governor and the Peacemaker."

Tamir sat and stretched her legs, making a point of looking comfortable in the chair and closed out the manifest file.

"I know we're still here," Flame continued, understanding what the Human motion was meant to convey. She had been half-raised by a Human, a fact Tamir took advantage of in the wordless communication. "I know it's not entirely logical for it to bother me, but it makes me worry what else I'm missing. That a Hunter would be behind it, or Hunters, combining with some other species to attack our own…I should have at least considered it."

"Not everything in the universe is connected. This is why we investigate—it's not some obvious point we ignored."

"But it's close *enough* that I want to shred someone's throat and then feed it back to him."

"Some trick." Tamir laughed, though there was little enough humor in it. "There's probably more ahead of us. At least we have a less recognizable transport."

"Less recognizable." Flame spat, looking around the galley that left little room for *her* to pace, never mind a Human more than twice her height. "Less everything. Who do we talk to next?"

"Ideally, we find a way to talk to the Cemarap Governor, given her friendship with both Hrusha and Sissisk. If she's retired, it should be easier getting to her without much notice."

Flame considered it, tapping through her wristpad to see what was publicly known about where the former Governor Kelket had chosen to retire. Surprisingly, GalNet supplied the answer right away. Security didn't seem to be much of a concern for Kelket then, which was good for them.

"Benabat. Cemarap planet, in the middle of nowhere. So, we figure out how to approach the sick retired Cemarap Governor on a backwards planet without anyone seeing us coming. Unless you think that attack at Capitol was some unrelated grudge?"

"They won't be looking for this ship." Tamir didn't bother to address the rhetorical question. "It's small and unremarkable enough to not pick up much chatter as we go, if it's seen."

"Looks like Benabat is relatively poorly traveled. Someone may notice us there, if they're concerned with what happened to Hrusha."

"Cochkala go to the system all the time, picking up new contracts," Tamir pointed out.

Flame weighed it over. "We'll have to damage the comms convincingly, depending on how you want to approach the planet itself, because neither of us can effectively impersonate a Cochkala."

Tamir shrugged, indicating that was the least of their worries. Flame paced for a few minutes more, then finally leapt to the table and settled across from Tamir.

"Is this our best option?"

"We have dead and retiring Governors, two d—missing Peacemakers, incoming and outgoing." Tamir almost flawlessly covered the slip that Hrusha and Reow were much more likely dead than off the interplanetary radar. "Records show three newly retired Peacemakers, two who had been rumored to be retiring, and one that had been sick for some time. A handful of new Governors across planets that go in for naming their new species representative ahead of the session. Your contacts are burned, and I don't have many more who are going to do much of anything that might bring them to a Governor's or Peacemaker's overly concerned attention."

"Then our best option *is* to track down the ailing former Cemarap Governor, who was close with both Depik Governor and Peacemaker, see if she's really dying, and see what she knows. Someone wants us dead. Whoever is behind the last attack, they almost definitely know you have a Hunter with you now, though probably not who."

"That sums it up," Tamir said.

For no reason Flame could have explained, Tamir's tone made her laugh. Her Human partner sounded unflappably calm at the depthless pile of shit into which they'd foundered.

Partner. The word snagged her thoughts, and she sat quietly while she turned it over in her mind. They'd saved each other's lives enough times already that they no longer sniped at each other over it, except to entertain themselves.

It had been easier than she had expected to adjust to another Human. She was different than Susa, but complementary with her Hunter disposition in an entirely other way. Idly, she considered Tamir's possible response to being offered a sigil and being claimed by a clan. By her clan.

She laughed again, and this time Tamir joined her, ruefully shaking her head. The woman stood, ducking her head. Though the ship cleared her height, something about the shape of it made everything feel close.

"Well. We've had more than enough for one day. The course is set, and we've time for research before we get underway."

"Or," Flame replied, her last laugh still wrapped through her voice, "we could practice."

"Practice?"

"I noticed your knife throwing could use some work," she said, dropping her mouth open and slow blinking to show it was a tease.

Tamir took it as Flame meant it, and she chuckled again. "We can't all hit an eye from across a dark hallway."

"On the run," Flame added innocently.

"I thought being a deadly assassin feared across the galaxy was enough for you. I didn't realize you had to brag about it, too."

"Where's the fun in that?"

* * *

"Here's what I know," the sweaty Human shifted for the thirty-seventh time since starting the conversation with Tamir. He pushed back his styled black and yellow hair, making it spike higher, leaned forward, and licked his lips, not saying anything at all.

Flame wanted to kill him and leave him as bait for the waste-eating antjes of her home planet, but he was only partly to blame for her simmering bloodlust. They had made five stops, with Tamir adopting an effective enough disguise, and Flame staying in her quintessence field. That had been enough to check in with some of Tamir's contacts, while ensuring they weren't being followed, and a calculated risk that it'd be few enough stops to minimize word of them oozing out into the galaxy. Comms couldn't be trusted, so their travel stretched longer.

They had seen no evidence of being followed, but they'd also learned absolutely nothing, and while Flame had become hopeful about every darkened hall and sticking door, there were no more teams of attackers waiting for them anywhere. Time dragged, Tamir asked questions, nobody got bloody, and Flame wanted to scream.

"I don't pay for dramatic pauses," Tamir said, and Flame's amusement helped her center away from the building rage.

"Right, yeah, yeah, so what I know. Human mercs are getting good, winning more than they're losing, you know?"

Flame didn't care. There was one Human in the entirety of the universe she loved, who she hadn't seen or smelled in far too long. There was a second Human she had become generally fond of, but the rest seemed like bumbling soft-shelled creatures cutting themselves on all the galaxy's corners. Maybe they'd form into something interesting someday, but if the species' overall skills hovered at the level of the five who'd tried to ambush Tamir in a hallway, Flame figured they still had two or three generations to go before they were worth more than a passing thought.

"Daron, you said you had something good." Tamir didn't react to his overall moistness. Flame wondered if the countless tiny beads of sweat coating his face were too small for her Human eyes, then wondered if she could wring the male Human out like a wet rag and shake him dry again.

"Yeah, yeah. It's just, some of the other mercs, you know, they haven't been nice, passing through. Like to shove us around a little more, show they can outdo us." Flame hadn't heard of anything dramatic happening, so it was probably less 'mercenary species were getting jealous of Humans' and more 'some company members had gotten restless on the station a couple of times.'

Tamir nodded, bored, and Flame could see the bounty hunter had come to the same assessment. Before she could finish off her drink though, Daron shifted and leaned forward again.

"Heard a couple of companies picked up a Depik leader to get them back on top." He said it with the air of one presenting an item of value, but he couldn't bear the risk of leaving it so subtle. "You got interest in those killer kit—"

"Don't be an idiot," Tamir cut over him smoothly, her posture still signaling the impending wrap up of their conversation. "What would assassins want with a merc contract?"

Reluctantly, Flame retracted her claws and turned her eyes from the male's throat. Killing him in public would be messy, especially if she rolled in his guts the way she wanted to, so she studied the bar around them. Dim colored lights and sticky tables seemed to be a deliberate style choice, along with low throbbing music that covered conversation but didn't hinder it. It was fine, for what it was, although it was full of smells just on the edge of souring. Maybe that was just Daron.

This should be their last stop before the former Governor's retirement planet, which meant she would have a break from Humans and their insistence on which Earth creatures Flame's race supposedly resembled. Even Susa had said it was true, to a point, but Flame had never agreed.

"I dunno. They like the company? Don't like other merc species? Just a fact I thought you'd want."

"A fact, or something you heard?"

"Yeah, yeah." He waved a hand, and Flame's attention focused back on him, tracking the idle gesture with an intensity it did not deserve. "'S'all I got on Depik. You wanna know more about Buma? This faction just got a trade agreement locked in with some Zuparti that chatter said was gonna fail and need some mercs, you know?"

"Daron, here's what I need you to find for me. You remember the drop box from before, where I pay you if you leave me something interesting in there?" She waited for his nod, not patient so much as thorough. "I want odds on who's taking the Peacemaker and Governor contracts for the Depik."

He snorted, finally leaning away from her.

"I'm serious. If you find it, let me know. Is that all you have now, some rumor of Depik teaming up with some mercs?"

"Yes," he sulked, shifting for the forty-second time.

Tamir's disappointed sigh set him moving on his chair again, and Flame seriously considered rupturing his spine so that he'd stop moving entirely. Or maybe flop entertainingly to the ground. To distract herself, she mentally pictured each of the Human vertebrae and assessed whether clawing it out would paralyze, kill, or lightly damage the overall body. She wondered what Tamir's coping mechanism was, though it couldn't be as fun as her own.

"You want odds on the other Governor and Peacemaker replacements?" Daron tried to hide his eagerness, only succeeding in small part. "You know there's at least five up for it, or about to be, and ten more we got numbers on, off chance."

Halfway through the thoracic region, Flame paused and turned her delighted, if invisible, gaze to Tamir. This explained why they'd come to talk to the greasy nobody in the corner of the Peco arm, and where Tamir had been guiding the conversation. Clever Human.

"Impress me," Tamir drawled, and the sweaty Human took out a different pad, unfolding the screen flat to press onto the table between them.

Flame sighed internally—she probably wouldn't get to kill anyone at all, this time.

* * *

"That went smoothly," Tamir said as they approached the Cemara planet Kelket had chosen for her retirement.

"Success is mostly preparedness," Flame said, moving her couch in lazy half-circles. "It's what caution is good for; it makes you take care on the front end."

"Care." Tamir turned enough to show her half-smile as Flame rotated. "Is that what you showed by wanting to murder each of my contacts over this last month?"

"They're all alive." Flame gestured with both a limb and her tail, dismissing the tease with a flash of humor. "And since most of them were a waste of our time, yes, remarkable self-discipline. You're welcome."

"Got it. The keys to assassinations are preparedness, caution to take care, not murdering everyone even if they deserve it for being boring, and...?"

"Execution."

Tamir turned to look at her fully, trying to gauge if that had been a deliberate joke. Flame held still for a long moment, then flicked ears and tail, dropping her jaw in a grin, and Tamir laughed.

"Fair enough," she managed after a minute, still rather breathless from the laugh. "I'm sorry there's been a lack of killing since Capitol."

"The hunt can be almost as satisfying," Flame said, tail flicking. "This part of our travel is likeliest to lead to whomever ordered the attack on us, so I took care to modify the drive. You took care to damage the comms, so no one will expect video packets from us, and static and voice boxes will keep us unidentifiable until landing. If someone pays overmuch attention to a small Cochkala transport, in this corner of the galaxy, I will eat an entire Oogar."

"After this, I should go into business as an assassin and put all my learning to use."

"Yes, you know enough to be a kit let *just* outside the den." Flame twisted her ears around again, the slow-blink turning the gesture into a fond tease. "Why leave all this glorious bounty hunting behind?"

"I have to do a lot of what you do, but I have to keep the target alive."

"Easier, wouldn't you say?"

"They *do* tend to do a lot of talking."

"And few are as entertaining as I am, right? Thank you, Tamir Alcuin. Your compliments truly make me feel appreciated."

"People will be so disappointed to know that Depik think they're funny," she answered, followed with a noise somewhere between a laugh and a snort. "Ruin that mystique of yours."

Benabat's flight control was brisk and efficient, registering their course of approach with little correction, given the relative lack of traffic. In keeping with their cover, they sent out a handful of written queries to pinpeck farmers and two traders, and a similar one to Kelket. She owned a fair number of the fruit farms, and their added reference to her old friend Diaden might increase the chance she'd reply to them.

"We realize our course and planetary heading lands us some time before local dawn," Tamir said, pitching her voice low even though the computer did the work of making her words sound like a Cochkala's voice box delivery. "This is not my or my trade partner's first visit to Benabat airspace, so please know we do not expect nor need anyone to welcome us."

"Very well, *Dimintina*. We will hand you over to local ground control, who will confirm your landing. Good trading."

"Confirmed, flight. Profits to you and yours." Tamir leaned back and stretched.

"Is that a Cemara saying, or a Cochkala one?" Flame asked, belting in more securely ahead of the maneuvering needed for a planetary landing.

"Neither, far as I know. But you know these smaller transports, always eager to leave a good impression."

"Is that what that is," Flame murmured, repeating in a much higher voice. "Profits to you and yours."

Tamir showed impressive self-control for most species, especially Humans, by utterly ignoring her, studying the automated systems as though they had something important to say to her.

Unfortunately for her, ignoring Flame only made her more entertained. They entered Benabat's upper atmosphere to the Hunter's singsong soliloquy about profits.

* * *

"It's possible that we're going to be ambushed on the ground, or that this is a dead end," Tamir said, arms crossed as they waited for the pressurization cycle to finish.

"Is there a possibility in which we are ambushed, and it's a dead end?"

"I think I liked it better when you were invisible and silent for days at a time." Tamir smiled as she said it, expression brightening when Flame splayed her claws in answer. "Hey, I listened to you make jokes about trading for three hours; you deserved that."

"Happy to oblige," Flame said with a sniff, pulling up her quintessence field.

"Oh shit," Tamir said, hunching protectively. "I was *joking*, Flame. Don't you dare—AAAH!"

Flame, perched invisibly on Tamir's shoulder, made a throaty noise of inquiry.

"I hope you get to kill someone on this planet," the Human muttered, flailing an arm but knowing better than to grab for the Hunter currently using her as a seat. "You have entirely too much energy you need to expel."

"I've been telling you that for ninenights," Flame answered, leaping down and releasing her field at the same moment so that she flickered into existence midair.

"Maybe the Governor will call security on us. You said you've never fought a Cemara?"

"I said," Flame replied with overdone patience, "I've never *killed* one before. I don't go around fighting as some sort of habit."

"No, brawls aren't really your style. Too bad—they can be fun."

Flame didn't see how that was possible, fighting with strangers you had to be careful not to kill. She'd adored wrestling with her littermates when she was young and play-stalking Susa, but brawls seemed too serious for play and not nearly serious enough for slaughter, which seemed dissatisfying on every level. Besides, just fighting, where she was visible, and there were rules, was hardly her strength. She had too many strengths not to cater to them.

The ship made an off-key series of beeps signaling an allowable pressure match, the noise sharp enough to briefly flatten Flame's ears, and make Tamir shake her head. The ship wasn't built for their hearing, and it was too much trouble to change.

They stepped into the briny night air, a susurrus of insectopods and the clicks of cooling metal welcoming them to Benabat. Proper etiquette was to either stay on the ship until trading opened for the day or to leave and seek on-world dens to ingratiate themselves with the locals. Anyone observing the ship would not be surprised to see it open, or for a single figure to step out and make the trip to town.

They may have been surprised to see a Human rather than a Cochkala moving away from the ship, but humanity was popping up all over these days, why not as a scout for a Cochkala trading group? Flame, her field pulled tight, amused herself by considering how that lack of surprise would move straight into shock, were the hypothetical observer to know a Hunter had left the ship as well, slipping into the automated transport behind Tamir, prowling the otherwise empty cart as it took them from landing grounds to town. Tamir stepped off when the transport arrived, glanced around the transfer point to familiarize herself for the next day, and Flame leapt out, stretching in anticipation of the hunt ahead.

The town itself was of little interest, set up primarily for Cemara to host deals for non-amphibious species. This part of the planet had more ponds and swamps for relaxation and rejuvenation, and they'd been able to confirm former Governor Kelket had retired to her fourth home here for the latter.

It was even odds she would respond to their pinpeck inquiry, so, to maximize their chances, Flame was to scout her security and get inside if possible—former Governors had a sliding scale of protection, depending on individual, species, and personal wealth which might make that difficult—and decide whether to leave a note, find Kelket's personal contact code, or have a spontaneous conversation.

Tamir was against the last option, but Flame kept it tucked in her vest, just in case. Sometimes efficiency won out, and recordings existed, so Tamir could still hear the same things she did. Granted, Tamir had mentioned three separate times that such an endeavor might end with Flame carving the retired Governor into bite-sized souvenirs out of frustration, but Flame was sure the Governor would know something and be savvy enough not to enrage her—the Cemara had been friends with other Hunters, after all.

Flame could have finagled transport, but Kelket's retirement ponds weren't far from the town, and after so long on ships and stations, moving in real gravity across real terrain made for an invigorating change. The thick air was saltier than Khatash's humid jungles, and this region's trees were short, spindly things compared to the endless stretches of her home. But for the moment at least, she would enjoy feeling the give of road and twining scents of more than bodies.

After the thrill of the unbound run, Kelket's security was a complete disappointment. Automated, with only two Cemara guards. Not even other species to make her work across various senses and strengths. She sighed, sulking a bit through the routine of splicing wires to make a gap, climbing the gate, invisibly parading past both guards—after following each of them on a round to see if there were any surprises—and jumping from each wall irregularity to the next to reach the roof. She paused for the view, distracting herself from her disapproval of how easy it had been. Tamir would be relieved, but Flame itched for a challenge, and this barely-secure compound obviously refused to provide one. The surroundings were nice, at least.

Benabat had three moons, one close enough to reflect a fair amount of light, one halfway to escaping its planet's pull and hurtling off into nothingness, and a third which left a faint crescent tear to the west of the other two. Each was a subtly different shade of gray. The orbiting station sparkled, and the occasional trail of a ship's drive closing in or breaking away was soothing in its way.

Closer to her, this part of Benabat stretched relatively flat, with curling trees dotting the landscape between the glittering purple-blue of the ponds and purple-green of the marshes that claimed more space than did the dirt. Mostly solid land served to connect pond to pond, or emerge from a marshy canal before being swallowed by another expanse of water. The Cemara home planet had been similar once, more wet than dry, but civilization brought changes to them all, and the Cemara had the profits to find a backup planet when their own had been wrung too dry.

In her immediate area, the roof angled and swooped in fanciful shapes. Walled off in the center of the marsh, a bright indigo pond stood slightly elevated from the darker water, with tree-high columns draped in gauzy covering. Dim lights studded the water and land mixed beyond the roof, allowing a line of sight for the guards without disrupting the night. The air carried the loamy scent of wet earth, with a sharp plant-like seasoning. The salt of the marsh and the bright copper of the pond mixed together in the moist breeze, and at least two different creatures had perched on this roof ahead of her this evening. A pleasant, if humid mix, and she closed her eyes for a moment to lean into the wind. Nothing that she could hear moved nearby, and she opened her eyes.

Flame hoped the Governor had retired inside the building, which would provide more challenge to get into than the pond, but she had a suspicion the Cemarap would sleep floating in her retirement pond. Why else go to the trouble of having an elevated, purified pond in the first place?

She made her way off the roof in much the same way she'd reached it, admiring the shine of the polished stone docking that transitioned the structure to the marsh. Invisibility wouldn't keep her from disturbing the water, so she stalked up and down the edge to determine the best path, finding a path of cleverly set rocks adjusted to just brush the top of the water. Invisible in their own way, which she could appreciate.

The sun hadn't yet lightened the horizon, so she took her time, moving on all fours and placing each paw perfectly to minimize disturbance. She was pleased to see the wall around the pond had another layer of protection, the faintest thrum of electronics telling her sensors had been placed all throughout. Weight, heat, life signs, no way to tell which from the noise of it, so she paused on the last stone of the path. Directly in front of her, the rounded wall was seamed, indicating it opened in waking hours. Given the marsh had its own creatures, it seemed unlikely there would be sensors in the swampy ground, so she went into the water after all, circling slowly around the raised pond. The wall had been built too high for her to see inside easily, but the brightness of Cemara scent told her Kelket was sleeping inside. Or she let other Cemara float in her pond, which was possible.

She could slip back to the house and prowl inside there, but that wouldn't leave her much time to come back out and break through if needed, so she committed to circumventing the sensors. It provided some amusement, finding the power source, splicing in to program a skip, and then timing her leap with the guttering of power.

Old standards remained for this long because they were so often successful. She paused at the top of the wall, looking for a solid surface to jump to rather than dropping into the water and potentially landing on governor-cytoplasm. There was mostly open water below her, with a small path across the way where the wall opened. Flame bolted, counting down the quarter seconds before the sensors locked back in. She was still short as the time dropped, so she bunched up for speed and threw herself into a long, low leap.

Three feet landed solidly on the landing, one just glancing the top of the water. The light splash was swallowed in the ambient noise of the night, but enough to hold her still for long moments to listen. No alarms built into the landing, which was short-sighted but on par with the light security in place. The water rippled behind her, receding from the long shape of a Cemara floating to the surface, cilia languid but moving.

Interested, Flame turned to watch, leaning closer. That slight disturbance of her trailing leg had been enough to rouse the Governor, though she didn't seem particularly alert or alarmed. Leaning back into a comfortable sit, Flame watched the cilia snake around, testing the area. Though tempted to bat the water and set them waving again, the Hunter watched until they slowed to bare motion, then sank under the water with the wider bulk of Kelket's body.

Tamir had better be grateful she restrained herself, she thought. It would have been so easy to strike up a casual conversation.

The Governor might not have found it so casual, given it would have meant yanking her the rest of the way out of her sleep cycle, but that would have been amusing, too. Waiting was the sensible, but disappointing, choice. She pushed away the resulting resignation and twisted around to open her bag. Flame pulled out the thin film that would become a temporary screen. She considered for a moment, composed a note, and sent it from her wristpad to the film. When the sensors' hum faded again, she pressed the film to the wall and stepped back to gauge the level. This should catch Kelket's visual spectrum when she woke up in the morning, though Flame rather wished she could make it blink or glow.

Highly motivated pinpeck buyer. Peacemaker compliments. Please return message at earliest ability.

Straightforward, related back to their innocuous query sent before they'd landed, and its appearance should cause enough upset that the Governor acted sooner rather than later.

And if not, well, Flame could just come back in again, and Tamir would have to miss out on the conversation. Worse things could happen.

* * *

Their comm rang out a series of notes, calling their attention to a live connection request rather than a delivered message, and Flame toasted Tamir with the remains of her breakfast.

"What do I win?" Tamir asked, accepting the connection as voice only. They'd wagered on the timing for the Governor's contact, and Tamir had it almost to the minute. *"Dimintina here."*

"This is Kelket, *Dimintina.*"

Flame pricked her ears forward, impressed. She'd expected an aide, not the former Governor herself to call.

"Governor Kelket," Tamir said, warming her tone significantly. "What an unexpected joy, receiving your attention so early in the day."

"Retired, *Dimintina.* Just a humble pinpeck trader now." The voice box Cemara used translated cilia motion and slight color changes to convey tone, and though nuance was still lost, the former Governor's tone sounded dry enough to empty her private marsh.

"And why we are so very honored to talk with you. Our business is of a highly profitable nature, Trader Kelket, and we should greatly value the ability to speak with you directly." Tamir's voice had never sounded so bright or cheery, and Flame tilted her head, observing this fascinating shift in her partner.

"You *have* come all this way." Wry now, and Flame thought she might like the former Governor, at least a little. "I'll send over directions and make time for an hour from now. Do you think you can find your way?"

Flame's chuff of amusement was too low for the comms to pick up, but Tamir shot her a look anyway. She rotated her ears toward the Human, all innocence, and jumped down from her chair to get ready.

"I'm sure your directions will be clear and easy to follow, Trader Kelket. Thank you so much, and we look so forward to seeing you shortly."

"Very well." The comm system beeped for the ended connection, and Tamir scrolled for a moment until the packet with directions arrived.

"She seems fun," Tamir said, standing and picking up her bag to drape over her midsection. "How do you think she'll take a Human arrival when she expected a Cochkala?"

"She didn't ask for any identification beyond the ship's name," Flame answered with a shrug before disappearing into her field. "Maybe she won't even notice."

* * *

She noticed. The Governor's cilia fluttered, a faint pink tinging through her upper region, though both eased after a moment. To her credit, Tamir showed an equal measure of surprise at being greeted by the Governor herself, rather than one of her aides.

"Welcome," Kelket said, scooting back from the gate. "Please come inside."

Flame paced between Human and Cemara, not needing to range ahead or lag behind because she'd already explored and could instead focus her curiosity toward where the Governor would take them.

Cemara could move across solid ground, but as benefited her age and ailing health, Kelket rode on a small wheeled platform that cupped her rounded form and kept her moving at a fast Human-walk pace. Multiple locks clicked behind the arched door as they neared it at the end of the path, and Flame gave herself a moment to mourn not taking the opportunity to sneak inside.

The interior of Kelket's dry dock consisted of an open room with a soaring, angled ceiling and a wall of windows looking out to the marsh across the way. Last night, the windows had been covered with stone indistinguishable from the rest of the structure. Flame cocked her head, surprised she'd missed it. Security overall was still lax, but it had some interesting wrinkles she'd missed. Marks for creativity.

Kelket turned them to the left, where the curve of the building took them to another multi-lock door. The room inside was bright, though windowless, comfortably full of various loungers for equally varied species. Around them, the air held an odd emptiness, missing something Flame couldn't identify. She turned her head at different angles, unsure what she was listening for, and stayed close to Tamir only with effort. She would have much preferred to paw at the walls and furnishings, and figure out what was missing around them.

"This is my private study," Kelket said, with a complicated wave of her right-side cilia that cycled the door closed behind them. "Recordings don't work, so you can be assured of privacy, though I'm afraid you will not be able to record your own notes, either."

Dampeners then, Flame realized, of a quality she'd never experienced—it flattened the flow of air around them. Governors handled sensitive business, certainly, but it piqued her interest all the same.

"I appreciate your—"

"Please, sit." Kelket leaned forward, waving her top cilia, and as soon as Tamir's bottom touched her chosen chair, she added, "How did you get into my pond?"

"I worked for Peacemaker Hrusha," Tamir said instead of answering the question. "I have questions that I didn't trust to messaging, no matter how well encrypted."

"Ah." Kelket sat back, cilia slowing to a gentle wave. "You're Tamir Alcuin. Diaden told me you were helping with the investigation."

"I hadn't realized you had retired, at the time."

"It's not a swift process, stepping down off-cycle. Concerns about my health helped move it forward, but I didn't want the investigation into my friend's death held up by my transition, so I waited to announce. Rather too late for some, I suppose. Diaden said you left suddenly."

"Cemara are not the only species who think Humans are abrupt." Tamir filled her voice with deference, and Flame thought it was working; Kelket appeared to accept the non-excuse. "Did he come to any conclusions?"

"Regrettably, it turned out to be exactly as it appeared. I thought I had grown to understand the Depik rather well, as well as one can from outside their kind, but I confess I still can't imagine a motive for Hrusha's successor to kill her."

"Did you know her successor?" Tamir asked. "Reow, yes?"

"No—outside of Peacemaker and Governor, I have yet to find a Depik who cultivates many relationships off of Khatash. She was relatively young; I remember Hrusha mentioning that. Liked Humans, maybe had one for a pet?"

Tamir stiffened slightly, and Flame resisted brushing against her in reassurance. Susa was hardly a pet in the way Kelket implied, and Flame wished she was here in this room to discuss her status as a sigiled member of the clan.

"Perhaps that's why Peacemaker Hrusha looked forward to Reow taking on the contract, given the Humans she employed?"

Kelket flapped her cilia forward and back in a shrug, offering no opinion on it either way.

"You were very good friends with Hrusha, Governor Kelket, from what I understand. How did that come about?"

"The investigation is closed, Tamir Alcuin. What purpose, or whose purpose, are you serving here?"

"As I'm sure you know, Governor, I worked for Hrusha for nearly my entire time with the Peacemaker's office. My last charge is a report to provide to her replacement, whoever that might be, which will be my case for continued employment. Even though you are now retired, you will be a potential great resource to the incoming Depik Peacemaker, and I thought, given your relationship with Hrusha, you would want to ensure a strong start for her replacement."

"Loyalty," Kelket mused, a slight purple tinging her body, her tone indicating she found Tamir adorable. "Very well. Hrusha had a fondness for pinpecks, which I believe she developed through her relationship with my old friend Sissisk, the Depik Governor. Oh, former I must say of her too. Still getting used to that. I provided Sissisk with pinpecks from my favorite farm, and met Hrusha through her."

"Did you have much in common?" Tamir sounded genuinely interested, as though it were a spontaneous and not purposeful question. Flame doubted Kelket would be fooled—the thought that Hrusha would have such an easily distracted bounty hunter on staff was laughable—but it served to continue building rapport.

"You don't see the connection between a Cemarap and a Depik?" Kelket's voicebox issued a laugh, her cilia rippling. "We tend to love games and winning them. It's not only mercenary species who compete." Her tone might as well have added 'little Human,' and Tamir stiffened again.

"Games?" she asked, forcing herself to loosen at the joints again. Flame admired her self-control, but wished it weren't so visible.

"Oh, yes, we wagered on everything. Projecting the profits on pinpecks, mercenary companies, and bounty hunter contracts. When our colleagues would retire or be called home." All her cilia drooped. "That one seems less fun now."

"Who won?"

"Here and there, we both did. What Depik would continue to play if it were always easy wins? I did much better on the pinpecks of course—shamelessly using my inside knowledge. I used to win almost half the time on the bounty hunters, but I don't think Hrusha paid much attention to most of them. Mercenary contracts—those I could never win against her. She liked you Humans, but usually bet against their companies, except when they won out on a big contract.

How she got so good at that, I'll just never know." A long pause. "Oh, and isn't that truer than it ever was."

"I am sorry to make you miss your friend, Governor."

Kelket dismissed it with a long wave of cilia, leaning back as though growing tired.

"Just a few more questions, I know you need your rest. Did you spend much time with Peacemaker Hrusha, near the—more recently?"

"Not as much. My health was already failing, and I didn't travel as much. She mentioned Sissisk was considering retiring, and so I spent more time with her, given my own looming transition. Sissisk never mentioned it, of course, but I showered her with pinpecks all the same."

"So kind of you, Governor," Tamir murmured, inclining her head. "When did you last see the Peacemaker?"

"I'm sure you have the exact date from your work with Diaden, bounty hunter."

"Of course, Governor. What I really want to know is, how was she? Did she seem glad Reow would be taking over for her? Concerned? What did you do? You saw her more recently than I did, so I suppose I'm mostly curious."

"She looked forward to the transition, though I know she would have preferred it otherwise, without our losing Sissisk. I hadn't expected to see her, and I will regret until my last day that I didn't have a gift for her."

"Oh?" Tamir leaned forward, a perfect example of Human surprise.

"A trade deal across seventeen civilizations was teetering, and my ship detoured to Capitol so I could fetch several involved parties. I wasn't going to step off the ship, but circumstances and..." Kelket trailed off, cilia fading to stillness, then sat back up abruptly. "Apologies, Tamir Alcuin. I woke with such a start this dawn, given the unexpected message. I will need to rest soon. Where were we?"

"Governor Kelket," Flame said, dropping her field on a whim and taking a moment to enjoy how immediately every one of the Cemarap's cilia snapped to attention. Shock and alarm made for quite the rejuvenation, no matter what wasting illness someone had. "I did not want to interrupt your conversation with Tamir, but as I caused your upset this morning, it seemed prudent to take that worry from you. How did you find Peacemaker Hrusha on your last visit with her?"

"I know you Depik value your privacy, but given your presence in my home last night and this morning, what is your name and clan?"

"No," Flame replied, quite politely. "In honor of your friendship with Hrusha and Sissisk, please know their interests are of great import to me."

The retired Governor showed no hint of her illness now, observing Flame so closely the Hunter almost wished she'd thought to disguise herself. But no matter how close to Depik Governor and Peacemaker she'd been, the Cemarap would have no reason to recognize the youngest Hunter of Night Wind. Tamir didn't look at her, but Flame could feel the Human's tension ratchet up every notch.

"She did not have much time, organizing both her move to Capitol proper and needing to ensure all was in order for her replacement. I admit I tried to dodge her, because I had no gift, but as I'm sure you know, Depik will always have their way, and she wanted to celebrate her latest win on our mercenary contract wager. We met for absorption—a drink for her, of course—at that corner place on the Capitol station, and all was normal, if rushed. I wish I had more to share, given your efforts to reach me."

"Is there anyone else you recommend we talk to, to best prepare the next Depik Peacemaker?" Flame asked, tail curling around her haunches. "Given the turnover on both long-term contracts, it's best we be thorough."

"Hrusha spent a great deal of time visiting a Tortantula company on Ziv Station. I would have thought she had invested in them, if Depik ever did such things. Talk with Chok, her partner is...Fisi. I believe they were friendly enough with Hrusha to keep from excreting in shock if a Depik appeared in front of him."

"Thank you for your time, Governor," Tamir said, standing. Flame did not have to turn her head to feel her partner's tension. "We wish you the best of health ahead."

Kelket's cilia splayed in several directions, then repeated an earlier gesture. As the door began to unlock, she wheeled ahead of them toward the opening doorway.

"Unfortunately, I am in a decline that ends in only one way, Tamir Alcuin, but I hope that your travels lead to great success for the next to hold the Depik contract. The Peacemaker's office has been glad to have you."

"As much as they notice a single bounty hunter," Tamir replied, so humble Flame nearly spit for the falseness of it. "Thank you again, Governor."

Flame disappeared before stepping outside the room. No need to leave an image, in case any other Hunter had the inclination and opportunity to access Kelket's records. She didn't regret showing herself, but she recognized it hadn't been the smartest thing she'd done so far. No need to compound it into an actual error.

* * *

They had talked in transit, and so had something of a plan.

Susa entered the office, and a young woman with almond-shaped eyes smiled up at her from behind a desk to the right of the entrance. A square of sunlight fell in through a window high in the left wall, beneath which sat a row of chairs. A single door stood opposite.

"Hello," the woman said. "May I help you?"

"My name is Dr. Susan Aloh," Susa said. "I have an offer of contract for The Golden Horde."

The woman behind the desk blinked, but showed no other form of surprise. Death admired her composure.

"I see," she said. "Please have a seat, Dr. Aloh. I will inform my supervisor you are here. May I offer you something to drink? Some water?"

"Thank you, yes," Susa said with a nod, and then took Death and sat below the window. The woman behind the desk smoothed her long, dark hair back from her face and tucked it behind one ear, and Death saw a metallic glint in the light as she stood to get the water.

"Interesting," she murmured, just barely loud enough for Susa to hear. "She has pinplants."

Susa shifted in her seat, her body language suggesting she'd seen it too. The neural implants that allowed a being to link directly in to the local information network, or even the full GalNet, were commonplace among Hunters. They allowed one to extend quintessential control to one's machinery, as she'd done with her Basreeni fighter. Not every Hunter had them, but many did, and it wasn't unusual to see them scattered throughout the other species one met in the galaxy.

But for a species so newly discovered and primitive as humanity? Well...that *was* rather unusual.

The door opened, and a man emerged from the hallway beyond. He looked completely unremarkable. Medium height, medium build, coloring a sort of midrange dusky blond or light brown. Death felt a twinge of appreciation. This man obviously knew how not to be noticed.

"Mr. Conason will see you now," the receptionist said, holding out a glass of water with a smile. Susa took the glass, picked up Death's carrier, and came to her feet.

"Dr. Aloh?" the man asked with a pleasant smile. "My name is James Conason. Would you please come with me?"

"Of course," Susa said.

"Katie here can keep your pet, if you like," Conason said, still in that pleasant tone.

"She is my companion, and it is necessary I keep her with me," Susa said.

"Ahhh...Okay. Is she, like, for emotional support or something?"

"Something like that."

"Well, bring her back, I guess. I don't think any of my guys are allergic to cats."

"I doubt she will be a problem in that respect," Susa said, and Death could hear the glint of humor underneath her words. Conason glanced at her sharply, but didn't say anything else as they walked down a short hallway and turned left into a small office. It, too, was lit only by a window high in the wall. Conason reached for a switch near the entrance, but Susa stopped him.

"If you don't mind, sir," she said. "Could you leave the lights off? I find I'm sensitive to light these days."

A wave of love surged through Death at her thoughtfulness. The sunlight on this planet *was* punishing, and in her guise as a domesticated animal, Death could hardly wear the goggles she would normally use when forced to be diurnal. The dark, fine mesh of the carrier helped some, but Death still found herself looking out through squinted lids, and her eyes ached with the brightness that stabbed into her brain.

"Of course, Doctor," the man said. "I apologize. What did you say your name was, again?"

"Doctor Susan Aloh, former professor of Xenobiology at the University of Texas," she said with a smile as she took the seat he indicated with a gesture. She paused for a moment while he seated himself behind a large, imposing desk, then added, "But you knew that already."

"I did," he said. "But I confess, I'm a bit confused."

"Oh?" she asked. "And why is that?"

"Because every record I can find says that Dr. Aloh died nearly ten years ago."

"Died? Or disappeared?"

"Excuse me?" Conason blinked. Death smirked, interpreting his reaction as surprise. Clever Susa.

"Do the records say I died? Or that I disappeared?"

"I believe both terms are used."

"Ah. Well. I did not die, as you will see when you analyze the fingerprints I've left on this glass," she said. She raised the glass to her lips and took a long sip, and then leaned forward to place the glass on the glossy top of his desk. Conason looked at it and then back at her. "I'm also willing to submit hair or blood for analysis if you would like, though I am working under a compressed timeline and would prefer you take me at my word for reasons which will become rapidly apparent. I am, of course, happy to compensate you for the consideration."

Susa removed a five-credit chit from the inside of her jacket and laid it down on the desk next to the glass with a *click*. Conason's eyes flicked down to the chit, and then back up to her face. He didn't move, otherwise.

"You didn't die, but you *did* disappear?" he asked slowly, suspicion in his tone. Susa let out a sigh.

"Yes. Do your records mention I was a member of Dr. Adelaide Black's expedition?"

"They do."

"Yes. Well, I was. Until I became addicted to an alien substance known as *Malluma Songo*. Have you heard of it, Mr. Conason?"

He nodded, his lips tight.

"Most do not survive, I am told. I did, though only through a series of strange happenstances. Are you familiar with the origin of the drug? The *Songo*?"

"No," he said. He began to tap his fingers in a short tattoo against the top of the desk. Susa, however, refused to be hurried.

"It comes from a planet known as Khatash, out in the Centaur region of the Jesc arm. Khatash is notable for only two exports, Mr.

Conason. *Malluma Songo*, and death. Khatash, you see, is the home world of the felinoid race known as the Depik."

"Dr. Aloh, I am not a child to be frightened by nursery tales of killer kitties," Conason said with a snort. "The Depik don't exist except in tales told to frighten rookie mercs."

Susa only smiled, and released the catch on Death's carrier. Death padded out on four feet, and then somersaulted to the desk, feeling a surge of dark humor at Susa's dramatic timing. She landed on her back two feet and stood, so as to better look Conason in the eyes. The Human mercenary sat back in his seat, eyes carefully blank as the "emotional support animal" turned out to be something very different.

"I, Death From Above of the Night Wind Clan, greet you, Human James Conason of the Golden Horde Mercenary Company," Death said in the Human tongue, reaching out her right paw in a mimicry of Human greeting customs. "Welcome to our negotiation."

* * *

Conason looked at Death for a long moment, his nondescript eyes flicking from her face to her outstretched paw. He glanced at Susa once more, and then leaned forward to place his hand under Death's fingerpads.

"A pleasure to meet you, Death From Above," he said. Death admired his bland nonchalance. She imagined he was working pretty hard for it. "Is that what this is? A negotiation?"

"Aren't all interactions between thinking beings?" Death asked. She tapped his hand once and then let her own hand drop as she settled into a sitting position on the desk. "Even if one is a mythical 'killer kitty.'"

"Perhaps especially then," Conason said. "I meant no offense. Your kind are not well known, and what we do hear is...legend. Rumor."

"I took no offense," Death said. "That is as it should be. As we designed it to be. One has a reputation to maintain, after all. It is easier if the reputation somewhat maintains itself."

"Circular, but logical, in a way," he conceded with a slight nod.

"It is, however, *your* reputation that brings us here today," Death said smoothly. "The Golden Horde is known throughout the Galaxy as an up-and-coming expert in the art of defense. Is your reputation deserved?"

"And then some," Conason said, without a trace of boastfulness in his tone. "But if you're looking to contract with us, this is not the usual way of going about it. We bid our contracts fairly and openly in the merc pits, per Guild customs."

"Yes, well, there are extenuating circumstances that make it impossible for us to operate through a standard Mercenary Guild pit," Death said. "Which is why we've come to you here, now."

"The Golden Horde is not looking to cross guild law. If you've gotten yourself on the bad side of the Merc Guild, I don't think we can help you."

"The Mercenary Guild has no quarrel with me," Death said. "I simply require a private contract. My quarrel is with my own people. You have characterized us as 'killer kitties,' and that is not entirely untrue. We are Hunters. We accept any prey, save our own people. Our lives alone are sacrosanct."

"So why are your people trying to kill you, then?" he asked, his eyes narrowing with interest.

"Because they think I, or a member of my family, killed another Hunter. They have placed my entire family under interdict, and all of our lives are forfeit if we are found."

"Did they do it?"

"Did who do what?"

"Did the member of your family kill another Hunter?"

Death drew in a deep, sharp breath. Betrayal pierced her chest anew. Mhrand hadn't asked that question, and yet this stranger on the other side of the galaxy did.

"No," she said, and it was nearly a whisper. "But I cannot prove that. Not yet. I need time, and safety to..."

"To do what?" Conason asked, as Death trailed off. Death turned and looked at Susa, suddenly unsure if she should confide all the details of her condition to this unremarkable, unassuming figure of a Human. Susa gave her a long look, and then a very slight nod. Death sighed and turned back to look Conason in the eyes.

"To give birth, Mr. Conason. I am carrying a litter of kits, and it is imperative that as many of them as possible survive."

Something that may have been confusion creased Conason's brow. Susa must have seen it, for she leaned forward to stroke Death comfortingly as she spoke.

"Mr. Conason, the Hunters, or Depik as you know them, are not like humanity. As a species, they are blessed with many natural gifts, but they are not prolific. The species has a staggeringly high rate of infertility among adult females, and those who do conceive often do not survive the birth process. Infant mortality, too, is disproportionately high among the Depik. In a very real way, the entirety of their society has been built around protecting the bearing mother, and giving her kittens the best chance at life possible. But now, with our home destroyed and our clan scattered, Death and I have nowhere to turn and no one to protect her as she goes through this most fundamental of battles. So, we turn to you in the hope that we might be able to hire your company to stand in for her brothers and sister…who may, in fact, already be dead."

Death swallowed hard and forced herself not to react to this naked, barbed truth. Thinking about the danger to her siblings wouldn't be productive at the moment, so she wouldn't do it. Right now, only her unborn kittens mattered. She resisted a sudden urge to crouch protectively around her middle and held herself motionless.

"'Our home?'" Conason asked.

Susa's hand on Death's back went still. Conason leaned his elbows on the desk and at Susa.

"Care to explain?" he added.

"It is not so hard to understand," Susa said lightly, but Death could feel her fingers tremble against her fur. "I have lived on Khatash with the Night Wind clan for over a decade. They have become my family. Their home has become my home."

Conason stared at her for another long moment. So long that Death figured he realized Susa wasn't telling him the whole story.

"The Golden Horde doesn't come cheap," Conason said eventually. He reached out to tap the five-credit chit that still sat on the desk between them. "As impressive as that is here on Earth, we charge galactic market rates."

"I think you will find we are good for it," Susa said. She reached into her jacket and withdrew something small enough to hold in her closed fist. When she opened her hand, the light from the window caught the object and refracted a glowing red beam against the far wall.

Conason stared at it, silently. He was, Death realized, really quite good. First an alien species he had thought to be a myth, and now an eyeball-sized red diamond worth more than the price of a luxury star liner, and his reactions had been confined to blinks and changes of breath. The man must be a talented gambler.

"This one is a signing bonus," Susa said into the silence of the room. "I can offer you another one of equivalent size for every month we spend in your care, payable upon completion of the contract. We require personal protection and defense for Death From Above, her kittens, and myself. We are willing to put ourselves into your care and follow whatever measures you deem necessary. We do require a secure GalNet feed, so that we may stay abreast of the developing situation. We are happy to pay expenses, above and beyond what you see in front of you now."

"What support will you need? In addition to the feed?" Conason's voice carried a rasp for the first time.

"Room and board. Some medical supplies for the birth. My training is sufficient to deliver Death's litter. Indeed, my background is rather more suited than any doctor you'll find on Earth, I wager."

"I'm sure you're right," Conason said. He still hadn't torn his eyes from the red fire in the heart of the gem on his desk. "So, we just have to keep you alive, is that it?"

"Yes."

"Against what?"

"I do not entirely know. Hunters are endlessly creative, Mr. Conason. And I'd wager another one of those diamonds that everything you've heard about them is true. But we are not without our own advantages. She can do everything an attacker can do. And she can do it better."

"And if she dies anyway? Childbirth or whatever?"

"Then you keep the signing bonus, and the contract expires without being totally fulfilled."

"Hardly seems fair."

"I am paying you in red diamonds for a reason, Mr. Conason. Very little about life is fair."

"Good point," Conason said.

"Do we have a contract, Mr. Conason?" Death asked. The Human man turned his attention from Susa back to the Hunter sitting on his desk.

"I believe we do, Death From Above," he said, holding out his hand. Death slow blinked and placed her fingerpads against his palm once more.

"Excellent. Please call me Death."

* * *

Conason, it turned out, was the detachment commander for the Houston office of The Golden Horde.

"Our main facility is in Tashkent, of course," he said as he led them out of his office after they finalized the details of the protection contract. He turned left to continue down the short hallway to a set of double doors at the end. The doors opened onto a utilitarian concrete stairwell that spiraled down. Conason held the door and waved for them to go on through. Death, back in her carrier for the moment, felt Susa's slight increase in tension as she stepped into the stairwell. It had no visible exits, merely wound down into the growing dark below their feet.

"I usually bring up the lights in here," Conason said as he stepped through with them. "Otherwise, it gets a little gloomy and creepy. But I can leave them low if you prefer, Doctor."

"Thank you," she murmured. He gave her a smile that managed to look both knowing and kind, and stepped deliberately past her, careful not to invade her personal space. Then he began leading the way down, picking up his lecture as if he'd never interrupted it.

"Tashkent, if you weren't aware, is in Uzbekistan. Bit of a ways away, but it's tradition, and it's home. But most of the other companies are headquartered here in Houston, and so we have to have a field office here. Problem is, we like to spread out. And in Houston, space is at a bit of a premium, as I'm sure you've seen. So, we dig."

"I see. An underground facility," Susa said, when it became apparent that Death wasn't going to respond. The Hunter wondered if most Humans felt the need to talk so much. Susa never had, but then, it wasn't hard to believe that among Humans, her beloved Susa was extraordinary.

"Exactly." By then they were approaching the bottom floor of the staircase. Another set of double doors stood in an otherwise unrelieved cinderblock wall. Conason pressed the bar that stretched across the doors and they both swung ponderously open.

Lights clicked on in the room thus revealed. Its footprint wasn't much larger than that of an average-sized Basreeni hangar bay, but the ceiling stretched several stories above their heads, giving the whole place a cavernous feel. The perimeter of the room stood ringed in huge, hulking shapes that appeared vaguely bipedal.

"We're not technically completely underground," Conason said. "I don't know if you noticed, but the front office sits on sort of a hill."

"What is 'sort of a hill'?"

"Large parts of downtown Houston were destroyed some years back. Riots and things. No one ever came in to move the rubble out, they just laid down dirt and built on top of it. The location of our front office used to be the fourth floor of a bank building. Anyway, this hangar opens out the back of that former hill."

"That seems...incredibly unstable..." Susa said, doubt clear in her tone. Conason turned to flash a surprisingly sunny grin at her.

"It was. But we're defensive engineers, don't you know? The City of Houston contracted with us to stabilize the downtown area, and we got this prime location as part of the deal."

"Interesting," Susa said.

"Still a doubter, huh?" Conason said. "Well, after nightfall I'll open up the doors and let you check out the view. It's actually pretty cool, and it suits our purposes to a 'T.'"

"No need for all that, Mr. Conason," Susa said quickly. "That seems rather an unnecessary risk. I'd rather we just focus on Death's security."

"Of course," Conason said, his grin fading to a more professional-looking smile. His tone didn't change, but Death saw a slight tension in his shoulders. Disappointment, perhaps? Was he that proud of the facility and the view? Death seriously doubted any vantage point Conason could offer would improve the ugliness of the Human city. Perhaps he read rebuke in Susa's words, rather than simply urgent concern. Whatever the reason, Death resolved to watch Conason closely.

Not that she would have done otherwise, in any case. It was, after all, the first lesson. Watch. Then find a way.

"This facility is the most securely defended in all of Houston," Conason was saying. "Unless you'd be willing to travel to Uzbekistan?"

"Perhaps eventually," Susa said. "Though I think it would behoove us to remain in the Free Trade Zone for a little longer to see what may be seen. I took steps, and it may be that no one knows we are here."

"That would make my job easy," Conason said. "I agree, I think it would be useful to know a bit more about what we're dealing with before making hasty decisions. We'll remain here for a few weeks, at least. Get an ear out on the GalNet and a few other less formal information streams. Size up the situation. Typically, the Horde is known for securing a position, though we have done executive protection details in the past. For now, your detail will consist of my staff here."

"How many Humans?" Death asked as she looked around and counted the giant metal monstrosities docked around the room. Eight.

"I have a staff of twelve. Eight CASPer drivers and four support staff. Would you like to meet them?"

"Yes, please," Death said. Conason nodded, and walked over to one of the CASPer bays. He punched a button, and a light began to flash. A door opened in the wall next to the CASPer, and a shortish man with a fringe of wiry fur on the bottom of his face popped out.

"Susa..." Death murmured in her own language as this new individual approached Conason. The newcomer moved with a kind of frenetic energy which was both fascinating and slightly disturbing. Death wanted to see more.

"Yes, of course, Little Dama," Susa responded in kind, and unfastened the door of the carrier once again. As Conason and the newcomer exchanged words, Death leapt up onto Susa's shoulder and pulled quintessence, cloaking herself in bent light.

"Dr. Aloh, Death From Above, may I present Brian "Bubba" Gnad, my mechanic. Bubba, our clients, Dr. Aloh and…where is Death?"

Susa smiled and shook her head. Conason's expression started to collapse into a slow frown, and Death let the cloaking drop.

"I am here, Mr. Conason," she said.

"How did you do that?" the newcomer, Gnad, asked.

"I cannot tell you that, Mr. Gnad. To do so would render your life forfeit."

"Now wait a minute," Gnad said, nearly vibrating with energy as he rocked forward onto the balls of his feet. His chest swelled and squared up, and his jaw thrust forward. "Client or not, you can't just go around threatening people—"

"My mistress meant no offense, Mr. Gnad," Susa said smoothly. "Hunters do not threaten as you know it. She was simply explaining the law of her people. The knowledge of Hunter abilities is a closely-guarded racial secret. She would not be able to share it and let you live."

"Who says she could—"

"Bubba, enough," Conason said, laying a hand on the other man's shoulder. He squeezed lightly before turning to look at Susa, the bland look back on his face. "Your mistress, is it?"

Susa froze and then let out a small sigh. Death began to stroke her hair in an attempt to comfort her. For some reason, Susa hadn't wanted to be specific about the nature of her connection to the clan. Death didn't understand it, but then, it wasn't her planet or her culture, and so she had respected Susa's attempts at discretion.

"Yes, my mistress," Susa said. "But before I explain further, I would like to invoke the confidentiality clause of our contract."

"All right," Conason said. "If you wish."

"I do."

"Fine. You have confidentiality. Dr. Aloh, what exactly is the nature of your relationship to Death From Above?"

"I raised her from kittenhood. I am her molly…like a nanny, but also a teacher."

"So, you're like a servant?"

"No, Mr. Conason, I am more than that. I am a sigiled being and therefore a member of the clan. Death's mother, her dama, is my dama as well. I am…well, the closest equivalent would be…a pet."

Death looked over at Conason and Gnad, reading shock in their eyes. She continued to stroke Susa's hair.

"Gentlemen, I love Susa and she loves me. She, and my offspring, may be all that is left of my family."

"You keep Humans as pets?" Gnad breathed.

"Only Susa," Death said with pride. "She is the only one. Our clan accrued quite a bit of status when Dama acquired her."

"But—"

Gnad shut his mouth when Conason nudged him.

"All right," he said. "That's your business, I suppose, Dr. Aloh. Now, shall we get on with our demonstration?"

"That would be lovely," Susa said, with a sad smile. Death looked from her face to those of her fellow Humans, but she didn't quite get it. Why was Susa suddenly sad?

* * * * *

Complications

Ziv Station meant another ninenight of travel, during which no more than seventeen words were exchanged. By the time they arrived, neither was angry, but stubbornness and habit kept them silent until they'd docked.

Flame went down to the airlock, lounging on two legs and adjusting her bag and vest as she waited.

"Are you going in visibly?"

It was the most words either of them had spoken since Benabat, and Flame was inordinately pleased it had been Tamir to do so. She preened a bit, rubbing the back of her front paw against each of her cheeks, and smoothed the fur showily before replying, making sure Tamir noticed.

"Yes. We'll know pretty quickly if they're used to Depik here, as Kelket mentioned."

"You don't trust the Governor?"

"Do you?"

"I'm just glad I'll be able to see you coming this time."

"Will you?" Flame asked, adding a slow blink that made it a tease.

Tamir relaxed further at the show of humor, and that felt like an entirely different sort of win. The airlock chimed, and Flame leapt to cycle it open before Tamir moved.

"I can't promise you no surprises, but I won't change the plan," Flame offered, pausing inside the airlock.

"A surprise already, Hunter." Tamir moved ahead, stopping only for the second airlock to open into the station and crossing over. "Thank you," she added, so softly a Human's ears would likely have missed it.

Flame made a pleased noise and charged ahead, staying tall rather than dropping to all fours.

"You're a Depik, huh?" The high-pitched voice that greeted them asked as soon as Flame left the airlock. It issued from a furry body about half her height, and Flame regarded this smaller presence with real interest.

The Flatar's fur was shorter than hers, somewhat puffier, brown and cream stripes compared to her own sleek black. While Flatars were deadly shots, Flame found herself rather impressed that one had come running to meet them alone, rather than riding its much larger Tortantula partner.

"I am. And you?"

"Nah, I'm no Depik." It made a chattering noise that Flame recognized as a laugh. "Flatar, name's Rill. You?"

"I'm Flame. This is Tam," she added as Tamir stepped out of the airlock in turn. "I greet you, Flatar Hunter."

"Pleased to meet you, Rill. Are you just passing by, or did flight control pass on our message?" Tamir was friendly but not too friendly, which Flame figured was a good call in Tortantula territory.

"Little of both. Who you here to see?"

"Chok and Fisi," Flame answered, trying to figure out if Rill's ease was because she was familiar with Depik, and maybe had known Hrusha, or because she was entirely confident on her home ground.

"Yeah, you go big, huh?" Rill whistled low, impressed. "Assassins keeping it real."

Flame cocked her head, unsure what the Flatar meant by it, but choose not to be offended.

"Come this way, they'll be in the pit. Some bidding going on, don't think you'll be able to meet them anywhere else."

They fell in with Rill, following her through the wide halls of a station built for Tortantulas. As they walked, one came around the curve, two legs appearing, then eyes and pointed talons, then eight more legs. The walkway was built wide enough for two to pass each other, so they weren't remotely crowded, but Flame slowed all the same.

Several eyes shifted to regard her, two top predators recognizing and acknowledging the other. The Tortantula was easily four times taller than her, and some fifty times heavier, and was one of very few beings Flame would agree had a chance at taking down a Hunter.

"Hey Guff," Rill said cheerily, flipping something like a salute and receiving a clacking of fangs in reply. Tamir kept her eyes caged ahead of them, which also seemed like a sensible decision.

They passed a number of other Flatars and Tortantulas in various combinations, and few others. Other galactic species who chose to spend time in Tortantula space were rare, which made sense. After they'd crossed three levels and several different walkways, Rill slowed, small rounded ears flicking rapidly. She tapped her ear, receiving a message, then typed something back on her slate rather than replying aloud.

"Changing it up," Rill announced, turning around. "Fisi says him and Chok are gonna meet you outside the pit."

Flame followed the change in direction, disappointed. She was ready to see half a company's worth of Tortantulas and Flatars all in a crowd. Something she hadn't seen before, a group of them at rest—as much as those species rested. Tamir's shoulders relaxed, only a touch, but enough that Flame figured the bounty hunter was relieved. Tamir had a healthy survival instinct. Flame could respect that.

They only backtracked half a hallway before turning down a new, smaller corridor and crossing another level.

"Short cut!" Rill announced.

"Is this a service tube?" Tamir asked, ducking her head as they walked. The ceiling cleared her height, barely. Dimmer lights lined the upper edges of the walls, and there was a distinctive woodier smell.

"Flatar tunnels." Rill pointed up with both hands, bringing their attention to a small, round hole in the ceiling as they passed under it. "Sometimes we want to climb."

Flame leaned back to check out the opening and noticed more ahead. She could fit, which was good to know, though there was no way Tamir could. Still, if things fell apart on this particular station to that point, Flame wasn't sure she could get them both out alive. Her attention sharpened further, excitement at the challenge rising. This was easily the most interesting place their travels had taken them.

"Tortantulas can fit in here," she gestured to the corridor around them, "they squash down pretty well. But mostly they leave this part for us."

"Much as we appreciate the tour—what's with the change of plans?" Flame asked, genuinely curious. A little hopeful it was to set up an attack, so she could really get a good stretch going, but mostly curious.

"Fisi said nothing good on the bidding. Small contracts, nothing with that wholesale slaughter upside. You know? We don't like to kill just one thing at a time." She glanced sideways at Flame, all mischief.

"No fun in the universe if everyone likes the same killing," Tamir interjected dryly, and Flame flicked her tail at the pair of them.

"Sure. Anyway, here you are. I gotta get back to the pit, see if they were exaggerating. Some of us would be happy just to blow some stuff up for decent pay. Not asking too much, huh?" The corridor deposited them in a much larger hall, and the Flatar pointed at the door across the way.

She did not, however, leave, which Flame noted. The little being kept her eyes locked on the doorway, and her fluffy tail nearly vibrated with something that might have been excitement or anticipation. Flame cut in front of Tamir to cross the hallway, waving idly behind her as though to say goodbye to Rill or keep Tamir back. Both, and thankfully Tamir picked up the hint and lagged back in the hallway.

Flame motioned the door open, making it look casual, but she was ready when two large, spike-haired legs slammed down precisely where she'd just been standing. Flame had already dodged, laughing, and lunged in, to get inside the Tortantula's reach and out of the line of fire for any Flatar rider.

In her peripheral vision, she saw Tamir duck and roll, coming up in a crouch with her gun pointed unerringly above the Tortantula.

Rill, hanging back across the hall, clapped.

"Nice moves, skinsuit. I still got you in range." The Flatar perched atop the Tortantula had a similarly high-pitched voice as Rill, but it skewed a lot crankier.

"Back atcha, furball." Tamir cocked her head, waiting.

"I mean, mine's bigger." Significantly so. The gun was bigger than the Flatar handling it.

"Yeah, size matters. Speaking of, I see your partner. You see mine?"

"Aw, shit." The Flatar kept his eyes on Tamir, but dropped a hand to tap the Tortantula. "She's under us, isn't she?"

"No," the multi-legged fighter replied, eyes looking in different directions.

"Hi," Flame said, tapping the Flatar on the shoulder. "Nice to meet you too."

"We were checking your reflexes," he answered, keeping the gun locked on Tamir with impressive discipline.

"I didn't think Rill would give you away if you were actually trying to kill us," Flame said, relaxed but not moving. "And I also think your partner would have followed up if she wanted to fight me."

At that, the Tortantula made a noise that wasn't exactly pleased, but didn't herald immediate death. Tamir straightened and slowly lowered her gun, and after a moment, the Flatar followed suit. Flame leapt down, further into the room, and only barely dodged the leg that snapped out after her.

"Yeah, yeah, reflexes are fine. Come on in, Human. Thanks for nothing, Rill."

"That's for cheating me off that last contract," she called back, more pleased than any of them.

"You almost blew up the CLIENT!" he roared back.

Flame examined the room—straightforward and mostly empty. There was a big screen, a very low, long table, and some small chairs. It was a workroom maybe, or a place to talk about their orders, and it was built more for the Flatar than the Tortantula; she supposed anywhere the giant predators decided to crouch was their spot, furniture or no.

Tamir entered the room with a hint of a saunter—she wasn't fully relaxed, but Flame might have been fooled if she hadn't spent so much time in close quarters with the woman. The Tortantula watched her closely, and Tamir angled well away from the huge killer. Smart decision.

The Flatar threw himself off his saddle, still grumbling, and fully swaggered over to the table. He made a show of swinging up his large gun and clanging it onto the table. Flame hopped onto the table, which was a better perch for her than the smaller chairs. Tamir took a moment to deliberately holster her gun, and the Tortantula turned to face them all, settling into a more comfortable position.

"Depik. Ever kill one of us?" the Tortantula said, her voice deep and thrumming.

Flame sat primly at the edge of the table, head tilted to stare back at her.

"Aren't a lot of contracts taken out on Tortantulas," she said, giving her the compliment of sounding regretful about that.

"Too bad. Be a good fight."

"You didn't set yourself up for success in the doorway," Flame said, not able to fully resist poking the giant being.

"That wasn't about killing. Could be." Her manipulators moved, welcoming Flame to come in close and try again. "Plenty of room in here."

Flame's tail lashed, once, and Tamir's hand moved ever so slightly back toward her gun.

"Eh. Give it a rest, Chok." The Flatar plopped down into a seat and waved at his partner. "We just wanted to make sure they were worth talking to, and Rill aside, if they just want to talk, we can give a minute or two."

The Tortantula made a noncommittal noise, but got more comfortable in her low crouch, and everyone else around the room relaxed slightly.

"I'm Fisi, that's Chok. Figure you figured, but let's make it official."

"Flame," the Hunter said, nodding, "And Tam."

"We appreciate your time," Tamir added, which received a dismissive tail flick from Flame and an equally bored fang clack from Chok.

"Nothing good to bid on anyway. Thought we'd see what brings a Depik to our station."

"Surely, you've met one before," Tamir said, convincingly surprised.

"One," Chok said, lifting and folding a leg to scratch under her abdomen. It was remotely threatening, but in the way most actions by a Tortantula were threatening. Any actual threat would have blood at the end of it, so Flame didn't pay much attention.

"Did he or she come around a lot? I hear some Depik have ties with the mercs, though not as much as they do with the merchant guild."

"Nah." Fisi's snort was much larger than his body should have been able to produce. "Only the once. Like you, she was too busy to play."

Flame wondered why the Governor had told them Hrusha had come here often. Neither of her two immediate theories were entirely satisfying. Perhaps the Governor's mind was ailing along with her body, and she'd become a bit addled. Or, perhaps Hrusha had come here often, but invisibly.

"Have a good talk?" Tamir had her hands comfortably at her sides, whole body at ease. She did keep Chok square in the corner of her eye for awareness, but had a solid air of relaxation around her.

"No," Chok said, eyes focusing on the Human. "She wanted to know about how we picked our contracts. Why we passed on some. What we'd heard about some of the other companies."

"She gave us some nice toys for talking with her," Fisi added, stroking the gun in front of him. "You gonna do the same?"

"No," Flame answered, ears pricked forward with interest.

"We'll pay the credits we offered in the message." Tamir didn't quite sound hasty, but it came close. Flame flicked the edge of her tail again, then realized Tamir was right to paper over the attitude. They couldn't afford a fight here. Or anywhere, yet. Killing a Peacemaker and maybe a Governor subtly didn't seem remotely in the style of a Tortantula and Flatar.

"When did she come here?"

"Uhhh, couple months ago now, probably? Six or so, I've had some time to break in little Onnie here." He patted his gun again, pleased with it.

"Anything come to mind about the companies you talked about? What she was asking for?"

"We missed out on a couple of contracts that went to the same Lumar company. No, we don't know why she cared about the Lumar company. Stupid brutes with a stupid name. 'Proud Fist.' Blech." He made a face that clearly communicated disgust. Flame thought it was adorable. "Uh. We got a big bonus for the multi-company contract we took with a Veetanho, and she asked some questions about her. Wanted to know who else we'd done jobs with in the last year or so."

"You got any info on that Veetanho and the companies you're talking about? I can push a few more credits your way."

"I'd rather a fun job," Fisi muttered, but shrugged a yes. "You having fun on your job, Depik?"

"Not as much as I would have if you had really attacked," Flame answered, looking at Chok. The Tortantula clacked her manipulators in agreement, and Fisi let out another chittering laugh that maybe also sounded the slightest bit nervous. Flame turned back to him and slow blinked her regret. "It would have been a spectacular fight. I'll have fun at the end of this job."

"Yeah, fair enough." He kept a hand on his gun, perhaps for reassurance. "Sending you over the info now. This helps you out, come back and play sometime, huh?"

Play so clearly meant bloodshed Flame almost shuddered in delight.

She really, really needed a hunt.

* * *

Flame and Tamir returned to their ship without incident, leaving Tamir relieved and Flame regretful. They dropped off the station and put in a course for the stargate, trying to figure out where they were going to go next.

"That was pretty useless," Tamir groused, unbelting from her flight couch and stretching. "Want something to eat?"

"I want to kill something and eat it," Flame muttered, but hopped down as well. "Fine."

"I wonder if Hrusha was wagering on the Tortantula company." The walk to the galley was short enough that Tamir had time to say the sentence, lapse into a thoughtful silence, and open her mouth to talk again just as they stepped inside it. "Think she was trying to figure out what contracts they might take so she could keep winning against Kelket?"

Flame tensed to spring onto the table and froze, ears swiveling as she thought. Tamir finished heating up two packets of food before the Hunter realized what had bothered her.

"Kelket said Hrusha always won their merc wagers."

"Yep," Tamir said, moving the packets to the table and gesturing for Flame to take her usual spot.

"Your old Human said Hrusha had lost the last round. And was angry about it. Would have been after she talked to the Flatar."

Tamir opened her packet with one hand, and tapped the fingers of her other hand against her bottom lip, remembering.

"Maybe Kelket was protecting her friend's memory. Letting her win that last one too," the woman offered, not entirely convinced by her own words.

"That sound like a Cemarap to you?"

Tamir shrugged, and Flame completed her jump to the table. As Flame settled in her usual corner, Tamir sighed.

"No, but she's slipping. Maybe she forgot."

"Maybe." They ate in silence, considering, and Flame pulled out her slate to pull up information on the companies Fisi had sent them.

Tamir started scrolling on her own slate, eating and occasionally making noises about this merc company or that.

"Human companies have been starting to post bigger profits," she noted, attention fairly evenly split between her food and her slate.

"Bad luck for Hrusha then, if she kept betting against them."

"No wonder she lost that last time—a couple of these got some big wins. Weird though, Proud Fist, that Lumar company Fisi mentioned? Bringing in a lot more credits than any other Lumar organization. Maybe they got a Veetanho to head them up."

"Who runs that company?" Flame asked, forgetting her food and snapping upright.

"Unclear," Tamir said, frowning. "Shouldn't be this hard to figure out..." she trailed off, scrolling and typing, then blew out her breath in frustration.

"Between an assassin and a bounty hunter, I am sure we can figure it out." Flame shoved her food aside, excitement at something happening replacing her appetite.

"Here's a thing," Tamir said after hours of almost total silence. Her voice held utter calm, but her hands tightened around the slate. "Proud Fist was bought with an investment from—get this—a conglomeration of pinpeck farmers. They were posting regular profits, then started going down, then about a year ago, steadily climbing again. Some big jumps, but mostly steady. Even through a change of command." She pulled up the change of command record, clearly filed on GalNet, and turned her slate for Flame to see. "From Veetanho Rhaabou to Human Alton Gage."

"Pinpeck farmers." Flame repeated the words with little inflection, studying the record. "From Benabat?"

"Weirdly, yes. Interesting, no?"

"Did Kelket send us here because Hrusha came here a lot, or because she wanted a Tortantula to eat us?"

"Kelket brought Sissisk pinpecks, an extravagant amount of them, soon before she died, but had no present for Hrusha." Now there was heat in her tone, building with each word. "Kelket maybe regularly lost merc company wagers to Hrusha, or Hrusha inexplicably lost to her, which Hrusha was suspicious about given their relative strengths. Hrusha even went to one of the most profitable merc companies to learn more." Her tail lashed behind her, picking up speed. "Lumars shouldn't be competing with Tortantulas, they're not remotely in the same class. You don't hire one for the other's kind of jobs. A Lumar company, bought with pinpeck money, loses their Veetanho and replaces her with a Human, and is bringing in a lot more credits than they should, given their contract ratio compared to other companies."

"Diaden tells her I'm poking around, she arranges some unrelated mercs to come take me out to try and keep it quiet." Tamir floated the question, letting them both consider the implications.

"A Governor would have that kind of reach. Maybe retires when it doesn't work, takes a step back." Flame should have thought the timing of the Governor stepping down suspect. Were Cemara often emotional enough to release influence because they lost some friends?

"It could be a whole lot of nothing," Tamir warned, knuckles white against the slate.

"Either way, we should go and thank Kelket in person for her help, wouldn't you say?"

"Oh, let's."

* * *

They burned with all possible speed back to Benabat, but no matter how fast they went, a particularly interested party would be able to see them coming.

"If she's in this, she'd be smart to run for it," Tamir said, still digging through the GalNet records. Trying to find all of a Cemarap's investments was like trying to count every piece of a Hunter's fur; it was a long process, even if they were cooperating.

"Find anywhere it looks likely she'd run?" They both knew an innocent former Governor would have no reason to care if they came tearing back into the system, and so would be unlikely to go anywhere. A former Governor who knew more than she was saying and potentially had a cilia or ten in the death of a Depik Peacemaker—and maybe Governor—would be out of orbit by the time they cleared the gate.

They wanted to flush their prey, but they needed to have an idea where their prey might flee, given the need.

"Anything on the scanners?"

"No," Tamir said with remarkable patience for someone who had been asked the same question for the seventeenth time. "And a small ship can use the curve of the planet and moons to avoid us almost entirely."

"We aren't going to miss her," Flame replied, grimly focused on her attempts to break into the flight control system and track ships that way.

"*Dimintina*," flight control's message packet spooled again, no different this time than the last two they'd sent. "You are not clear for planetary landing. Accept the packet to change your course for the mid-orbit station Exabet. Confirm receipt."

"We are not equipped for a fight," Tamir said, also not for the first time.

And again, Flame ignored her. On the bright side, they wouldn't have the same conversation again. On the not so bright side, a ship was hurtling toward them, and their scan showed it was almost definitely taking shots at them.

"Incoming," Flame said calmly, pulling Tamir's concentration off the slate and back to the controls.

"Well." Tamir matched Flame tone for tone. "Shit." She programmed an evasive course that would almost definitely keep them whole, and studied the course of the fleeing ship that had briefly attacked them.

"What do you think? I'm guessing that's not the Governor."

"Agreed. A bit obvious for her, and we could probably still catch this one. Looks like an in-system hopper that was left out here, can't see an approach for it before it shot at us."

"Waiting in the dark," Flame noted. "Bold. And cover, I'd guess."

"Meaning the Governor had a plan in case we came back, and could already be on the move."

"Let's see who went through the gate recently, shall we?"

"So glad this system is a backwater," Tamir said, picking up her slate. "I'll match the courses to what we've turned up in investments...Damn me, but some of these ships are positively *ancient*—" She broke off, her eyes wide and face pale.

"Tam?" Flame asked, sitting all the way up and abandoning her idle watch over their path, now slowly diverging from that of the projectiles aimed for them. Her ears pricked up, alert for the threat as her fingerpads closed instinctively over the hilts of her two favorite knives.

"Fuck me straight into entropy," Tamir breathed, slamming her slate down against the edge of her couch. "I know where she's going! Hrusha told me, before she sent me to Khatash, that there was a place...a bolt hole, she called it. She and Sissisk built it out in the ancient debris field in the Capitol system. Didn't tell anyone but the kind of friends who might need a place to escape to..."

Flame felt her fur rise on end. It seemed like a big jump, but Hrusha had known something—maybe everything—and if she'd planned something like this...

"Fuck it." Tamir said. "Want to take a risk?"

"Only way to catch the good stuff."

They'd watched. They'd found a way. The chase was on.

* * *

"Ah, but that's a good point, Hunter friend of mine. Perhaps I could save you just a credit or two on—"

Blade leaned forward, pleased to have managed a bargain with Fip on such a fine set of knives, when a faint scent pulled his attention sideways, just as the interruption solidified.

"Chirruch, come with me," Ichys demanded, with a brief nod to Fip that both acknowledged the Sipset trader and effectively closed him out of the conversation.

Blade's pulse lifted for action. In the months since he and Ichys had taken each other's company, she had rarely commanded him, and invariably found it amusing when he asked questions rather than blindly following her. She thought it indicated an indulgent dama, somewhere north in the jungles, and considered it charming. Blade, however, had never jumped to do a dama's bidding simply because she was dama—his dama he followed without question, because he still had much to learn from her. While he respected his sisters, he had ever been their leader. Following a female simply because of who she could become had never interested him.

All that came to little and less, because her tone made him leap now, bargain and knives forgotten. Fip fluted a farewell, and Blade absently lifted a hand in response, his attention focused on the leashed energy all but vibrating through Ichys.

She said nothing while they cleared the maze of stalls and merchants, and still nothing as they made their way through the twisting halls of Whispering Fear's den. Once they'd reached Ichys's alcove, she shoved him down on their shared nest of cushions and fabric, and closed them inside. He was fairly sure this meant neither attack, nor that he'd been found out, nor that she'd simply needed to mate, and so he waited, watching the surge of nerves and emotions ripple through her.

"The simplest way to join a clan is by being taken as a mate," she said, pacing in the small space, her eyes fixed on his.

"I would hardly call it simple, if done properly," he demurred, wondering if she was about to ask him something formal. Wondering what he would say if she did.

"No jokes." She waved at him impatiently, paced two more paths through the alcove, then came to a stop and took a breath. "I'm pregnant."

Shock struck, his every claw briefly extended, ears flattened in confusion. He stared back at her for several long moments, not a

single thought moving through his usually busy mind. Then he realized the import, and moved, launching across the room, stopping
just short of her, and winding his body around hers.

"I did it all to secure a life with Whispering Fear," he said in her
ear, taking the buffet of her front leg against his head as his due for
such a ridiculous comment. He wanted, more than anything, to tell
his dama, and to see Susa's face brighten in that Human way it had
when they had unbearably good news. The inability to do so, to not
even discuss Susa with Ichys, made him want to leave the room, find
Dirrys, and bury his claws in her gut.

But in perfect distraction, Ichys turned her head so their noses
touched, slow-blinking a smile and grabbing his face in both front
paws. They stood in that manner, celebrating silently, until thoughts
of his true home ebbed. For now, with Ichys, this could feel like
home.

If only for this moment.

* * *

Blade did not have the privilege of being in the room
when Ichys told her dama the news. How Death and
Night Wind had done things was not exactly how Dir-
rys liked to learn of significant updates to the future of her clan, so
Blade was left to pace in a waiting room, restless and alone.

Until he wasn't.

"Such tension, young Hunter." Arow sat comfortably on a perch
near the ceiling, as settled as if he had been there the whole time.
Blade was sure the deo hadn't been in the room moments ago, but

he hadn't so much as sensed another presence before Arow spoke, which left him even further off balance.

"Deo," he said, forcing himself to stop and sit, embarrassed at both his own surprise and his overly transparent attempt to hide it. He felt entirely off-center, and this inability to deal with Arow's sudden appearance pushed him further from true.

"Is this not a time for joy and celebration?" he asked, tail slipping from his shelf and slowly waving in the air below him.

"Deo?" Blade asked, confused, and uncomfortable being so.

"Ichys's news. It has been some years since we have had a pregnancy in Whispering Fear. Some of us worried we may have seen our last one."

"Whispering Fear did not grow old and ancient by luck." Blade tilted his head, grasping for his equilibrium. "Surely there are many females to follow the dama in time."

"I can see why you might think such a thing, jungle Hunter. Even the largest of clans can falter, and as you know from your hunts, success takes skill, yes, and luck as well. Whispering Fear has been lacking in that of late."

"Luck? Or skill?"

"Ichys being pregnant will change things. Our dama is talented in many things, but she does not love change."

"Even that which makes the future of the clan more secure?"

"The clan, yes. But not everyone in it." He leapt from his perch more easily than one of his age should be able to, and crossed close to Blade. "Consider who this changes things for. You, and Ichys, and..."

If Dirrys were truly mad—and Blade believed to his core she was—an official Heir to the clan could be read as a threat to her position as Dama. Especially if Dirrys had offended enough influential clan members, treating them the way she treated Arow.

Blade did not know Arow well, but he knew enough not to push the older male to say explicitly what he was so clearly implying. Instead he dipped his head, and Arow's pupils contracted in satisfaction.

"Clever, for a little jungle Hunter. Walk the paths carefully, kit— the highest canopies have the loosest vines. I heard you were being considered for an off-world contract. That's the best place for the two of you, as soon as you can go."

"I'm not in danger," he said, distracted by trying not to protest being called a kit.

"It's not you I care about," Arow replied, staring directly into his eyes. "She's not my kit, Chirruch, but she could have been. This matters for our clan. She matters most of all." He slipped past Blade and left before Blade could summon a reply. Every time he thought he had a handle on how deeply Dirrys would pervert their few unassailable rules, she found a new low. What dama was weak enough to be threatened by her own offspring, by the natural order of clan, damas, and Hunter life?

Killing her would be a service to all Khatash.

* * *

Not long later, Dirrys summoned Chirruch. He entered the audience room on light paws, attempting to convey both confidence and nervous deference at once. The effort of finding that balance kept his rage and disgust well-buried.

When the dama looked up to acknowledge his presence, she bared her teeth in a gesture that could result in joy, but left Blade further on edge, regardless.

"We will gather all of Whispering Fear who are on-planet, to celebrate Ichys, and what her pregnancy means for the future of our clan."

"Dama, wouldn't it be better to wait until we are sure of a live birth?" The tip of the damita's tail twitched, and Blade wished he could comfort her as she worked to control her emotions. "Of course, you should announce as you see fit, but to wait to celebrate—"

"You're being ridiculous, Ichys. You shall announce your news, and I will confirm you as Heir in front of all the clan. You are pregnant, which means you are fertile, which means this pregnancy or the next, this mate or another, will succeed. We will have a path forward, kits to secure our next generation."

"Dama—"

"You have certainly waited long enough for us to have this moment, Ichys. Perhaps I should send your younger sister to the northern jungles, given their stock. Do you have a brother, Chirruch?"

Ichys was trying and only partially succeeding at hiding her frustration, so Blade stepped forward, ears pointed toward the dama, eyes lowered. He could tell his show of respect pleased her, especially given Ichys's apparent stubbornness. He tried to modulate his tone to convey enough deference to please her, but he was afraid he only got as far as cordial, perhaps even pleasant. He would have to work harder, given how high the stakes of this game had become.

"No, Dama, there was just me. We were not as lucky in kits or adopted Hunters as Whispering Fear has been."

"Lucky?" Dirrys snorted, tail lashing. "We are not lucky, Chir-ruch. We are *good*. Bloodlines last as long and as well as ours only with skill and determination." She lost interest in him as quickly as she'd taken it, turning her too-wide pupils back toward Ichys.

"Speaking of determination, if certain contracts fall our way as they should in the near future, I will be able to leave much of the clan in your fingerpads, Ichys, rather than keep it all on my own shoulders." Dirrys didn't seem to realize how her inability to still her tail and her darkened eyes made that sound like a bad thing. Blade wanted to throw himself between dama and kita, though no threat was clear.

"I will always serve as you need, Dama," Ichys said, her own eyes aimed at the floor. Blade read from her posture it was more about hiding frustration than lowering herself, though Ichys was better at hiding her emotions than her dama in this moment.

"Of course," Dirrys replied, shaking herself and settling her fur back into place. "I will speak with our elders at the celebration, and see how well they will trust our new Heir, to take more of a role."

As she gestured for them to go, Blade knew Arow was right. The knowledge sank into his gut like a river stone; there was no avoiding the danger they were in. If the elders showed any enthusiasm about Ichys taking over from or for Dirrys, she would strike. He needed to take Ichys off-world, immediately, or he would soon see a new level of the depth of her perversion.

And while that would, perhaps, be the proof he needed to restore his clan, he knew to his marrow he wouldn't sacrifice Ichys to do it.

* * *

"**H**e's an official delegate holding up a critical trade agreement," Blade recited dutifully, aware of Ichys's unblinking regard. "His aide gets the vote if something happens to him, and she is more sympathetic to the trading party. The aide is not the client and is very loyal, so it must be an accident as far as the aide is concerned, but the trading party needs to know it was deliberate, in order to give a more competitive rate to the client. The delegate has a number of risk-taking interests, but never indulges when on an exploratory investigation. He always eats the same thing, and poison is the aide's top fear."

"You've just memorized the contract," Ichys said, flicking her ears toward him and away in a blatant tease. "What do we do about it?"

"The aide should witness the accident, so her guilt and own perception will keep her from pushing for an investigation. Also, an invite should be sent to the trading party, implying a matter of great interest, to make evident that it is planned without leaving a real path for the aide to follow, at least not before the vote."

"You studied the aide! Overachiever. I see why Arow likes you."

He gave her a showy little fillip of his tail, and she very deliberately curled her own tail around so that it brushed her chest. On the edge of suggestive, but he didn't take the bait. She had run him through hundreds of different scenarios as they approached their target, and though she greatly enjoyed flirting with and teasing him, she also took his 'training' very seriously—meaning if he broke his concentration to answer her almost-invitations, she would slap him down. She wasn't very gentle about it, but it still took him more times to learn the lesson than it should have. Served her right, for being tempting, even though he was the one who ended up with the bruises.

"So, what should we do?" she prompted, seeing he wasn't taking the bait.

"Give them the sort of off-temper day that has them sniping at each other, ensure an argument on the stairs, and I'll trip him from inside my quintessence field just as he turns to yell at her." He delivered it over-earnestly, rewarded by one of her soft barks of a laugh. "Send her threatening messages from the opposing trade party, telling her to stop influencing the delegate against them, and then set up the assassination to aim at her, but take out him. She might end up working out a bonus for the client, just to spite the opposing party."

"It won't work in this case, with the opposing party full of pacifists, but I was always sure that's what happened on Sakall with those Sikar a few years ago." She made a chuffing noise of pride, and he came back to himself with a start. He'd been so interested in entertaining her he'd outlined one of his own contracts, from exactly a few years ago. It had been needlessly complicated, but he'd needed a bit of flair for the client, and that didn't matter. He needed to stop showing off for her, and make a plan a rookie off-world Hunter would suggest.

"His respiratory organs are weakened. We treat some of his files with ackleen spores. When she brings in his new files, he breathes in the spores, in the next hour while he's doing his customary reading his system fails, he dies, she feels terrible. We wait in the room, and if anything seems to go off, we just make sure he gets a more direct dose. Ackleen is native to Elgon IV, and it's not out of season for blooms, so if it looks like it just leveled up in his body over their time there, she'll feel terrible for not noticing his state along the way, and we'll be sure to send an ackleen plant to the client directly before he dies."

"An asset to the clan," she said, making an approving noise and dropping to all four feet to gesture a break. He bounded across the room to her without a moment's hesitation, to reap his reward.

* * *

The contract itself had gone well. While Ichys and Blade waited in the delegate's temporary office, wrapped in their quintessence fields, the aide noted her delegate had been sounding raspy, and reminded him to take his medicine.

Because the updated stack of bylaws was unusually thick, he ignored her. It wouldn't have mattered if he had taken his medicine, but when he quietly choked to death half an hour later, he had to have wondered about it. For the briefest of moments, Blade considering dropping his field, so the delegate could die knowing his own death wasn't his own fault, but it was a passing notion.

He had made sure the client saw a flash of him when the ackleen plant arrived, and Ichys praised that inspired bit of improvisation as they made their careful way halfway across the planet to their well-hidden dropship, invisible and silent for most of the trip. Let word get out a pair of Depik had been seen wandering anywhere near the sudden death of a key vote, and the aide's suspicion would outweigh her guilt.

As they made their final approach to their dropship, they walked the perimeter to ensure nothing had been disturbed. The dropship itself was camouflaged well, an extravagant part of the even nicer ship tucked away well above them.

Dirrys had proclaimed in front of the clan that Ichys must help herself to the finest ship Whispering Fear had, rather than her own usual sleek ship. *Of course, the Heir must bring her mate, must be entirely comfortable on this last contract before she dedicates herself to pregnancy and the protection of her young. Of the clan's future!*

The dama had nearly shouted this last, and it had drawn sounds of approval from the gathered Hunters.

It had been awkward, but the dropship had been a luxury that eased their approach to the target, and Blade was sure he could talk Ichys into taking a detour rather than returning directly to Khatash, given all the time they'd saved.

With the perimeter of their landing site secure, they were finally able to drop their fields, given its distance from civilization and the lack of disturbance.

Ichys threw herself at Blade, tumbling them both to the springy moss-covered ground, making such approving noises Blade stopped thinking about the world around them entirely.

"The deep jungle prepared you for this better than I could have hoped," she said, touching the tops of his ears with the very edge of an extended claw. "Confirmation of a bonus from the client is already tagged to our account, you clever little kit."

"Chirruch the mighty off-world Hunter," he said, twisting under her to send them rolling again, wrestling with all the excited energy of successful Hunters. "You would be lost without me."

She opened her mouth to retort, and but he froze, looking around. He shoved her and they sprang apart. Just in time, as a sizzle of energy blasted between them, leaving the air hissing in its wake.

Ichys pulled her quintessence field up and vanished, Blade bounding for the closest overgrowth of vegetation to draw fire away from their ship. He wished for the endlessly tall trees of Khatash which would give vantage and cover, but made it behind a hillock of moss and pulled his quintessence field. To his surprise, the shots turned to scatter, spraying the area around the vegetation, as though anticipating he might come back out, unseen—was he being attacked by another Hunter?

Not a very good one, if so; they had to have lost track of Ichys. Another burst of scatter spray spat back the way they'd come.

Blade raced away from his cover, just missing a long shot and taking a long circling loop around, using the ship now that the shooter couldn't follow him. He leapt onto the curve of the lower part of the ship, jumping to the lower and stubbier of the pair of wings. Movement in the trees, but nothing visible other than the broad barrel of the gun. Cursing himself for losing focus even after the contract had been completed, he made a plan that accounted for the worst-case scenario—if they were being stalked by fellow Hunters. He'd circle further, come in as quietly as the sprawling vegetation allowed, and—

The sound of the small explosion was so perfectly familiar he froze, every bit of his mostly formed plan disappearing. The probes at their den had had that same pitch—the tortured mechanical shriek followed by the inner pop, then the larger external corruption of the globe itself ratcheting apart.

Dirrys. The realization should have launched him into motion, but for a long moment disbelief held him to the ship as though electrified in place. She hadn't hesitated to come for their clan, and that had been bad enough even though there was the slightest chance she might not have known Death was pregnant. But this, her own kita, her own offspring and the future of her clan, definitively pregnant…to attack her betrayed every tenet of their species so deeply he couldn't process it, even knowing how dangerous she was. But this…this madness was complete, at a level he couldn't…

With a curse he threw himself from the ship, moving as fast as he ever had to loop behind the shooter, just as the gun went silent and disappeared.

"Ichys," he said through their comms, unsure if he was out of earshot of their invisible opponent and uncaring, "it's a Hunter. At least one." Blade smelled nothing, heard nothing. Whoever had been sent after them might not be the best of the clan, but they were more than skilled.

Still, he'd trained all his life against his siblings, and Flame could vanish more thoroughly than almost any other Hunter he'd encountered.

"Arilys!" Ichys trumpeted, flickering into and back out of sight, daring their attacker. "I smell you, traitor. I feel the pull of your quintessence like muck against my fur. Take your death as you deserve. Meet me!"

"You betrayed the clan!" a male voice, on the move, and Blade changed direction instantly, angling for what would, with luck, intersect with his path, counting on Ichys's challenge to distract him. Had he met Arilys? No—one of the off-world Hunters, who'd been out on a contract since before the attack on Night Wind. Devoted to the dama, no surprise that, and either loyal enough Dirrys could count on his silence after taking out Ichys, or expendable enough that she could kill him too, if he were successful.

Why would she reveal herself so obviously?

No, he'd wonder later, after they handled this threat.

Blade missed the direct intersection with their attacker's path, but he was sure Arilys remained nearby. Ichys flickered in and out of the visible spectrum once more, and the softest yowl of frustration sounded from Blade's left. He leapt unerringly, with the briefest flash of gratitude for the many lessons with his siblings, and rammed into the other Hunter's back. They went down silently, Arilys struggling to roll over and get purchase against his attacker. Blade found the gun and ripped it free, throwing it clear of their fields. The motion caught Ichys's attention, and she released her light-bending, racing their way.

"Betrayed! How?!" she demanded, causing Arilys to stiffen in rage and twist harder under Blade's determined grip. Blade let the quintessence go, so she could see better where he ended and Arilys likely began, allowing her to grasp her clan member hard around his neck. "Betrayed how," she said again, more growl than words.

"You and the dama know what you did. She'll kill you as soon as you return." Arilys dropped his own field, revealing his lightly-striped gray fur and the seething hate in his green eyes.

"Arilys, I'm bearing kits." Ichys shoved her face into his, and despite everything he momentarily quailed in the face of an angry damita. "She named me Heir to Whispering Fear and gave me her own ship. Why would she do that if I betrayed our clan?"

Blade wondered at her attempt to reason with him. Fondness for an old friend? Disbelief that her dama would do such a thing? Or, best of all, tightening his hold on the other male's legs, proof? Keep Arilys from scrambling and removing himself from the board, bring him back to tell his story to the clan.

"She gave you the ship so I could track you," he said, thrashing more under Blade's hold. His tone remained vicious, "She always knew you didn't take the future of the clan seriously, but to lie that you were pregnant, knowing you've always been infertile—"

Between his last word and the breath it took to continue, his body went limp against Blade, and even his finely-honed Hunter instincts faltered in catching up to what had happened.

Ichys stood over them both, claws dripping, eyes wide and so wild Blade defensively crouched back away from the sudden corpse. Silence held the mossy cove for some stretch of minutes before Ichys shook herself and blinked her pupils back to normal size. Blade stood tall the moment after, tilting his head at her in a silent question, and she dropped her gaze to consider her bloody claws. He wondered if he would have acted with such finality, without thinking through a single consequence, if Dirrys rather than Reow had been his dama. He thought how much easier it would have been to bring Arilys back to Whispering Fear to make Dirrys's failures and betrayals plain to all. He weighed a hundred thoughts, all of which brought him no answer, but served to distract him from crossing over to comfort her.

"I should not have done that." The admission was impressive for a Hunter; for a damita, even such a newly confirmed Heir, it landed heavily enough Blade knew he would forgive her.

"Should we scramble his DNA and leave him behind?" he asked, choosing not to remark on her statement. They both knew it was true, and they both knew it changed nothing. "It would only tell your dama that he failed, and give her time to plan against our return, but transporting him makes it possible for her to say we have killed him without cause, and declare our lives forfeit."

"Take him," Ichys snapped out the word as she pivoted and moved toward the ship. "I'll call for Arow before we get to Khatash. He'll be an asset against the dama."

Whether because she said 'the' instead of 'my,' or that her eyes had been cold, Blade hesitated before following. He knew something was off, and experience had long taught him to trust his instincts. But all his training and experience had never prepared him for a newly pregnant damita reacting to the complete and bone shockingly unexpected betrayal of her dama, so in this case perhaps he was wrong.

Flicking his ears to dismiss that trail of thinking, he lifted Arilys's corpse and followed his mate into the ship.

* * *

As they maneuvered toward the stargate, putting Elgon's space behind them, visible tension passed through Ichys's frame, and she turned her gimbaled couch to face Blade's, set just behind and to the left of hers.

He thought they would finally talk about what had happened with Arilys, and how they would approach Dirrys, but he was incredibly wrong.

"Were you going to tell me?" Ichys asked, claws embedding themselves in the thick hide cushioning the couch's arms for just such a purpose.

Her words snapped him out of his reverie, and he blinked rapidly, focusing on her face, only to see her anger aimed squarely at him. His ears flattened in instinctive, immediate deference. His mind raced through her possible meanings—she couldn't possibly know of

Blade, or Night Wind clan, or what had truly brought him to her notice in a merchant's tent some months ago.

Could she?

"What did you want to know?" he asked, his tone careful. He was only a temporary mate, not even part of the clan, and so he must speak with caution to the angry Heir.

"Tell me now *Chirruch,* or I will kill you before we get back to Khatash." Ice in her voice and bearing, and for the first time, he saw her dama in her.

The emphasis on his name, his entirely false name, shot adrenaline and dread through him. His tail lashed once, his fur lifted all down his back, and he was perfectly balanced between fleeing and fighting. Neither was possible. Neither would help. How had she found him out? How—he cut off the useless string of thought, understanding that his life hung in the balance. If he wanted to figure anything out, he had to survive this moment, locked in a small spaceship with a pregnant Heir he wasn't entirely sure he could best in battle.

Or if he would try.

"I would have told you," he said, surprising himself how much he meant it, even while buying himself a little time, on the slim chance she was talking about something else. "How did you know?"

"You're no deep jungle yokel," she snarled, holding herself in place with her claws sunk deep into the arms of her chair. "You knew how to prepare for a contract, Arow said you notice too much to be new to clan politics, and your reaction during the attack...you're good, but you're not that good. You were expecting something." The words pushed out of her in a rush. Had she been calmer, she never would have revealed so much.

"If my dama can betray all we are," she continued, biting off the words in bitter, sarcastic satisfaction, "it shouldn't be a shock that you did too. Why. Are. You. Here?"

He lowered himself in further deference, forcing himself not to cross the space between them and rub against her fur. He could see her teetering on the edge of control, breaths away from striking him. He should have had a story ready, some explanation, another layer away from the truth—his life would be just as forfeit once she knew who he was at it was in this moment.

"Your dama destroyed my clan," he said, tail flattened and utterly still.

"Clans break all the time," she said scornfully, anger shading into disgust for such a weak excuse. "Lack of offspring, bad trade deals, less successful Hunters."

"Not mine," he snapped, momentarily shocking them both into silence. He took a deep breath, and then another, trying to control his own anger and succeeding in at least calming his tone. "My dama raised all four kits she bore to maturity. My dama grew her clan into success, taking on so many successful contracts she came to the Peacemaker's attention. My dama did not kill the Peacemaker she was nominated to replace, because she was not insane, and so she, and my clan, are not anathema."

"Night Wind," she said, her voice strangled and low.

"Someone did this to us," he said, as though she hadn't spoken, his eyes fixed on the floor between their couches, the muscles in his limbs jumping with the release of the truth. "Someone with power and control, but who wants more, always more. Someone who imagines threats so she can destroy then. Someone who believes competition must be destroyed. Someone who finds unspeakable means acceptable. Someone who didn't think twice about causing the death of a pregnant damita. Someone who would kill the Heir to a clan."

Blade felt the tension jump between them, the frisson of recognition of what Dirrys had so recently done.

"My littermate was pregnant, and Dama had just confirmed her as Heir. I couldn't believe one of us would do such a thing, but she's just done it again…to her own kita."

"And so, you came to destroy my clan, in revenge?" So many emotions twisted her tone, Blade knew his life still balanced between them. Ichys's rage at her dama's depthless betrayal had to go somewhere. But at least she had delivered it as a question, leaving him some room to shift the scale.

"No. Her. Her, and any of your clan broken enough to have been a part of it, if they knew." He slumped in his chair, then turned his head and bared his throat to her. She would take the invitation or she wouldn't, but for the first time in his life, Blade decided not to fight.

The silence stretched through the confines of the bridge, and he was not so resigned to death that he didn't sense each of the three times she tensed to launch herself at him. But he neither flinched nor changed his posture, and ultimately neither did she.

"When would you have told me?" She was not calm, but death had retreated enough that he turned his face back toward her, eyes still lower than hers.

"When I had proof. Before I killed her, but with enough distance that you couldn't have stopped me."

The truth of it resonated between them.

"I would have stopped you," she said finally, retracting her claws.

"No. I needed enough proof to clear my clan's name, in case...for any of my siblings who live. You wouldn't have liked it, but it would have held you."

"And do you have any idea where you'll get that proof?" She didn't argue; they both knew how the fight would have gone if she had attacked this day, and both were just as conscious of Arilys's body in the hold.

"She tried to kill you, Ichys. Is it too hard to believe—?"

She snarled across his words, and he cut himself off, watching her closely as she leapt from the couch to pace across the bridge. Not toward him, though when she stopped she faced him fully, standing on two legs with her arms at her side, leaving her midsection open. Still angry, but not coiled to attack, nor tensed to protect against one.

"Not proof for *me*. I know she tried to kill me. What proof will you find to restore your clan?"

He dropped from his couch, crossing to her. If she cut him, still it was worth the risk. He bent to rub the top of his head under her chin, then straightened to rub his cheek against hers, ears swiveled toward her. A hand bristling with slightly extended claws pressed under his arm nearest her, but he held the side of his face to the side of hers, and breathed in her scent.

"She never deserved you," he said, meaning only to think the words rather than whisper them aloud.

"Neither do you," she replied, and the claws briefly pierced his skin.

She was worth the blood. He stayed close, and after a moment she withdrew her claws, and rubbed back against his face once before pacing away.

"Cunning Blade," he said, cutting her pace short. "I greet you, Hunter."

The pause stretched between them, the traditional greeting also a reminder of their first meeting in Fip's stall. Finally, she nodded, accepting his name, and then stared until he returned to her question of proof.

"Before the last council, she put some trade agreements in place by implying she would be named either Peacemaker or Governor. Despite the collapse of the *Malluma Songo* and some disastrous contracts, the clan had a profit in the season before, one that grew out of proportion to the contracts and agreements over the same time period. If I can get access to the files to see where those credits came from—"

"As impressive as Night Wind was becoming, your clan was tiny compared to Whispering Fear. We have so many old investments and agreements she can justify anything in the accounts."

"I don't think so. It was careless to suggest she'd be offered either of the two biggest off world contracts, and I think she's been unchallenged as Dama for so long she isn't at her cleverest in hiding her tracks. I've also heard her with Arow, she doesn't always consider what she says. And she's panicking now—why else attack her own kita?"

Ichys spat, disgusted at the reminder, her pupils narrowing and widened as she struggled to leash her emotions. Blade put to words what he'd been weighing since they left Elgon IV's atmosphere.

"Chirruch," he said, flinching back slightly when she focused on him. He shook his head, lifting a hand in silent apology. "An inexperienced Hunter on his first off-world contract should have made our job take longer."

"It would have given Arilys more time to set his trap." Her tail lashed, and she glanced toward the hold where the other Hunter's body remained.

"And at the least, I would have been a distraction to you."

"You—Chirruch—wouldn't have given us that moment before he shot. Chirruch had no reason to believe we were in danger."

"He had some." Blade's ears flicked back, acknowledging how weird the sentence was. "Arow warned me, to get you off-world. He warned me Dirrys wouldn't like this change."

Ichys growled, low in her throat, and looked away again.

"He thought—I thought too, that you'd be safe out of her reach. It's messy, involving another Hunter. Dirrys isn't making good choices." He sat back on his haunches, trying to still his twitching tail. Dirrys making terrible choices could mean either she would become more dangerous, or easier to shake off course. Or both, which, while not ideal, gave him something to work with.

"But she thinks I'm a threat to her." She growled again, touched her abdomen as though to reassure the growing kits, and flexed her claws.

"I think she's beyond wariness and good choices, Ichys. I think she's mad."

The words dropped into the silence between them, heavy stones sinking to the bottom of a river. Ichys stared at him, her angry eyes boring into his.

She blinked, then drew in a breath to snap the silence.

"It's not enough. Maybe we can convince the other clan members that this attack on me was hers—"

"Of course we can!" Blade's surge of excitement sent him racing back to his couch, just to move. She'd said 'we,' and she'd given him an idea. "She's not panicking, she's *mad*. I don't know if it's jealousy or age or if she's always been crazy, but the clan were all so happy you are pregnant. More than celebration for the natural progression of a clan, for the joy of new life. The Hunters are losing patience with her, and now, with you, they see an end."

Ichys snarled, but didn't argue.

"We can use that, to push her. We can get all the proof we need."

"Arow will meet us at the station. It won't leave us much time before she knows of our return, but his traveling to the suborbital wouldn't raise her attention as much as his leaving Khatash without a contract. It's our best option, as long as she's tracking our ship."

"I've seen Dirrys push him—if Arow had any proof against her that would stick, he would have used it."

"Arow has never been so motivated to take action as he is now," Ichys replied dryly. "And what would he have done, after pushing the dama out? Let Whispering Fear wither like a cut vine, without leadership?"

"Arow is a deo, and could have held the clan on course until you or Sivand threw a litter."

"And if we never did? What clans would take risks on partnering with us, with only an aging deo at the head and no breeding dama?" She scoffed at his naiveté, adding, "You really were raised by a Human, weren't you?"

The sharpness in her tone made clear he was not yet entirely forgiven, and his hiss of protest could have been for either that or the slight against both Susa and his dama. She showed neither regret nor apology in the face of his evident anger, and so he ignored her last comment entirely.

"Then I'm sure he'll know enough to make up a story for having Arilys' dead body in our cargo bay," Blade replied, the tip of his tail flicking in disapproval. Perhaps he hadn't entirely forgiven her, either.

* * *

For a long time, it looked like Susa's plan had worked. Though another Hunter could have (and probably did) track Death's ship, they'd abandoned her in orbit above Skradchar before taking a passenger transport to Piquaw, and from there to Earth itself. For a plan conceived on the fly, it had yielded good results. Most of Death's gravid season passed uneventfully and quietly in the bowels of the Golden Horde's Houston complex.

"You look like you swallowed a football," Tony Connor, one of the mercs, said one evening, as Death leapt gingerly down from her preferred daytime resting place. He and Conason were sitting nearby, inspecting pieces of their personal gear.

The inside of the CASPers that lined the walls were tight for a fully-grown Human mercenary, but they were just about the perfect size for a den. Intellectually, Death knew her constant drive to seek out small, tight places was the result of hormones and bearing instinct. That didn't make it any less imperative. At first, the Human mercs had not been comfortable with her messing around in the CASPers, but she had demonstrated over time that she wasn't hurting anything, and they eventually relaxed.

Or she wore them down. Whatever.

"I do not know 'football,'" Death said, padding closer to the merc and his commander on all four feet. Despite their professional relationship, she had decided that she rather liked James Conason, and so she took the time to rub her head and the left side of her body along his calf in greeting. He reached down from the chair he occupied and scratched under her chin in a most delicious way.

"Football is a game we play here on Earth. It's played with an inflated, oblong ball," Conason said, still scratching. She pressed her head into his hand in a mute appeal for more. "It's a lot of fun. I grew up playing it."

"Ah. And you move this ball with your foot?"

"Sometimes. Mostly though you just pass—throw it—or run with it through the other team to try and score."

"Oh. So why is it called football, then, if you do not always use your feet?"

"No one knows. I think it was originally played with a rugby ball, which is almost the same shape. Rugby clubs are sometimes called football clubs. But really, only people in America call football 'football.' Everyone else calls it 'American football,' and reserves the term 'football' for a game we call 'soccer.' Soccer is played with a round ball that you kick. No hands, unless you're the goal keeper."

Death slow blinked and backed up off of his caresses for a moment.

"You Humans make no sense," she said. "But your scratches are nice."

Connor pointed his finger at his commander and laughed.

"She's got you there, boss," he said. Conason just shook his head and chuckled. Death dropped her jaw in an answering smile, and they seemed quite cheery when Susa emerged from the office that had become her sleeping quarters and work area. Death turned and ran to her, leaping up into her arms and nuzzling her head under the woman's chin. Susa's scent filled her nostrils. As always, she smelled of home.

"Good evening," Susa said. "Mr. Connor, Mr. Conason, Little Dama. I'm glad to see you're all so happy."

"James was explaining about footballs," Death said, rubbing her face against Susa's collarbone. "There are quite a few of them, it seems."

"There are," Susa said, and turned her smile on Conason. "Are you a football fan, Mr. Conason?"

"I am," he said, and returned Susa's smile. Death didn't think her molly noticed the faint reddening of Conason's ears as he spoke. That had been happening a lot lately whenever Conason interacted with Susa. "I played a bit in school. Wasn't good enough to go pro, though, so I took my VOWS."

"Who is your team?" Susa asked.

"What? You like football?"

"I used to," Susa said. "It's been decades since I saw a game, of course, but I grew up a fan of the Texans. And, of course, I went to UT, so I rooted for the Longhorns in college ball."

Conason's ears got slightly redder. Death rumbled a bit to herself in amusement. She glanced over at Connor, but he was studiously looking down at his gear. A bit too studiously, and his lips curved in a small smile. Was 'football' part of some obscure Human courting ritual?

"The Texans still play here in Houston," Conason said. "I could get tickets, if you wanted to go, sometime."

"That's a lovely thought," Susa said smoothly, but Death noticed a definite cooling in her voice. "But it's not possible right now. I couldn't leave Death for that long, not so close to her birthing-time."

"Of course," Conason said. He kept any bit of disappointment out of his tone, but Death was certain he was feeling it anyway.

"In fact, Little Dama, we should take a look at your progress now," Susa said, turning back toward her office.

"Why do you discourage him?" Death asked in her own language as she looked over Susa's shoulder at Conason. He remained in his chair and lifted a hand in a wave, while Connor clapped him gently on the back. She slow blinked back at him and then turned to look at the composed lines of Susa's face. "It's obvious that he likes you. Don't you like him? I confess, I don't know exactly what passes for 'sexually attractive' in Human males, but he's certainly intelligent and personable enough. Is he ugly?"

"Not at all," Susa said, shutting the door of her office behind herself. "By Human standards, Conason is quite handsome. Our tastes vary, but most Human females appreciate symmetrical features in a male, as well as a defined musculature and strong bone structure as indicated by the jawline. Conason has all of those qualities."

"So why are you not interested in sex with him? I can't imagine you find his personality objectionable."

"No, his personality is just fine. He's an entirely likeable man, Death. It's not him I object to, at all," Susa said. She carried Death over to her worktable and let her hop down, then turned away to begin gathering the primitive diagnostic equipment she'd been able to source here on Earth.

"Then what is your objection?" Death asked, speaking gently. It was obvious that Susa didn't want to talk about it, but it was equally obvious that something was amiss. She was Dama, she couldn't take care of her clan if she didn't know what was wrong with them. Susa let out a sigh and then turned around to meet Death's eyes.

"Before Dama found me," she said, "I was a *Songo* addict."

"I know that," Death said.

"Yes, you do. But I don't think you realize some of the ramifications of that experience. Suffice it to say, Death, that what I did…and what I allowed others to do to me in pursuit of my next high has complicated sex for me. I like Conason a lot. And I know that he likes me. But for now, sex is…off the table."

Death looked at Susa for a long moment and then slow blinked.

"I love you, Susa," she said, because it seemed like the appropriate thing to say.

"And I love you, little Dama. So, let's see how these kittens are coming along, shall we?"

* * * * *

Found

I t was several days before Deluge was able to leave 'Tlor. Once the credits were transferred to the Goka company, they pitched in and began working side by side with Gage's Lumar to repair and refit the headquarters building. Deluge watched Gage curiously during this time, but he seemed to be handling the situation. If his jaw occasionally clenched, and he spoke in a slightly clipped manner, it was likely that only Deluge noticed anyway. No one else had enough experience with Humans to pick up on those cues.

"What will you do now?" Gage asked as the two of them stood on a loading dock, supervising the loading of supplies onto a shuttle bound for the station where *Iora* was docked.

"That depends on what Rurranach finds out," Deluge said. "The Hunter who attacked me said that my whole clan was under interdict, which is something I've never heard of before. Interdict is reserved for the worst criminals of our race...but to my knowledge, it's only ever been levied against individuals, never whole clans. Things are strange, and I must find my dama and sort it out."

"And the Sidar will go with you?"

"Yes," Deluge said, slow blinking even as he sighed. That had been an unlooked-for development. "Apparently, he feels an obligation to me, since I saved his life. He asked me for a sigil."

"What does that mean, a sigil?"

"It's the symbol of my clan," Deluge said, reaching into a pouch to pull out the metal symbol he'd picked up from an artisan at the starport the evening prior. He held it up so it caught the light for a moment and then stowed it safely away. "It means he's sworn to my family, to obey us and stay with us as a companion and servitor."

"You mean he asked to become your slave?" Gage asked, his eyebrows rising in surprise.

"Not exactly. Not as you know the word. It's more like…" Deluge racked his brain, trying to remember what Susa had said about her role within the family. "Like a beloved and useful pet."

"Oh. A pet. And that's better than a slave how?"

"Judge me if you like, Gage. It was Rurranach's choice."

Gage harrumphed and followed it with a sigh.

"Well," the Human said. "If the Proud Fist can ever be of service to you, Choking Deluge, simply call."

"You have already been of great service to me," Deluge said, turning to look up at the Human who stood beside him. "You fought to defend me and lost some of your Lumar in the process."

"Not very many," Gage said. "Uban was pleased."

"Yes, but still. Some. I did not ask you to do that, and you were under no obligation or contract. So, it means a great deal to me. I owe you a debt."

"They were attacking us too, remember."

"Because I was here," Deluge said, reaching into his pouch once again. This time, he drew out a flat metal disc and handed it to Gage.

"What is this?" Gage asked.

"That is a token of my debt," Deluge said. "Do not lose it, for they're incredibly valuable. My pawprint there indicates I owe you a favor. A killing, perhaps, or a fortune in credits, or some other thing you might need. Keep it, and if you ever have need of me, simply get this to a member of the merchant guild who deals in recreational substances. It will get back to me or my clan, and we will do all that we can to get you what you need."

"Del," Gage breathed, unconsciously using Rurranach's nickname. "This is a blank check...are you sure?"

"I have nothing else I can give you, my friend. I owe you a debt."

"You've already given me a freaking mercenary company!" Gage said, waving a hand at the busily-working Lumar. Deluge dropped his jaw in a laugh and twitched his tail.

"That was a contracted exchange," Deluge said. "I needed someone to take over the company, you needed a company to lead. Zero sum. No dice, as Humans say. Take the token, Gage. If you don't use it, pass it to your heir. It might come in handy one day."

"All right," Gage said, closing his big fingers around the disc. "I will. Thank you."

"Thank you, my friend," Deluge said, and reached out with his head to rub against Gage's calf.

"You...ah...you're leaving this evening?" Gage asked. He appeared a bit nonplussed by Deluge's expression of affection, which made Deluge slow blink a smile.

"Yes. As soon as the sun sets. I may not have a destination in mind yet, but I feel it would be good to get moving. There are bound to be others hunting me, and the longer I stay here, the less secure I am."

"Plus," Gage added, "it puts us in danger."

"Yes, but you're a fully-grown mercenary company. You can handle it."

That caused the big Human to throw back his head and laugh so hard he couldn't speak. He was still laughing when Rurranach approached from a side door. The Sidar moved with a slight hitch as his wounds continued to heal, but his progress improved daily.

"You found something?" Deluge asked, eagerness flooding his tone.

"I did, my...Del," Rurranach said. For some reason or another, the Sidar had the stupid idea that being sigiled to Deluge's clan meant that he should treat Deluge with a lot more formality. The Hunter was quick to point out the idiocy of that stance, given that they were essentially partners in this venture. He had told Rurranach in no uncertain terms to address him as a friend, except for the rare occasions when Deluge might give him a direct order. In which case, it was probably a matter of life or death, and no one should care about the niceties anyhow. Rurranach had let out his chittering laugh and conceded, but he was still working on being comfortable with their changed dynamic.

"Excellent," Deluge said. "What?"

"Perhaps...aboard *Iora*? It might not be safe for Commander Gage and his Lumar if I speak too freely."

"We're just about done here anyway," Gage said, his friendly tone indicating he took no offense at their need for privacy. "We can say goodbye here, and you two can hop a transport of your own to the shuttle station."

"Excellent," Deluge said again. "Goodbye, Gage. Good luck. Remember the token, if you need it."

"Just like that, huh?" Gage asked, his mouth twisting in a grin. "Goodbye, Del, Rurranach. Take care of this crazy cat, Sidar. He's liable to get himself killed, otherwise."

"I will do my best," Rurranach said, and reached out the tip of his wing to tap Gage's outstretched hand. "Please give Uban our regards."

"Will do. Be good." With that, the Human merc commander turned back to overseeing his Lumar troops, leaving Deluge and Rurranach to their own devices.

"This way, Del," Rurranach said, extending a wing to point toward the front of the building, where hordes of vehicles flowed in semi-orderly patterns to and fro across the cityscape of 'Tlor.

"Still hard for you, is it?"

"What's that?"

"Not calling me your lord or master or anything like that."

"A bit. You are, you know. You saved my life. Therefore, it belongs to you."

"Here," Deluge said, stopping in his tracks and pulling out the metal sigil again. "Put this on around your neck and don't take it off."

"What...?"

"It's my clan sigil. It means that you belong to Night Wind Clan. Not just me, the whole clan. You're part of the family now, Rurranach. Not a slave...a pet."

"Is that better?"

"Susa seemed to think it was."

"Ah...your Human molly. She's sigiled too, is she not?"

"She is. You should talk, after this is all over. I think you'll like her."

"I'm sure I will. Thank you," the Sidar said, and fastened the chain around his thick neck. "Now, perhaps we should go?"

Deluge slow blinked and leapt to Rurranach's shoulder. The Sidar seemed startled for a moment, but adjusted quickly and began moving purposefully toward the stream of vehicles. It was time to get back aboard the ship and get to the bottom of whatever was going on.

* * *

Rurranach refused to speak until they were safely aboard *Iora* and established in an orbit away from any docking stations.

"It seems," the Sidar said, tapping the pad to bring up still images on the ship's viewscreens, "that your dama was implicated in the death of Hrusha, the Depik Peacemaker."

"That's impossible," Deluge said. "Dama would never do such a thing."

"As you say," Rurranach said. "But this is the GalNet feed that would indicate otherwise."

A video feed flashed up on the view screen. The scene was an open area on what Deluge recognized as the major orbital shuttle station above Capitol. He saw Reow and another Hunter wearing a harness with a Peacemaker badge walk out of the shuttle dock and down a short corridor to enter an airlock that led to Reow's large ship, the *Sarru*. *Sarru* pulsed her way back from the station's docking arms, clearly visible through the external view cameras. A moment later, an explosion blossomed across the black, blotting out the stars and the view of Capitol below. Deluge watched, his chest tight, and wondered why his claws hurt.

He looked down and realized he'd buried them in the side of his couch.

"I am sorry," Rurranach said gently. "I didn't think. That must be difficult for you to watch. I know you were close to your dama."

"Am close," Deluge said quietly. "And she's your dama too, now."

"Del—"

"No," he said flatly. "She is not dead."

"That footage was screened by every program my banking house has. It's authentic."

"Maybe so, but Dama isn't dead. And I can prove it."

"What? How?"

The truth broke open in Deluge's mind like the moon breaking over the horizon. His jaw dropped slowly open in a smile and he slow blinked as he turned to look at the Sidar seated beside him.

"Because," Deluge said. "We're in her ship."

"Yes, but—"

"No, listen. I'm about to tell you one of those truths that would kill you, were you not mine and sigiled. We Hunters are linked to our ships, via our quintessence field."

"Quintessence."

"It is energy. Non-electromagnetic, non-baryonic energy. It is how we do many of the things that no one understands. Our nervous systems are redundant in their operation. Our neurons fire both baryonic signals and quintessential ones. It would take too long to explain further, but take me at my word. That is a secret that we Hunters will kill to protect."

"Ah...I see..."

"You don't," Deluge said, laughter and delight in his tone. As much as watching that footage had hurt him, realizing the truth of the matter buoyed him up ten times more. Clever, clever Dama! "But take it on faith for now, if you must. The point is, we are keyed in to our ships via our quintessence. Once keyed, our ships register our presence, our location. They can be used to track us down if necessary. Like her ghost in the machine."

"What?" the Sidar asked, his tone confused. "Ghost? I thought you said she wasn't dead."

"Never mind," Deluge said. "Obscure Human reference. The point is, the ship would register if she were dead. And according to this, she isn't."

He tapped his fingerpads against the control interface, and the navigation screen came up. On it, marked in bright green, was a direct course across the Void, angling in toward the center hub of the great spiraling arms of stars.

"What is that?"

"That, my friend, is an unflyable course." Deluge scrolled the view along the green line, following it to a neighboring arm of the galaxy. "But it is the direct line to where my dama awaits. And it appears…yes. She's not far from Capitol."

* * *

They couldn't follow the course that *Iora* set. Not directly. The little ship didn't have its own hyperspace shunt—its tiny mass made using one impossibly cost-ly—so they had to follow a far more indirect and slow route, facilitated by hitching rides on the great behemoth ships that regularly crossed the void.

Deluge didn't mind. Truth be told, a meandering course suited him fine, as it made them harder to track. *Someone* had set that explosion on *Sarru*. *Iora's* databanks confirmed that *Sarru's* quintessential transponder signature was gone. The ship's death had been very real, even if Reow's was not. Deluge had no idea how this was possible, but he didn't worry about it too much. He'd find Reow, and the mystery would solve itself.

Or not. It didn't much matter to him. Finding Reow was all that mattered.

After enough transits that he'd lost count, Deluge and Rurranach finally arrived in the Capitol system. Much to their relief, the trail didn't lead them in to the planet itself, but rather to a wide swath of debris orbiting the system's primary.

"Dama must be hiding in the asteroid belt," Deluge said as he set *Iora's* course to intercept the trail from the hyperspace emergence point.

"That's not an asteroid belt," Rurranach said. "It's the lost fleet."

"What?"

"Remember your Union history, Del," the Sidar said, giving him a small grin. "During the great galactic war, one faction in the First Republic built a fleet to defend Capitol against the other faction. It was the largest fleet ever assembled, on both sides. They battled for months, slugging away until almost every ship was destroyed. The debris left over coalesced over the intervening years into this belt."

"Susa never told me that story."

"Likely, she didn't know it. It's nothing but an obscure anecdote now. But some of us remember. For all intents and purposes, though, you're right. It's an asteroid belt. Just don't plan to land on any of the 'rocks.'"

"Got it."

However, it looked like that was exactly what they were going to have to do. The green line pointed unerringly toward one of the larger chunks in the center of the deadly field. Deluge took a deep breath, toggled off the autopilot, and brought the command helmet down over his head, engaging his pinplants. *Iora* would be faster and more maneuverable if he flew her himself.

And maybe they'd survive.

"This is crazy," Rurranach said, letting out a chittering laugh. Deluge dropped his jaw in a grin, but didn't otherwise answer. Right now, he needed to fly.

Iora entered the belt at a roughly 45-degree angle of intercept. It wasn't exact, of course, but it did the job of providing Deluge with maneuvering options as soon as he needed them.

Which was right away. A chunk of twisted metal came hurtling at them right at eye level. With a thought, Deluge engaged the energy shielding to burn away the smallest pieces of debris and slammed the ship into a hard bank to the right. He watched as the chunk glanced through the shield, turning red as it heated up, missing them by a few bodylengths. Small flashes of white or blue indicated that the shield was doing its job against the tinier pieces, but there were plenty of big ones to worry about.

Deluge relaxed and sank into the feeling of piloting the ship. He let her thrusters become extensions of his own thoughts. He banked, pulled, and wove his way through the deadly obstacles, maneuvering in three dimensions at once. It was like stalking through tall grass or the leaves of jungle canopy: ducking here and there, twisting around the obstacles, but always coming back to that shining green line, the trail that led to his quarry.

"Del!" Rurranach breathed. "Look! It's...it's a whole hulk! It's not in pieces!"

Deluge blinked, and his awareness snapped back to the view screen directly in front of them. Sure enough, the massive behemoth they'd been chasing turned underneath them, revealing its apparently intact structure. He snapped out a quick thought, and *Iora* ran a scan, her results spilling over the view screen as she reported no electromagnetic activity within the hulk. It was dead, a derelict ship left over from an era long gone.

"I don't understand," Deluge said softly. "There's no life support or anything. How could dama be here—?"

Alarm bells screamed in his head, and audibly through the cabin as well. Rurranach flinched, and started tapping commands on his interface as he tried to slew the ship's external cameras to identify the new threat. Deluge swatted his hand lightly and did the same thing, faster, with his own mind. He also pinged the ship on baryonic and quintessential channels, looking for identification. *Iora's* thrusters fired in obedience to his commands, and the ship herself turned just in time for the two of them to catch the visual of a ship hurtling toward them.

"Hail it?" Rurranach asked, his voice low and stressed.

"No," Deluge said. "Look."

He threw the results of his transponder query up onto the view screen.

"That's a Hunter ship," he said. "It carries a Khatash registry, and it returned a signal when I hit it quintessentially. That ship belongs to a clan called Whispering Fear. I think this is another attack."

"Do you have a plan?" Rurranach asked, his voice eerily calm.

"No," Deluge said, slow blinking. "I'm just going to wing it."

With that, he judged the chasing ship had come close enough and he gave *Iora* the command to fire. The ship jerked as her twin "defensive armament" missiles fired at once, streaking through the black toward the still oncoming ship. He'd keyed them in to the ship's transponder signal, so that even when she tried evasive maneuvers, the missiles tracked unerringly to her heart. First one, then another tiny star erupted as the miniaturized nuclear payload exploded, rendering the attacking ship down to nothing but atoms in the debris-choked field in front of them.

"*You were carrying ship-killers?*" Rurranach asked, his eyes wide, his tone shocked. Deluge looked over at him with a grin.

"Just little ones," he said. "They're excellent for self-defense, as you see."

"That's illegal!"

"Not at all," Deluge said. "It's just not really accepted. But then, neither is killing for hire. We're a race of Hunters, my friend. Nobody expects us to play fair."

Rurranach opened his mouth as if he would say more, but just then, their comm system crackled with an incoming message, and it made both of them freeze in surprise.

"Blast it all to Entropy, Del! You ruined our whole case!"

* * * * *

Convergence

Arow had a room in the far end of the orbital station, and Blade had to trust that the older Hunter kept it clear of any listening devices. Dirrys would know they were back shortly, if she didn't already, and time pushed at them all.

Blade followed Ichys to Arow's corner, the two of them not quite walking together. They separated as they threaded through the few other beings in the halls, but came back to the same small distance when they were past them. He could feel the edges of her fur against the barest edges of his, and when he wasn't careful, his eyes tracked her motion rather than their path ahead. Were they to be ambushed now, as they had been on Elgon IV, he would be useless.

By the time they reached Arow's door, Blade was as jumpy as a kit first out of the den, sure there were dangers everywhere and unable to focus on a single one. When the door irised open to the mid-sized alcove, Blade tensed, and Arow's gaze landed on him with tangible weight, shocking him back into himself.

Arow moved back into the room without saying anything, Ichys following without hesitation. The old deo greeted the younger damita by brushing her cheek with his paw, his eyes landing back on Blade as the other male stepped inside. The door closed, and they all stood there, silent.

"She told me who you are," Arow said, displeasure clear in his tone.

"And about Arilys too, then." Blade said, keeping his tone neutral.

Ichys stayed next to the older male, across the room, and Blade knew he was supposed to feel that it was them against him. He stood upright, arms at his side, inviting the attack—a silent 'get on with it then.'

"She told me." Arow revealed a flash of amusement for Blade's daring, there and gone as fast.

"Dirrys is an enemy to each of us."

"Is it only Dirrys that is your enemy?"

Blade preferred subtlety, maneuvering until the preferred outcome was the only logical course. Watch. Then find a way. In other circumstances, with other species, especially with individuals who didn't know they were the target of a contract, he had the luxury of time and far greater skill. In this room, he couldn't be sure he was the cleverest or the strongest, or even the one who wanted Dirrys's downfall the most. They each had reasons to be here, and now he had to trust that would be enough.

"I thought Whispering Fear might be my enemy. I came to the clan to learn who was truly to blame. Unlike Dirrys, I have no interest in wiping out a clan to suit my ego. Unlike Dirrys, I do not hunt my kind. Unlike Dirrys, I am not a traitor to all we hold inviolate. If there are others in the clan like her, they are my enemy. And they should be yours."

Arow settled back on his haunches, still in position to lunge if needed, but more comfortable and less poised to attack than before. He considered Blade's aggressive demeanor, weighing more than just these moments.

"Dirrys is a rot in our clan," the deo said, after letting the moment stretch. "And she spread to some, but not many, of the clan. Disappointing that Arilys was corrupted, but there are not many more. What did you think you would accomplish, latching onto the clan you suspected, not knowing how deep the rot went?"

"Build proof to clear Night Wind's name. Proof enough that makes her life forfeit, and those of any of her allies in this. She destroyed my clan. She attempted to destroy her own pregnant heir. She has profits where the clan should show losses, and it's not from good business. She betrays what we are and what we claim to be every minute she breathes, and once the proof is presented, that wrong will be rectified."

"And if you couldn't?"

"I would have."

"If you couldn't." Ichys this time, less a question, more a demand.

"Kill her." There was no bravado or false confidence in his voice. Blade meant it as deeply as he'd meant anything.

"And die in the attempt?" Arow again, tilting his head in curiosity.

"A possibility, but an unlikely one."

"Don't discount her ability because of her madness. If anything, it makes her deadlier in self-defense."

"I don't underestimate her." Blade's expression tightened with disgust, lips drawing back from his teeth. "She is lashing out without thinking. Whatever cunning served her these past years, she's losing it in her desperation. Attacking Ichys was stupid, and that anger would drop her at my feet."

"That anger would take you with it." Arow flicked his tail dismissively, neither impressed nor mocking.

"It is the last option," Blade replied, with a gesture echoing the older male's. "I'd prefer to ruin her first, clear my clan, have Ichys fix your clan, then we can draw lots to decide who kills Dirrys."

He locked eyes with Arow, who met his gaze unblinking. His heartbeat rammed through his senses, and he was sure they could hear it. Would this be the end of his work? He tore his gaze away from Arow to meet Ichys's eyes. Her dark ones on his, her shining fur a knife in his chest. He wanted her with him. He wanted to be by her. It didn't matter to him which of them led, so long as Dirrys was destroyed. He would follow her anywhere. When he next spoke, Blade couldn't keep his tone entirely smooth. His ragged emotion tore at his words, and all his cunning wasn't enough to hide his pain.

"I need to know," he said, "Are we in this together?"

In the stretch of this third long silence, Ichys took a step, and then another. Slowly, she crossed the room again to stand next to Blade.

After another handful of breaths, Arow nodded.

* * *

"I didn't have access to the official financials," Blade said, starting with the obvious as he unlocked his files to display them for Arow and Ichys. "This is what I put together based on merchant accounts, what I heard of off-world contracts, trade agreements I knew about, and results from standard record searches. I couldn't go to any of my contacts, so it's still sketchier than I'd like, but even still, the picture doesn't match with Dirrys's approach to spending, nor her repeated confidence that Whispering Fear is stronger than ever. I would have thought it just hubris, except that her spending supports it, and overall the health of the clan seems assured."

"No outsider could be sure of the full contracts," Arow said, but not as though he were arguing. Thoughtful, he pulled up his own files. After scanning several, he moved a summary document to display—Blade noticed with deep satisfaction his estimates on spending matched very closely to the official records—and they all stared at it for a stretch of silence.

"These aren't the clan records," Ichys noted, glancing back to Arow.

"An excellent lesson for a dama." Arow studied the display, but flicked an ear toward her in amusement. "You control the overall finances, but your smarter clan members will keep their own copies. Our fortune is tied to the clan's, and you know Hunters like access to information that affects a job, or their possible comfort."

She answered with a fond snort, and, despite the tension around them, Blade relaxed slightly. With what he had put together, and these critical partners, he wouldn't have to haunt Whispering Fear for years. His clan could be cleared in the very near future, and Dirrys removed.

"The credits in and out don't match up," Blade said, leaning toward the display.

"Determined to share the obvious with us today, aren't you, jungle kit?" Arow's clipped tone reminded them all of the strain in this alliance, and Blade knew better than to argue the jungle kit designation. Arow had suspected him, but learning the truth from Ichys rather than Blade himself had been a misstep. Blade should have argued harder to tell Arow himself—it would not have made everything perfect, but the older male had clearly lost much of whatever respect he'd had for 'Chirruch.'

"There are older investments, such as our *Malluma Songo*, that don't always accumulate in a pattern, and I tend to add those in at once each year. And of course, Dama keeps some contracts for herself, of which we rarely learn the details."

"The hit you took on *Malluma Songo* was so big it came up in the last council." Blade shook his head, studying the numbers. "Pending profits there couldn't possibly account for this. A strong dama can bring in plenty of credits on her own, yes, but Dirrys has only left Khatash three times in the last six months. Unless her contracts were more lucrative than the Peacemaker contract, she doesn't fill in these gaps either. And," he continued, sure they were close to something, tail lashing behind him, "she would not have been so set on the Peacemaker contract if she had contracts like that in her vest."

"Then where is Whispering Fear's money coming from?" Ichys asked for them all, gesturing for Arow to share all the files with them. He did so, and they each reviewed silently for a time.

"This," Blade said suddenly, sitting up in interest. "No transfers came in around the time of Peacemaker Hrusha's death. The balance doesn't change. But shortly after, the clan took in money from a large sale of *Malluma Songo*, tasked back to the field that failed. Are there old stores still being sold off?"

"Yes," Ichys said, flipping through her notes. "But small quantities, only enough to keep our connections dealing. How big was the sale?"

Blade moved his file to the display, and they regarded it. After a moment, Arow returned to his own scan and took over the display with a new file.

"When is this?" Blade asked, seeing a similar bump with little to justify it.

"After the Governor died."

Everything Dirrys had said, when he'd eavesdropped, when she'd lost control after Ichys's announcement, when she showed off for the clan...everything solidified for Blade in that moment.

"She killed the Governor, so that she could take either the Peacemaker or Governor contract. She killed the Governor *on a contract.*"

Killing another Hunter was anathema, except in certain proscribed circumstances. Killing another Hunter by accepting a contract on one's own kind?

"Who would have asked for such a contract? She could have killed them just for asking."

"Should have." Blade shrugged; without making much effort, he could imagine a hundred scenarios where someone in the galaxy was desperate enough to try and secure a Depik to kill the Depik Governor. He was less worried about that than he was consumed with the pieces falling together in front of him. "But she didn't. And she didn't get the Governor contract—Peacemaker Hrusha did. Then she didn't get the Peacemaker contract—my dama did. So, she killed them both and destroyed Dama's clan to clear the board."

"Whoever requested the contract has—or thought they had—the power to influence those contracts." Arow's pupils narrowed to slits, his gaze fixed on some middle distance. "Dirrys wouldn't have taken such a risk on trust."

"Is this enough?" Blade asked, though he suspected the answer.

"No," Arow said flatly.

"But now we know where to dig in our claws." Ichys, for the first time in days, slow blinked a smile. "We have her ship. And her ship's logs. Of everywhere she's been over any time period we like."

"We don't have to worry what Dirrys will do now that you're back," Arow interrupted, looking up from his wristpad.

"Has she already done something?" Blade tensed for action, though there was little he could do to prepare if Dirrys had already put something into motion against them.

"Unlikely—she'll have something more pressing. A council has just been called. Time to see who's taking the Governor and Peace-maker contracts, and from Dirrys's message, she knows one of them."

Blade took a moment, looked over their notes once more. The records they'd collected, the trail they'd recreated. Now or never.

"Want to go to the council?"

* * *

Arow had been an off-world killer longer than most Hunters ever lived. Blade had heard stories of Hunters who grew very old, of course, and some were likely even true. To be so old, and still so lethal, imbued Arow with a sense of gravity Blade had rarely experienced, even among damas. For all that to be true of a male meant that Blade kept some part of his focus on Arow even when the older Hunter simply walked them toward his ship.

The ship itself served as a reminder of the privilege of such a long career as Arow's. It was not new, but it was exceptional. Blade wanted to see it from the outside, wanted to linger inside rather than just pass through to the dropship. It was that beautiful.

"Jeha built this?" he asked, forgetting his awe and wariness.

Arow swiveled one ear toward him and away. His silence reminded Blade that no matter how they were allied, they were not friends. Ichys brushed the back of Blade's hand with her own, then bounded ahead of the males, leaving them to walk in their own tension.

"Arow," Blade began, weighing his words.

"Dirrys decided I failed her when our litter did not survive through birth," Arow said, musing, as though Blade were not there, hadn't spoken. "I should have seen who she was then, when she hated me. I thought she was young and grieving, but that was never who she was."

They moved down the main corridor of the ship; the lights held a steady warmth, and the air smelled clean and only of Ichys's recent passage. Blade glanced at the older male and away, unsure of the moment and not wanting to interrupt it.

"Her second mate bragged that his strength would overcome her luck when she became pregnant again. He died on a hunt before she gave birth. He was older, but still impulsive; no one was surprised he'd been careless. Then, I didn't think she'd done it. Now, I still don't know how she managed it. Two kits survived birth, only Ichys grew to be weaned. Dirrys basked in the achievement. I taught Ichys to hunt."

They neared the second airlock, and Arow's steps slowed. Blade kept his pace to the older male's, skin jumping under his fur. Had

Dirrys always been mad? What did it say of them, to elevate such a Hunter to run a clan, all because she could bear young?

"Her dama bore other young, but the other kita she had disappeared. I would lay that at Dirrys's feet as well, if I could. She is the worst of us and wants only for herself, and she will kill you today if she can."

"She won't," Blade said, confident in his youth, strength, and cunning.

"She can." Arow flicked both ears at him, dismissing the confidence. "She has not survived this long by being weak. She killed the Governor, the Peacemaker, and your dama. Do not underestimate her because she is mad."

"They didn't see her coming." Blade turned to look at Arow, willing the older male to meet his eyes. Arow glanced at him, held his gaze for a moment as they walked. "I know who she is. I know she'll fight like a cornered Tortantula. She didn't destroy my clan, though she tried. She didn't destroy you or Ichys. She won't win."

"No," Arow said, softly now, turning away. "She will not."

Just before they reached the dropship, Blade stopped and reached his hand just short of Arow. The older male felt the gesture and turned.

"Ichys is good," Blade offered. "The best of us. Thank you for that."

Arow clucked in reply, and cuffed Blade on the side of the head—not gently.

"That's her doing, not mine, jungle kit. You are lucky to know her." Without waiting for a reply, the deo cycled open the door to the dropship and vanished inside.

Blade looked around at the beautiful ship once more, steadied himself with a breath, and followed.

* * *

"Ichys, Heir of Whispering Fear," she announced herself, gaze at the center point between the two Hunters in front of the door. Beyond them, the council would momentarily begin, or had just done so. They had timed their arrival to get the best chance for Dirrys to be distracted, so they could make their final approach. Given Dirrys's schemes, a public setting gave the safest opportunity for confrontation. As long as the gathered elders from other clans didn't summarily move to execute them.

"My mate." Ichys added the last casually, not sharing his name. He mattered because she mattered. Flame could have sneaked past the guards, her lightbending undetected, but they'd decided it was better for Blade not to risk it.

"You are late," the larger male replied, unimpressed. He examined Blade and shrugged. "Your dama will not be pleased."

"No," Ichys agreed, aggressively pleasant. She rested her fingerpads on her swelling abdomen and stared at him, until his companion cleared his throat.

"Enter, Damita, and do not interrupt the proceedings. The Speaker has begun discussion of the Governor and Peacemaker contracts."

He did her a kindness by telling her what she would find inside. Unfortunately, she would not return the favor by heeding his advice.

They moved inside, Blade two steps behind Ichys until the doors closed behind them. Ichys pulled up her quintessence field, and Blade continued alone through the curving corridor that deposited him at the back of the large audience chamber.

It had been more than a season since he'd first walked that aisle with his dama, and it felt like years. He let the loss of her, and his corresponding rage, wash over him. Acknowledge it, and pack it away. He would need that anger soon enough.

Etiquette dictated he should stay in the back of the room until there was a break in the proceedings, but he walked directly down the main aisle, passing elders of the most accomplished clans of Khatash. Any of them could lunge at him for such hubris, but luck, shock, or a light-bended hunter on his side prevented any of that.

When he reached close enough to the front that the Speaker paused, lifting a hand in silent question, bemusement coloring her expression, he stopped as well and lowered his head to her. He held it for a breath, two, then turned unerringly toward the reclining Dama of Whispering Fear.

"Dama, I challenge you." Blade stepped forward, fully facing her, for once not cataloguing the reactions of everyone in the room.

"I am Cunning Blade, of Night Wind Clan." A yowl of shock answered that, somewhere to his left, but he trusted in Ichys and ignored it. "You attempted to murder my clan. You murdered Reow, Dama of Night Wind. Hrusha, Peacemaker for the Hunters. Sissisk, Governor for the Hunters. You accepted a contract on another Hunter, and I name you anathema."

Blade's bold words, confidently delivered, fell into the most dangerous silence he had ever experienced. Every eye of the foremost assassins in the galaxy fixed on either him, or Dirrys. The dama had not even stood to meet the challenge, the black tips of her gray fur supremely still, her ears canted toward him in polite interest.

The moment held, then her pupils went wide. Ichys dropped her field and stepped in front of Blade. Her pregnancy had begun to show, and many eyes dropped automatically to observe it.

"Dirrys, I challenge you." Ichys stood tall, eyes steady on her dama. The lack of title was deliberate, and the faintest of stirs moved through the crowd. "You have betrayed our kind. You sent a clan hunter to kill me." This received the most dramatic response yet, with two males coming fully to their feet before they controlled themselves. "You are anathema. I claim Whispering Fear."

Now, finally, Dirrys reacted. She stood slowly and stretched indulgently. Her laugh echoed through the room. While she endeavored to look relaxed, Blade saw the tension in each major joint, the readiness to lunge.

"Little Damita," she said, pitying, tail curling behind her. "I know it is shocking to find your mate is a traitor. Arilys ran to your side when we discovered who he was, to kill him. I am sorry this…creature," her gaze didn't so much as flicker to Blade, she knew which threat was more dangerous to her in this moment, "dragged you into his treachery. You can still recover, my kita. Come to me and be safe. You bear Whispering Fear's future inside you."

"I am Whispering Fear's future, Dirrys." Ichys's voice did not waver, her posture pinpoint focused on the hunter who had borne her. "It will be secured with your death."

"Speaker," Dirrys began, turning to look at the dama above them. Blade was impressed how quickly she had turned his identity to her advantage and didn't want to know what other truths and lies she would spin together in this room. He didn't have to find out.

Directly behind Dirrys, breathing over her shoulder, Arow released his field.

"No, kita. There is no squirming out of this. Speaker, we have sent you proof, in the financial records of Whispering Fear and the ship logs of this betrayer that prove what these Hunters say."

The proof was not incontrovertible. Compelling, damning, but it hung on several conjectures. Dirrys could ridicule them, relax, and likely some in this room would believe her.

Such was not Dirrys's way.

The Speaker conveyed interest in every line of her form as she reached for her slate. At that motion, when the Speaker did not dismiss this out of hand, the dama took matters into her own claws.

She blurred into invisibility mid-leap, but Blade was expecting it. Dirrys would not attack Arow first, nor a pregnant damita. Blade expected she thought him the weakest link, having seen him fight and stalk, having heard of him from her hunters.

She had seen Chirruch. Not Blade.

He vanished into his field and spun, taking the fight from where he had been, too close to Ichys, and closer to the pedestal where the Speaker still stood. Around them, hunters moved back, but there was no chaos. No scrambling.

A challenge had been issued.

A challenge would be met.

Dirrys screamed in frustration when she missed Blade, flickering in and out of her field in her frustration. He lunged for her, projecting where she would land, missing whatever warning Ichys shouted.

It had been, of course, a trap. Dirrys met him midair, expecting him to take the bait, clawing him across the face so deeply he forgot to breathe.

Don't underestimate her, Arow had said, more than once. The words echoed in his head again as he shook off the blood. It wouldn't clear his vision, the blood kept coming, but it centered his thoughts.

He reached, as he'd sometimes been able to reach for Flame, for that whisper hint of another field. She knew she'd wounded him, she wouldn't have gone far.

There.

Blade lunged with front claws extended, connected and dug in, piercing through fur and skin. Before he could bring his hind legs to bear, to disembowel her, she twisted away, leaving strips of flesh in his claws.

They both bled too much to effectively hide in a field, and Blade could barely see out of one eye.

Fast. Savage. No hesitation or quarter. He would finish this.

For his dama. For his family.

She saw the determination in him and sneered.

"Do you know how to best kill Cheelin? You let them bleed, slowly, over time. A wound here," she darted forward to slice him, and while he spun out of the worst of it, she raked his haunch. He rolled and lashed at her, barely missing. "A wound there. If you're lucky, they take you back to their den, and you get a whole brood."

Blade flickered into his field, dodged where he thought she'd strike, and rammed into her, knocking her askew. She laughed again, rolling with the new momentum, and struck a glancing blow on his side. He'd winded her, perhaps cracked a rib.

He mustered himself, crouching low enough his quintessence field would hide the drops of blood scattering around him, and considered. Wrestling with his littermates had prepared him in part to fight another Hunter, and he knew he was better than this. He could win. He needed to account for her complete disregard of injuries. She didn't move sensibly, protecting herself. She opened herself for injury, to hurt him worse.

He had play-fought his siblings. She had killed other Hunters.

As he fought to develop a plan, a blur of motion between him and Dirrys distracted him. He felt it more than saw it.

Arow had entered the field.

He did not move as an elderly Hunter might. He moved like air through the tall canopies, the current of the river. Natural, inevitable. Dirrys rose to meet him, claws extended.

They were hard to follow, blurring in and out of quintessence. Now the gathered elders moved away, as Dirrys and Arow covered broad distances in their conflict. Someone pulled Ichys back, protecting her kits above all.

A spray of blood here.

A grunt of pain there.

Limbs appeared and vanished. A snarling face. Two bodies, locked.

Blade's depth perception struggled to adapt, given the blood congealing on his face, but he knew this would be hard to follow even were his vision clear.

After a stretch of time, minutes or months, the flickers of motion and sprays of blood stopped. Three breaths. Four. Blade stumbled forward, not sure what he was going to do, and then they appeared.

Arow's back left leg was buried in Dirrys's lower midsection, his front paws occupied controlling her head. He bled freely from so many wounds it was astonishing he still lived.

And Dirrys, dying, stared up at his face. And she laughed. Spat blood at him. Laughed again.

"Should've frozen you," she said, beginning to go limp. Blade would have missed the words if he hadn't kept lurching forward. He'd forgotten he'd been moving, staring at the tableau in front of them.

"What did you say?" Arow's voice was nearly as faint as hers, but he shook her, slamming her head against the floor.

"You know exactly what I mean." Her laughter was ragged, but the hatred in her eyes shone clear. "Froze you. Thought you hid your tracks, but I found it. Built it. Used it, you clawless kit. You never even knew I'd hacked your ship, did you? All these years, you thought you were hiding from me. I was there in the programming, always tracking your field. You can't get away from me, Arow. How'd Sissisk die?" She spat again, blood and bitter anger boiling out of her. "Frozen in place. Staring at me. Just like you."

Hatred carried her out of the world, the dregs of life oozing from her body.

Without looking, Arow reached for Blade, grabbed him, dragged him closer. The old deo's breath was labored, and he struggled to stay upright, but when he turned his face toward Blade, his gaze still landed like a blow.

"Search everything she's ever owned. I killed a Human, years ago. He found a way to freeze us in our fields. If she had it. If it exists…"

"I will," Blade said, his mind lumbering to catch up, his head heavy.

Arow blinked, acknowledging him, and looked around, searching for something. Someone. Blade knew Ichys was pulling away from the Hunters protecting her, trying to come to them.

The old Hunter saw her, relaxed, tried to speak, and died instead. He slumped to the ground, and Blade belatedly reached for him, feeling something tearing deep within.

It overbalanced him, or maybe he'd already been falling. Dirrys was dead. It was over. The elders would agree…

He never felt Ichys catch him.

* * *

A ninenight or so after their conversation about Conason and sex (it was hard to keep track—Humans used an entirely different way of reckoning time, and Death found it easier just not to care) Death went into labor.

It started benignly enough. It was the middle of the day, and she woke from a bizarrely vivid dream. In deference to the mercs' training needs, she had holed up in one of the non-operational CASPers for the day. The technicians were waiting on some part or other to fix it, and so she had been confident of an undisturbed sleep.

But something had pulled her to wakefulness. Death felt a trickle of wetness from between her back legs, and looked down to see what was going on. She wasn't relieving herself, that was certain, and she wasn't bleeding, from what she could tell.

Suddenly, her entire middle contracted like a fist. She let out a gasp and instantly heard it echo throughout the large hangar bay that housed the Horde's CASPers as the internal mic picked it up. A mutter of voices that she hadn't noticed until then stilled, and she panted her way through the contraction.

"Death?" Conason's voice came through the speakers inside the cab of the CASPer. "Is that you?"

"Yes," Death said, drawing in a deep breath as the contraction eased. "Please get Susa. I think I need her."

She heard the muffled sounds of CASPers moving quickly outside the cabin, and concentrated on breathing and relaxing. Slowly, she realized she was generating a low, rumbling purr, which helped to ease her trembling muscles. She'd just gotten her breathing back under control when two things happened—another contraction ripped through her, curling her up into a ball on the seat of the CASPer—and an explosion rocked the building, causing her temporary den to rattle from side to side in its storage rack.

"Horde!" Conason's voice shouted through the speakers. "Breach in the south wall! Bubba, Connor, cover that—!"

The rest of his orders were cut off by another deafening *boom*, followed by the distant repetitive thumping of some kind of automatic projectile weapon. As she forced herself to breathe through the contraction, Death spared a thought for Susa, hoping she was safe and under cover.

The contractions came faster and harder. Death panted in between, sucking in air and trying to force her body to a calm, relaxed state. *Hunters have been giving birth for thousands of years*, she told herself, *your body knows what to do.*

She steadfastly ignored that Hunters had been dying in childbirth for just as long. That wasn't a helpful fact at this particular moment.

Her body coiled itself up tightly again, but tighter than before…and this time, much to her surprise, she felt an overwhelming need to push back. So, she did. Lying on her side, half curled into a ball, Death bore down and pushed out with all of the considerable strength she had to muster. More explosions and projectile fire shattered the space outside her CASPer, but she focused her attention down to a single word, a single action backed by her iron will. Push.

Something released and slid from her body. Death looked down to see a tiny, wet newcomer resting on her lower thigh. She dragged in a breath and reached down to touch this most precious of gifts. It gave a small "mew" and turned instinctively towards her warmth.

Another contraction hit as Death gathered her first kitten up into her forelegs. She closed her eyes and pushed again, feeling the movement inside her as the new one's littermate moved closer to the outside world. Above her, there was a great sucking sound, and daylight flooded in, violating the dark sacredness of her hiding place.

"Death?" Susa asked, her voice strained and frantic

"Here," Death managed to croak as the contraction raged inside her body. She closed her eyes tighter and hunched over her kitten, trying to protect it from the hammering light. "They are coming."

"Entropy!" Susa cursed, and Death heard the sizzle of an energy weapon fired in atmosphere. Something heavy hit the outside of the CASPer. "They're already here. We have to fall back."

"Can't," Death panted, and once again, she pushed down and out. Another release, another slide, and another kitten wriggled out into the world. Death reached down to gather it up to her chest as well, and for the first time, she tasted smoke in the air.

"The building is on fire," Susa said. Death squinted her eyes open to see her molly climbing awkwardly over the lip of the CASPer cabin. Susa hooked her leg on the internal structure and reached in toward Death. "We can't stay here. Come on, kita, we've got to go."

Death pulled her two kittens in close to herself and felt Susa's gentle hands slip under her bulky, useless body. Birth was so debilitating! She should be fighting, protecting herself and her newly born kittens…but another contraction hit and all she could do was let out a small cry.

"I'm here, little love," Susa whispered as she pulled Death close. "I'm right here. *CONASON!*"

Death closed her eyes once more and heard the sound of another CASPer stomping close.

"Looks like they're neutralized for now," he said. "But this building could come down at any moment. We have to get out of here. I can carry you in the CASPer arms until we get to a vehicle." His voice was amplified through the external speakers of the CASPer, and it made Death's head ache. She closed her eyes against the uncomfortable swaying as Susa climbed from one CASPer to another, and then fought not to push through the next contraction.

"Death?" Susa asked.

"Two," Death panted. "Are here…Another…wants out."

"Oh, sweet merciful…okay, kita. Hang in there, I've got you. Conason, could you step on it?"

A tiny corner of Death's mind wondered what, exactly, Susa wanted Conason to step upon. Certainly, the big CASPer was capable of crushing something, but it didn't seem the most efficient way of taking out a threat. And then her mind went blank of any thoughts at all as they surged forward in a horrible, jerking, swaying motion at speed.

Death retched, and emptied the contents of her stomach all over Susa.

She felt the molly flinch, and then hug her even tighter. Death's body wrenched into another contraction and this time she couldn't stop herself from pushing back. She felt Susa reach and jerk to catch the third kitten that crawled from inside her. A great sob escaped from Death's tightly closed lips.

"I've got it!" Susa said, her exultant words barely audible in the wind of their lurching passage. "Oh, so tiny! It's beautiful and strong, Death! I've got your kitten!"

Death felt Susa try to nestle the third kitten up close to her belly, where she held the other two. The first kitten was busily rooting and kneading to find a source of milk, but the second one had fallen still. Death tried to speak, tried to tell Susa about it, but another wave of contractions hit, and she was paralyzed.

She didn't notice when the swaying and lurching stopped, for her focus had once again drilled down to a single pinpoint intensity.

Push.

Get them out.

Make them live.

Push.

Somewhere, distantly, she heard Susa's shout, and a rumbling that sounded like mountains falling all around them. Blackness crowded in from the edges of her vision, and Death spiraled down…

"No! Stay with me, kita! Your kittens need you awake!"

Another lurch, along with the panicked sound of Susa's voice, brought Death back to awareness. The blackness receded as her body's latest contraction eased, and Death blinked her eyes against the punishing light of Earth's primary star.

"Bubba!" Conason yelled, his voice booming from the external speaker of his suit. "Are our people all out?"

Death panted during the short respite and swiveled her head to see the mechanic, now soot-stained and weary looking. He stood next to the leg of Conason's CASPer, while the other suited mercs gathered around.

"All that were living," Gnad said. "I think I'm the only one not in a suit who made it out—"

"Mr. Conason," Susa said, her voice low but urgent. "My mistress is still in active labor. I must get her somewhere safe immediately."

"I know, Doctor," Conason said. "We have a fallback location, but it is not in this immediate vicinity. I don't think carrying you the whole way would be wise, and all of our vehicles were lost in the garage when the building came down."

"I've got a truck, Boss," Gnad said. Conason stilled, then turned his cumbersome, suited body to face the tired and bedraggled figure of the mechanic.

"You do?"

"Yeah, it won't fit inside the garage entrance. I was going to ask you about parking it in the CASPer bay, but then we got this contract." Gnad said, grinning. Death slow blinked toward him, though she didn't think he could see her very well. Since their rocky meeting, she had actually come to like the mechanic very much. He told amusing tales and had a way of scratching behind her ears that was *most* delicious.

"Get it, Bubba, thanks. The rest of you, I don't know who sent those drones, but it's obvious they're after our client. So, this is now a vehicle escort mission. Doctor, you and your mistress will have to make do in the back of Bubba's truck for a little while."

Susa looked as if she'd protest, but Death lifted her head slightly.

"That is well, thank you, Mr. Conason," she said. Her voice was raw and hoarse, but he must have heard her, because that ended the discussion.

"Right. Form up on me, then kiddies. Let's get this cat and her kittens to safety!"

* * *

The second kitten, the one that had gone so dreadfully still, started to move again as Bubba drove up in what had to be his truck. Death felt a wave of relief crash over her as she guided the tiny (so impossibly tiny!) body to her abdomen to nurse.

"What is that?" she heard Susa say, cuddling Death close while trying not to jar her or the greedy kittens. Even the little latecomer began nursing enthusiastically, once it figured out the logistics. Again, Death turned her head to see past the barrier of Susa's arms. At least Conason had finally set them down on the solid ground.

They stood on the dirty, cracked concrete that fronted one of the downtown roads. A white vehicle with Human writing on the side pulled up to stop in front of them, causing the CASPers to aim their weapons at it. The door opened with a thick *ker-chunk*, and Bubba Gnad stuck his bearded face out from behind a tinted window.

"Don't shoot! It's just me!" he said, with a grin. Even from this distance, Death could see a distinct pinkness to his ears and face. He was blushing?

"Bubba, what on Earth is that thing?" Conason bellowed through his speakers. "'Biological Emergency Response Team'? Are you kidding me with that zombie bullshit?"

"Just because you got no taste in literature is no reason to crap on mine!" Gnad shouted back. "*Black Tide Rising* is a classic! Besides, it's a truck, ain't it? And look, I even put a few toys on it."

He must have toggled a switch or something, because the large cross arm mounted to something piled on the back began to spin, and a hatch opened in the front side fender of the truck. From this hatch, a six barreled, belt-fed weapon emerged.

"See? I got twin miniguns on either side! I figured an area of effect weapon might be helpful in clearing a path, you know what I mean? I got a few other surprises, too. And with the radar on top, I can keep track of you guys in your CASPers—"

"Okay, Bubba, we get it. You like your toys. Let's get the clients loaded in and get gone, please! I doubt that's the last we've seen of those drones," Conason said. Gnad nodded, and reached to open the rear door of the cab. Susa carefully laid Death on the back seat, and then climbed in beside her and began gently prodding at her abdomen, away from the nursing kittens.

"Little Dama," Susa said lowly, using the Hunter language. "Have your contractions stopped?"

"I…" Death said, thinking back. "The last one was in the hangar, when you pulled me out…"

"I still feel one more kitten inside you, sweetling."

Panic rose up within Death, and she swallowed hard to push it down.

"You must get it out," she whispered. "If the fluid sac has broken, the kitten must be born, else it will die inside. You told me this."

"Yes," Susa said softly. "And were we at home, or even back at headquarters, I could go in and get it. But here, now—" she broke off, her tone frustrated as Gnad turned the engine over, and the strange truck roared to life.

"I don't care," Death said, gritting her teeth. "Bubba! You have a knife?"

"Course I do, Kitty," he said. He'd taken to calling her that at some point over the last season.

"Little Dama! You can't be serious? Here? In a moving vehicle with no sanitation? No anesthetic? I could kill you because his tire hit a bump!"

"No need to worry about that," Gnad said, up front. "I modded this suspension myself. It's the smoothest ride you'll feel."

"Still not helpful!" Susa snapped over her shoulder at him as she twisted in the seat to look at Death.

"Yes, it is," Death said. "You can give me nanites later. After we get to the safe house. If the Horde doesn't have them, I would be very surprised."

"If you live that long!" Susa cried.

"Susa. I require this."

"Death, no!"

"Yes."

Tears streamed from the Human woman's eyes. She swiped the back of her hand viciously across her eyes and reached across the back of the seats.

"Give me your knife, Bubba," she said, her voice soaked in sorrow.

"Thank you, Susa."

"Shut the fuck up, Death," Susa snapped. "I love you, and I don't want to hear from you right now. This is going to hurt. A lot."

"I know," Death whispered. "I am ready."

But she wasn't. She really wasn't.

She'd been hurt before, but nothing could have prepared her for the feeling of being ripped open and having her last kitten pulled from inside of her. To Gnad's credit, he drove as smoothly as possible, but he used plenty of speed, and every bump, swerve, and turn ratcheted up Death's agony even higher.

"Stay with me, kita," Susa whispered. "I'm sorry I was mad. We're almost there. Just stay with me!"

Death tried to concentrate on her three nurslings, and on keeping them away from the lower part of her body where Susa worked. Bright spots appeared in her vision, brighter even than the cursed Earth sun. She found herself taking short, choppy sips of air.

"Got it!" Susa cried, and lifted a small, wet, bloody mass up. Death blinked and squinted at it, trying to see the kitten within. Just then, the truck hit a bump, and Death screamed as pain lanced through her.

"Watch it, Bubba!" Susa yelled.

"That wasn't me! We're being attacked! Keep your heads down, ladies! I got this!"

The night split open with the ripping sound of six thousand rounds per minute blasting out either side of their truck. Gnad's wild laughter drifted back to them, while Susa ripped off her outer shirt to wrap the still form of the littlest kitten. She tucked it next to Death, within easy reach of a free nipple, but the tiny thing didn't move.

"Come on, little one," Susa said, her voice ragged from all the stresses of the night. "Come on! After all that, you've got to nurse. You've got to…shit!"

More thumps peppered the side of the truck, but Gnad just hit the accelerator, and they surged forward. Death felt a gray nothingness gather at the edges of her vision, pressing inward, pushing her down toward the oblivion she'd escaped earlier.

"Susa…" she whispered. "I'm trying…"

"Damnit! NO! Stay with me, kita! Death!"

"Here!" Gnad's voice was faint, barely audible over the ringing in Death's ears. "Heard her mention nanites, earlier. Didn't want to interrupt, but I always keep one of these in my truck. It's nonspecific, so I don't know if it will work with her biology…"

"Give it to me!" Susa screamed. She sounded so far away. The grey closed in on Death, making her lose everything in the nothingness and the formless ringing sound. Somewhere, a thought drifted. There was something she had to do before it was too late…oh yes. Scramble. She started to bite down on the toggle switch in her back molar. She was so weak, it didn't actuate right away. She kept at it, knowing that if she didn't, her entire race would be compromised. As would her precious kittens. She had to scramble her DNA. She had no choice.

She bit down again.

A tiny pinprick. So small she barely noticed. Fire flowed into her body from the site, though. Searing, acid, burning fire as millions of nanoscopic healing machines located her hurts and began to repair them faster than thought. Something shoved itself into her mouth, holding her jaw open, preventing her from actuating the tooth switch.

"Don't you dare scramble on me," Susa hissed in the Hunter language. "Don't you do it, Death! I'm not letting you die, do you hear me? These kittens need you. I need you. I am *not* letting you die!"

Something heavy hit the front of the vehicle, and, suddenly, they were airborne.

Though the nanite agony continued to blaze its way through her vessels and tissues, Death managed to curl her body around the tiny, warm bodies of her four kittens. She felt Susa hugging them close, attempting to shield them from the impact as the truck flipped end over end and landed on its roof with a tremendous, world-shattering crash.

"Death?" Susa's broken whisper penetrated the awful silence that followed.

"Susa," Death mewed. "Yes. Here."

"Bubba?"

"Here, Ladies," their driver answered. His voice sounded oddly calm, all of the gleeful mayhem of earlier gone. "You'd best scooch out that back window if you can. I lost contact with the CASPers when the drone kamikazied into us, but some of them are probably still alive out there."

"Conason? The others?" Susa asked.

"I don't know," Gnad said. "No telling. Best go now."

"What about you?"

"Not going anywhere," he said. He coughed wetly. "Got a piece of metal through my chest. Prob'ly going to hurt real bad in a minute. You just get them babies and Kitty, and run. Hide off the road somewhere. Conason will find you."

"Oh Bubba…"

"Just go now, Doctor. That's a good girl."

"Thank you, Bubba," Death roused herself to croak. "Thank you for my life, and those of my offspring. You will be remembered in my clan."

"Well, that's nice," Gnad said, his voice sounding faint and pinched with pain.

"Come on, kita," Susa said, and began scooting across the glass-strewn, crumpled ceiling of the truck. Death felt her kick out to clear a bigger hole in the window, and then Susa squirmed through, holding Death and the kittens close to her chest. Once outside the car, Susa crouched low and began a sort of shuffling run off toward the side of the road. Death could see the hulk of a fallen CASPer there. Susa headed for this and collapsed, weeping, against its metal side.

Something pinged in Death's awareness. The nanite burn continued, though it was easing, and she was able to turn and look back at the wreck they'd escaped. A crumpled metal mass that must have been the drone lay half-buried under the inverted hood of the truck. As she watched, a line appeared in the mass, and a door slid smoothly open.

It wasn't a drone. It was a ship designed to look like a drone and still function even after being deliberately piloted into another object. It was a Hunter ship.

And as she watched, a grey-striped Hunter emerged from the opening and climbed up onto the wreckage of the truck.

"I greet you, Death From Above, of the Night Wind Clan," the Hunter, a male, said in their language. Susa started to sob harder, her body shaking. Death felt her hands wrap around the precious weight of the last kitten, still wrapped in her shirt from earlier. With a quick pull, she detached the kitten from Death's nipple and put it up under her shirt.

"It may not live," Susa breathed in English, in between sobs. "But maybe I can save one of them."

Death dragged in a breath so filled with love that she thought she, too, might weep. She swallowed hard and pushed away the last of her fear and pain, buried it in a box, and turned to face her adversary.

"I greet you, unknown Hunter," Death said, in English. "Congratulations on finding me and defeating my mercenary guards."

"They were more challenging than I expected," the Hunter said. "These machines of theirs are fascinating! I had to remain cloaked lest they shoot me out of the sky. You are to be congratulated on finding such worthy protectors."

"They are worthy," Death called out, hoping Gnad would hear her words if he still lived. "I think you will find Humans to be full of surprises."

"You think so?" the Hunter asked, flicking his tail in amusement. "I wonder—"

Boom!

Death curled into Susa, who ducked down behind the dubious shelter of the CASPer's leg and pressed herself to the metal as Bubba Gnad revealed one of his truck's other surprises—an explosives package that sent a column of flame into the midday sky. The shockwave rippled outward, echoing off of the derelict buildings that surrounded them and setting Death's ears to ringing all over again. She felt flattened by the noise and the heat...and then panic hit.

Her kittens?

She looked down, frantically patting their still little forms. Dead? Or merely stunned by the blast and everything else?

First one, then two moved, and began mewling pitifully and rooting for the teats they'd lost. The third little body, alas, remained still. It was one of the small ones. The third one she'd delivered. An ache unlike anything she'd ever felt pierced through her. Death closed her eyes and lifted her head to scream her loss at the too-bright sky.

"Death?"

Connor's voice. Ragged and hoarse, but low enough to cut through the tinnitus and Susa's quiet sobs. Death squinted her eyes open and looked at him, battered, bloody, wearing a strange smile that didn't touch his eyes.

"Susa?"

"I'm here," the woman said, her voice wet. She reached under her shirt and removed the fourth kitten, who still squirmed weakly, and put it back with its living siblings. The lost one she gently took from Death's fingerpads. "We lost one."

"Oh…Death, Doctor Aloh, I'm so sorry."

"Bubba died too," Death said, her words almost angry in her grief. "He was trapped in the truck when we wrecked, and then he blew it up to save us."

"That sounds like him," Conason's voice was sad as he limped up beside his fellow merc. He, too, was missing his CASPer. Death idly wondered if it was the one they hunkered beside. "He was a good man and will be missed. I'm so sorry about your baby."

"More than your man?" Death asked, because she had to know.

"He was a man. And more, he was a merc. He died doing his job. That's what we do. Now come on. Tony, lift them up. The cavalry's here. I knew the home office would send a detachment as soon as the Headquarters building came down. They tracked our CASPers, and now they're here. So, come this way, and we'll get you on a plane to Kazakhstan."

* * *

"There's another ship incoming quickly," Rurranach said, reading the display that scrolled across the view screen. He didn't need to say it, as the ship's external sensors had transmitted the same information directly to Deluge through his pinplant link, but his subdued voice served to cut through the shocked silence that permeated the cabin.

"It's not registered to Khatash," Deluge said. "No quintessential transponder, so it's not a Hunter ship…but the only people who call me Del are family."

"Del. I know you're there. It's Flame. Please tell me my readout is wrong, and the Governor's ship is somewhere out here."

"Could it be a trick?" Rurranach asked.

"It could," Deluge said, his voice tight. The voice sounded enough like Flame's to be legitimate, but there was enough electronic distortion that it could have been faked as well.

"Do you have any more of those ship-killers?"

"No. Usually, the drill is kill one ship, and if there are more, then turn and run."

"Maybe we should do that, then?" the Sidar said.

"But what if it really is Flame?"

"Give her a test."

"What?"

"Ask her a question only she would know. Something that can't be faked. Maybe something that happened just between the two of you?"

Deluge thought about it for a moment, his brain swirling. How had Flame come to be here of all places? And what was this about a governor?

"Unidentified ship," he said, transmitting slowly. "If you are who you claim to be, please authenticate with the full Human name of our molly."

"Dr. Susan Aloh." Even thinned by the interference, frustration colored her tone. "She's from Texas, on Earth. You threw blood on me after our first hunt, and I covered you in intestines later that night. You took my last contract and better have completed it. I still owe you for throwing me on the table in the den. If you shoot my ship, I will strangle you with your own intestines."

"Well, hi, littlest!" Deluge said, slow blinking. "What brings you to this wasteland of space ghosts?"

As he spoke, Deluge was busy continuing to maneuver through the bits of metal. This close to the derelict hulk, most of the debris was small enough that he could take it on the shield, but a few of the larger pieces had to be avoided.

"We are chasing the former Cemarap Governor. Did you blow her up or is she in that debris field?" Her voice sounded intense, shaded by shock and joy, but very focused on his answer.

"I don't know anything about a governor. The only ship out here besides mine and yours was carrying registry from home and came up as belonging to a clan called Whispering Fear. You know about the interdict, right? I was attacked while on contract. That's why I came here."

"I know." Three breaths worth of a pause. "They blew up our den. Where's the ship?"

"You're in its debris field," Deluge said, allowing exultant joy into his tone. "I wasn't going to let them come at me first. I took them out with my defensive armament. All that's left is the dust burning off our energy shields."

"Fuck." Her curse was low and vicious. "She's behind what happened with Dama and the Peacemaker. We've been tracing her blasted trail for a season and then chasing her for the past three days and now…Del, you've ruined everything!"

"Me? What was I supposed to do? Let her shoot me out of the sky? You weren't there on 'Tlor, Flame! The Hunter who attacked me hired a *Goka mercenary company* to help her get to me! Dama taught us to survive! How was I to know that you were chasing after some overgrown paramecium in a ship *that had Hunter registry*?"

"Children."

The voice that cut through their rapidly escalating argument made Deluge go very still. Apparently, there was someone else out here in the black.

"I am certain I did not teach you to argue in public on an open communications channel. Neither one of you has the full story. Bring your ships in to dock, and I will fill you in."

"Dama…?" Flame's voice on the channel was barely a whisper as the hulk next to them suddenly came alive with lights leading to a docking entrance. "You're…"

"Not dead," Deluge said, and because he couldn't resist, he added smugly, "I knew it the whole time."

* * *

Deluge knew he was smirking—he couldn't help it—as vindication surged through him, nearly ruffling his fur. Reow was alive, and more, she was *here!* His plan had worked, and now he and Flame would know the reason why everything had happened the way that it did.

What a fun contract this had turned out to be!

"Master," Rurranach said lowly from his seat next to Deluge's.

"Who?"

"Ugh. Del," Rurranach corrected himself, sighing. "It just feels wrong to call you by name!"

"Get used to it. You were, before. Did you want something?"

"Yes," the Sidar said, rustling his wings. Deluge looked over at him, surprised to find that Rurranach lacked any trace of glee in his demeanor. "Have you considered, *Del,* that this, too, may be a trap?"

"What do you mean?" Deluge asked, some of his glee draining away. "How could it be a trap?"

"How could it not be?" Rurranach countered. "We're out here in the middle of an ancient floating debris field. Two ships show up, racing at us, one with Hunter registry—"

"And I blew that one up."

"And so you did. But then the other appears to carry your sister, and now your mother's voice comes across the transmission channel? Doesn't it appear just too convenient to you?"

"You've got a nasty, suspicious mind, Rurranach," Deluge said, slow blinking as his good mood returned.

"I do. It's why I'm still alive."

"Fair point. Okay, I don't think this is a trap, because, remember, we were tracking Dama's quintessence field out here in the first place. So that's two independent indications that she's really here. One, her field and two, her voice."

"But it doesn't make any sense!" Rurranach protested, shuffling his wings again. "Why would she be out here in this forsaken waste?"

"We'll be sure to ask her," Deluge said, slow blinking a laugh again. He jerked his head toward the display screen, currently carrying the visual feed from the ship's external sensors. "It's our turn to dock."

Since Flame's ship had the best approach vector to the derelict hulk that turned out to not be derelict at all, she'd docked first. In the meantime, Deluge maneuvered *Iora* around and got her headed in the correct direction as well. It had taken a small amount of time, but now they were closing in and ready to begin docking procedures. He gave the docking command through his pinplants, and the agile little ship moved smoothly to obey.

* * *

Tamir rocked up on her toes and back to settle her center of gravity, and Flame watched her with interest. The bounty hunter's restless energy ramped up when they realized they were flying through the miniscule specks left of Kelket, and had only increased while they docked. She fairly vibrated, waiting for the airlock to finish matching their pressure.

"We're not getting attacked," the Hunter said, amused. "Dama's alive! And Hrusha. This is good news."

"Is it?" Tamir did not reach for her gun, but twisted her wrists, loosening the joints as though in preparation.

"Did you secretly have a falling out with Hrusha that you hadn't mentioned?"

"What? No."

"Then it's good news." Still, Tamir's tension affected her excitement, and Flame's ears swiveled, trying to pick up anything on the other side of the airlock. Reassuring both herself and her partner,

Flame stretched out her claws, demonstrating she was ready, if something unexpected waited for them.

"Besides," the Hunter added, tone brightening considerably, "if it is some kind of trap, Del is docking nearby. He's better than me in a brawl." She shared that without embarrassment—Flame knew, straight through her core, exactly the measure of her strengths, so it offered no threat to recognize where others excelled.

The airlock finally clunked, singing out its odd medley, and Flame paused before opening the lock. Tamir wasn't convinced, so she offered what she could.

"If no one is out there, we'll wait for Del and whoever is with him before we go any further into this."

Tamir frowned, doubtful, but as ever she didn't hesitate. Settling into her calm, alert stance, she nodded.

Flame toggled the switch, and the airlock door irised open.

Reow awaited on the far side, another Hunter behind her.

"My kita," she murmured. "I greet you with love and so very much pride."

"Dama." Flame shuddered from the tips of her ears down through her tail. With the briefest of glances up to Tamir—she hoped it communicated 'told you so' clearly, she stepped slowly into the hall. It took every bit of control she had, not to throw herself against her dama. Had it been only Tamir to witness, she would have.

"Dama, Peacemaker Hrusha. I greet you." Keeping her tone steady used all the discipline she had left, and she kept moving until she could finally, finally rub the top of her head under her dama's chin.

Reow closed her eyes and leaned into the caress, turning her head so as to rub her own cheek against her smallest child's skull.

"I had no idea," Dama murmured, her voice low and sad, pitched for Flame's ears alone. "I never imagined they would go so far as to interdict all of us. I knew you would likely survive, but I have so feared for you and your siblings. Does everyone live?"

"I don't know." That admission hurt far worse than complimenting another's skills ever could, stabbing through her with every regret she had of not finding her siblings. "They all survived the initial attack on the Den. I couldn't look for them, though, and risk drawing attention."

Reow pressed harder against her kita for one more breath, and then lifted her head. "Peacemaker Hrusha, this is my youngest kita, Silent Flame."

Flame stepped back from her dama, the motion screaming her unwillingness to do so, and looked up at the Peacemaker.

Hrusha flicked her ears politely at Flame, then turned to regard Tamir closely. Tamir, who blinked at her in stunned silence. The Peacemaker tilted her head, huffed a small laugh.

"You are amused, my friend?" Reow asked. "This is your Human bounty hunter, is it not? The one you sent to my Den under the pretext of finding me, when you knew I was already gone?"

"I am understanding why you sigiled one of them," Hrusha said, and Flame stiffened slightly. Would Hrusha claim Tamir? "She always did good work, this one, but this has exceeded my expectations." There was something more than pleased in her tone—smugness? Flame wondered at it, and subtly put herself between Tamir and Hrusha. Not a challenge, but if there was a claim here, Flame wanted it.

The warning chime sang out again, and a sliding hiss heralded the arrival of the second ship. The airlock door had only irised halfway open before an orange figure dived through, landing in a roll and coming up on his back feet with a grand flourish. Behind him, in quiet contrast to these dramatics, a cloaked Sidar stepped into the ever-more crowded corridor.

"I knew it all along!" Choking Deluge cried, his glee ringing through his words and rippling out from him in near-palpable waves.

"How?" Reow asked, her tone calm and dry with just a touch of amusement. "How did you know?"

"*Iora!*" Deluge exclaimed, nearly shouting in his excitement at having solved the puzzle she'd set for him. "She still carried your quintessence signature. That's why you let me take her! So one of us, at least, would know that you still lived, even when the whole Galaxy thought otherwise!"

"Clever Kit," Reow said, slow blinking. "Well done. I am very proud of you."

Deluge let out a loud, victorious yowl, and launched himself at his dama, not caring about the presence of strangers. He needed to press against her, and feel her love and warmth and approbation.

Behind him, the Sidar remained very still, except to pull out a chain from around his neck and let its pendant sit above his cloak. It caught the light in the hallway and glinted at Flame. It was the sigil of their clan.

Flame turned her head, examining the Sidar silently as Del made his usual Del show. She was glad to see her brother, but fully distracted by his companion.

"You made a friend," she said, using the Human phrase naturally. It wasn't the most pressing issue, but it mattered to her, all at once. That they *would* have their clan back. That sigils could be given. Because their clan would exist.

"I did," Deluge said, backing up from his enthusiastic rubbing against Reow's cheek. "Everyone, meet Rurranach. He's a Sidar and a money genius and just the right amount of unscrupulous. Rurranach, meet our dama, and my sister-kita Silent Flame, and...her friend...and...oh! Hello Peacemaker! I, Choking Deluge of the Night Wind Clan greet you. I'm glad to see you looking so alive."

Rurranach stepped forward under this effusive introduction and bowed in the manner of his kind. That is to say, he swept his cloak off and bent at the waist, extending his wings out to either side, showing off their impressive span as best he could in the narrow hallway.

"I greet you, Dama," he said simply, his chittering tone high with what was probably nerves.

"Welcome to our clan, Rurranach," Reow said, slow blinking at the Sidar. "I look forward to getting to know your unique skills in our service."

Flame glanced at Tamir, but resolved to revisit the matter later. She looked over this group, studying Hrusha in particular, and finally asked the question she'd been obsessed with since hearing Reow's voice over the comms.

"What, happened?"

"Perhaps we should make ourselves comfortable?" Hrusha said by way of answer, flicking her ears to gesture down the corridor.

"Yes," Reow said. "Our sitting room is this way."

She turned and began walking past the airlock doors. At the end of the corridor, she turned left and headed into a low, comfortable room with the dim, green-tinged lighting reminiscent of Khatash. Chairs, cushions, pedestals, and other various seating surfaces clustered in conversational groups throughout the space. There was even a small pool in the center, something suitable for an elderly Cemarap who wished to relax, perhaps.

Deluge watched the others follow his dama and hung back to enter beside Flame.

"Hello, Littlest," he said, rather more quietly than earlier. "This ought to be interesting, no? You're all right?"

"Happy to see you," Flame answered, brushing her shoulder into his arm fondly. "And ready to understand…all of this." She nodded ahead, gladder than she could express to have her littermate there. It made the absences of Death and Blade cut deeper, but she had Reow, and Del, and Tamir, and had to believe the rest would follow.

She nudged her brother-kit again and followed the rest, meaning to observe this odd space around them, but eyes drifting back to her dama instead. As everyone settled themselves, Flame tore her gaze to Hrusha, her *want* to know vibrating through the room.

"Where should I begin?" Hrusha asked, turning slightly toward Reow.

"Perhaps with the late Governor," Reow said. "What you told me when I arrived."

"I have known Sissisk since we were barely grown kits, new to the jungle." Hrusha sat back in her cushion, tail curled around her. The tip flicked once, then stilled. "She became friends with Kelket years ago, soon after Sissisk discovered pinpecks. Last year, Sissisk mentioned a falling out she'd had with Kelket. Our Cemarap friend had invested in a number of merc companies, and didn't care for how quickly the newest mercenary species was gaining ground." Her tail flicked again, ears briefly flattening.

"Sissisk mocked her, as would any of us who know the value of competition. They did not talk for months, until Kelket left her an enormous gift of pinpecks. Sissisk took it as an apology, and then died a ninenight later."

"Was there reason to link these events? I had not heard any rumblings of foul play connected with the late Governor's death," Rurranach said from his cushion in the corner. He sat with his wings tucked close, swaddled once more in his great cloak.

Deluge slow blinked at his friend, then turned to Reow.

"See, Dama. I told you he was a genius."

"I never doubted, my kit," she said, then flicked her eyes at Flame as well. "I never doubted any of you."

"No." Hrusha drew out the word, heralding the next, "But it was suspicious to me. Sissisk was getting older, but I had hunted with her days before. She was in perfect health. A peaceful death in her sleep was her future. And Kelket's gift was so extravagant. As though she were guilty."

Flame turned toward Tamir, remembering half-whispered rumors gleaned from a dark corner of a shipyard designed to be forgotten. The kind of place one would float contracts against targets no Hunter would touch.

But what if one did?

"As you note, Sidar, it was not much, but enough that I paid attention. Mercenary companies were at the root of Kelket and Sissisk's disagreement, so I took our friendly wagers and applied them to the profits and successes of several major or growing companies. I mostly won, until Kelket started betting on the fortunes of a Lumar company known as the Proud Fist."

Deluge sat up very straight, his ears pricked forward in interest.

Hrusha slow blinked. "This company was winning contracts that no Lumar company had business even bidding upon. As I'm sure

Deluge can tell you, the Lumar are brawlers, good for a dust-up and not much else. So why, then, were they snatching fortified assault contracts from the jaws of much more capable Tortantula companies?"

"Rhaabou, their former commander," Deluge said softly. "And her sister, Apeya."

"Yes," Hrusha said. "Their Veetanho commanders were undercutting the bids, winning the contracts, and soaking up the losses while their pinpeck farmer masters raked in the attrition bonuses."

"They paid them out, too," Deluge said. "We've got the financials from the Proud Fist mercenary company. They were paying out combat bonuses and refitting fees to companies owned by the same pinpeck farming conglomerate. The whole thing was a credit laundering scheme, but Rhaabou got greedy and started skimming off the top. So, her sister, Apeya, who is on the board of the farming conglomerate, got the bright idea to take out a contract on the greedy commander."

"You can thank me for that," Hrusha said, slow blinking. "You do have clever offspring, Reow. I congratulate you."

"Thank you," Reow said.

"You see," Hrusha said, turning back to her rapt audience. "I knew something wasn't right with those contracts, so I went to talk to a few of the Tortantula companies to find out what they knew about the Proud Fist. All they could tell me was that they'd undercut the bid, and that they'd been nearly annihilated for their trouble by the Golden Horde. The entire station was abuzz with the gossip. Apparently, you Humans have developed a new kind of battle suit." She turned to look at Tamir in inquiry.

"They have," Deluge said, before the bounty hunter could speak. "They call it the CASPer Mark 3. I talked to one of the designers. And one of the survivors of that battle. He said they were quite deadly."

"Yes, well, they certainly did make the upstart Human mercenary companies sound much more effective. Almost everyone in that pit was talking about it. It was exactly the kind of example Sissisk said Kelket used as to why Humans shouldn't be allowed to petition for membership.

"In any case, I needed to know more about the Proud Fist. So, I did some research, and discovered the same thing you did, Deluge. Rhaabou was skimming off the top, and her sister, Apeya, was displeased. I sent her an anonymous message, strongly recommending that she seek a contract with a member of the Night Wind Clan on Khatash. And then I requested your dama by name as my successor."

"But *why*?" Flame burst out, unable to help herself. "Why us?"

"Because," Hrusha said. "If my friend Sissisk *was* murdered, it had to have been by the hand of another Hunter. She would have suspected anyone else and would have survived. But *someone* from Khatash got to her.

"Your clan is small. You have taken in no outsiders, and every one of you had a legitimate alibi. I could be reasonably confident none of you were involved in her murder, and I needed more information. So, I sent Tamir to you, to be on site and to see what developed. You see, I knew that there was threat to my life, and likely Reow's once she arrived. So, we decided to let our enemies think they had succeeded in taking us out. Once that was done, and once Rhaabou and Apeya were taken out of the picture, we expected they would make a move."

"A moment, Peacemaker," Deluge said, holding up a paw as he interrupted her again. She slow blinked and flicked her ears in permission for him to continue. "The contract was only for Rhaabou. How could you predict that I would eliminate Apeya as well?"

"I didn't," Hrusha said. "The contract was originally offered to and accepted by your sister, Silent Flame. Her record of successful contracts indicated she had the personality traits I desired...she hated waste, and wouldn't appreciate the kind of dynamic those two Veetanho sisters had. I gambled she would act as you have done. I am a very skilled gambler," she added, dropping her jaw to show all her teeth.

Deluge inclined his head in agreement.

"Also," Reow said, coming to her four feet. "You must understand, we never imagined you would all be put under interdict. I knew eventually you would find my quintessence field via *Iora*, and I thought that you would at least be able to communicate and coordinate your efforts with one another. We never anticipated our enemy's response would be as vindictive as it was."

"But who *is* the enemy?" Tamir asked, leaning forward. "Governor Kelket was behind the plot, but who was she paying? Who is the assassin?"

"I have an idea," Reow said. "But no proof. One of the reasons for our masquerade was to try and draw her out."

"Her?"

"Yes. My instinct tells me that it is a particular dama. One who argued vociferously against my posting here. Dirrys, of the Whispering Fear Clan. But again, I have no proof," Reow's tail twitched as she allowed those present to see her frustration.

"So, what do we do now?" Deluge asked.

"We must obtain proof. Though I don't know how we're to do that without Kelket," Hrusha said.

"Go home," Tamir said.

"What?"

"Your clan is under interdict because they think you killed the Peacemaker, right?" the bounty hunter said, turning to Reow. "But if you and Hrusha arrive on Khatash, they'll have to acknowledge that no crime was committed. And if it is this Dirrys, we can see how she reacts. Maybe she'll trip herself up when you return. Especially when you come back bearing the Proud Fist financial statements that establish a credit trail from Kelket's pinpeck collective to her clan."

"The statements aren't that clear," Rurranach said.

"Yes, but she doesn't know that, does she?" Tamir replied with a grin.

"Apparently, I'm not the only gambler in this room," Hrusha said, her voice threaded through with approval as she looked at her longtime associate.

"Not even close," Tamir said, and for some reason, turned to grin at Flame.

"When do we leave?" Flame replied, slow blinking and flexing her claws. "Tell me now works."

* * *

Flame made herself a target.

They had announced their return to Khatash while still in route. *Iora* flew alongside *Dimintina* and the

Peacemaker ship *Aloru* with clear signatures, on a direct course. They had Hrusha, alive. The interdict was entropy and rotten waste. Their return dared Whispering Fear's Dama to come for them.

Flame hoped she would.

More often than not, when faced with a threat or a target, Flame prowled, a moving target impossible to sense in her quintessence field. She would stalk, and wait, and strike from nowhere. Not this time.

She stood directly in the airlock as it opened, giving the impression of ease, ready to strike.

And froze, when the hall in front of them revealed…

Blade.

Blade, a livid scar burned across half his face. Less an ear and an eye, from when she'd last seen him.

"I greet you, littlest," he said when it became clear she wasn't moving.

"Blade," she said, abandoning the greeting. She had been ready for anything, always, braced herself for any number of confrontations upon their arrival to Khatash's suborbital station. Not this. Not him. Aware she was floundering, she crossed into the station, her hand lifting to touch part of his scar before she'd meant to do anything.

"You've been busy," he said, and there was humor in his voice.

That fact stabbed against her so painfully she took a ragged breath, and then another, steadier one. Blade. He was alive. That made three of them.

"So have you, biggest. What…"

He flicked an ear, interrupting her question, and leaned forward to rub his unmarred cheek against hers.

"How did you convince Dama to let you dock first?"

"I didn't. She made us keep this stupid ship, so I asked Tamir to get fancy and cut *Iora* off just enough to slow her down. I wanted to be here first, in case—"

"In case Whispering Fear attacked." Blade finished her sentence, and she nodded, wondering as his tail waved. As though he had a secret. "No worry on that front, littlest. I'm mated to their dama."

"BLADE." She stepped back from him, thoroughly thrown. "Tamir!"

The Human leaned around the edge of the airlock, and Flame knew she'd have a hand on the holster of her gun, the other hand loosening its wrist.

"Standby," Flame continued, staring at her brother. "We may still have to kill everyone." She didn't mean it, but she was at such a loss she could do nothing but joke. Del would have appreciated it.

"*Iora* will finish depressurizing in a minute. Walk with me."

She did, gesturing for Tamir to follow, unable to tear her bemused gaze from Blade. Behind them, Tamir muttered about manners, or Hunters, but Flame couldn't focus on her. She knew the Human would repeat herself, as needed, louder and more to her face later. If the ground stopped shifting under her long enough to reach a later.

Waiting outside *Iora's* dock was a female Hunter—a damita, Flame corrected herself, taking in the visible pregnancy. Her fur was a cloudy gray, and her eyes focused first on Blade, then Flame, and finally Tamir.

She was demonstrably not Dirrys, and Flame didn't have time for a greeting before the airlock clunked and began to cycle open.

"That was a nasty trick you pulled with *Dimintina*, Littlest," Deluge said, his ears flat as he leapt through the opening. "You're lucky *Iora's* so maneuverable. Blade! I greet you, big brother! What in entropy happened to your eye? And...I, Choking Deluge, of Night Wind Clan, greet you, Damita. I surely hope you're not going to try to kill me, not with a litter growing."

"I greet you, Hunters." The gray damita pricked both ears forward, amused by Choking Deluge and apparently pleased by his jump to preventing violence. Flame felt the realization crash the moment before the other Hunter said the words, "I am Ichys, Dama of Whispering Fear. Blade has told me much about you." She turned her eyes to Flame. "Both of you."

"Dama," Flame said, dipping her head slightly in respect, "I greet you." At least a hundred questions crowded in her throat, but Blade was flipping his ear at her again, and habit made her hold them.

A series of chimes announced that the third airlock had begun to open, and the group of them turned to face it. Out of the corner of her eye, Flame caught sight of Del's Sidar stepping out and to Deluge's side.

Then she carefully watched Blade's face and ears as their dama emerged into the hallway.

Blade took two sudden steps toward their dama, as though he hadn't truly believed she'd be there until he put eyes on her. His ears pricked toward her, back toward Ichys, and back toward Reow again, and he stared at their dama hard enough Flame wasn't sure he'd noticed Hrusha at all.

"Dama," he said, the rest of the greeting stalling in his mouth.

"I greet you, my kit," she said, slow blinking. She crossed the remaining distance to him and took a moment to rub her cheek hard against his uninjured one. "Does the one who hurt you still breathe?"

"No," he said simply. "But I did not kill her."

"He wounded her, Dama, and she fell to another of my clan's Hunters." Sorrow touched the younger dama's tone on only the last words.

"Dama, I introduce to you Ichys, Dama of Whispering Fear."

Reow turned to face the younger dama and gave her a long, measuring look.

"And so," she said. "Dirrys is dead?"

"As I said," Ichys replied.

"And will you continue your clan's enmity toward mine?"

The question dropped like a stone in the sudden silence that followed. Flame glanced at Blade, at Deluge and his Sidar, at Tamir and Hrusha, and lastly at Reow and Ichys. Ichys did not blink, and there was no hesitation in her. She paused only to touch Blade lightly with one hand, and rest the other on her midsection.

"Blade is my mate. I would prefer to move forward as allies." Her voice remained calm, outnumbered in that hall by many who had cause to hate her clan. In that moment, Flame decided she liked her brother-kit's new mate, though the realization made her miss their remaining sibling even more.

Reow stared for a moment longer, and then slowly blinked her eyelids in a smile.

"Then I greet you, Dama of Whispering Fear and beloved of my kit. Congratulations on your litter." She turned to gesture for Hrusha to come forward. "And I introduce you to Governor-elect Hrusha, who was nominated before the council, and as you can see, is very much still alive. I imagine we will all have many questions and much to discuss. Shall we proceed to the council's meeting chamber, so that we can explain everything only once?"

"Dama." Ichys inclined her head, conveying agreement and respect, and turned to Hrusha. "Governor-Elect, I greet you. I know all await your words with interest." She led them down the hall, where Flame was sure a dropship waited to take them to the surface. And to the many questions from very-invested clan leaders.

She had never been so happy to be home.

* * * * *

Epilogue

I t was over.

Susa drew in a deep, shuddering breath as the airlock began its opening sequence.

"Nervous?" Conason asked, next to her. She looked up at him with a small smile.

"Not exactly," she said. "Overwhelmed, perhaps, but in a good way. Your mission is almost finished, Mr. Conason. It was good of you and Mr. Connor to escort us all the way home."

As she spoke, a soft mewling sound came from underneath her outer jacket. A small, black-furred head poked out of her collar and looked directly at Conason.

"Dama?" the little one squeaked.

"I am here, Bubba," Death replied, behind Susa. She had regained her liquescence of movement in the time since she'd given birth, and the molly was glad to see it. "Where are your sister-kitas? Susita? Caspr?"

An orange kita appeared on the floor next to Conason's booted foot, looking perfectly smug with herself. Conason bit off a curse and bent to pick her up. As he did so, a grey-striped head poked out of the back of his shirt and climbed out onto his shoulder, prompting more curses.

"Damn your sharp little claws, Susita!" the Human merc said, reaching around his neck to pull the striped one forward to join her sister and brother. On Susa's other side, Tony Connor smothered a chuckle.

Susa thought about admonishing the kits to be good, reminding them of their manners and greeting, but those thoughts fled as the airlock door finally irised open and she saw them.

Del, orange as the sunrise and dropping his jaw in a grin, standing beside a sigiled Sidar.

Blade, battered but happy, wearing the air of command as he stood firm while his very pregnant mate leaned against him.

Flame, the littlest. Always the best at hiding and stealth, now nearly shining with confidence and resting on the shoulder of the Human bounty hunter.

And in front of all of them, Reow. The one who'd saved her from herself so long ago. The one who'd taught her how to love. The one who'd given her a family.

"I greet you, clan of my heart," she found herself saying. She couldn't say more, for her words felt choked with emotion. She cleared her throat and blinked overfilled eyes while Death rocketed forward to embrace her dama and littermates.

"Susa," Reow said softly after a moment. "You saved her, and her kittens."

"Only three," Susa said, bending down, and gesturing for the mercs to follow. "We lost one, but here are Bubba, Susita, and Caspr. Kits, greet your dama."

"That's not Dama!" little orange Susita snapped. "Dama's right there!"

Reow laughed.

"I am your dama's dama," she said. "She was once a tiny kita in my hands, just as you are now. I greet you, lovely little ones, and welcome you to the family."

Her beautiful blue eyes tracked up to meet Susa's.

"Welcome home."

# # # # #

Glossary

Basreen—a smaller predator native to Khatash. Also the Hunters' preferred aerial/orbital supremacy fighter, named after the above species.

Cheelin—a large, dangerous prey animal native to Khatash.

Clan—the Hunter's family structure and business framework.

Cooz—a fermented Khatashi beverage made from the poisonous sap of the tree by the same name. The drink is much prized by Hunters, though it is fatal to any other species.

Dama—the Depik word for both mother and queen. The head of a clan.

Damita—a lesser Dama, a female Hunter who has borne kittens and is a leader within the clan, but not the head of the clan.

Deo—a male elder of the clan.

Elder—any of the Damas, damitas or deos who convene to discuss/decide on matters that affect the race of Hunters as a whole.

Hunter—the Depik word for themselves.

Khatash—the Depik home planet.

Khava—a predatory fishlike aquatic species native to Khatash.

Kit—a male kitten.

Kita—a female kitten.

Malik—a species of tree native to Khatash. The fruit is poisonous.

Malluma Songo—a psychotropic, highly addictive drug derived from a Khatash plant of the same name.

Molly—an infertile Hunter (or rarely, Sigiled being) who raises a clan's kittens. A combination nanny, tutor, nurse, and coach.

Quintessence—the non-baryonic energy that Hunters and other species native to Khatash have evolved to use alongside electromagnetic pulses in their neuroanatomy.

Pinpeck—a meaty fruit. Known by Humans as "the jackrabbit fruit of space."

Rizel—a species of tree native to Khatash. The leaves are poisonous.

Sigil—the mark of a Depik clan, indicating ownership by/membership in that clan.

Distances on Khatash

(approximate)

Khatash—Metric
1 tailtip = 0.25 centimeters
1 span = 5 tailtips or 1.25 cm
1 bodylength = 0.5 meters
1 bound = 10 meters or 20 bodylengths
1 sprint = 10 bounds or 100 meters or 200 bodylengths
1 tensprint = 1km
1 half-range = 80 km
1 range = 160 kilometers

Metric—Khatash
1 cm = 4 tailtips
1 meter = 2 bodylengths
1 km = 1 tensprint or 10 sprints or 100 bounds

Time on Khatash

The Depik calendar is based on factors of 9. The Khatashi day is based on the planetary rotation, which lasts roughly 27 Earth hours. Due to their largely crepuscular/nocturnal nature, Depik divide that day into 3 equal periods called Mrurs, which roughly translates to "Prowls."

3 Mrurs = 1 night
9 nights = 1 ninenight
1 month = 3 ninenights = 27 nights
1 season = 3 months = 9 ninenights = 81 nights
1 year = 3 seasons = 9 months = 27 ninenights = 243 nights

The Khatashi year lasts 3 seasons, and is therefore quite a bit shorter than our own Earth year. For that reason, and their relative life spans, Humans seem particularly long-lived to the Depik.

About the Authors

Kacey Ezell

Kacey Ezell was born in South Dakota in 1977. Her parents joined the US Air Force in 1984, and she grew up around the world on various military bases. When she was seven, her mother gave her a copy of Anne McCaffrey's Dragondrums, and shortly thereafter, Kacey decided that she wanted to be a dragonrider when she grew up. In 1999, she followed her parents into the "family business" and attended the United States Air Force Academy before going to pilot training. As dragons were in short supply at the time, she reasoned that flying aircraft was the next best thing. She earned her wings in 2001, and has over 2500 hours in the UH-1N and Mi-17 helicopters.

From the time she was a small child, Kacey made up stories to tell to her friends and family. In 2009, while deployed to Iraq, she wrote the military-themed supernatural story "Light," which was published in the Baen Books anthology Citizens. She was asked to consult on John Ringo's 2015 novel Strands of Sorrow, and wrote the cover story for the Black Tide Rising anthology set in Ringo's zombie apocalypse universe. That story, "Not in Vain," was selected for inclusion in the "Year's Best Military SF and Adventure Fiction" anthology produced by Baen Books.

Kacey writes science fiction, fantasy, horror, noir, romance...she writes fiction. She lives with her husband, two daughters, and two cats.

* * * * *

Marisa Wolf

Marisa Wolf was born in New England, and raised on Boston sports teams, Star Wars, Star Trek, and the longest books in the library (usually fantasy). Over the years she majored in English in part to get credits for reading (this...only partly worked), taught middle school, was headbutted by an alligator, built a career in education, earned a black belt in Tae Kwon Do, and finally decided to finish all those half-started stories in her head.

She currently lives in Texas with three absurd rescue dogs, one deeply understanding husband, and more books than seems sensible.

* * * * *

Connect with Kacey Ezell Online

Website: www.kaceyezell.net

Amazon: https://www.amazon.com/Kacey-Ezell/e/B0195040QU/

Facebook: https://www.facebook.com/AuthorKaceyEzell/

Twitter: @Sevillalost

* * * * *

Connect with Marisa Wolf Online

Website: https://www.marisawolf.net/

Amazon: https://www.amazon.com/Marisa-Wolf/e/B077K8V2J5/

Facebook: https://www.facebook.com/marisawolfauthor/

Twitter: @marisa_comeaux

Instagram: @bookdogs

* * * * *

The following is an
Excerpt from Book One of The Psyche of War:

Minds of Men

Kacey Ezell

Available from Theogony Books

eBook, Paperback, and (soon) Audio

Excerpt from "Minds of Men:"

"Look sharp, everyone," Carl said after a while. Evelyn couldn't have said whether they'd been droning for minutes or hours in the cold, dense white of the cloud cover. "We should be overhead the French coast in about thirty seconds."

The men all reacted to this announcement with varying degrees of excitement and terror. Sean got up from his seat and came back to her, holding an awkward looking arrangement of fabric and straps.

Put this on, he thought to her. *It's your flak jacket. And your parachute is just there,* he said, pointing. *If the captain gives the order to bail out, you go, clip this piece into your 'chute, and jump out the biggest hole you can find. Do you understand? You do, don't you. This psychic thing certainly makes explaining things easier,* he finished with a grin.

Evelyn gave him what she hoped was a brave smile and took the flak jacket from him. It was deceptively heavy, and she struggled a bit with getting it on. Sean gave her a smile and a thumbs up, and then headed back to his station.

The other men were checking in and charging their weapons. A short time later, Evelyn saw through Rico's eyes as the tail gunner watched their fighter escort waggle their wings at the formation and depart. They didn't have the long-range fuel capability to continue all the way to the target.

Someday, that long-range fighter escort we were promised will materialize, Carl thought. His mind felt determinedly positive, like he was trying to be strong for the crew and not let them see his fear. That, of course, was an impossibility, but the crew took it well. After all, they were afraid, too. Especially as the formation had begun its descent to the attack altitude of 20,000 feet. Evelyn became gradually aware of

449

the way the men's collective tension ratcheted up with every hundred feet of descent. They were entering enemy fighter territory.

Yeah, and someday Veronica Lake will...ah. Never mind. Sorry, Evie. That was Les. Evelyn could feel the waist gunner's not-quite-repentant grin. She had to suppress a grin of her own, but Les' irreverence was the perfect tension breaker.

Boys will be boys, she sent, projecting a sense of tolerance. *But real men keep their private lives private.* She added this last with a bit of smug superiority and felt the rest of the crew's appreciative flare of humor at her jab. Even Les laughed, shaking his head. A warmth that had nothing to do with her electric suit enfolded Evelyn, and she started to feel like, maybe, she just might become part of the crew yet.

Fighters! Twelve o'clock high!

The call came from Alice. If she craned her neck to look around Sean's body, Evelyn could just see the terrifying rain of tracer fire coming from the dark, diving silhouette of an enemy fighter. She let the call echo down her own channels and felt her men respond, turning their own weapons to cover *Teacher's Pet's* flanks. Adrenaline surges spiked through all of them, causing Evelyn's heart to race in turn. She took a deep breath and reached out to tie her crew in closer to the Forts around them.

She looked through Sean's eyes as he fired from the top turret, tracking his line of bullets just in front of the attacking aircraft. His mind was oddly calm and terribly focused...as, indeed, they all were. Even young Lieutenant Bob was zeroed in on his task of keeping a tight position and making it that much harder to penetrate the deadly crossing fire of the Flying Fortress.

Fighters! Three o'clock low!

That was Logan in the ball turret. Evelyn felt him as he spun his turret around and began to fire the twin Browning AN/M2 .50 caliber machine guns at the sinister dark shapes rising up to meet them with fire.

Got 'em, Bobby Fritsche replied, from his position in the right waist. He, too, opened up with his own .50 caliber machine gun, tracking the barrel forward of the nose of the fighter formation, in order to "lead" their flight and not shoot behind them.

Evelyn blinked, then hastily relayed the call to the other girls in the formation net. She felt their acknowledgement, though it was almost an absentminded thing as each of the girls were focusing mostly on the communication between the men in their individual crews.

Got you, you Kraut sonofabitch! Logan exulted. Evelyn looked through his eyes and couldn't help but feel a twist of pity for the pilot of the German fighter as he spiraled toward the ground, one wing completely gone. She carefully kept that emotion from Logan, however, as he was concentrating on trying to take out the other three fighters who'd been in the initial attacking wedge. One fell victim to Bobby's relentless fire as he threw out a curtain of lead that couldn't be avoided.

Two back to you, tail, Bobby said, his mind carrying an even calm, devoid of Logan's adrenaline-fueled exultation.

Yup, Rico Martinez answered as he visually acquired the two remaining targets and opened fire. He was aided by fire from the aircraft flying off their right wing, the *Nagging Natasha*. She fired from her left waist and tail, and the two remaining fighters faltered and tumbled through the resulting crossfire. Evelyn watched through Rico's eyes as the ugly black smoke trailed the wreckage down.

Fighters! Twelve high!

Fighters! Two high!

The calls were simultaneous, coming from Sean in his top turret and Les on the left side. Evelyn took a deep breath and did her best to split her attention between the two of them, keeping the net strong and open. Sean and Les opened fire, their respective weapons adding a cacophony of pops to the ever-present thrum of the engines.

Flak! That was Carl, up front. Evelyn felt him take hold of the controls, helping the lieutenant to maintain his position in the formation as the Nazi anti-aircraft guns began to send up 20mm shells that blossomed into dark clouds that pocked the sky. One exploded right in front of *Pretty Cass'* nose. Evelyn felt the bottom drop out of her stomach as the aircraft heaved first up and then down. She held on grimly and passed on the wordless knowledge the pilots had no choice but to fly through the debris and shrapnel that resulted.

In the meantime, the gunners continued their rapid fire response to the enemy fighters' attempt to break up the formation. Evelyn took that knowledge—that the Luftwaffe was trying to isolate one of the Forts, make her vulnerable—and passed it along the looser formation net.

Shit! They got Liberty Belle*!* Logan called out then, from his view in the ball turret. Evelyn looked through his angry eyes, feeling his sudden spike of despair as they watched the crippled Fort fall back, two of her four engines smoking. Instantly, the enemy fighters swarmed like so many insects, and Evelyn watched as the aircraft yawed over and began to spin down and out of control.

A few agonizing heartbeats later, first one, then three more parachutes fluttered open far below. Evelyn felt Logan's bitter knowledge that there had been six other men on board that aircraft. *Liberty Belle* was one of the few birds flying without a psychic on board, and Evelyn suppressed a small, wicked feeling of relief that she hadn't just lost one of her friends.

Fighters! Twelve o'clock level!

* * * * *

Find out more about Kacey Ezell and "Minds of Men" at:
http://www.kaceyezell.net/

* * * * *

The following is an
Excerpt from Book One of the Revelations Cycle:

Cartwright's Cavaliers

———————————

Mark Wandrey

Available Now from Seventh Seal Press

eBook, Paperback, and Audio Book

Excerpt from "Cartwight's Cavaliers:"

The last two operational tanks were trapped on their chosen path. Faced with destroyed vehicles front and back, they cut sideways to the edge of the dry river bed they'd been moving along and found several large boulders to maneuver around that allowed them to present a hull-down defensive position. Their troopers rallied on that position. It was starting to look like they'd dig in when Phoenix 1 screamed over and strafed them with dual streams of railgun rounds. A split second later, Phoenix 2 followed on a parallel path. Jim was just cheering the air attack when he saw it. The sixth damned tank, and it was a heavy.

"I got that last tank," Jim said over the command net.

"Observe and stand by," Murdock said.

"We'll have these in hand shortly," Buddha agreed, his transmission interspersed with the thudding of his CASPer firing its magnet accelerator. "We can be there in a few minutes."

Jim examined his battlespace. The tank was massive. It had to be one of the fusion-powered beasts he'd read about. Which meant shields and energy weapons. It was heading down the same gap the APC had taken, so it was heading toward Second Squad, and fast.

"Shit," he said.

"Jim," Hargrave said, "we're in position. What are you doing?"

"Leading," Jim said as he jumped out from the rock wall.

* * * * *

The following is an
Excerpt from Book One of The Kin Wars Saga:

Wraithkin

Jason Cordova

Available Now from Theogony Books

eBook, Paperback, and Audio Book

Excerpt from "Wraithkin:"

Prologue

The lifeless body of his fellow agent on the bed confirmed the undercover operation was thoroughly busted.

"Crap," Agent Andrew Espinoza, Dominion Intelligence Bureau, said as he stepped fully into the dimly lit room and carefully made his way to the filthy bed in which his fellow agent lay. He turned away from the ruined body of his friend and scanned the room for any sign of danger. Seeing none, he quickly walked back out of the room to where the slaves he had rescued earlier were waiting.

"Okay, let's keep quiet now," he reminded them. "I'll go first, and you follow me. I don't think there are any more slavers in the warehouse. Understand?"

They all nodded. He offered them a smile of confidence, though he had lied. He knew there was one more slaver in the warehouse, hiding near the side exit they were about to use. He had a plan to deal with that person, however. First he had to get the slaves to safety.

He led the way, his pistol up and ready as he guided the women through the dank and musty halls of the old, rundown building. It had been abandoned years before, and the slaver ring had managed to get it for a song. In fact, they had even qualified for a tax-exempt purchase due to the condition of the neighborhood around it. The local constable had wanted the property sold, and the slaver ring had stepped in and offered him a cut if he gave it to them. The constable had readily agreed, and the slavers had turned the warehouse into the processing plant for the sex slaves they sold throughout the Dominion. Andrew knew all this because he had been the one to help set up the purchase in the first place.

Now, though, he wished he had chosen another locale.

He stopped the following slaves as he came to the opening which led into one of the warehouse's spacious storage areas. Beyond that lay their final destination, and he was dreading the confrontation with the last slaver. He checked his gun and grunted in surprise as he saw he had two fewer rounds left than he had thought. He shook his head and charged the pistol.

"Stay here and wait for my signal," he told the rescued slaves. They nodded in unison.

He took a deep, calming breath. No matter what happened, he had to get the slaves to safety. He owed them that much. His sworn duty was to protect the Dominion from people like the slavers, and someone along the way had failed these poor women. He exhaled slowly, crossed himself and prayed to God, the Emperor and any other person who might have been paying attention.

He charged into the room, his footsteps loud on the concrete flooring. He had his gun up as he ducked behind a small, empty crate. He peeked over the top and snarled; he had been hoping against hope the slaver was facing the other direction.

Apparently Murphy is still a stronger presence in my life than God, he thought as he locked eyes with the last slaver. The woman's eyes widened in recognition and shock, and he knew he would only have one chance before she killed them all.

He dove to the right of the crate and rolled, letting his momentum drag him out of the slaver's immediate line of fire. He struggled to his feet as her gun swung up and began to track him, but he was already moving, sprinting back to the left while closing in on her. She fired twice, both shots ricocheting off the floor and embedding themselves in the wall behind him.

Andrew skid to a stop and took careful aim. It was a race, the slaver bringing her gun around as his own came to bear upon her. The muzzles of both guns flashed simultaneously, and Andrew grunted as pain flared in his shoulder.

A second shot punched him in the gut and he fell, shocked the woman had managed to get him. He lifted his head and saw that while he had hit her, her wound wasn't nearly as bad as his. He had merely clipped her collarbone and, while it would smart, it was in no way fatal. She took aim on him and smiled coldly.

Andrew swiftly brought his gun up with his working arm and fired one final time. The round struck true, burrowing itself right between the slaver's eyes. She fell backwards and lay still, dead. He groaned and dropped the gun, pain blossoming in his stomach. He rolled onto his back and stared at the old warehouse's ceiling.

That sucked, he groused. He closed his eyes and let out a long, painful breath.

* * * * *

Find out more about Mark Wandrey and Jason Cordova at: https://chriskennedypublishing.com.

* * * * *

Made in the USA
San Bernardino, CA
08 April 2019